DARK
ISLE

'Clare Carson delivers a meaty, beautifully written and original thriller featuring an engaging central character.'
IRISH INDEPENDENT ON ORKNEY TWILIGHT

'*Orkney Twilight* is an original, haunting thriller about fathers, daughters and the ghosts of the past. The author cleverly weaves the political struggles of 1980s Britain with the beauty of Orkney... a clever take on crime fiction.'
ABERDEEN PRESS & JOURNAL ON ORKNEY TWILIGHT

'This is an unusual book with an unusual heroine. Clare Carson has a rare insight into the world of the undercover cop... The plotting is clever and keeps up the suspense to the end.'
CRIME SQUAD ON THE SALT MARSH

'I was utterly entranced from start to finish, not only by the strength of the characterisation, but by the lyrical prose and the beautiful realisation of location throughout... Outstanding.'
RAVEN CRIME READS ON THE SALT MARSH

'An intelligently written, highly suspenseful and wholly engrossing read.'
BOOKISH JOTTINGS ON THE DARK ISLE

'Beautifully written... with superb storytelling, clever and convoluted plotting, and a wonderful sense of time and place.'
CRIME REVIEW ON THE DARK ISLE

CLARE CARSON is an
anthropologist and works in
international development,
specialising in human rights.
Her father was an undercover
policeman in the 1970s.
She lives in Brighton.

THE
DARK
ISLE

CLARE CARSON

HEAD
of ZEUS

For Rosa, Eva and Andy

'These our actors,
As I foretold you, were all spirits and
Are melted into air, into thin air.'

—PROSPERO IN *THE TEMPEST*, ACT IV SCENE 1

PROLOGUE

Orkney, August 1976

'BLOODY HOY,' JIM shouted. He wasn't going to that poxy island again tomorrow or the next day or any other day ever. He'd had enough of Hoy. He stomped across the shingle to the saltmarsh at the head of the bay and left his family sitting on the beach. They had arrived there early. The heatwave had spread far enough north to transform their usual dank and windy summer break into a Mediterranean beach holiday. Helen and Jess, at least, were determined to make the most of it. They had badgered Jim to drive them over to Waulkmill Bay again because they hadn't been there for a couple of days and he had eventually conceded even though, he had said, he wasn't in the mood for swimming. The tide was in, the cove deserted. They clambered over seaweed-matted rocks, parked themselves on the lip of sand and watched the ocean retreat, run-off channels glistening in the sun. The rise of Hoy's mountains was dark and hazy, a sleeping giant guarding the horizon. It was Liz who had pointed across Scapa Flow, said perhaps they should all take the ferry to the island the next day and have a look around. She seemed perplexed by his bad-tempered reaction, although she didn't respond to his tirade. Helen was less restrained.

'Miserable git. What's got his goat?' she asked as they watched him disappear over the ridge dividing beach from midge-infested marshland.

'God knows,' Liz said.

Sam said nothing, eyed the island that had sparked Jim's fury.

'Let's go for a swim,' Jess said. She nudged her younger

sister. 'You too, Sam. Come on.'

Liz told them not to go too far out, then stuck her nose in a book. The three sisters ran across the sand, chased the tide, jumped the waves, searched for crabs in the kelp tendrils undulating in the currents of the crystal water. Their bodies adjusted to the chill and they swam further out to sea. Sam was enjoying herself, floating on her back, the surface calm, the sun on her face; she wasn't a bad swimmer, she reckoned, for a ten-year-old. She drifted. The splash-landing of a cormorant made her look up and she saw she was on her own, Helen and Jess far away, their heads black and round like distant seals. She put her feet down. There was no bottom. She was out of her depth, going under, water closing over her head. She panicked, splashed and flailed, seaweed tangling legs, swallowing brine, couldn't breathe. She was sinking. Drowning. Lungs bursting. Head pounding. She'd had it. Everything went black. And then a light exploded, and for a second she thought she was dead before she realized she had surfaced. She spluttered, gulped air desperately, waved her arms, almost sank again, bobbed back and forced herself calm. She wasn't going to die. Not then anyway, not there in Waulkmill Bay. She trod water until she could breathe normally, flipped on her back and headed to the shore.

She was halfway home when she heard shouting. Jim. She looked around. He was right ahead, between her and the beach, water lapping at his abdomen. She put her feet down, toes touching sand this time, head and shoulders above the waves. In the five minutes it had taken her to realize she was out of her depth, panic and recover, Jim had run across the bay, waded through the shallows, met her halfway. He was angry. Face twisted, jabbing his finger in the air, yelling. She was stupid, swimming so far out. What the hell did she think she was playing at? He swung the flat of his hand at her, made her flinch, but the water broke the force of his movements anyway, converted whacks to splashes. His tirade stopped abruptly and he dived headlong into the waves and swam off to the open sea. She watched him do his purposeful front crawl, passing the spot where she had panicked and believed, for a moment or two, that she had copped it. She wanted to cry. Not because of going under, but because of Jim's reaction; his shouting had been far worse than the near drowning. She waded back to the beach, trudged across the sand, wrapped a damp towel around her shoulders, wiped her nose on her forearm, and sat next to Liz.

'Not waving but drowning,' Liz said. 'That's us. That's this family.'

'Sorry?'

'It's a poem by Stevie Smith.'

'Oh, well, I was not drowning but waving. I was OK until he started shouting at me.'

Liz was staring at her page and Sam thought she wasn't taking any notice, then she rested the book on the sand, open with the pages face down. Liz was always telling them they should never do that with books, it would break the spine. It was usually Jim who failed to practise what he preached. Liz gazed across the sea, the sun catching her pretty features in a troubled configuration, and raised her hand to her brow, searching until she caught sight of Jim, a buoy floating far away. She waved at him and Sam could see with her eagle eyes inherited from her father that he was waving back.

'So is he waving or drowning?'

Liz heaved a deep sigh. 'Why ask me? I'm just his wife.'

CHAPTER 1

Orkney, September 1989

SAM STROLLED THROUGH the graveyard to the shore, hoping to escape the sense of being watched, but the shifting outline of Hoy made her uneasy. She stared at its treacherous north face of stacks and caves, shrouded by spray where the towering cliffs plunged into the sea and met the breakers rolling in from the Atlantic. The twilight made the isle appear more cloud than land, a storm gathering across the water. She trailed the high tide mark, her eyes still drawn to the island rather than watching where she was placing her feet, and almost tripped over the rusty corpse of the seal among the bladder wrack, starbursts scarring its abdomen where the body had bloated and exploded leaving the brine to preserve its hide. She leaned and stroked the leathery skin then parked herself by the dead creature. The still presence gave her strange comfort. She waited. A pipistrelle flitted past. The mountains of Hoy blurred with the darkening sky. The North Star gleamed. Surely he would have disappeared by now. She decided to risk it, stood and retraced her steps inland along the burn. The sea breeze buffeted her from behind and she tried to hold the gusts in her mind, but the wind slipped away, rattled the deadheads of the cow parsley lining the path. Left her with a knot in her stomach.

She reached the graveyard and heard the hurried footsteps of somebody retreating as she pushed the gate. She cut through the grey tombstones, past the yellow walls of the Round Church, surveyed the Earl's Bu and the field beyond for signs. The Norse Earls had made their home here in Orphir on the southern edge of Orkney's Mainland, the settlement recorded in the *Orkneyinga Saga*. A place of deaths and ghosts. There had been dusky evenings when she had stood here and thought she'd glimpsed the shadows of pissed Norsemen fighting among the ruins of their great drinking hall, but this evening she saw nothing apart from a hooded crow pecking among the stones. He was there, though, she could tell. Watching. She had been aware of his presence all summer. She had tried to ignore the constant prickle at the back of her neck as she grappled with the gradiometer, the new-fangled piece of kit they were using to try to locate the buried remains of the Norse settlement. They couldn't dig because the ruins ran under the cemetery and they didn't want to disturb the graves. Geophysical surveys were a good way of detecting sub-surface features without excavating and causing damage, the archaeologist in charge of the site had said. Like water dowsing, she replied. He laughed and said if they didn't find anything with the equipment, perhaps she could have a go with her hazel divining rods.

The initial results were not promising. Too many anomalous spikes in the data, either because the ruins lay too deep to be detected or, as the archaeologist suggested when the monitor went haywire, there was some strange force buggering up the readings. He had looked at Sam when he said that and accused her of having supernatural powers that interfered with the magnetic fields. It had taken her a couple of seconds to realize he was joking. She was the one who had mentioned water dowsing after all. The archaeologist had invited her to come back the following summer to help with another survey, if they could find the funding. She had recently finished a history degree and now, at twenty-three, was about to start a doctorate. She would love to write her thesis on the Earl's Bu, she had said. It would be a relief, she had added – four years of academic study. He had raised an eyebrow. A relief? She had corrected herself. More of a retreat than a relief. A retreat from what, he had asked. Her father's dodgy legacy, she had wanted to say; Jim had been a police spy, killed five years before, and she'd never quite escaped his shadow. She shrugged instead of speaking. He had eyed her shrewdly and said retreating was fine as a temporary strategy but eventually you had to turn and face the ghosts, assess the ruins that lay below one way or another. She wasn't so sure. She had volunteered for the archaeological project in Orkney, drawn back by the happier memories of childhood holidays here with Jim, the darker recollections buried deeper. The presence of the watcher made her fear that somebody else was digging in the murkier corners of her family's history, unearthing events best forgotten. Her return to Orkney had disturbed ghosts of a more solid and ominous kind, she feared, than the spectres of long dead Norsemen.

She spotted a merlin perched on a fence post beyond the Bu, its gold-flecked belly bright in the gloom. Something startled the bird and it fled. She scanned nearby for the cause of the disturbance and her eyes locked on the figure in the mauve shade of the sycamores at the end of the path, facing her as if he wanted to be sure he could be recognized. He waited, turned and hobbled away. Her heart hammered. She had never seen him close up, but she had little doubt about his identity. Lanky. Military bearing. Limp. Tradecraft – picking his moment to reveal himself. She had known in her gut all along it was him. Pierce, the wounded hero. The Fisher King.

She sprinted past the ruins, along the track and reached the lane just in time to see the rear end of an ancient navy

Volvo estate driving towards Stromness. Still the same car. She ran to the derelict pig shed where she had parked the crappy Honda 50 she'd borrowed from the archaeologist, squashed the helmet on her head, wheeled the bike on to the pitted tarmac, swung her leg over, twisted the ignition key, kicked the start pedal. The engine spluttered and died. Fuck. Idiosyncratic, the archaeologist had said, but useful for island hopping because it was light enough to lift on and off the passenger ferries. Borrow it for the summer, he had added; he'd bought a second-hand car. She kicked the pedal again. The engine chugged, the bike leaped forward and she found herself driving in the wrong direction, away from the croft that was her temporary home, following the Volvo's trail.

She came to the Houton turnoff, spotted the Volvo parked by the jetty, dumped the Honda on the verge, sidled down the hill, breathless for no real reason. A lighthouse blinked its distant warning. He stood beside his car, facing the water. The ferry docked. Ramps clanked, incoming cars and vans drove past. Engines revved. Cars edged forwards. The Volvo last in line. He turned and stared straight at her again before he clambered into his car and drove aboard. She stood rooted, watching the ferry as it crossed Scapa Flow, heading to the dark isle. She had resolved not to dwell on her own history and yet here she was unwinding the past, drawn back by the lure of the Fisher King. Was he still lying low in Hoy after all this time? How many years had he been exiled in his far-flung hideaway?

She had seen him twice before, both times in the summer of '76; that was thirteen years ago when she was ten and Jim was – Jim was forty-six when he died in 1984, which made him thirty-eight in '76. Grumpy old man, she had thought at the time, but now thirty-eight seemed almost young. Not old anyway. Grumpy maybe – he'd been in one of his deeper troughs that summer, his bleak mood cranking up the pressure, adding to the edginess of the sweaty, rainless days. The summer of the heatwave had left a dark mark in her memory and, although she had only ever glimpsed him briefly, the figure of Pierce coloured those troubled recollections. The first time she'd seen him hadn't been here in Orkney but in south London, standing outside her childhood home. Funny word – home. The place she grew up was still home in her mind, despite the fact she no longer lived there and it was furnished with the memories she wanted to leave behind. Perhaps it always would be home for her, that ordinary suburban house. Jim had billed Pierce as his colleague, a fellow member of the secret state's shadow family. A spook. Did all spies park their families in the suburbs, she wondered, the bland domestic surroundings part of their subterfuge, a cover for their cloak-and-dagger lives? He had arrived in a navy Volvo, dropped his wife and his daughter Anna on their doorstep then disappeared because, it turned out, his life was in danger. And he had left Sam to befriend Anna in the relentless sun and heat.

CHAPTER 2

London, July 1976

THERE WAS NO shade and it was way too hot for a bike ride. She wished she'd stayed at home – but her sisters had told her to eff off when she had stuck her head around Helen's door to see if she could join them. Liz had taken their side, urged her to find something to do by herself. She pressed her weight on the pedals, calf muscles aching, throat dry, forced the Raleigh up the hill, past the Rock and Fountain, the line of mock Tudor piles with long drives and high privet hedges guarding green lawns. Rotten Row, Jim called it. How come the hose restrictions didn't apply to them? That was the worst thing about the drought as far as she was concerned: no sprinkler in the back garden, no running through the cool spray, squelching wet grass between her toes. It wasn't fair. The front wheel wobbled. She was sweating but she didn't want to take her hands off the handlebars to wipe her face, she had to keep going until she reached the top. She couldn't give in. Under the pylon cables, sighing in the still air, past the donkeys looking sad in their makeshift animal rescue centre. Out of breath, jelly legs. Finally, the summit. The very end of London, the dirty rim; the silver stream of the bypass heat-hazy in the distance and beyond that, the green belt. But this was still the edgelands, the neither here nor there.

She turned the bike around and hurtled down the hill, faster and faster, freewheeling, almost losing control around the bends.

She reached the bottom, the bike slowing as it hit the far slope of the dip, and wondered whether she could be bothered to cycle back to the top so she could repeat the exhilaration of the descent. She couldn't. She pootled along the level, swerved right into the road that led back home. A car overtook. Brown Cortina. Jim. He had been away for months. He often disappeared, doing whatever stupid things it was that he did for his secret job that they weren't supposed to talk about, but he had been gone for longer than usual this time, leaving them to swelter. And now he was home without warning. He pulled in ahead. She cycled up beside the door. He wound the window down, his wiry black hair plastered to his forehead.

'Do you want to get yourself killed?'

'No.'

'Why don't you use hand signals then?'

He hadn't even said hello. 'I do use hand signals.'

'You didn't just then.'

'I didn't realize there was a car behind me.'

'Exactly.'

He swerved away. She waited until he had disappeared, turned her bike around and pedalled furiously back up the steepness of the hill.

The tarmac was still sticky despite the dusk. Jim's Cortina parked on the verge. Liz's car not in the garage. Liz was often out these days too; she had been appointed as a lecturer in the English department of one of London's colleges at the beginning of the year and Roger, the head of the department, was always calling meetings. Jim had said that meetings were for poseurs and procrastinators. Liz had replied she wanted to make a good impression in her new post, so she went.

The tinny notes of Helen's transistor radio whined through her open bedroom window. Jess and Helen had spent the afternoon smoking and doing the tarot, she reckoned. Helen was fifteen and in the last six months had taken to thick black eyeliner, punk and anything to do with the occult. Jess was thirteen and followed Helen's lead. Helen had bought a pack of tarot cards from Martin, the hippy, who sold joss sticks and bags of weed to those in the know from his poky shop behind the shopping mall. Helen entertained her mates to tarot readings in her bedroom – the Devil, the Hanged Man, Death – Jess her willing assistant.

Sam entered the kitchen, grabbed a glass, crossed to the sink. A presence behind made her turn. Jim.

'It's like the Sahara out there,' he said.

Her tongue clammed in her mouth, thick from the exertion of cycling. She filled her tumbler, took a sip, savoured the water, eyed him over the rim.

'I spotted a camel wandering down the High Street when I was driving home this afternoon.'

He was trying to be friendly, making up for shouting at her about hand signals. She wasn't sure she was prepared to play along. He did sometimes take her side in arguments with her older sisters, though, which was more than could be said for Liz.

'One hump or two?'

'One. Never trust a camel.'

Never trust anyone or anything, according to Jim.

'Do you think it will ever rain again?' she asked. The drought. Neutral territory.

'I hope so.'

'But why hasn't it rained for so long?'

He gazed out the window at the wilting garden, the yellow grass. 'It's the Fisher King. He's sitting wounded by his dwindling stream, hoping somebody will help him break the curse.' Jim often talked like that – answered questions with stories instead of facts. She was used to it. Accepted it as part of the way he was, his secrecy, his background she supposed, growing up with the joshing of the Glasgow bar where his father was the publican. Or, at least, that was the story he told about his childhood. She had no way of knowing whether it was any more truthful than any of the other stories he told; she'd never met any of his family and he didn't have much of a Scottish accent so for all she knew he could have been making it up.

'Who is the Fisher King?'

'An ancient Celtic lord.' He stepped to the sink, twisted the tap. The pipe spluttered. Jim caught some water in a glass, held it to the light. Brown particles whirred. Dirt from the bottom of the reservoir. Or were they insects? He sipped, swished the water around his mouth, swallowed.

'He was guarding the ancient treasures of his clan. But he was attacked and wounded. Then his enemies stole the treasures and his land was cursed, and it became a barren wasteland.'

Like water-restriction south London.

'How did he break the curse?'

'He didn't. He's still sitting there fishing, because he's too badly hurt to hunt. He's waiting for help. Hoping one of his children will come along and give him a hand.'

She scowled when he said that, sensing he was manipulating the story, nudging the conversation around to some favour he was after, something he wanted to tell her. There was an awkward pause. She wanted to retreat to her room and read a book, but she felt obliged to stay. He asked, 'Do you want a friend to do stuff with over the summer?'

Why was he asking her that? She looked down, examined

the cracked lino, a column of black ants marching across the floor with captured sugar grains clamped in jaws.

'I thought you might like to meet the daughter of somebody I know.'

What was he on about? She could find her own friends; she didn't want anything to do with any of his arrangements. Although Helen and Jess weren't much fun these days.

'What's her name?'

'Anna. You'll get on with her. She likes doing the kind of things you like doing.'

How did he know what she liked doing? He was never there.

'She's the same age as you. She's twelve.'

'I'm ten.'

'Close enough. She might be staying for a couple of weeks.'

'Why?'

She suspected she was more likely to get a thick ear for impertinence than a straight answer.

He replied, 'Her dad has to go away. Anna and Valerie, her mum, need somewhere to stay.'

'Why do they have to stay here?'

'I want to help them.'

'Why?'

'Because her dad is a colleague. We're all part of the same family.'

The way Jim said *family* made her shudder.

'Which family is that?'

He hesitated. 'The shadow family.'

God, her own family was bad enough, she didn't want a shadow family too.

'Pierce. Anna's dad. He's always been a bit of a hero.'

'Hero?' That was a funny word to use and it didn't seem quite right coming from Jim's mouth.

14

'That's what I said. Hero.' He was beginning to sound irritated. She'd better try a different tack.

'Why does her dad have to go away?'

'Because he's damaged.' He reconsidered the word he had used. 'Injured. Wounded.'

'Like the Fisher King?'

He took another glug of water.

'Yes, I suppose so, like the Fisher King.'

That was why he had told her the story; he wanted to let her know she had to be nice to this girl Anna because her father was sick. What was wrong with him anyway? Car crash? Cancer? Well, she didn't care if Anna's father did have bloody cancer, she still didn't want her staying here, with them.

'Anna's got a bike. You can go cycling with her.' He drained the last drops from his glass, pulled a face, spat in the sink. 'Jesus, that tastes disgusting.'

'I think it has insects in it,' she said, but he was already sauntering away, left her feeling cross. *Anna and Valerie.* The names rattled around in her head and she played with the story Jim had told her; Anna's father was the Fisher King and his wound had caused the heatwave. The drought. The grittiness in the air, the bugs in the tap water, the yellow grass, and the hose restrictions that meant they couldn't even use the sprinkler. All because of Anna and her damaged father. Their fault.

They shuffled around to make room for Anna and Valerie. Her sisters weren't happy with the arrangements. Jess had only just moved out of Helen's room and now she had to move back so that Valerie had somewhere to sleep. Sam had to jam all her things in the corner cupboard of her box bedroom to make space for a mattress on the floor. Liz was indifferent. If they needed somewhere to stay, she said, they needed somewhere to stay, but she hoped nobody expected her to hang around every evening cooking. Jim said he didn't expect her to do anything. It was a favour, a temporary fix while Valerie and Anna looked for something permanent. The sisters huddled in Helen's bedroom to discuss the situation; the reek of hairspray and fag smoke tickled the back of Sam's throat. Helen laid the cross of the tarot on the floor.

'I don't get why they have to stay here,' Jess said.

Helen said, 'Because of Jim.' She reached over, plucked the top card from her arrangement. 'The Magician.' She waved the card triumphantly. 'The player of tricks. The deceiver. That's Jim. He's behaving like a right tosser at the moment.'

'Maybe it's because of the heat,' Sam said.

Helen pinched her bare arm. 'Why are you making excuses for him?'

Anna arrived two days later. Sam skulked behind the window and watched the navy Volvo estate ease along the verge. She didn't know much about cars but she knew that a Volvo estate was better than a crappy Cortina. If Valerie and Anna could afford a Volvo, why couldn't they pay for a hotel? A titchy woman clambered out of the passenger seat. A pair of long legs ending in shorts and plimsolls emerged from the back. Anna was lanky. Sam glanced at her own muscly calves. She looked stumpy in her shorts, not elegant. Not willowy. There was something confident about the way Anna slouched on the pavement, hands in pockets, and surveyed their house as if she were deciding whether it was good enough. She must have seen Sam's face in the window because she stuck her tongue out. Sam's stomach fizzed with anger. Sam returned the gesture, gave her a two-finger up-yours sign. Anna mirrored her V. Sam was about to intensify the hostilities, go for the one-finger salute when she realized Anna was laughing, which made Sam feel silly. She smiled too, although the anger was still bubbling away inside. Jim's whistle heralded his descent from upstairs; one of his jovial tunes.

'Aren't you going to answer it?' he said. 'You can't leave them standing outside on the pavement.'

Sam opened the door, came face to face with Anna; porcelain skin, freckles bridging her nose, big front teeth with a gap between, unlike Sam's overlapping fangs. Anna's hair was short, dark and curly and her eyes were blue, like Jim's, with black eyelashes and thick eyebrows. Sam's eyebrows were pale and sandy, almost invisible in fact, which Jess said made her look like an alien. Or a Midwich cuckoo according to Helen, because her khaki eyes gleamed golden in certain lights. Maybe Sam was a cuckoo and Anna was the real daughter of Jim. She was being stupid. That couldn't be right anyway because Anna was tall and lanky and Jim wasn't. Neither was Valerie. She was a sparrow, a twitchy mouse. Jim took the case Valerie was holding. He waved the guests inside.

'Jess, put the kettle on.'

Anna and her mother edged through the porch, dragging their bags.

'There are still a few things in the car, I'm afraid,' Valerie said.

Sam couldn't help feeling sorry for her; she sounded so apologetic. Unlike Anna.

'My bike is in the back,' Anna said as if she expected somebody to fetch it for her. Bloody Princess.

Jim directed. 'Go and have a drink in the kitchen. Sam, help me with the rest of the cases.'

She trailed after Jim, scuffing her plimsolls along the floor, hating Jim for ordering her around in front of Anna. She hung back at the top of the front steps, skulked underneath the twisted laburnum tree that was already dropping its poisonous seed pods on the pavement, the stress of the drought speeding up its natural cycle. The door on the driver's side of the Volvo creaked. A tall and wiry figure appeared. He had to be Anna's father. Pierce, Jim had called him. He walked around the back of the car to greet Jim. He was limping. Perhaps that was why he didn't help with the cases. Was it the wound Jim had told her about? The damaged Fisher King. And he was like a king, Sam reckoned as she watched them talking; Pierce commanding, looking down on Jim. Her father stood at ease, sharing a few pleasantries, she supposed, with his colleague from the secret state.

She crouched, tickled their cat that was sunning itself on the shrivelled marigolds and edged down a few steps, close enough to identify Jim's voice, if not quite close enough to hear everything he was saying '... whatever I can do... until it's safe...' Pierce nodded, made some reply in a low voice she couldn't hear and she guessed that was the end of the conversation, but then Pierce leaned over Jim and started talking in a sharper tone that struck her as out of order when her dad was obviously doing him a favour. She snatched at a couple of Pierce's words. '... problem... not sure how...' He must have caught Jim by surprise too because he shrank away. 'It wasn't...' Jim said. Pierce interrupted. 'I'm not saying...' his voice dropped again '... whose fault...' Her stomach lurched. *I'm not saying... whose fault...* She couldn't tell whether he was warning her father about something or pointing the finger at him, accusing him of something for some reason. She strained to hear. '... used water...' Pierce continued. *Water.* Was it something to do with the drought? The curse of the

Fisher King? The cat purred, untroubled by the exchange. Pierce placed a hand on Jim's shoulder in what looked to her like a friendly gesture, as if the concerns he had voiced had evaporated in the evening heat. Perhaps she had imagined the tension. 'Thanks... I know I can rely...' Jim didn't reply. Or if he did, she didn't hear him. She repeated Pierce's words to herself and the sounds bounced around her brain. *Water, fault, water, fault.* They didn't make much sense.

'Sam.'

Jim's call startled her.

'Come and take this bike.'

She stood and smiled at Pierce but he had already looked away, limped back to the car without a smile or a hello and left her feeling invisible. Jim heaved a racer from the boot of the Volvo, plonked it on the pavement.

'Come on, you dozy lummox. I don't want to stand here all day.'

She had a sudden urge to kick the bike and run away. She hated Jim. Hated his mates. Hated the way he treated her when he was in a bad mood, when he was with other people. Hated him full stop. Helen was right, she shouldn't be making excuses for his behaviour. She took the bike, wheeled it up the drive and through the garage, the pedals catching her ankle, making her madder. A proper racer, with dropped handlebars and loads of gears, the saddle way too high for her short legs, she noted enviously.

Jim was in the kitchen, making Valerie a cup of tea. Jess had ignored his order to boil the kettle.

'Sam, show Anna her room,' Jim said.

It wasn't Anna's room, it was Sam's room. Jim shouted for

19

Liz to come down. No response. The door of Helen's room remained firmly shut as they passed along the landing. Sam opened her bedroom door at the back of the house.

'You've got the mattress.'

Anna dumped her bag on the floor. She farted. 'That's a smelly one.' She wafted the air with her hand.

Sam suppressed her giggles, unwilling to reveal she was amused by Anna's lack of stuffiness.

Anna asked, 'Does your dad always do that funny whistle when he answers the door?'

'Yes.'

'So does mine.'

'What's happened to your dad?'

'Pierce? He has to go away.'

Sam perched on the edge of her bed. Anna sat down next to her. Sam noticed the side of Anna's thumbnail was bleeding where she must have nagged the skin.

'Does your dad work for the police?'

'No.' Anna's blue eyes glinted through her black curls. 'He works for the Firm.'

'The Firm?'

'That's what he calls it. Intelligence. MI6. He's a spy.'

The statement caught Sam off guard; she wasn't allowed to talk about her dad's work, and yet here was Anna casually mentioning that her father was a spy. She couldn't decide whether she was annoyed or impressed by Anna's brazen disregard for the rules.

'My dad's a spy too,' she said. 'He works for the Force.'

'He can't be a proper spy if he's a policeman. That's different.'

Anna's comment riled her. 'My dad is a proper spy. He works for some secret part of the Force. He's always going away on missions. Sometimes he grows a beard and I asked him once

20

whether it was his disguise and he said it was. Actually, he said the disguise was when he shaved it off. But he said I wasn't to tell anybody.'

She'd never revealed so much about her dad's work to anybody before; it left her with a hollow in her stomach. Still, Jim had said they were all part of the same family, so why should it matter if she shared their secrets with Anna?

'Who does he spy on?' There was a note of disbelief in Anna's voice.

'I don't know.' She dug around, searching for something to say, retreating from her openness. 'He told me once he tries to stop people who use violence. He said that was why he did it, to stop innocent people getting hurt, and that's why I shouldn't say anything because otherwise we might get hurt.'

A wood pigeon cooed in the back garden.

'Who does your dad spy on then?' Sam asked.

'Arms dealers, terrorists. That kind of thing.'

Sam wanted to say that was what her dad did too, but she wasn't sure whether it was true. She said nothing.

'That's why Pierce has to go away. We've moved out of our house because it's too dangerous to stay there. We don't know where he's going.'

Anna lifted her thumb to her mouth, chewed her nail and Sam felt bad for being cross about her staying.

CHAPTER 3

Orkney, September 1989

THE AIR WAS chilly beneath the clear sky, stars dusting the moonless night. She batted away the crane flies, torn between retreating to the cosiness of the croft and sitting here in the meadow a little while longer, making the most of the last few evenings before she returned to London. Peewits called from the shore below, waves gently lapped the shingle; the sounds of dwindling summer. She stared across Scapa Flow to Hoy, followed the beams of a car travelling north and attempted to identify the source of the magnetic pull. Was it Pierce or his daughter Anna? Or something deeper. She hugged her knees. Introspection made her edgy. Her father's long absences, filled with anxieties about when and whether he would return, had taught her to cauterize her emotions – focus elsewhere; nature, school, protests, music, the best way to roll a spliff, anything other than her feelings. Be like a spy, keep your true self hidden. Her father's sudden death had blown the lid off her cover and she had lost it for a while, swamped by grief and anger before she had regained her balance. She liked to believe, though, that she had emerged from the turbulence with a maturity that enabled her to reflect on the depths without sinking in sheer panic. And now, when she analysed her desire to follow the Fisher King, she could identify a shadow – a mark like a bruise inside herself. A fear about her father. *Water.*

Fault. Had he done something wrong? Was he the cause of Pierce's damage? She shuddered. She might have matured, but still she was gripped by unease when she thought about that summer. The tense conversations. Anxieties intensified by the heatwave. She pushed herself to her feet, trod the soft grass to the croft.

She rose early, drank her coffee outside, the cool breeze clearing her mind. The sky overhead was sapphire, but in the far distance she could see the cumulus gathering. Showers later, she reckoned. She found her cagoule, stuffed it in her backpack, kickstarted the Honda and drove to Scapa Pier – the car ferry to Lyness took a different route on alternate days. She clanked over the gangplanks, parked the bike at the side of the car deck and went to sit on the passenger walkway above, kept her eyes fixed on the choppy water, blanked her mind, fearful of dredging up confusing emotions which might discourage her from seeing this through.

The emptiness of Lyness surprised her. She had expected something more – a shop, a post office, police station, a sign that the people who lived on the island had a visible means of support. But there was little beyond the remains of the old army barracks. How many people had been stationed on this island during the Second World War? Thousands. Hard to believe. She rode through the straggle of houses and turned right, heading north. Hoy was separated from Mainland by a narrow stretch of water, and yet it felt as if it was part of a different archipelago. Mainland was an emerald glowing in the ocean. Hoy was dismal; wind-lashed crags littered with boulders and scree. But as the road dipped to the lush green and gold of Pegal Bay, she was reminded that the barren mountains nurtured unexpected fern-fringed burns and coves where rowan and ash trees flourished. There was something bewitching about these glens, enchantments that could easily blind the unwary to the dangers of the waves and wind and cliff-edge drops to the water.

She left Pegal Bay behind, passed the solitary headstone marking Betty Corrigall's grave, the story of her sad death playing on her mind as she crossed the moor. A buzzard circled overhead, searching for rabbits in the ling and moss. She took the road to Rackwick, an inland cut through the mountains, kept her eye on the tarmac – the vertical walls of the valley made her dizzy – and breathed a sigh of relief when the moraine gave way to the wild tangle of Berriedale. The view ahead brightened; a hollow of blue sea and sky caught between soaring cliffs. A scattering of crofts littered the dip and the northern slopes of the bay; ruins, most of them, left to crumble. The road became a bumpy track then dwindled to a dead end in the middle of the deserted hamlet. She wheeled the Honda into a roofless bothy, parked it among the rosebay willow herb that had colonized the interior, returned outside and leaned against the wall. Sight of the Volvo parked beside the highest croft knotted her stomach, although now she had satisfied herself that he must still be living here, she wasn't quite sure what to do. She needed an excuse, even though she knew he would see through any casual deception. She surveyed the low building, with its whitewashed walls and blank windows staring warily from underneath the turf roof. She had the feeling she was being watched. Was he waiting for her? She fished an apple from her rucksack, crunched, spat the pips, rested the back of her head against the stones. The autumnal sun warmed her face. She closed her eyes and pictured the cumulus clouds hanging over the Atlantic, drew them nearer, imagined their colour shifting from white to mercury and lead. The pounding of the waves and mews of gulls lulled her. She was startled by a spit of water on her face. She squinted; the sky above was overcast, threatening rain. A sudden shift in the weather. She willed the clouds to dump their load on Hoy.

She followed the path winding through the crofts. One or two were occupied, wood smoke curling from chimneys, gardens fenced and ordered. A few more people living here, she reckoned, than there had been in '76. But not many more. She reached the final bend before the track became steeper and climbed the cliff. She was level with the whitewashed croft. She paused, turned and surveyed the bay below; fulmars gliding over a garnet crescent of sand, a copper burn burbling through the peat. She detected a movement in the furthest corner of her vision. He was standing at his door. He had been waiting. Watching. Her head swivelled when she felt his gaze on her face, too late to pretend she hadn't seen him. Even from here, she could tell he was attractive in the same way as Anna; the couldn't-care-less-what-anybody-else-thinks confidence, hands in sagging jeans, baggy jumper, the ease that made him seem as if he belonged anywhere and everywhere. He did the same head scoop as Anna as well, a movement that gave the impression he was looking up at her even though he must be nearly a foot taller.

'Good day for a stroll,' he said; the bantering tone she recognized from her encounters with old Etonians at Oxford.

'Do you think so? I was worried it might rain.'

He twisted his eyes in an exaggerated movement, looked at the sky. 'Oh that's nothing. If you worried about a few clouds here in Hoy you'd never get anything done.'

'Right.' She mimicked his body language, stuck her hands in her pockets.

'Just here for the day, are you?'

'Yes.' She wondered which of them would blink first, acknowledge they knew the other's identity.

He made his move. 'Did I see you yesterday at the Earl's Bu?'

'Yes, I was there.'

'The Earl's Bu. And the Round Church, built by Earl Hakon to atone for the murder of St Magnus, a place of penance for past sins I always think. Are you a penitent?'

She smiled; the spy's ability to put you on the back foot, bypass any small-talk and ask a barbed question as if they were asking the time of day.

'No. Not a penitent. I've been helping with an archaeological survey. How about you? What were you doing in Orphir? I thought I recognized you from somewhere.'

'Indeed.' He raised one eyebrow. 'You thought correctly. And I think you're after something more than a glimpse of the Old Man. Am I right?'

She bit her lip, wondered whether she should back off now, leave it while she could, finish her walk. Keep her distance. A raindrop splattered against her cheek, then another and another, hammering the path.

'Well I never, you were right about the rain,' he said. 'That came out of nowhere.' He pulled a bamboozled face, and she remembered Anna's comedic flair, her lanky limbs made for slapstick. 'Perhaps you'd better come in until it's passed.'

He stepped back, held the door.

Over the threshold into a gloomy space that served as kitchen and living room. The darkness surprised her after the brightness of the day. There was only one window, overlooking the bay. The floor was stone flagged, a wood burner nestled in the hearth, armchairs either side, a bookshelf in one corner. He lived here alone she guessed, a hermit. A simple life.

'Have a seat.' He gestured at a chair in what Sam suspected was as much an attempt at confinement as an offer of hospitality. She perched on the chair opposite the one he had offered; a small act of assertion. He strolled to the sink, filled a kettle, placed it on the hob, leaned back against the kitchen table, folded his arms. He had a prominent Adam's apple which bobbed as he swallowed and was the only sign she could discern that he was even slightly apprehensive about her visit.

'Let me guess.' He paused, nodded. 'You're Jim Coyle's daughter.'

'How did you work that one out?'

'You're taller, but you haven't changed that much.'

He had taken some notice of her then, that day in 1976.

'Sam,' she said.

'Good to meet you properly after all these years. And as I'm sure you know, I'm Pierce. Anna's father. So, Sam... what brings you to this remote spot?'

He spoke in a jocular voice, the knowing tone of double bluff she remembered Jim using – the refusal to be serious because he wasn't going to pretend that he was entirely straightforward and, because he had acknowledged the shadiness of his persona, he was, in effect, suggesting he was honest. Conversation for a spook was, she suspected, always a game of stealth. And here he was tipping the conversation around, implying she was the one with a hidden agenda, even though he had been watching her all summer. Although now he was asking, she realized she hadn't prepared an answer. What *did* bring her here? The rain pounded the window.

'I suppose... I suppose I was curious. I wanted to find out what had happened to Anna.'

'Anna.' He rubbed his stubbled chin. 'Well now...' The kettle rattled on the hob. 'Tea? I'm afraid I can't offer you coffee. I don't drink the stuff myself. Gives me palpitations.' He scoffed when he said *palpitations*, as if he were deriding his own frailties; she suspected the display was a diversion, an attempt to head her away from the subject of Anna.

'Tea is fine. Thank you.' She wasn't that fond of tea, but in the absence of proper coffee she would drink it. 'Milk no sugar.'

He messed around with a mug and some tea bags, handed her the brew, sat in the chair opposite, stretched his long legs, crossed them at the ankle.

'You picked the best chair. The one with the spectacular view.' Her small act of defiance hadn't gone unnoticed. 'At least, it's spectacular when you can see it.' He gestured at the window, the downpour curtaining the cliffs. 'Rackwick Bay wasn't exactly where I expected to end up, but there are certainly worse places to be confined.'

'Are you confined here?'

'Ah. Like your father. Cut through the crap.' He was buttering her up for some reason. 'Confined is probably the wrong word. I suppose I am my own gaoler. I prefer to stay on Hoy. I take the ferry to Stromness every couple of weeks, do some shopping, make a few phone calls...'

'Don't you have a phone?'

'No. No phone. I still rely on the telephone box in the valley. No television. No electricity.'

He pointed to a flickering paraffin lamp on the table. 'The old crofts were built to keep the heat in, so there aren't many windows. Sometimes I have to light the lamps during the day.'

The lamp cast a pale arc, failed to dispel the murk.

'To be honest, nothing much has changed since I washed up here in '76. A couple more neighbours in the summer. Running water, which is a blessing. I have a radio for company. The World Service. Thank god for the BBC.'

He nodded his head at a battered Bush radio with a red dial sitting on a desk. 'But I live a solitary existence. I make the trip to Stromness, then I return here and pull up the drawbridge, draw the curtains.'

She wasn't entirely convinced; ex-spies never completely retreated. If there was one thing an old spy couldn't bear to relinquish, it was the inside track on information. They always had to be in the know, share their whispers and conspiracies, enjoy the feeling of superiority over lesser mortals who were oblivious to the conversations behind closed doors. He rapped his fingers on his mug; his nails manicured – short and clean. He lived this simple life in a deserted fishing village without the basics that most people took for granted, but he still managed to exude this sense of good living. Perhaps it was in his genes, the air of the upper classes.

'Doesn't it get lonely here in the winter?'

He flashed a well-maintained smile. 'Oh, I've lived in worse conditions.' His irises gleamed, the same cornflower blue as Anna's, although his eyeballs bulged more than hers, which made him seem more intense. He leaned forwards, caught her gaze. 'I heard Jim... died.'

'Yes.'

She shrugged, nothing more to add. She didn't want to go into the details, she assumed he had heard anyway – the stories, official and unofficial. He furrowed his brow and nodded sympathetically; an acknowledgement of bereavement, an indication that he would keep a respectful distance from her feelings about her father's passing. He leaned down, rubbed his ankle. The old wound perhaps. She cast her eye to the window, the deluge easing enough for her to spot the dark wings of a skua gliding over the valley, and she wondered why she had come here. Anna. Stick to Anna.

'Biscuit?'

He offered her an unopened packet of Digestives. She shook her head. She tried again.

'Anna. How is she?'

He winced when she said her name.

'Anna, yes. Being a spy doesn't always sit comfortably with family life. I'm not sure many people have successfully combined the two. As you may know, Anna and her mother went their own way.'

Her mother, that was an odd way of describing Valerie. They'd obviously drifted apart, as marital partners often do. Especially if one of them goes into hiding on a remote, windswept island. But surely his daughter was different. She persisted. 'You keep in contact with Anna?'

He sighed, stood, crossed to the window, locked his hands behind his back, shoulders sloping. She found her gaze flitting around the room, alighting on the shelves, searching in the gloom.

'It seemed better to make a clean break at the time.' He was talking to a point on the other side of the rain-splattered pane, halfway up the sandstone cliff.

'What, you mean you haven't seen her?'

'Not since the day I drove her over to your house. The summer of '76.'

She sat in stunned silence for a while, listened to the gurgle of water pouring from the downpipe. Pierce had stopped seeing his own daughter. How did that happen? Jim had broken away from his parents too. Maybe all families had these unbridgeable chasms, or were the families of spooks particularly prone to fracture? The double lives, the secrets and deceptions. These were the foundations of any relationship with a spy, even if the spook happened to be your father. Sam thought of Liz and Jim, the arguments, the standoffs, the long disappearances, the drinking and tension when he was at home. She sometimes wondered how their family had managed, why Liz hadn't walked away. Maybe it wasn't that simple. And anyway, in the end, Jim made an effort. 'Haven't you contacted her at all?'

'I've spoken to her a couple of times over the phone. A few years back...' He took a deep breath. 'I know, Anna's been playing on my mind too, to tell you the truth. I'm getting old.' He was still talking to the rain clouds curtaining the bay.

'You can't be that old.'

'Sixty.'

Jesus, he was well preserved for sixty. She'd imagined he was, what, fifty-odd. 'Sixty isn't old.'

'No, but time passes more quickly once you're past the half-century mark, and you can never be sure how much more sand you've got left to run. We never know when...' He stalled, his voice wavering. He turned and looked straight at her and she could see his eyes were glistening in the watery daylight. She was momentarily surprised and touched by his reaction, the tears of somebody who was a professional at covering his emotions. She thought of Jim, the tears in his eyes the night before he died, foreseeing his own death, trying to reach out to her and bridge the gap that had grown between them over the years. Too late. Her eyes were blurred, she blinked and wiped the dampness with a finger. Grief was like that – she thought she was over it, striding along happily, and then she lost her footing.

'You've got to contact her again,' she blurted. 'You've got to contact her before it's too late.'

'Yes, of course. You're right. I know you're right.' He sniffed and she didn't know what to do, too shy to put her arm around him and offer him comfort, more inclined to behave as she would have done with her own father and play the chin-up, no-crying game, pretend she hadn't noticed his tears.

'Hang on a moment,' Pierce said. 'Let me find a hanky.'

He limped to a doorway which, she presumed, led to his bedroom and closed the door behind him. A moment's privacy, a chance to regain his composure. She stood too, still disturbed by his revelation that he had lost contact with Anna, wandered over to the bookshelf, examined his clutter absentmindedly. The artefacts of a traveller; a woven basket with *karibu tena* stitched in its base, a tiny carved wooden figure pounding some grain in a bowl – West African, she guessed – a carved gourd pot, a string of cowrie shells, a bejewelled elephant from India perhaps, or Thailand. She was looking for something else, though, something from closer to home: the white mosaic tiles. She couldn't see them on the shelves. He would have them somewhere, she was sure, because those tiles, she realized now, must have been Anna's last gift to him. Those precious tiles, the ones she and Anna had found at Blackstone. Found. Stolen, more like.

CHAPTER 4

London, July 1976

ANNA HAD BEEN at their place for nearly a week when they went to Blackstone. They had run out of things to do; they had cycled to the park, dared each other to go higher on the swings, fed apples to the gypsy horses tethered along the bypass, taken the bus to Tooting and been swimming in the lido. Well, it was hard to swim in the lido because there were too many people. They had splashed about in the fountain and found a space to lie on their towels and picked the hundreds and thousands off their Fab lollies and licked the melting strawberry ice cream from their sticky hands, ignored the boys showing off with their shouting and diving into the pool. Anna was a weird mix, Sam had decided, somewhere between her and her sisters, a not quite teenager. She felt flattered that Anna hung out with her, didn't try and edge in on Helen and Jess's occult pursuits unless she was invited. Sam was happy to keep Anna to herself; she didn't want to share her with her sisters or her friends even though her air of superiority and her mocking digs sometimes rankled.

'I'm bored,' Anna announced.

'Let's cycle to Blackstone,' Sam said. Blackstone was at the top of the steep hill, beyond the line of mock Tudor mansions. Rotten Row. 'We could go to the Roman villa.'

'Is it a real Roman villa?'

'Yes. Actually, it's a ruin. But there's a big mosaic.'

'OK. Let's go and look.'

Jim was sitting with Valerie in the kitchen. Since Anna and Valerie had arrived he had been at home more than usual. He had the air of somebody who was skiving off school. Liz had made herself absent; preparing for lectures, important meetings about the future direction of the department. Jim looked around with a guilty expression when Sam entered. It annoyed her a bit, the way he was with Valerie, all calm and understanding. He wasn't like that with Liz, at least, not much of the time.

'We're going for a bike ride,' Anna announced.

Anna was more assertive than her. Sam had developed a habit of not telling anybody what she was doing or what she thought, because then it couldn't be contested.

'Use some bloody hand signals,' Jim said.

'Yes sir,' Anna said. She saluted and Jim smiled and Sam wished she could acquire some of her easy charm.

'Where are you going?' Jim asked.

'Blackstone,' Sam replied.

'That's too far. The clouds are building.' His tone returning to his usual brusqueness now he was talking to Sam. 'You don't want to get caught in a thunderstorm.'

She didn't care for Jim's peremptory orders and, anyway, she didn't think it would rain.

'Have you got your torch and penknife?'

Her cheeks reddened. Jim always insisted she took a penknife and torch with her, a command she was happy to obey, but hearing him utter his orders in front of Anna was embarrassing; made her feel that there was something odd about Jim and his insistence that she should always be prepared for disaster, even if she was doing nothing more adventurous than cycling past the golf course. The Coyle family, survivalists in the suburban jungle.

The sky was grey for the first time in weeks, the air heavy. She was determined not to let the bike wobble as her sweaty hands slipped on the handle grips and she forced her legs to move. She didn't want to be the first one to admit defeat.

'Can we walk the last bit?' Anna shouted from some distance behind.

'Yes, if it's too steep for you.'

She dismounted, caught her breath while she waited for Anna. She arrived panting and pink, curls sticking to her forehead, still managing to look pretty in her tomboyish way. What was that word? Gamine. They pushed their bikes up the last stretch, blackbirds trilling alarms from the wilting oaks.

The car park was empty apart from a couple snogging in the back seat of a battered Austin. A crow strutted around the rubbish bin, undisturbed by their arrival. They padlocked their bikes together and found the path that cut through the woods to the valley. A black bra dangled bat-like from a holly bush; there were always pieces of women's clothing littering these woods, lying torn and abandoned. Not far out enough to be rid of all the nutters, too far out for anybody to hear the screams. Sam was glad to have Anna's company. The sultry air was humming with midges and flies, dead leaves and dropped branches crunching underfoot. An emerald woodpecker hammered the scabby trunk of a silver birch, a streak of green among the drabness of the parched plants. The wood darkened as the clouds above them thickened.

'Do you think it is going to rain?' Anna asked.

Sam sniffed; she couldn't smell the rain coming, no tang of oily roots in dry soil.

'No. I can't smell the plants.'

Anna looked at her curiously. 'You're weird.'

Sam said nothing, tried to contain the clouds in her mind, hold back the precipitation. They reached the bottom of the hill, a line of willows and ash cutting across the valley floor.

'There's a river down there,' Sam said. 'It runs past the villa.'

'Come on then, let's follow it.'

They scrambled through the yellow grass, the curly nettles and toppled trees, reached the steep bank. 'Oh, it's gone.'

The river had been reduced to a sluggish stream, water sucked away by the heat of the sun. Sam jumped down into the bed, exposed banks and tree roots above her head. The smell of stagnant water was overpowering but there was still enough cooling green in the roof of limp branches to give the river a magical air, a hidden grotto. She squatted by a shallow pool, water boatmen skimming its thick surface. The evaporating brook had left a mat of decaying vegetation and floundering insects.

'Come here.'

Anna slithered down the bank.

'Dragonfly nymph.' She pointed to an ugly brown larva clinging to a drooping reed. 'I hope it hasn't dehydrated in the heat.'

Anna sat beside Sam, wrapped her arms around her lean legs. The smooth flesh of her thighs caught Sam's eye. She turned away, scooped a handful of water boatmen stranded in the dwindling pool, dropped them into the silted trickle. 'They'll have more of a chance there.'

'How come you know so much about insects?'

She considered her response. She enjoyed flipping stones and watching the uncovered insects scurrying away. She collected beetles and kept her prize specimens in labelled matchboxes in a shoe box under her bed. Best not to say anything about it to Anna; other girls always thought it was odd.

'I know about nature,' she said, 'because I'm a Druid.'

'You really are a weirdo.'

Sam scooped another handful of water boatmen out of their death trap, set them free. She could tell Anna was assessing her.

'Your dad said you were a bit odd.'

'No he didn't.'

'Yes he did.'

She had a surge of anger that took her by surprise, an overpowering desire to thump Anna in the mush. She twisted around to face her and saw she was grinning.

'Actually he said you liked reading books.'

She knew Anna had been lying; Jim wouldn't say she was odd, she was sure.

'And collecting beetles.'

'He told you I collected beetles?' She scraped at the drying mud with her fingers. She felt betrayed.

'He said you were like Charles Darwin because he collected insects too, and he thought that one day you might be a great scientist.' That made her feel better; Jim had been boasting, not mocking his daughter's interests; he didn't think her beetle collection was odd. He had compared her to Charles Darwin. There was a hint of admiration in Anna's voice, which chuffed her. 'What are you doing anyway?'

'I'm digging a channel between this pool and the main stream. Or what's left of it. An escape chute for the stranded water boatmen.'

Anna joined in. They kept digging but the water from the pool trickled into the new hollow then disappeared in the cracked clay.

Sam sat back on the heels of her plimsolls. 'It's not going to work.'

'Never mind. Who were the Druids anyway?'

'They were Celts; they knew about nature and magic. You know like Getafix in *Asterix*.'

She liked Asterix because he was a Gaul and the Gauls were Celts and sometimes she thought of Jim as a character in an *Asterix* story – Getagrip. That was what he was always telling her. Get a grip, you've got to get a grip. Getagrip, in her mind, was an axe-wielding fearless Celtic warrior.

'*Asterix*. I like those cartoons. Weren't all the Druids men?'

'No. Women were allowed to be Druids, they were called the bandrui.'

She had read about them in a book of Celtic myths.

'Can I be a Druid too?'

'If you like.' She said it in an offhand way because she couldn't tell whether Anna was taking the piss. 'But you have to swear to respect the insects and the birds and trees and plants, because they all have spirits and they are sacred.'

'Fine. I swear. Wasn't Boadicea a Celt?'

'Yes.'

'I want to be Boadicea then, and you can be my trusted Druid adviser.'

Sam grinned. 'OK. We are the Iceni. Although they lived in Essex, but that doesn't matter.'

'Iceni?'

'That was the name of Boadicea's tribe. Oh my god, look at that.'

The buzzing of flies had caught her attention and through the wilting reeds she had spotted a body in the next bend of the river bed; a vacant eye staring, brown and green scales peeling back to reveal rotting flesh and bone. She scrabbled around the silt and reeds, crouched to examine the corpse. She had an urge to prod the serpentine body, but even in death its needle-sharp teeth were a deterrent.

'Pike.'

Anna ambled over. 'Yuk.'

Sam's finger hovered above the head. 'The Druids wrapped themselves in dead animal skins when they wanted to contact the spirit world.'

'That's disgusting.'

'It's not disgusting... it's... it was because they were close to nature. They got their magic powers from the earth and the creatures and elements.'

'Why did they have to use dead animals?'

'They needed a bridge, a way of connecting with the other side, so they could prophesy, understand what the spirits were saying.'

She could tell Anna was pulling faces behind her back, but she didn't care. She held her palm flat, skimmed her hand above the length of the scaly body, the lateral fins, the gills – heat rising from the decomposing flesh – reached the head, the fearsome jawbone, the needle teeth, the grey, grey staring eye and she saw the trunks of oak trees, dense woodland, a hut in a clearing, thatched roof, a woman with hands on her hips, shouting, warning her about playing in the river, the water spirits.

Anna poked her in the ribs, made her jump. 'What does the dead pike tell you?'

'The pike tells me...'

'What?'

'That this is a sacred place, the home of the water nymphs.'

Anna leaned over her. 'And?'

Sam closed her eyes, held her palm above the pike's eye. Nothing. She'd have to make something up. 'The Romans have stolen the ancient treasures of the Fisher King.'

'Who's the Fisher King?'

'The Fisher King is...' She didn't want to say she thought that Pierce might be the Fisher King, because she was afraid Anna would laugh. 'The Fisher King is a Celtic king.' She was going to have to do a Jim, improvise a bit to make the story fit in with the villa. 'He was wounded and when the Romans attacked their settlement,' she waved her hand at the woods behind, 'he couldn't protect the sacred treasures he was guarding, and the Romans ran off with them and hid them in Blackstone villa.'

'Blackstone villa? The villa here? Is that true?'

'Yes.' She was almost starting to believe her own story. 'When the sacred objects were stolen his land was cursed, there was a terrible drought and all he could do was sit in this piddly stream and fish.'

'Where is the villa anyway?'

She pointed along the cutting.

'You and me,' Anna said, 'we are sisters of the Iceni. We have to retrieve the sacred treasures of our tribe.'

Sam was enjoying this. She hadn't expected Anna to play her games; not many of her friends did these days, they were all more interested in shoplifting mascara from the makeup counter at Miss Selfridge.

'What kind of treasure is it?'

'A chalice.' Sam rubbed the back of her neck; a chalice wasn't going to work. They'd never find a chalice. She glanced down at the dried-up river bed and spotted the glistening surface of a broken flint. 'No, it's not a chalice. It's some precious stones.'

'Magical stones.'

'Yes. Magical. They protect the person who keeps them.'

Anna's blue eyes stretched wide. 'We have to retrieve the stolen treasures. We are blood sisters of the Iceni.'

'Blood sisters,' Sam repeated.

'We need something to prick our skin.'

Sam stuck her hand in the back pocket of her shorts, produced her small red Swiss Army knife, flicked open a blade. 'I'm not sure I can do it.'

'You're such a weed. Give it to me.'

Sam handed over the penknife. Anna nicked her thumb without flinching, squeezed the skin until a ruby bead appeared.

'Give me your hand.'

Sam obeyed. Anna jabbed the point of the knife into her skin, yanked. Blood bubbled along the slit.

'Now what do we do?'

Anna pressed their thumbs together, lifted her thumb and drew it across Sam's lips.

'You do the same to me.'

Sam wiped Anna's mouth gently, left a trail of red.

'Now lick.'

Sam ran her tongue around her mouth, tasted iron, watched the pink tip of Anna's tongue following the lines of her fleshy lips.

'We can never betray one another, even under pain of torture or death. We are blood sisters.'

The intensity of Anna's voice scared Sam, but it reassured her as well to have such a fierce bond with a fellow traveller in the scary world of spies and secrets which they both inhabited. The oath was a bind, but it also felt like a lifeline. They were in it together, come what may. She could do with a friend, somebody she could talk to.

'We are blood sisters.' A rumble of thunder made her wonder whether she had been wrong about the rain. 'Do you think we should go back to the car park and cycle home?'

'No. Come on. I want to go to the villa.'

They paddled through the dribble of the river, reached the

41

wooden building with a flat felted roof, a solitary Hillman parked in the gravel courtyard.

Sam pointed. 'That's it. Or at least, that's the building that covers its remains.'

'Do you think we can go inside?'

'I don't know whether it's open.'

'Let's go and have a look anyway. We've got to try and find the treasure.'

Sam read the sign taped to the door. 'Closed until further notice due to emergency repairs'. The door was ajar.

'Let's go and look inside.'

'I'm not sure we're allowed.'

'We can just look.'

Anna was like Boadicea, a fearless warrior queen. Sam wanted Anna to think she was fearless too. She followed her through the door.

Inside, wire-trailing hanging bare bulbs illuminated the excavation trenches and walls of the Roman settlement. A bearded man was staring at them from the middle of the site.

'Weirdy-beardy,' Sam whispered. 'Come on, let's go.'

He shouted, 'We're closed. Can't you read? There's a sign on the door.'

Anna clasped her hands in front of her, tilted her head to one side. 'We're so sorry. We saw the notice but the door was open, and I wanted to look at the villa. My friend told me there was a beautiful mosaic here.'

She was really hamming it up. He fell for it, though, smiled. Or perhaps he leered; it was hard to tell what was going on under the beard. His reactions made Sam uncomfortable. Anna wasn't bothered. Maybe she was used to eliciting that sort of response. He shambled over, hands in pockets of brown cords. He reminded Sam of Roger, the head of Liz's English department. He didn't suffer fools gladly, Liz had told them, and Helen had said, well, how come he's so bloody fond of himself then? The site curator couldn't take his eyes off Anna. Sam stood behind, invisible.

'We've had to close the site to do some checks. The drought has caused some cracking and collapse of the earth banks.' His voice was gravelly; too many fags and mugs of Nescafé. 'We need to strengthen them to make sure they are safe and no long-term damage has been done. I'm waiting for the local authority to call back and let me know if they have any emergency funds.' Anna looked up at him through her fringe of black curls. He cleared his throat. 'But if you want a quick look at the mosaic, it's this way.'

He smiled again, nicotine-stained teeth visible through his beard. Why did anybody grow a beard? Jim grew a beard as a disguise, which made her wary of hirsute men. Beards were a sign of something to hide.

'We'd love to have a look at the mosaic,' Anna said. 'Thank you.'

They followed him across to the far side of the site. Sam had seen the mosaic before. It was impressive, but she wasn't sure whether she liked the image: a naked woman riding a bull through the sea, flanked by two cherubs. It gave her a funny feeling. The colours were still vibrant, despite its age; the figure of the woman picked out in red against the white of the bull, the sea a deep blue.

Anna surveyed the mosaic. 'It's amazing.'

Sam couldn't work out whether she meant it, or was just enjoying twisting her creepy admirer around her finger.

'What are the tiles made from?' Anna asked.

'You mean the tesserae?'

The tesserae. Plonker.

43

'Is that the proper name? Tesserae?'

'Yes. The tesserae come from a variety of places. The blue ones are made from local flint. The white ones come from marble the Romans brought with them from Italy, and the red tesserae are made from some kind of ironstone, which we believe may have been taken from sculptures or icons they found in the structure that was here before the Romans built their villa. A temple, a shrine to a water deity.'

'A Celtic temple?'

He displayed his ratty teeth again. 'You are a very intelligent young lady.'

Sam poked Anna's thigh with her finger. Anna ignored her.

'And what's the mosaic about?' Anna asked. 'The naked woman doesn't look very happy. Where's the bull taking her?'

'It's a depiction of...' His sentence was interrupted by a distant ringing. 'Was that the phone?'

'Yes, I think I can hear something,' Sam said.

He looked at her as if he was surprised to find that she could speak.

'I'd better go, it might be the council returning my call. I'll be back in a minute.' He headed towards a door near the exit, opened it, disappeared. Anna grabbed Sam's arm, her eyes glinting. 'Now's our chance,' she said.

'What are you going on about?'

'The revenge of the Iceni. We are the blood sisters. You walk over there towards the exit. Cough very loudly if you hear him returning and make something up, delay him.'

'Anna...'

'I'm Boadicea.'

'You what?'

'Tell him I went to look for a toilet. Go.'

Anna skittered along the pathway around the mosaic, head

44

down as if she were searching for something. Sam watched her, open-mouthed, wondering what on earth she was up to, nervous in case the curator reappeared.

'I said go.'

Anna jumped down from the walkway, disappeared from view. Jesus. Sam didn't have any choice. She had to follow Anna's instructions and intercept him as he was coming out of his office. She made her way over to the exit, eye on the door, hoping Anna would finish whatever she was doing before the phone call finished. She could hear him talking crossly on the phone. *I don't think you quite understand the...* She glanced over her shoulder, but Anna still hadn't reappeared. The phone clicked; the curator had replaced the receiver. She coughed. The door cracked open and she started hacking as loudly as she could. He emerged, frowned. She cleared her throat, returned his stare, tried to hold his gaze. She managed to lock him in for about five seconds and then he turned his head. She did too. Anna had materialized and was tripping towards them. She panted, 'I was just looking for a toilet.'

The curator's face blushed below his beard.

'Oh, it's...' he waved his hand. 'The public one isn't very salubrious. Perhaps you'd like to use the staff...'

'It doesn't matter,' Anna said. 'I can pee in the woods. I'm sure the plants will appreciate a bit of liquid.'

She didn't care what she said, she knew she could get away with it because she was so attractive. Anna linked her arm through Sam's, frogmarched her to the entrance.

'Bye,' she said over her shoulder and was out and pulled the door shut before the man had time to question her.

They ran across the courtyard, jumped the fence, thrashed through the nettles, skidded down the bank to the river.

'What was all that about?' Sam demanded.

Anna grinned and stuck her hand in the pocket of her shorts. 'Guess what I've got.'

'I can't.' And then she realized. 'Anna. You can't do that. You have to take them back.'

'Don't be a spoil-sport.'

'But that's stealing. It's an ancient monument.'

'Nobody will notice. I've only got a few. Anyway, they belong to the people. Not some stuffy man with a beard. You heard him. The Romans stole them from the Celts. It's like you said, the treasures of the Fisher King.'

'Anna, I was… You've got to take them back.'

'I don't want to.'

'I will.'

'You can't. Are you going to tell on me? Are you going to betray me? You sodding traitor.'

Sam opened her mouth, astounded by the onslaught.

'I thought we were friends,' Anna said. 'Blood sisters.'

'Why did you take them?'

'It was your idea. Your story. Anyway, he was a creep. His beard was disgusting. Did you see all those bits of food that were clinging to the hairs around his mouth?'

'Yes, but you…'

'I what?'

The grumble of thunder cut their argument.

Sam said, 'God, we shouldn't be out here in a thunderstorm. Under all these trees. This is the worst place to be. Let's go back to the villa.'

'No, come on, I'm not going back to that old perv. I'm going to find my bike.'

Anna ran along the river bed, lanky legs picking through the rocks and dying reeds.

Sam chased after her, thunder rolling as they hounded

through the oaks, struggled up the hill. The car park. The Cortina was sitting there, windows down, Jim scowling.

'For fuck's sake, hurry up. Get the bikes in the boot.'

Even Anna's presence was not enough to charm him. They clambered into the back seat. Jim swivelled around, directed his face at Sam's.

'Do you ever do anything you're fucking told?'

She didn't answer. His face had gone a peculiar colour, a whiteness made sickly by the yellow storm light.

'Anything could have happened.'

She sat there fuming, couldn't quite work out what all this was about. It wasn't Jim's grumpiness that surprised her, but the fact that he had bothered to come and pick them up. His random warning. *Anything could have happened.* They drove back in silence. The thunder had stopped by the time they reached home. Not even a drop of rain, she wanted to point out to Jim. But she didn't. Jim dumped them and the bikes in front of the house without a word, drove off somewhere. Valerie was waiting in the kitchen. Her face was pale and there were dark rings under her eyes that made her look ghostly.

'I'm going upstairs for a rest,' she said. 'Why don't you get yourselves something to eat?'

Sam made cheese and salad cream sandwiches and they ate them in front of the telly. *Blue Peter.*

'I prefer *Magpie*,' Anna said. '*Blue Peter*'s wet. All they ever do is make houses for Cindy dolls from shoe boxes. I've never had a Cindy doll in my life.'

'Neither have I. Sometimes they do other stuff which is quite good, though. Did you see the time capsule?'

'The box they buried in the *Blue Peter* garden with all those things in it?'

'Yeah.'

Anna stuck her hand in the pocket of her shorts, rummaged.

'That's what I'm going to do with these. I'm going to give them to people I know, tell them to bury them and then in thirty years' time I'll go around and dig them all up.'

'How many did you get anyway?'

'Seven.'

'Let me see.'

Anna opened her cupped hands, Sam peered. Seven dusty mosaic tiles. Four deep red, two marbled white and one glassy flint blue. Barely half an inch square, if you could call them square because all of them were misshapen with faint cracks marking their surfaces like fingerprints.

'They were on the edge, loose. I just reached down and grabbed them and they came away in my hand.'

Sam prodded the blue tile with the tip of her finger; a tingle ran up her arm.

'I'm going to give a red one to Liz.'

Anna said it with determination, as if she had already planned how she was going to distribute her bounty.

'Liz? Why?'

'I think she's cool.'

'Do you?'

'Yeah. I like the way she does her own thing.'

Sam hadn't thought about Liz that way before. Cool.

'And two red tiles for my mum – one for her and one for her baby.'

Sam squealed. 'Baby?' She didn't know anything about a baby.

'She's pregnant.'

'Pregnant?'

'Didn't you realize? That's why she's spending so much time in bed.'

'Oh.' Sam mulled over this piece of information, felt dumb

for having failed to notice, and concluded that Liz must have known, which was why she made sure Valerie had her own room. Liz was quite thoughtful sometimes, she supposed. Or, at least, more thoughtful than she sometimes appeared. She was surprised Anna hadn't said anything about the baby before. Perhaps Anna was annoyed that she was about to be lumbered with a much younger sibling.

'Is it going to be a boy or a girl?'

'It's too early to tell yet.'

Anna gave her a you're so stupid look, which made Sam decide she wouldn't ask any more questions about Valerie's pregnancy.

'I'm going to keep the blue tile,' Anna continued. 'And here. This one is for you. My blood sister.'

Anna took her hand, squashed it tight. Sam opened her palm and stared at the red Roman mosaic tile lying across the crease of her lifeline, radiating warmth. 'This must be one of the tiles made from the statues the Romans found in the old Celtic temple.'

'Exactly,' Anna said, and Sam sensed again that she had some plan in mind, telling a story with the mosaic tiles, weaving some kind of magic. Her body pulsed with the thrill of being a piece in Anna's design.

'That leaves the two white ones.'

'Those are for Pierce.'

'Why two?'

'Because that's what I've decided.'

'What about Jim, doesn't he get one?'

Anna held her hand flat, rocked it; a gesture of iffiness. 'I'm not sure about Jim.'

She wasn't either, she thought. Nobody was sure about Jim.

CHAPTER 5

Orkney, September 1989

PIERCE FILLED THE kettle, placed it on the hob. She stood by the window, watched the rain moving out to sea, a shadow on the ocean. He had regained his composure, although now she had seen below his cover, she found she was looking at him differently, less easily able to dismiss him as a toff, more sympathetic to his upper-class English banter which was, after all, the crutch of his generation and class. Retreating to his bedroom to express his emotions. Perhaps that was what he had done with the tiles, hidden them away in a bedside drawer, too personal and precious to leave lying around.

Pierce returned to his chair with two mugs. She sat down again too, mirroring his moves; a game of human chess.

'I know I should contact Anna again,' he said. 'In fact, I'm desperate to be back in touch with her. But of course, it's not that straightforward.'

'Isn't it?'

He reached for the packet of Digestives, removed one, broke it in half, held a piece in each hand.

'Nothing is ever straightforward when you are a spook. Or even an ex-spook.'

He dropped a jagged fragment in his mouth. She reached for a biscuit too, caught his eye, blue and clear, and was reminded of Anna's directness. She had never heard Jim refer to himself as a spook or a spy, although that was precisely what he had been for a large part of his life. She dunked the Digestive in her tea, the liquid seeping into the biscuit, dissolving its edges. She was warming to Pierce; he might be an old spook but he wasn't afraid to reveal his emotions, wasn't ridiculously secretive about his work, didn't talk in riddles and fairy tales.

'Did Jim ever tell you why I had to exile myself to Hoy?'

'Jim never told me anything.'

He noted the tone of her comment. 'You shouldn't be too harsh on your father. He was of a generation that believed in public service, duty, the importance of keeping the state's secrets.'

'He was a younger generation than you.'

Pierce leaned back in his chair. 'I've had time to reflect.'

His generosity about Jim reassured her.

'Jim was a great help to me,' Pierce continued. 'All in all,' he added. He swallowed the remainder of his biscuit.

All in all – a more ambiguous judgement. It was where she had ended up on Jim and his work as well; all in all, in the final analysis, all things considered.

'We were colleagues, as you probably know.'

Colleagues not friends. Not like Jim and his old mate Harry.

'Different employers of course, but same line of work, and we ended up being chucked in the soup together. Quite a complicated story...'

A gust of wind whistled down the chimney, fluttered the stack of old newspapers waiting to be folded into kindling bricks.

He stood, walked to the window, checked outside as if he were looking for watchers, returned to his seat, his limp noticeable even in the few steps he took across the room.

'You know I worked for MI6 – foreign intelligence?'

'Yes, Anna told me you worked for the Firm.' She grimaced as soon as she said it, afraid she had betrayed Anna, revealed his daughter had passed on his secrets. Traitor.

'Don't worry,' he said. 'I was probably more open with Anna about my work than I should have been. We're not supposed to say anything, but it can become ridiculous, as you must know, trying to maintain that level of secrecy with your nearest and dearest. In the end, we're all part of the same family.' *The family*, that was the phrase Jim had used as well.

He flicked a crumb from the arm of his chair.

'All these events are long past, so I don't think there's any harm in telling you, obviously I wouldn't want you to...'

She interrupted. 'I find it easier to say nothing than to talk.'

He nodded, approvingly. 'As I thought. One becomes a good judge of character in this game, and my sense is that you are trustworthy.'

She reddened, flattered but uncertain whether she merited his confidence.

'My area of specialism ended up being the illegal arms trade. Gun running. Rifles in the banana crates, that kind of thing.' His brow furrowed. 'It's a rum old world, the world of the illegal arms trader, that heady cocktail of money and violence and glamour.'

She glanced at his manicured nails, his spotless white shirt.

'Everybody knows everybody else. You wouldn't get anywhere without the contacts. It takes a while to work your way in, set yourself up.' He nodded, remembering the time when he was a player, she supposed.

'Do you know Czechoslovakia's main source of foreign currency?'

'No.' She had no idea, although Czechoslovakia rang a muffled bell.

'Firearms and Semtex. Major exports. They've never been too fussy about the buyers, as long as they've got the readies. Back in '76, there was this Czech arms dealer who was selling the stuff and some terrorists who wanted to get their hands on it.'

Terrorists. She reached for the tea, her hand shaking as she lifted the cup to her mouth. She'd lost her nerve. Four years ago, a conversation like this would have excited her, the thrill of secret information, seeing below the surface of the shadow state; but now it worried her. She'd learned her lesson, had her fingers burned. She wasn't as fearless as she used to be, or perhaps she was just less naïve.

'Are you OK?'

She took a sip, gulped it down. 'Yes, I'm fine.'

'Tell me if I'm telling you things you'd rather not hear.'

'Honestly. I'm fine.'

She appreciated his sensitivity to her reactions. But she had come here because she wanted to know.

'I'm not giving you any details that could get you into trouble. None of it is news. Seventy-six. History. The Red Army Faction. Better known as Baader-Meinhof. I'm sure you've heard of them.'

She had; the name Baader-Meinhof had cropped up regularly on the news in the seventies. Even as a child, she had picked it up and remembered the reports of assassinations and bombings. 'Weren't they a gang of West German terrorists?'

'Yes. They called themselves anti-fascists – protesting against ex-Nazis employed by the West German state and in private companies. There was a lot of sympathy for them until they started killing people – industrialists, military personnel. Cold-blooded assassinations. And then there were bombings. And hijacking.'

He shook his head, sipped his tea.

'So why did you have anything to do with them if they were doing all this in West Germany?'

'Well, the original gang were rounded up in the early seventies, but some of the more extreme followers got away – on the run from the West German authorities. They were trying to make contact with other terrorist groups. The Palestinians. The Provos. We had to step in; they were threatening our national security. The Firm wanted to set up a sting – lure the leaders of this particular breakaway faction into an arms deal and then spring the trap. This Czech dealer...' He stalled. 'My role, my part in the chain, was to liaise between the Germans and the Czech. It was a long-drawn-out operation. The Red Army Faction – they were very excitable. Trigger-happy. I spent a good year establishing my cover. Stressful, of course, but like most people who do that kind of work, I enjoyed it. Playing a part. Doing my bit. One of the unseen and unsung who take the risks so ordinary people can sleep peacefully at night.'

He said it with a note of self-mocking irony, but she found herself drawn along by his story.

'And it was all going very smoothly.'

He rubbed his leg.

'I finally arranged a meeting between the Czech and the Germans in Paris. But then, somehow...' He emphasized the *somehow* and stared at her when he said it, which gave her an uneasy feeling... 'somehow, the Germans got wind that there was something rum going on. And then the Czech heard from his sources that the meeting was a trap and he didn't show up. Of course, as the middle man, some of the suspicion fell on me. There was a bit of... bother. I thought I'd got away with it – escaped without too much damage. Then I heard word they were on to me, found my name and number.'

'The Red Army Faction were after you?'

He looked blank.

'No,' he said. 'No. Not them.'

She felt reprimanded, too slow to follow the plot, and then he smiled as if he'd just worked out what she was asking. 'The Red Army Faction? I dealt with them.'

She wondered what that meant, *I dealt with them.*

'No, it was the Czech I was worried about. It was the Czech who had a bullet in his Glock with my name on it. He was the man with the connections and cash. Ruthless.' His Adam's apple bobbed. 'No qualms.'

She squashed the last piece of her biscuit against the roof of her mouth, turned Pierce's story over in her mind, and tried to mesh his account with the pieces she already held, her fragmented recollections from the summer of '76. *Water. Fault.*

'How did Jim fit into all of this?' As soon as she asked, she wished she hadn't. Pierce gazed into the middle distance, as if he didn't want to meet her eye, and was debating what he should say. He took a deep breath, shifted in his chair to face her.

'Jim was working for some secret part of the Force that did undercover operations, of course. You knew that, didn't you?'

She did. Or at least, if she hadn't known the details at the time, she had discovered them after his death.

'And the Force, in their wisdom...' His mouth twisted into a smile. 'Well, put it this way, it all got a bit complicated. It didn't necessarily help...' He trailed off.

He was leaving her to join the dots.

'Did he... did Jim...'

Pierce closed his eyes and leaned his head against the back of the armchair. She began to fear she had said the wrong thing, revealed that she knew too much, hit on a raw and painful nerve.

'I'm sorry,' she said. 'It's none of my business. It's probably not something you want to talk about. It must have been…' Her sentence tapered. 'So you came to Hoy,' she said.

He didn't budge, eyes tight shut. A knot of gulls bickered above the bay, their squawks filling her head. Eventually he blinked and said, 'Yes, that's right, I came to Hoy. This magical island.'

'It is a magical island,' Sam agreed. 'I remember Jim saying he thought Hoy was like the island in *The Tempest*.'

'*The Tempest*? Shakespeare's *Tempest*?'

He sounded surprised; perhaps he hadn't expected Jim to know anything about Shakespeare.

'Yes. It's my favourite, in a perverse sort of way.'

'Oh right. I see. Hoy is like the island in *The Tempest*, an enchanted place to which I have been banished, because of my brother's treachery.'

She twitched when he said treachery. Was that a dig at Jim, or was he just recounting Shakespeare's plot? She twiddled her hair around a finger. Pierce crossed to the kitchen, filled the kettle again. He gave her a reassuring smile, and she could see something of Anna in the generosity of his mouth.

'I suppose I'm like one of those Japanese men hiding out in the jungle. It's probably been safe for me to come out for ages. These dealers, they move on. Find new markets, new targets. And anyway, the Cold War is all but over. Times are changing. They've elected a bloody non-communist government in Poland for god's sake. Moscow has new puppet masters now.'

Was he going off on a tangent with Moscow, she wondered, or were they part of the story too? 'Was the KGB involved in the arms deal in some way?'

A shaft of sunlight pierced the rain-smeared window. He twiddled the paraffin lamp on the kitchen table, extinguished its feeble glow. 'We don't need that any more. KGB? No,' he continued. 'Not the KGB. They didn't have anything to do with it. The Czech – he originally worked as some functionary for the StB – that's the Czech secret police. He was checking end user certificates for Omnipol.'

'Omnipol?'

'Sorry. The state-owned arms manufacturer. But then in 1969, after the Prague Spring and the Soviet invasion, the KGB had a purge of the StB and the Czech had to move out pretty quickly. Of course, he kept his contacts in Omnipol – his guest pass into the arms game. But he went freelance. Private arms dealers, much worse than the state-run show, I'm afraid. More ruthless. It's their own capital at stake after all.'

He winced, walked to the door, opened it, the damp, salty air blasting the room, shut the door. Restless. He sat down again. 'You know, hardly anybody knows I'm here.'

She almost laughed. 'Surely everybody knows you're here. You can't keep anything secret in a place like Orkney.'

He laughed too. 'Of course, everybody knows I'm here, but nobody knows my real identity.'

'You use a false name?'

'Steven Hill.'

'Don't you ever slip up?'

'No. I've had so many identities in my life. I'm used to it, moving from one persona to another. The trick is to make sure you believe in your own character, then you can inhabit the part. Steven Hill is a reclusive writer, which is, in fact, quite true.'

He gestured at a desk in a corner of the room, a typewriter, reams of paper.

'He came here after a painful divorce from which he's never quite recovered.'

'And nobody's ever questioned your story?'

'No. Why should they? There aren't many people around here to ask questions anyway – a couple of old fishermen with nothing much more than whisky to see them through the winter. And then there are the creative types who rock up in the summer – a violinist, a photographer. I talk to them, but we respect each other's privacy.'

'So Pierce disappeared, and nobody knows his location?'

'Not quite. There are a couple of people in the Firm who know where to find me, a couple of other colleagues in different parts of the show. There was Jim, but he's dead. And then there's you.'

He gave her the sharp-edged stare from under his brows and she tried not to be drawn in, but she couldn't help feeling flattered that she was in the club, a trusted member of the inner circle.

'Keep it tight. That's always the best way. In the family.' He nodded at her. 'I would like to see Anna again, but as I said, it's not straightforward. I have to tread carefully.'

'Surely you can trust Anna?'

'Of course I can trust Anna. The thing is...' He sighed, stood, crossed to the cooker, removed the boiling kettle from the hob. 'More tea?'

'OK, thanks. What's Anna doing these days anyway?'

'She went to university – Cambridge – like her old man.' He beamed, the proud father, and she felt a stab of jealousy – her dad was no longer around to laud her achievements. 'She got drawn into all that Footlights stuff. Which is great, of course. Fantastic. And now she's acting for a living. So I hear.'

He didn't sound that impressed with Anna's career choice but Sam couldn't help smiling; Anna was a natural actress, somebody who would thrive in the spotlight.

'I'm sure she's a brilliant actress,' Pierce continued. 'But some of these actors – creative people, dreamers, idealists – they don't understand the real world. Easy to manipulate. And she has obviously got carried away by some of them.' He returned to his chair with the steaming mugs. 'Look, I don't want you to take this the wrong way because I suspect you've done similar things yourself, but she's involved with all these hard-core politicos herself these days.'

'Who is she hanging out with then?'

'This bunch of protestors against the poll tax.'

'Poll tax protestors?' Sam couldn't help the tone of incredulity. 'They're just ordinary people who think it's unfair to be slapped with a massive tax bill they can't afford to pay.'

'Of course, I'm not saying they don't have a good cause and I'm sure some of them – like Anna – are well-intentioned and genuine. But I wouldn't want word leaking out that Anna's old man is a spy and he's been involved with all sorts of stuff and he's hanging out in Hoy. God knows who might get to hear.'

'I'm sure Anna wouldn't say anything if she thought it might harm you.'

He leaned forward.

'Sam, all I'm saying is, I have to tread carefully. Let's not be naïve. The poll tax campaign might be a good cause, but there's always some hard-line group lurking, scheming and prodding behind the scenes. Militant, for example. They see the poll tax as their big moment, the chance to overturn the state etcetera, etcetera.' He offered her another Digestive. 'You've not had anything to do with them by any chance?'

'The anti-poll tax campaign?' She took a biscuit. 'No.'

He was giving her his incisive stare again.

'I haven't got time these days...' she faltered. Actually, now she came to think about it, she remembered her housemate

Becky mentioning a poll tax meeting. Becky, her best mate from school. The friend she always trusted. No nonsense, training to be a doctor Becky. She had shouted up the stairs as she headed out the door, *See you later, I'm just off to this meeting about the poll tax.* When was it – early June, just before she set off to Orkney for the summer. She hadn't taken much notice because she had other things on her mind, and anyway, why should she take much notice? Pierce drooped one side of his mouth, a hammed-up expression of sheepishness, held his hands palms to rafters.

'I'm sorry,' he said. 'I should probably come clean.'

Her jaw dropped.

'It's not as bad as you think. Somebody on our side was just keeping a check.'

'MI6 was watching a bunch of poll tax protestors?'

'Not the Firm. MI5. Domestic brief. Nothing heavy-handed, a list of names, that's all.'

'Why was anybody spying on them?'

'It's not straightforward.' He smiled. 'There I go again. But it's not. The problem is that if our side didn't keep an eye on them, that would give the other side free rein to turn up and manipulate and use innocent people as vectors for all sorts of... unpleasantness.'

She'd heard it all before, the justifications for spying. Commies. Reds under the beds. She could see the need for watching would-be terrorists, and she could understand that Pierce's experiences might have made him suspicious of lefties. But poll tax protestors?

'Don't you think the other side has got more pressing things to do at the moment than manipulate a bunch of students and unemployed actors who are protesting against the poll tax? I mean, seriously, you yourself pointed out that the Soviet

Union is collapsing – surely their spies are more concerned with protests on their side of the Iron Curtain.'

She couldn't disguise the disdain in her voice.

He raised an eyebrow. 'You'd be surprised.'

She leaned back in her chair.

'What I'm saying is, I still know people and they tell me things and I hear what Anna's up to.'

It gave her the creeps, the way these spooks used their networks to keep an eye on their offspring, a secret state nannying service to fill the gaps in their inadequate parenting.

'And last time I spoke to one of my contacts, they mentioned your housemate. They laughed about it, funny, the fact that this woman who was attending the same meetings as Anna shared a house with Jim Coyle's daughter.'

Bastards.

'I don't go to any of those meetings any more, I've stopped doing all that kind of stuff, so how does anybody know who I'm sharing a house with? Why is my name still on anybody's list?' She sounded like a whiny teenager, but she didn't care. She'd tried so hard in the last couple of years to keep below the radar, she'd not been on a single protest or a march and had focused on her studies. Yet here she was, still on somebody's bloody watchlist. Maybe she was being naïve to think her name would ever be erased. She was, after all, the daughter of a police spy.

'Look, don't worry. You're not on a list per se.'

Per se, what did that mean?

'People know your father's name. They might know who you are, but there's not necessarily any black mark attached.'

Not necessarily, that wasn't particularly reassuring.

'It wasn't anything official. I was chatting to this contact, and they knew Jim and your name came up as the housemate of this person. What's her name? No, no, don't tell me. I don't need to know. First rule of espionage. Information strictly on a need-to-know basis. Anyway, I simply enquired – curious, I suppose – what you were doing these days. And this contact told me he'd heard on the grapevine you'd had a rocky couple of years after Jim's death, but you'd found the right path. You were studying archaeology and, funnily enough, he'd heard you were back doing some work in Orkney. So of course, it was interesting to discover that you were on my doorstep. And then when I saw you in Orphir...'

'Were you looking for me?'

'No. Not at all. It's one of my favourite places. The Round Church. I spotted you there one day, early summer it must have been. July perhaps. Please don't be cross with me. I should have said something straight away of course, but I have to be careful, and I'm just desperate to see Anna again.'

He rubbed his hands. 'I was hoping you might help me.'

Here we go; he was after something. Of course, she'd known he was the one pulling the strings, watching her, reeling her in.

'I can see I've blown it.'

His eyes were wet again. God, she shouldn't be so brutal.

'But how could I help you?'

'Look here, I don't want to demand too much of your time and energy. I just wondered if you could test the waters. Find out whether Anna is up for a meeting. I haven't seen her for thirteen-odd years. I don't want to call her out of the blue, say here I am, hiding out in Hoy, let's meet. Who could blame her if she blew up in my face, told me to sod off, ranted to her mates?'

She extracted another biscuit, bit into its edge.

'I believe she was very fond of you. I heard you got on well.'

Sam blushed, she couldn't stop the ends of her mouth curling into a smile. Pierce latched on to her reaction. 'I thought you might like to see her again. What do you think? Would you be prepared to do it?'

She wanted to steer clear of Pierce's spying networks, but she'd be lying if she said she didn't particularly want to see Anna again.

'If all this makes you feel uncomfortable, say no. But don't worry, I'll make sure you don't end up on anybody's list. In fact, I could find out whether there are any old files with your name on them, just to be sure. Wipe your slate clean.'

A tempting bonus – it would be a relief to know her name had been removed from the cavernous vaults of the secret state.

'You wouldn't have to do much. Go along with your housemate to one of these meetings perhaps. See if she turns up. And if she does, you could say hello. You'd have to be careful how much you revealed, you couldn't tell her you'd met me here, in Hoy. Not until I'm sure it's safe. Just find out whether she's interested in being in contact with me again, that's all.'

There didn't seem to be anything too difficult or underhand in his request.

'Obviously, you can't simply phone me and report back. Or write. I mean, I wouldn't want anybody else to know... I was wondering...' He rubbed his chin, the silvery bristles glinting. 'Is there any reason for you to come back to Orkney this autumn? Will you still be doing whatever it was you were doing at the Earl's Bu?'

'No,' she said. 'The work is over for the summer. I'm hoping to come back next summer to help with another survey. I'm going to make the Earl's Bu the subject of my PhD. I wasn't intending to come back before then, not least because of the cost.'

'Cost?' he said. 'Oh, don't worry about that. Aren't there some archives you need to consult?'

'Archives?' Sam's voice lifted; she hated to admit it but there was nothing she liked better than digging around in archives. 'Well, I will have to check the archives at the library at some point to see what I can find out about the history of the area and previous excavations.'

'There we go,' he said. 'A visit to the archives. I'll pay you. I'll cover your costs to come back and report sometime this autumn when you've had a chance to talk to Anna.'

'Really?' The prospect of a paid-for return visit was definitely tempting.

'Of course, I wouldn't want you to be out of pocket. I can give you some cash now.'

He turned and disappeared through the door on the far side of the living room before she had a chance to object. She gazed out the window. The rain had stopped, the clouds had cleared and the sun was beaming, the sand golden, the ocean turquoise. A solitary raven flapped past, its feathers emerald in the rays.

'Here.' Pierce had returned, waving a fistful of tenners, his face more relaxed, the lines softened. He really was incredibly good-looking, she thought. Like Anna.

'Oh, this is like old times,' he said. 'I feel like a case officer again.'

'Case officer?'

'Handler.'

She must have blanched at the word.

'Handler, you're right, it's not a very pleasant term. Spook talk. I was a case officer for the Firm before I decided to go off piste. Into the field as it were. Set myself up as an arms dealer. So it's back to the good old days for me. You're my source, the one doing the demanding stuff, digging out the information.'

His words were tumbling out, relaxed now he'd come clean with Sam and sealed the deal. 'I'm the one sitting back, dishing out the readies, waiting for you to deliver the product. You're an invaluable asset. Sorry, old habits die hard. I can't help thinking in those terms. I'm going to have to give you a code name.'

'A code name?'

'Yes, a code name. Always give your source a unique code name, especially if you're handing out cash. I've learned the hard way, I'm afraid. Jotted a name I shouldn't have done next to some payment. Wasn't thinking.' He raised an eyebrow, shook his head, momentarily distracted by the memory. 'Gave me plenty of sleepless nights, that's for sure. Still, I seem to have got away with it.'

'What did you...'

'Enough of the questions now.' She was momentarily taken aback by the sharpness of his response.

'What am I going to call you? Let me think. Hmmm,' he continued pleasantly, which made her wonder whether she'd imagined the sudden edge to his tone.

'Hah, I know. You can be Ariel.'

She was being sensitive; there was nothing fierce about his manner now.

'Oh. Ariel. We could all have code names from *The Tempest*.'

'Good idea. I'm old man Prospero stuck on this island, and you're Ariel the free spirit who seems to be able to conjure rainstorms out of thin air.'

'OK. And Anna is Miranda, your beloved daughter.'

'Yes indeed. And I'm afraid she is in many ways just as innocent as Miranda, which is precisely the problem. I don't want her to be used or manipulated by scheming Trots or desperate Eastern Bloc spooks going for one last jab at their

Western counterparts, so let's do it this way. Keep it between you and me. In the family.' And what was Jim's code name in this drama, she wondered. She was afraid he might be Antonio, Prospero's scheming brother, whose treachery was the cause of his exile to the island. Pierce flicked through the notes in his hand. 'There. Three hundred.'

Her eyes widened.

'If you spend more than that, keep the receipts. Let me know how much.'

He stepped over to his shelves, returned with a notebook and biro, flicked to the back page, scribbled, ripped the page out, handed it to her. 'That's a PO Box, where you can contact me to let me know you're coming. Give me a date and sign it Ariel. That's all. It's not a direct line, so to speak. It will take a week or so for a message to get to me. Oh, and don't forget, my name is Hill. Steven Hill.'

He flipped the pages again, jotted *Ariel, £300* and then the date. *10th September 1989.* 'Anal, I know,' he said. 'I like to keep a note of cash flows.'

He pointed the biro at her. 'We need a name for the operation.'

'Operation?' She was trying to pretend she wasn't enjoying this, the code names, the secrecy, but part of her was having fun.

'The mission for you to contact Anna. Operation Tempest? No, that makes us sound like a bunch of storm troopers.'

'How about operation Fisher King?'

'Fisher King?'

'It's a story Jim told me – that summer when Anna stayed – about a damaged king who can't guard the treasure he's supposed to be looking after because of his wound, so his precious chalice is stolen and the land around him is cursed. I remember seeing you limp that afternoon you dropped Anna and Valerie, and somehow in my head I associated the story with you. You were the wounded Fisher King and the drought was the curse.'

Pierce's mouth opened, lost for a reply, and Sam wondered whether she had put her foot in it, overstepped some boundary. Unforced error. She often misjudged these things, hung back too much and then made a bad move to compensate for her awkwardness. Pierce recovered himself.

'The Fisher King.' He chuckled. 'Yes, Jim was always a bit of a storyteller. Aren't we all in one way or another? I like that. Operation Fisher King. Mission objective – contact Anna. Code name Miranda. No mission creep.'

'No. Definitely not. No mission creep.'

She couldn't help warming to Pierce. He was OK. Open. Sensitive, relatively anyway. A wave of maudlin self-pity hit her; Anna had a caring father. A living father. She felt herself sinking. She had to move, breathe fresh air, clear her head.

'I'd better get going, I want to stop off at Pegal Bay on the way back to the ferry.'

'Of course,' he said. 'Of course.'

He held the front door open; the sun poured in, the crescent of Rackwick Bay spread below and she wondered, as she crossed the threshold, whether it was possible to find a more enchanting front-door view, anywhere.

'Oh, one more thing I forgot to tell you.'

She turned.

'She's changed her name.'

'Anna?'

'Yes. Changed it to Hilary Bird. Don't ask me why, I'm not sure it was necessary, I'm the target not her. But there we go. We all overreact, I suppose. I just wanted to let you know.'

'Right. Hilary Bird.' She wanted to laugh; she couldn't imagine Anna as Hilary, it didn't seem right. Quite odd, in fact, but then being the daughter of a spy was strange, and she had done odd things herself in response to perceived dangers. So now Anna had three names: her real name Anna, Hilary her cover name, and Miranda the cipher that she had to use with Pierce to ensure that neither of the other two names were revealed. This was going to be a laugh. Or maybe it wasn't.

'Knew I could rely on you. Like your father. Trustworthy. Smart. Ariel,' he added. 'Fitting.'

She didn't look back as she traipsed down the path. She could tell he was still standing there, watching. Reassuring in some way to have his eyes on her back.

Through the grey valley, the sun brightening the northern slope, right on the coast road, past Betty Corrigall's grave, white against the heather. Enticing Pegal Bay. She pulled over, scrabbled through the chest-high bracken, reached the gurgling burn, removed her plimsolls, dipped her foot in the clear water, retracted it immediately. Freezing. She swirled her hand in the stream, searched, pulled out a glassy black rock, scratched it, saw the red streak on her hand. Jim had told her about the hermatite that summer. He was on the phone arguing with somebody as she entered the kitchen to fetch a couple of ice pops from the freezer – one for her, one for Anna. He slammed the phone down. Bloody personnel department, he had said and he waved his hand dismissively. Fucking pen pushers, he added. He'd never be one of them. He'd find something else to do without their bloody help. And then he asked, how do you get blood out of a stone? Look for a rock made of iron oxide, he said, without giving her a chance to think of an answer. Hermatite. You can find it at Pegal Bay. Hoy. God only knew where all his odd nuggets of information came from.

Jim. Police spy. Storyteller. Getagrip the fearless Celtic warrior. She thought she had him settled in her mind and then somebody said something or other and she saw him from a different angle. *Fault*. She tossed the hermatite into the water. It splashed and sank leaving a faint trail of red on the burn's surface, reminded her of the red mosaic tiles Anna had taken; they were made from ironstone the creepy curator had told them. Bloodstone. She sat back on her heels, wiped her wet hands down her coat. Ariel. She liked her code name; fitting, as Pierce had observed. Ariel the storm maker. The free spirit. Except Ariel wasn't a free spirit at all, she remembered now, not until he'd done Prospero's bidding.

CHAPTER 6

London, September 1989

PIERCE'S CASH HAD already come in useful; she had treated
herself to a bed on the overnight train to London and she
had the two-person berth to herself. The Cairngorms rolled
past the window, purple against the night sky. Moonlight
whitened the ghostly limbs of the silver birches lining the single
track. She had a sudden urge to leap from the train, roll down
the embankment and hide away out here, the middle of
nowhere. She thought about Pierce, alone in his remote and
poky croft, estranged from his family and friends. Had fear of
some Czech arms dealer really kept him there, lying low all this
time, or was there something else, some hidden wound that
bound him? She dug around in her backpack for the cheese and
tomato sandwich she had bought in Inverness, peeled the top
layer of soggy bread and regarded the paltry red crescents. She
had worked in a café one summer and had been instructed in
the art of laying two thin slices of tomato along the diagonal
line of the sandwich cut, ensuring that the exposed edges
promised more tomato than the sandwich delivered. Everyday
life was full of petty deceptions of one kind or another.
Everybody maintained a cover of kinds, the blank looks,
unanswered questions, half-truths, white lies, mis-directions.
Spies, like Pierce and Jim, they wove those petty deceptions
into something different, another persona, a separate identity.

And sometimes, she suspected, even they could not tell the difference between the real and the fake. If you lived a lie long enough, did it become the truth?

There had been moments, when Jim had been alive, when she had questioned her own existence, wondered whether she was merely part of his legend, a convenient prop for his undercover life. But now he was dead, she wanted to retain the good times with her father, let the bad memories slip away. She wolfed the last corner of the sandwich. Would Jim have done what Pierce did, she wondered, and gone to live in a remote hideaway without contacting them for years on end? Perhaps if he thought it was better – safer – for them. Or perhaps she was kidding herself about Jim, seeing him through rose-tinted glasses because it was too painful to remember him any other way. She washed the sandwich down with a cup of water from the tap above the tiny sink, peered through the grimy window as she drank, caught the moon rippling in the black water of Loch Insh. There was one dark fear about Jim that still lingered. The bad memory she couldn't forget. Her meeting with Pierce had made it more solid, illuminated its outline. Was Jim guilty of harming Pierce? Had Jim played the part of treacherous Antonio to Pierce's Prospero and betrayed him in some way? She couldn't let go of the nagging doubts, the questions. She sensed she had a duty to help Pierce reunite with Anna because both Jim and she had played a part in their fractured relationship. She was Ariel, slave to her master on the enchanted island, until she had completed the task.

She humped her rucksack on her back, decided to walk home from the station. Walking was good for the soul, as well as being cheaper and more reliable than any other form of transport in London. Euston to Vauxhall, one hour she reckoned. There weren't many journeys she needed to undertake in London that couldn't be covered in one hour. By the time she reached Vauxhall Bridge, the sun was belting and she was sweating. Vauxhall had been Jim's favourite bridge. Always a bit of a hotspot, he had said, a place where three rivers meet – the Thames, the Effra and the Tyburn. Jim had died on the south side of the bridge; the green patch behind the railway arches near the Royal Vauxhall Tavern.

Sam lived just beyond the bridge in a ramshackle hippy square. The first time she had lived there was in '85 when she had taken a year off university to recover from her father's death. She had suggested the square to Becky when she was looking for a cheap place to live so she could complete her medical training. Then Sam had moved in with Becky after she had finished her history degree that May. Sam had always thought of Becky as the senior partner in their friendship. Becky was confident and pragmatic; got on with her medical course at King's College while all her mates were hand-wringing and wondering about their place in the world. But as Becky was approaching her final year of study, she decided to have a break and signed up for a course on forensic science. A taste of the other side; investigating death rather than preventing it. She had enjoyed it more than her medical training, she admitted to Sam, and was wondering whether she should continue with the doctor's training at all. For once their roles were reversed. Sam had a four-year plan while Becky was dithering.

'Don't you mind living so close to the place where Jim died?' Becky had asked when she had offered her the room. Sam didn't mind, she found comfort in the river. In the aftermath of her father's death she had wandered the foreshore near Vauxhall

Bridge, searching for his presence. She had lost hours to the leaden flow of the Thames. Waiting for the jagged wooden stumps of the Bronze Age jetty to appear as the water ebbed, contemplating the violent death of her father, the hidden reach of the secret state. Submerged history, only revealed between the tides. It was harder to walk the Vauxhall stretch of the river now because, after many years of plans, false starts and delays, a construction company was digging foundations on the derelict land below the bridge, and access to the muddy banks had been blocked by some heavy-duty chainlink fences and a twenty-four-hour patrol complete with snarling Alsatians. Offices she presumed, although god only knew why they needed such aggressive security to guard a building site.

She was relieved to reach the coolness of the Vauxhall house. Old, damp, south London terraces, left to rot by Lambeth Council, the housing co-op granted a short-term lease on the square. Everyone was afraid that rocketing property prices meant the council would sell it off to the highest bidder. Their house was three storeys high, but Sam and Becky were the sole occupants because the top floor was a wreck.

Becky and she had very different habits. Becky was a collector of crap – second-hand clothes, magazines, ornaments from aunties. Sam couldn't stand owning things – she didn't voluntarily acquire stuff and if anybody gave her anything she waited a few weeks then gave it away. Liz had given her a spider plant to brighten up her college room and she had spent weeks battling the conflicting urges to water it and to let it die so she had an excuse to chuck it. In the end, she had let it die. It was a relief to bin it, although once she had dumped the withered thing she had felt guilty, wondered whether it revealed some deep streak of indifference that she couldn't even manage to care for a plant. But she did hang on to some objects, if they

73

meant enough to her. And she did keep hold of some friends. Becky being a case in point.

The front door snagged on the floorboards.

'Becky, I'm back.'

No answer. She dumped her bag, wandered into the sitting room, surveyed Becky's junk, walked over to a stack of newspapers by the sofa. She was snooping on her friend. No. She wasn't snooping, she was just looking at her magazines. She grabbed a couple from the top of the pile, made herself a coffee and sat on the kitchen step down to the small backyard. Home, she suspected, to a family of rats. Late-morning sun fell through the leaves of the rowan tree and gathered in yellow puddles on the mossy paving stones. She sipped her coffee and glanced at the cover of one of the magazines: *Marxism Today*. She flicked through the articles, unable to work up much interest. A couple of years ago she might have read this kind of leftie verbiage with more enthusiasm. She had forged her friendship with Becky on CND marches and trips to Greenham. Becky came from a family of liberal Jewish politicos and had moved through the cabals of the left as a teenager, but even she had given up attending the activist meetings when she started her medical course; too knackered by her studies for comrades and committees. Or, at least, that was what Sam had assumed. The course on forensic science had allowed Becky more free time and she had obviously been filling it with activist stuff. *See you later, I'm just off to this meeting about the poll tax.* Sam hadn't questioned Becky's renewed interest when she cheerily shouted goodbye up the stairs, but since Pierce had mentioned it, she had been wondering whether Becky was going to these meetings for the politics, or whether something else was driving her interest.

She took another mouthful of bitter coffee. What was she doing, questioning the motives of her best mate? This was what happened when she associated with spooks; their sneaky ways started infiltrating her life. Tradecraft. She stared at the ivy creeping under the back fence. That was where the rats were nesting, in the roots of the ivy. They should get a cat. She grabbed another paper, not a glossy mag like *Marxism Today*. *Militant*. Marxism Yesterday. She scanned the pages; the Polish election, strike action by the dockers, and at the back a page of reports and grainy photos of meetings. She scrutinized the pictures. There, sitting in a row behind a table decked with a home-made banner proclaiming *No poll tax* was Anna. Hilary Bird. Miranda. The details were blurred, but the curly black hair and pale face stood out from the grey. Unmistakably Anna. She folded the paper, tucked it under her arm, ran through the kitchen, the hall, up the stairs to her bedroom.

She searched the spines of her books, located the one she wanted. *The Secret Island*. A fat, thick-paged hardback she had inherited from her uncle. He had hollowed the pages out when he was a boy and he had handed it to her when she was seven. *The Secret Island*, very appropriate. Ha ha. She used it to store her stash and the precious mementoes that had survived the successive culls of her possessions. She opened the front cover, flipped the first two pages to reveal the roughly hacked-out rectangular hidey hole. She removed the Bryant & May matchbox, couldn't resist pushing the tray out to admire her prize specimen – emerald dung beetle, still glittering after all these years – placed the box on her desk. The envelope was wedged in the bottom of the hollow. She dislodged it with her fingernails, checked its contents – a used chequebook and a small school photo. She removed the photo, compared the face against the picture in the newspaper. Anna then and Anna now. As beautiful as ever. She replaced the photo in the envelope, jammed the envelope back in its hiding place, fitted the Bryant & May matchbox back on top, wiggled the book back into its space on the shelf, skipped down the stairs and resumed her position on the back step, dropped *Militant* beside her foot.

A sparrow pranced around the courtyard, searching for insects. The front door scraped. The sparrow fled to a topmost branch of the rowan, hopped and bobbed on its matchstick legs.

'Hello, Becky. I'm home. I'm out here.'

Becky stuck her head around the door.

'Good to see you. All right?'

'Yeah, I'm fine.'

'Find any skeletons up there in Orkney?'

'No. What about you? Had a good summer?'

'Not bad.'

She clattered around the kitchen, re-emerged clutching a mug.

'Shift yer bum.'

Sam shuffled over, Becky plonked down beside her. Becky was larger than her, a broad frame on which her flesh was smoothly moulded; chocolate eyes, chestnut wavy hair and olive skin. She nodded at the newspaper.

'What are you reading that for?'

'I wasn't reading, I was flicking. I'm so dozy. I couldn't sleep on the train. I needed something to keep me awake.'

'I would have thought *Militant* would have the opposite effect.'

Becky swiped a fly away from her face.

'What do they do anyway?'

'Militant? Oh, you know, Sam, what do any of these groups do? Sit around, talk about the evils of capitalism, make grand plans to overthrow the system, go to the pub.'

Sam's thigh felt hot against Becky's.

'Are they the group that's been organizing these meetings about the poll tax?'

'Not organizing. You know they're one of these parasite organizations.' She waved dismissively at the newspaper. 'Entryists. Why are you asking anyway?'

'I was curious that's all. Wondering why you were going to these meetings.'

'Because I'm fucked off with the poll tax.'

'Fair enough.'

'And because I'm interested in somebody.'

Sam drained the dregs of her coffee. 'You mean you fancy somebody?'

'Yes.'

'Male or female?' Becky had always said she went out with whoever she fancied; she didn't want to be defined by who she slept with.

'Female.'

Sam could see the inevitable coming, it made sense. Anna always was the kind of girl who everybody fancied. 'What does she look like?'

'Tall, leggy, dark curly hair, blue eyes. Gorgeous actually.'

Sam shivered, jolted the coffee cup in her hand.

'Are you OK?'

'Yes. Just tired.'

The spooks were monitoring Anna and whoever was watching her old friend had also spied on Becky. She wondered whether Becky's crush on Anna had been noted, passed on to some faceless case officer who had passed it on to Pierce. Should she tell Becky? Let her know she was being watched? Maybe not until after she'd managed to speak to Anna.

'What's her name?' Sam asked.

'Hilary.'

'Oh.'

'Where did you meet her?'

'She was handing leaflets out at King's, I got chatting to her, and she invited me along to one of their meetings.'

Sam picked the paper up, flipped the pages, pointed at the picture of Anna. 'It's not her, is it?'

Becky scowled. 'Yes. How did you know?'

'I guessed. I was flicking through the paper and I saw her picture. I thought I recognized her. Somebody I knew when I was a kid. And then your description fitted the bill. Except the girl I knew was called Anna.' Was that a mistake, revealing Anna's real name?

Becky pushed herself to her feet, ambled over to the rowan.

'Well, it must be a different person.' She sounded huffy.

Sam fumbled for another tack. 'Have you given up fancying men then?' God, that was clumsy. Becky didn't seem to care; she had always been open about her sex life, couldn't be bothered with coy secrecy.

'I've not given up fancying them – but I've given up having relationships with them.'

'Why?'

'It's a probability calculation.'

'Probability?'

'Yeah, I mean if you are going on a long train journey and there are two seats available, one next to a woman and one next to a man, which do you choose?'

'The one next to the woman.'

'Right. Because you don't want to run the risk of sitting next to a jerk. You know it's more likely that the woman will be OK. It's the same with relationships, as far as I'm concerned. I fancy men and women, but why take the chance of ending up with a tosser?'

She shrugged. 'You could reduce the risks by following the rules.'

'What rules?'

'Never go out with a man with a beard, because they're always hiding something.'

Becky grinned. 'Any others?'

'How about, once a bastard always a bastard.'

'Where did you get that one from?'

'A women's refuge.' She'd volunteered in a refuge when she was a student, and the first night she worked there the manager, a tiny black woman, took her into the office and showed her the notice pinned on the wall. *Once a bastard always a bastard*. You'd better be clear about that, the manager had said, because I've met so many women who thought it didn't apply to them, who believed it when the man who beat them up said he'd never do it again, and in some cases, it cost them their lives. Don't ever think there are exceptions. Working class, middle class, upper class, black, white, it doesn't make any difference.

'Once a bastard always a bastard. Very sound,' Becky said. 'I've got another one.'

'What?'

'Never trust a man from the West who insists on travelling by himself to Thailand.'

'Why not?'

'Seriously, Sam – you don't know?'

Sam shook her head. Becky had travelled around Asia in the summer of the previous year; Sam hadn't been outside Europe. Becky's experience sometimes made her feel naïve.

'Maybe I'm being judgemental, but it seemed to me that if you met a Western man travelling by himself in Thailand, there was usually only one reason he was there, and that was to buy sex. Half the time with underage girls.' She pulled a face of disgust.

'Jesus,' Sam said. 'I'll definitely add that one to the rule book then.'

'What about you?'

'What about me?'

'Relationships.'

'I've given up on them full stop. I want to get my PhD.'

'That's a bit drastic.'

'Maybe.'

She sensed Becky was over her huffy reaction to Sam's questions about Anna; she thought she could risk another move. Operation Fisher King commences. 'Could I come along with you to the next poll tax meeting?'

Becky lodged her hands on her hips, an edge of aggression in her stance.

'I suppose so.'

Sam ran her toe along the crack between the paving stones, chiselled the moss and damp earth. What was she doing this for? Jeopardizing her friendship with Becky for contact with somebody she hadn't seen for thirteen years. Lying through her teeth, digging up her past even though she had resolved to leave her murky family history undisturbed. She was a mole. A snoop. No, she wasn't; she was trying to help reunite Anna with her father, because if Anna didn't talk to him now, she might regret it later. She was a go-between. She was Ariel, using her magical powers to heal the bond between Miranda and Prospero, reunite them on the enchanted island of Hoy. What was wrong with that?

'By the way, your mate Tom kept calling while you were away.'

'He's your mate too.'

'He used to be.' Becky had fancied him once, a long time ago, but he didn't fancy her. Becky and Sam had met him on a CND march in London. Sam had stayed in contact with him and he had come with her and Jim on holiday to Orkney the week before Jim died. He had been curious about Jim, which, at the time, had annoyed her. Now the fact that he had met Jim was a bond Sam didn't want to relinquish. She was still hanging on to this relationship which had always been awkward, even when it was running smoothly. He asked too many questions for her liking. Tom was a journalist. He would, she reckoned, report on his granny if he thought he could get a by-line from it; always after a story. Coppers and journalists, he had once commented, had many similarities. Exactly: never trust any of them with a secret.

'What did he want?

'To see you.'

Becky stretched her arm above her head, twanged the lowest branch of the rowan, dislodged a shower of golden leaves and sent the sparrow fleeing skywards. 'Why don't you have a relationship with him? He hasn't got a beard. He isn't a creepy male sex industry tourist.'

'He spent six months in Afghanistan by himself.' Stringer for Reuters, reporting on the tribal rebels fighting the Soviets.

'Afghanistan is a conflict zone. That's a different form of perversion. Attraction to danger. He's obviously keen to see you. You should find out what he wants.'

Sam could read the subtext; *concentrate on your own social life*.

'Last time I spoke to him he was about to move. Did he leave his number?'

'Yep.'

'OK. I suppose I'd better call him.'

CHAPTER 7

London, September 1989

SHE HAD ARRANGED to meet Tom at the South Bank. She followed the Thames downstream, the autumn sun low in the sky, the damp breeze rustling the papery leaves of the overhanging plane trees. Remembering Jim. The first years after his death she had been haunted by him, glimpsed him on the Vauxhall foreshore at low tide, a solitary figure traipsing the river's edge. Five years on, he didn't occupy her mind in the way he had done in those early days and when he did materialize he was a more benign presence: a swagger, a whistle on the wind, a jaunty wave of the hand, a comic cop's string of expletives. Perhaps she had just become more adept at locking away the ghosts. She had learned to deal with the shadows by becoming more like a spy, compartmentalizing, retreating into herself. She had once asked Becky whether she struggled to resolve her inner and her outer selves, and Becky had given her the blankest of looks, which made her think that some people negotiated their demons with greater ease than she did. Or maybe they had yet to stumble across their cupboard full of skeletons.

The South Bank was the middle-class version of the brutalist housing estates that littered London; a concrete ziggurat that people visited for entertainment before they went home to their cosy Victorian terraces. The café was under Waterloo Bridge.

She was there first. She was always everywhere first, she couldn't be bothered with being fashionably late. She parked herself at an outside table. A bedraggled pigeon hopped along the wooden rail marking the boundary of the café's premises, shat down the slats, flapped away and sheltered on the rusty girders on the underside of the bridge. She tried not to inhale too deeply – she didn't want a lungful of the petrol fumes from the traffic crawling overhead. Loops of white lights strung along the embankment swayed in the gusts, made the deserted riverside seem more melancholic than magical; a party which nobody had bothered to attend. Tom was late, as usual. She watched him approach; buzz-cut apricot hair like a mangy chick, tall and gaunt with a cautious stride as if he was worried about treading on a landmine. She wondered whether he was putting it on, this air of war-beaten vulnerability, and then felt bad for doubting him. They exchanged greetings, his accent still audible. He came from Bolton and made a big deal of his northern roots.

'Let me buy you a drink.'

She used to drink whisky with her father. Since his death she hadn't consumed much alcohol. She preferred dope. Tom had always been critical of her pothead tendencies, which she found a bit rich given his drinking habits. Drinking, apparently, went with the Fleet Street territory – another similarity between cops and hacks. She fancied a glass of something, though, to warm her insides.

'I wouldn't mind a red wine.'

He returned with two plastic beakers, sat opposite, gave her a meaningful look. He had brown eyes and pale lashes. His eyebrows were almost invisible, like hers. Eight years ago, when she first met him, she thought gingery hair and pale eyelashes were unattractive. She had never been able to tell whether he fancied her or not. Jess would have said of course he did, but then she thought sex was the prime motivator of all men. She suspected he didn't; he had other reasons for seeking out her company. She took a sip of wine, the plastic beaker squishing in her hand. Vinegar. Yuck. It was also, she realized as her brain reacted instantly to the alcohol, a tactical error.

'What have you been doing all summer then?' Tom asked.

'Nothing much.'

'You've been away, though. I called your place a couple of times. Becky told me you were in Orkney.'

'I was.'

'What were you doing there? Or is it a state secret?'

'Of course it's not a state secret.'

'You're so cagy about everything. I sometimes wonder whether you've had the old tap on the shoulder.'

He was right; she had been tapped by Pierce, turned when she felt the eyes on her back, roped into the manoeuvres of an ex-spook. She flushed.

'If anybody tapped me on the shoulder, I'd tell them to fuck off. I was doing a geophysical survey of the site of a Norse settlement mentioned in the *Orkneyinga Saga*.'

She hoped bringing Norse literature into the conversation would deter him from asking further questions about Orkney.

'God. Is that what you're researching for your PhD?'

'Yes.'

'Spare me the details.'

'OK. What about you?'

He grinned; they were both more comfortable talking about him. 'I've got a staff job at the *Sunday Correspondent*.'

'The which?'

'The *Sunday Correspondent*. It's a new paper. It's just been launched.'

'I know. I was joking.'

'Oh. I should have realized. I'm on the investigative journalism team.'

'Team?'

'There's two of us.'

'What are you investigating?'

He scratched his head. 'I've got a couple of ideas on the go.'

'Like what?'

He glanced over his shoulder, leaned forward conspiratorially. 'They want me to do something on the demise of the Eastern Bloc.'

She nodded. 'Go on.'

He scrunched his face. 'Actually, I'm finding it hard to think of a good angle.'

'Not like you, not sure of your story. No burning leads to follow.'

The pigeon landed on the table again. He shooed it away.

'I need a killer idea. I feel a bit out of my depth, truth be told.'

'What, with the subject?'

'No. The paper. It's a clique. All these Londoners who knew each other at Oxford.'

'You could have gone to university.'

'I know, but I didn't. And I wouldn't have got in to Oxford.'

'You didn't try. And anyway, you've been a war correspondent in Afghanistan. Doesn't that give you an edge of rugged glamour?'

'I was a stringer, not a war correspondent.' He sucked his top lip. 'An Oxford degree would have been better.'

She took another glug of wine; the embankment fairy lights blurred.

'I haven't found that an Oxford degree is the golden key to everything.'

'That's because you're…'

'What?'

'Oh, I don't know. Nothing.'

'Thanks.'

He always did this to her, riled her in some way, egged her on. She leaned forward now. She had an idea. Should she be doing this? There were pros and cons but her mind wasn't clear enough to assess them. The Czech arms dealer. What had happened to him? Was he still a threat to Pierce? Where was he? Perhaps Tom could ask around, see what he could discover.

'Why don't you investigate what's happening to all those Eastern Bloc spies who can see which way the wind is blowing? Are they digging in, retrenching, or are they breaking free and looking for other sources of income?'

He tapped his fingers on his mouth. 'That's quite interesting. But it's… woolly.'

'It was just a thought.'

'I need something more tangible.' He tipped his face to the pigeon squatting under the bridge, back at her.

'Didn't you once tell me that your dad hung out with KGB officers?'

It was true, she had told him her stories about Jim and the KGB. He used to work at Tilbury docks checking the boats coming in from the Baltic; he went on regular vodka-drinking sprees with his KGB counterparts. She didn't want Tom going after stories about her father. She had to train him on the Czech.

'Jim did hang out with KGB officers, but they were bottom of the ladder. Grunts. Not really worth the effort. Maybe you should start somewhere else. Somewhere a bit less hard-core than the KGB. Somebody told me about this guy, a Czech.' She was being reckless, she knew it. But all secret missions involved some kind of risk, and if she was going to complete Operation Fisher King successfully, she should take a calculated chance right now.

'A Czech? What about him?'

'He used to work for the StB. That's the Czech state security service.'

'I know that. Státní bezpečnost,' he added.

'Exactly. Anyway. He was a front man for Omnipol.'

'Oh, they sell guns and explosives to everybody. They don't give a shit. What happened to him?'

'He got booted out after the Soviet invasion in 1968, so he went freelance.'

'As an arms dealer?'

'Yep. And then he got involved in this arms deal in 1976. Well, in fact, it might have been a set-up, an MI6 sting, and then the set-up was blown.' She showed him her palms in a there-we-are gesture.

His eyes flickered under his pale lashes. There was something gratifying about his interest. 'Is that it?'

She tutted. 'Isn't that enough?'

'No. It's a nothing. It's like all your stories, it's a hint of something sinister with nothing solid behind it.' His tone was accusatory, as if he had paid her for information she'd failed to deliver.

'I thought it was quite a good story. The collapse of the Soviet Union and the privatization of the state monopoly on violence.'

'Well, yes, it would be if there was some substance to it. Some facts. But at the moment there's nothing there. The story you've given me isn't even from this decade.'

'It's a start. A way in.'

'I need a lead.'

Did she have a lead? The funny thing was, she might have one, from that sweaty day in Lewisham.

'There is a lead actually.'

'Yeah?'

'Yeah.'

He clasped his hands in front of him on the table. 'Are you going to tell me then?'

She drained her beaker.

'I'll get you a refill.'

Tom returned with a brimming cup, squirmed on to the bench opposite, the moon rising behind his head, vast and orange.

'So, this lead?'

'I'm not certain it is a lead. And even if it is, it probably won't go anywhere because, as you said, it's so long ago now.'

'What is the lead?'

'It's a name and address. Somebody who knew the Czech. Possibly.'

It was only a possibility, but it seemed like a good guess. Pierce had been working on a sting which involved a Czech arms dealer. The woman in Lewisham she'd spotted that day with Anna was Czech. She toyed with the name and address, wondered about the ethics of revealing them to Tom. Her rationale. She wanted to see if he could dig up anything on the Czech. The worst that could happen would be that Tom would go to the address, ring on the door bell and whoever lived there now would tell him to sod off.

'Go on then, tell me.'

'Karina Hersche. Castle Street. Number Fifty-two C. Lewisham. She was living there in 1976, so she's probably long gone.'

He eyed her shrewdly. 'You always did have a good memory.'

He reached for the notebook he always kept in his top pocket, a pencil parked in its spiral binding. 'Karina. How do you spell Hersche?'

'H.E.R.S.C.H.E. Will you look at that harvest moon?'

He twisted. Looked back.

'How did you get hold of the name and address?'

'It's a long story. It was the summer of '76.'

'The heatwave?'

'Yeah, I was with a friend, Anna.' Tom's pupils dilated. She shouldn't have dropped Anna's name. But what could he do with a Christian name? 'Anyway, my friend's father... might... have had something to do with this MI6 sting. And we discovered the name and address of one of his contacts. A young Czech woman. Or at least she was young then, in 1976.'

'And?'

'As I said, I was with a friend whose father...'

'Anna. Whose father was a spy. Your childhood must have been...'

She had given too much away. It always ended up like this between her and him; she couldn't resist the urge to show off, prove she had newsworthy secrets. And then she regretted it.

She pointed at the moon. 'That's the second red moon in a row.' The first had been a blood moon on 17 August. She had stretched out flat on her back in the damp grass at Orphir and watched the shadow of the earth seeping over the milky lunar face, tinging it red, casting the meadow in a womb-like darkness and she had wondered whether it was an omen.

'Do you think this Czech dealer could still be at large?'

'Don't know.' She fixed her gaze on the moon, imagined its trajectory low over the black water of the Thames.

'So go on. How did you find out about this contact?'

'I can't tell you.'

'Nothing?'

She gulped the last of the wine. 'No.'

He drained the last of his coffee. 'Do you want me to walk you home?'

'No.' He had curtailed their meeting too quickly; he'd got what he wanted and now he was keen to scarper. 'Thanks for offering, though.'

She ambled homewards along the river. A jogger brushed past her, a woman in tight trackie bottoms that clung to her thighs, headphones clamped to ears, Walkman attached to her belt. What was with all the joggers around here? There weren't any joggers in Vauxhall when she first lived here in 1985 and suddenly they were everywhere. Yuppies, that's what they were. Up ahead, the moon hemmed the far corner of the Cold Store, the rotting warehouse by Vauxhall Bridge once used for storing meat and now frequented by gay men searching for late-night thrills. The darkened lift shaft was a regular death trap. Why were people so dumb? Was it because they enjoyed the danger, or because they didn't see it until it was too late?

She strode under the railway bridge, reached the square, heard Becky replacing the phone receiver as she shouldered the front door.

'You've just missed Tom.'

'I've just left him.'

'I know. He told me. He called from a phone box.'

Perhaps he'd called to see if she got home safely. 'What did he want?'

'He said he needed to check something; the only Castle Street he could find was in Catford, not Lewisham, and was it the right one?'

Typical. Tom the hard-nosed hack had gone straight to his *A to Z* and checked the address she'd given him. Well, he could work it out for himself. She called it Lewisham. Perhaps it was Catford. They merged into one another on the ground and in her memory, those grotty south London neighbourhoods. The moonlight spilled through the kitchen window, solidified on the hall floor, cast her shadow on to the front door. Funny how one piece of information – Pierce's revelations about the Czech arms dealer – made other fragments of her past seem clearer. Anna had been convinced at the time that the woman they trailed across Lewisham had been one of her father's contacts. She had doubted Anna at the time, but now it seemed quite likely she was right. What was it with these spies? Did they really think if they said nothing to their families, dumped them in the suburbs while they gallivanted around playing their games of subterfuge, their children wouldn't be able to work out what they were doing?

CHAPTER 8

London, July 1976

HELEN AND JESS and their mates were under the apple tree, wasps buzzing, kneeling around a body, flat on the ground with a jumper over its upturned face. Helen had moved on from the tarot and was doing levitation. Chanting. *Welcome to the House of Levitation. This girl looks ill. This girl is ill. This girl looks dead. This girl is dead.* Liz had been indignant when the mother of one of Helen's friends had complained that her daughter was having nightmares and suggested she should clamp down on Helen's occult tendencies. Occult tendencies, Liz had repeated later. Hadn't the woman read *Macbeth*? Marlowe's *Faustus*? Didn't she know that some of the finest plays in the English language were full of death and ghosts and witches? If Shakespeare had occult tendencies, she was fucked if she was going to stop her daughters having them too. Sam and Anna had been allowed to join in with the ritual, but after the third round Sam was getting bored.

She nudged Anna. 'Let's go for a bike ride.'

Anna said, 'It's too hot for cycling. Why don't we do something else?'

'OK. What?'

'I don't know.'

Sam had an idea. 'My gran gave me a book token for my birthday. We could get the bus to Lewisham, there's a bookshop near the shopping centre. You could buy a book too if you want, I've got enough.'

'OK.'

Helen shouted after them as they tip-toed away. 'Where are you two going?'

'Lewisham.'

'When will you be back?'

'Before tea.'

In the absence of a functioning adult, Helen generally took command. Jim had gone out, god only knew where. Liz was at some literary conference with Roger. Valerie wasn't functioning. She was in her room. Anna went upstairs to say goodbye. She returned looking anxious and was quiet on the walk to the bus stop. Perhaps it was the heat; the dustiness of the streets made you want to keep your mouth shut.

They sat at the front of the top deck, Anna still subdued.

'Are you OK?'

'I'm worried about my mum.'

'Is she sick?'

'Maybe it's because she's pregnant. Women feel sick when they're pregnant, don't they?'

'I think so, yes.'

The dead man's fingers of the silver birches scratched the windows as they drove along the common. Anna glanced over her shoulder, Sam did too. There weren't many people on the bus: four boys about their age giggling over some porn mag, a couple of suedeheads in Sta-Prest trousers sucking the straws of their McDonald's thick shakes. A McDonald's had just opened in Bromley. Sam had never been; Helen and Jess said the French fries were weird – not like proper chips. Anna pressed close to her.

'I think I know where my dad is staying.'

'Do you?'

'I think he has another house. Just before we left our home, I spotted a gas bill on the table. There was a name on it I didn't recognize.'

'What name?'

'Davenport.'

'So?'

'It might have been a false name my dad uses. Spies do that kind of thing.'

Anna seemed to know a lot about spies. More than she did.

'The gas bill might have been for a house he uses when he is working – it's called a safehouse, I think. He snatched the bill away when he saw me looking at it. I remembered the address, though. It's in Lewisham. Do you want to see if we can find it?'

Sam fiddled with her lip.

'I want to give him the tiles. I want him to have the magic protection of the Fisher King's treasures.' She glanced out the window. 'I want to tell him Mum's not well.'

Maybe it would cheer Anna up to have a look for the house, even if Pierce wasn't there. 'What is the address?'

'Backhouse Road.'

'Oh, I know that road. My friend Bridget lives there. She used to be in my class but they moved, and she had to change school. It's not far from the bookshop. We could go and look if you want.'

Goose bumps prickled Sam's arms; the excitement of being part of Anna's plot. The danger of heading into forbidden territory.

There was a derelict break between two lines of terraces. Second World War bomb hole Sam reckoned, the gap filled with sun-burned lilac and the castoffs of the intervening years; rusty twin-tub washing machine, portable record player in a cracked mint-green case, deflated orange space hopper. Davenport's house – Pierce's safehouse if Anna was correct – was the first of the second stretch, joined on the far side to another house and on the nearside to an overgrown garden that would have looked as if it were part of the bomb hole if it wasn't for the garden fence. The rambling garden was the only interesting thing about what would otherwise have been a regular suburban house; the long grass, already turning to straw, a great place for a den. They strolled past. Netted windows, grey door, a rubbish bin standing beside the bay window with its lid off, emptied by the binmen and not used since. She wondered whether the bin lid was a sign – spy code for nobody at home.

'It looks deserted,' Anna said.

Sam nodded, relieved that they had managed to do what Anna wanted without anything terrible happening.

'That's Bridget's house.' She pointed across the road, another row of identikit Victorian terraces, eager to distract Anna from the safehouse now.

'I'm desperate for a toilet,' Anna said. 'Can we go and see her?'

They crossed the street, rang the bell. The door was answered by Bridget's mum; she was small and bustling and Sam immediately regretted calling. Bridget had gone swimming with a mate, she would be back any minute, so why didn't they come in and wait? Hard to say no without sounding rude. They ended up sitting in the front room, feeling awkward, with a glass of lemonade and some Custard Creams, while Bridget's mum clanked pots in the kitchen. Sam was edging to get to the bookshop, but Anna seemed quite happy to perch on the uncomfortable sofa. Sam finished her lemonade. 'Maybe we should go.'

Anna shook her head. 'Let's stay a little longer.'

'Why?'

Anna nodded at the window. Sam clocked – Pierce's safe-house was in full view. Anna had been watching it surreptitiously while she drank. Sam wiped the back of her neck, sweaty even out of the sun. Anna's quiet intensity was unnerving. She had some concealed agenda, Sam was sure. She was out of her depth. She had thought she was moving of her own volition, but now she was aware that Anna had manoeuvred her here, nudged her in this direction. Sam squirmed on the sofa, trying to find a comfortable position.

Bridget's mum shouted through from the kitchen, 'Anybody want another drink?'

Sam said no before Anna had time to say yes. Anna scowled. Bridget's mum stuck her head around the door. 'I don't know where Bridget has got to, she should be home by now.'

'We'd better go anyway,' Sam said. 'I want to get to the bookshop before it closes.'

'I'm sorry you've waited for nothing.'

Anna said, 'The lemonade and biscuits were very nice. Thank you.' Bridget's mum beamed. Anna always managed to say the right thing at the right moment. Sam couldn't think of anything else to say, so she repeated Anna's thank you and grinned inanely as they made their way along the hall.

Bridget's mum opened the door. 'I'll tell Bridget you called.'

Sam felt Anna nudging her in the ribs, misunderstood the message.

'OK. Thanks for having us.'

'Any time.' Bridget's mum wasn't looking at Sam. She wasn't even looking at Anna. Her eyes were focused over Sam's right shoulder. Sam glanced too, took in a woman with long peroxide hair strolling slowly past Pierce's house across the road. She kept glancing around, conscious of their gaze perhaps. Bridget's mum whispered, 'That's the third time I've seen her here today. I wonder what she's doing.' She raised one eyebrow. 'This street isn't what it was. There are loads of funny people moving in. I've seen all sorts of men hanging around.'

Anna asked, 'What sort of men?'

'Swarthy.' She peered down the road. 'I hope Bridget's back soon. You be careful now. Don't go talking to any strangers.'

She retreated, closed the door firmly, left them standing. The blonde woman had passed the house and was heading to the far end of the road.

'Let's follow her,' Anna said.

'Why?'

Anna gave her a furious glare. 'Because I want to. I'm sure she's got something to do with my dad. She might know where he is staying.' She jumped down the steps, through the front gate, along the pavement. Sam fumed. She didn't want to be left standing on her own in the middle of Lewisham. She ran after Anna.

'I've always wanted to be a spy,' Anna said. 'Haven't you?'

'No.'

'It's fun. We can trail her.'

They crossed the road, kept their distance. Sam reckoned she was quite young. Or at least not as old as Jim or Pierce. She reminded Sam of a rich friend's French au pair she had once met. Young, pretty, cool in her tight faded jeans and stripy tee shirt. The woman glanced around as she walked.

'She thinks somebody is following her,' Sam said.

She must have clocked them over her shoulder but their presence didn't seem to bother her. Maybe she was worried about somebody else. She turned left at the main road. They turned too and saw her standing at a bus stop.

'Let's get on the same bus as her,' Anna said.

'Don't you think that will make her suspicious?'

'No. We're just two schoolgirls.'

'We could end up anywhere.'

'We can always get off if we think we're going too far.'

A double-decker trundled past them, destination Catford. The woman edged to the kerb. Anna started running.

'What about my book token?'

The bus juddered into the stop ahead. The woman stepped up to the back platform. Anna shouted to the bus conductor. He folded his arms in mock impatience.

'Hurry up. I haven't got all day.'

The conductor pinged the bell as they jumped on board. The woman edged on to a seat downstairs near the back exit. They shuffled past her, squished on to the next bench along. Close enough to hear her asking for a ticket to Ladywell. Sam heaved a sigh of relief; she wasn't going far at all – a couple of stops.

'Any more fares?' The conductor loomed. 'Where to?'

'Ladywell,' Sam said.

She paid for both of them. He twiddled the dials on the ticket machine dangling around his neck, whirred the handle, handed the paper strip to Sam. Anna was staring out the window.

'What's wrong with your mate then? Got the hump, has she?'

Anna didn't react. Sam shrugged.

'School holidays. Too bloody long if you ask me. Any more fares please.'

The bus dawdled along the main road, chugged into a stop, dawdled away, lethargic in the heat. Another stop. Sam glanced behind; the blonde woman was edging down the aisle.

She nudged Anna, but she was already standing. They made it to the back and jumped to the pavement as the bus pulled out. The woman turned. This close, Sam could see her scarlet lipstick and sad dark eyes. She looked away and carried on walking. They lingered by the stop, pretending to examine the timetable.

'I think she's Czech,' Anna said.

'What makes you think that?'

'Her face. I was looking at her reflection in the bus window.'

Anna knew all the spies' tricks.

'She took a book out of her bag. I'm sure the writing on the cover was in Czech.'

'Czech? How did you work that out?'

She doubted Anna could even see the writing on the woman's book, let alone recognize that it was Czech.

'It was the same alphabet as the wrappers on the chocolates my dad brought back from Prague.' She said it huffily, irritated by Sam's challenge to her authority. 'I'm going to follow her. Are you coming with me or not?'

'OK.'

Sam couldn't resist the game. Anna had played along with the Iceni and the Fisher King's treasures after all, so maybe it wasn't fair to question Anna's story. The blonde woman took a left and they scampered after her, found themselves in a treeless street of vast bedsit converted mansions; basements with barred windows, cars parked bumper to bumper, someone playing 'Love Hangover' at top whack. The woman opened a gate ten or so houses ahead of them, skipped up the steps, paused, looked around while searching for a key, didn't seem to notice them, unlocked the door and disappeared. They followed, strolled past the house. Anna wanted to go and examine the name tags on the column of labelled bells by the door.

Sam begged her to leave it, she'd had enough; the grimy heat was getting to her. Anna reluctantly agreed. They turned back the way they had come, the bonnets of the cars shimmering, ants swarming from the cracks in the paving stones. Anna elbowed her ribs.

'Postman.'

He was advancing down the road, mail bag slung across his chest, pausing to check envelopes before pushing through front gates. Sam could almost hear Anna's brain whirring as he passed. She was such a schemer.

'Hang on. I've got to do something.'

She turned, sauntered after the postman. Sam opened her mouth, closed it, followed Anna. The postman had reached the steps of the house the woman had entered. He rummaged through his bag, pulled out a pile of mail, trudged up the front steps, rang on a door bell, leaned back. A sash window opened on the first floor, a face topped with an Afro leaned out.

'Parcel,' the postie shouted. 'I need a signature.'

'I'm coming down.'

Anna had reached the house and was bounding up the steps, made the top as the door swung open. Sam stood at the bottom, bewildered. The postman was handing over the parcel. Sam could hear Anna breathlessly explaining that she had to run up to give something to her aunt. She slipped inside. Sam fidgeted. The door closed. The postman descended, gave her a half smile as he strode away. Sam couldn't quite believe Anna's audacity; she got away with everything. There was something about her appearance, her perfectly pitched confidence. Sam was worried, though; she had no idea what Anna was doing. The sash window scraped shut. The man collecting the parcel had returned to his flat. Where was Anna? Sam's scalp was prickling. She was beginning to feel faint, standing on the baking street. She was considering the possibility of ringing on door bells when the front door sprung open and Anna bounded down the steps. She grabbed Sam's arm, propelled her back to the main road with a triumphant gleam on her face.

'What were you doing in there?'

'Looking.'

'For what?'

'Anything.'

'And did you find anything?'

Anna stuck her hand in the back pocket of her shorts, produced a white envelope, waved it in the air. 'I went up the stairs to the second floor, waited until that man had gone back to his flat, then went back to the hall. There were loads of letters on the shelf above the radiator.'

'You went through other people's post?'

She nodded, still grinning, pleased with herself. 'I found one with a Czech stamp on it. It's addressed to somebody called Karina Hersche. She must be the woman we followed.'

'You took the letter.'

'Yes.'

'It's not addressed to you. You can't do that.'

Sam wanted to cry. She didn't know who or what was upsetting her – Anna, Pierce. Or maybe even Jim, for a reason she couldn't put her finger on.

'I wanted to see her name and address.'

Anna flashed the envelope in front of her face; she clocked the stamp, *Ceskoslovensko* beside a red and gold hammer and sickle flag. Sam imprinted the name and address in her memory.

'Please, Anna. Put it back.'

Stealing mosaic tiles from an ancient monument was bad enough, taking other people's letters was too much. Anna cradled the envelope in her hand for a moment, and then she ran back and stuck it through the letterbox, returned to Sam.

'There. Happy?'

Sam's eyes were brimming. She didn't want Anna to see her tears. She was so hot and confused. She marched straight ahead. Anna caught up with her. Sam turned and glared and saw the dirty tracks down Anna's cheeks. She had been crying too.

'Are you OK?'

'Yes, let's go home.'

They sat on the back seat of the upper deck. Sam wasn't going to mention the woman again, but Anna said, 'She was one of Pierce's contacts. I'm sure.'

'Contact?'

'Yes. You know.' She was whispering. 'Somebody who gives him information. Maybe she knows somebody Pierce is watching.'

Sam gave her a doubtful glance, uncertain whether this was a game or whether Anna really believed what she was saying.

'She's definitely one of his contacts,' Anna said and nodded, as if she was confirming this observation to herself, and smiled, but not in her usual megawatt sort of way.

CHAPTER 9

London, September 1989

SHE WAS NERVOUS about seeing Anna again after all these years. The poll tax meeting was in the Crypt, Brixton. The last time she had been here was with Becky as well; 1987 and she had come down from Oxford to spend the weekend with her mate in London. There had been an all women's night, and somebody had been playing the guitar and massacring 'Only Women Bleed' with great sincerity. They had got the giggles and had to leave and retreat to the Prince Albert on Coldharbour Lane for a shot or two. Were any of London's churches actually used for worship these days? It wasn't that she believed in God but she didn't believe in mammon either and they were all being converted into offices or cafés or expensive flats, as far as she could tell. The steps were slippery, carpeted with soggy leaves. There was no light. Becky was acting aloof, keeping two steps ahead, making it clear that she didn't want to be associated with Sam, she was merely tolerating her presence at the meeting. Sam stumbled, a pain jolting her leg, and almost decided to go home. An evening with a twisted ankle and a bunch of old Trots calling people comrade and boring everybody to death with their talk of neo-imperialism; hardly an enticing prospect, she thought as Becky disappeared. Apart from the possibility of seeing Anna.

*

A burly bouncer in a puffy green bomber jacket guarded the door. Something about his penguin feet shrieked copper. He gave her a once over and handed her a clipboard.

'Name and address.' She glanced at the list; Becky had written her real details. Seriously. She couldn't believe it, she thought Becky was more sussed; hardly surprising that the spooks had been able to work out a connection between Anna, Becky and herself. Sam grabbed the pen and wrote *Minnie Mouse, Dick Street SE1*, handed the clipboard back. He gave her a dirty look. They huddled in the back row of the darkened room that reeked of smoke and corpses and she wondered whether the whole meeting was run by the secret state, a lure to flush out the revolutionaries. She was edgy. She shouldn't have come here, drawing attention to herself in this shadowy underground meeting.

'Will you stop acting like a toddler who needs the toilet?'

Becky wasn't bothering to hide her irritation, narked with her for tagging along. She attempted to control her nervous fidgeting, distracted herself by surveying her fellow conspirators. A clutch of chain smokers in anoraks huddled near the front. Misfits. Social no-hopers. The spooks and Militant members, she decided. The rows at the back were filled with people who looked more normal – like herself. Women, young people. Old people. Black and white. Locals. No sign of Anna. Sam was almost relieved; she'd done what she could, she should go now before the meeting started, leave Pierce to sort out his own problems. She nudged Becky. 'I think I might go home.'

Becky brushed Sam's arm away. 'Suit yourself.' She wasn't paying any attention, eyes glued on the woman who had emerged from a side door. Sam gawped too. More attractive than she had been when she was younger because her face was sharper, squarer. Arresting. Sam suppressed the urge to stand

and wave her hand in the air, shout hello to her old mate, her blood sister. Anna. Hilary. Miranda.

She stood at the front, next to a dome-headed man with a dark rim of hair and a pointed Lenin goatee.

Anna spoke first. 'Hello, my name is Hilary.'

Her accent was the same – Sam was relieved she wasn't doing a fake Cockney – but her voice was sombre. She reeled off a potted history of the poll tax – Thatcher this, class that. Blah blah blah. Sam glanced around the room again. Anna was holding people's attention; an enchantress, even in this earnest reincarnation. Anna sat. Goatee beard stood and rambled on about smashing the state. Sam stared at Anna; she must have felt her eyes boring into her face, but she didn't look her way. Sam nudged Becky.

'Is that the Hilary you fancy?'

'Yes.'

'I'm sure she's the girl I used to know.'

Becky tutted. The Lenin lookalike churned on.

'Yada, yada, yada, yawn.' Becky folded her arms.

The man in the green bomber jacket was puffing a fag in a corner and watching her. The straightforward personal mission to find her childhood friend and reunite her with her father seemed more complex in this damp crypt filled with spooks and cops and informers. She needed to be careful.

Lenin's speech came to an end. Anna stood.

'OK, any suggestions? Comments?'

A show of hands. Sam's brain clunked, searching for a suitable question; not because she wanted to join in the discussion but because she wanted to make her presence known to Anna. Becky was leaning forward, elbow on knee, chin resting on hand, ogling Anna. Sam raised her hand. Anna failed to meet her eye and nodded instead at a man in an anorak. He rattled on about leafleting rotas. Other hands shot up; awareness raising. Non-registration. Non-payment. Sam gave up, retracted her hand. God, she'd forgotten how much she hated this kind of meeting. The length of time people spoke inversely related to the interest of anything they had to say. The discussion petered out. Heads nodded, seats shuffled. Anna announced the date and venue of the next bash. Sam had to move quickly. She stood, ignored Becky's hand on her arm, squeezed along the row, working out her greeting as she went. She didn't want to use Anna's real name, not in public anyway. She reached the front of the room, a cluster of the committed gathering, and stood behind like a schoolgirl trying to attract the attention of the teacher. Anna ignored her, conversed with her followers. The gaggle thinned.

'Hi.'

Anna directed her large blues eyes at Sam's face, smiled politely.

'Can I help you?'

Sam was thrown by the blank.

'I wanted to say hello. We know each other.'

'Do we? Oh, I'm sorry, I'm not very good at remembering faces.'

Liar. Anna remembered everything she wanted to remember. Sam played along.

'We met when we were kids. You came to stay with my family in the summer of 1976. My name's Sam.'

Anna raised her eyebrows. 'I'm sorry. I think you must have the wrong person.' Her eyes flicked away, focused over her shoulder, registered interest, smiled the warm and generous smile Sam remembered. Sam spun around. Becky was standing behind her.

'Hi Becky, nice to see you.' Her voice instantly lifting from monotone to flirty.

'Hi Hilary, lovely to see you too. That was a great discussion. You're really good at public speaking,'

'Do you think so?'

'Yeah, you're great.'

'Thanks.'

Sam had a feeling of creeping invisibility. Insignificance. She coughed loudly. Anna's eyes flicked in her direction, back to Becky.

'I'm sorry I have to run. Are you coming next week?'

'Definitely.'

'Maybe we could go for a drink afterwards.'

'Sure.'

'It's a date.'

Becky flushed. In all the years Sam had known Becky, she had never seen her redden before. Anna marched away through the side door.

'Well?' Becky's brown eyes gleamed.

'Well what?'

'Well, she's not your old mate Anna.'

Sam raised her hands in exasperation. 'It is her.'

'She didn't recognize you.'

'She did. She was pretending she didn't.'

'Why would she do that?'

'I don't know.'

The man in the shiny bomber approached. 'Time to be leaving, ladies.'

Ladies. Giveaway. Sam had to stifle a cynical tut. Honestly, couldn't Her Majesty's finest do a little better than that? Standards really were slipping since her father's day.

The street lamp hummed, her bedroom sulphurous in its light. A car alarm blared. In the back bedroom, Becky snored. She was irritated with Becky for refusing to believe that the woman she fancied was Anna, not Hilary. She was irritated with Becky for fancying Anna full stop. Becky was her best mate. She didn't want her trolling off with bloody Anna. She didn't want to be the fucking gooseberry in an Anna–Becky lovefest. And she was annoyed by Anna's total lack of recognition. It was painful to think she might not have left any lasting impression on Anna or, worse, Anna did remember her and was not interested in renewing their friendship. The idea stung more than she would have expected. Whatever the explanation, she should drop it. Operation Fisher King was not going according to plan and now was a good time to abort the mission. Leave Prospero and Miranda to work it out for themselves. She didn't owe Pierce anything. Apart from three hundred quid. The estrangement between father and daughter was not her fault. Even if she suspected it might be Jim's. She tutted, kicked the quilt away, sat on the edge of the mattress, head in hands wondering what to do. Leave it? Follow it up? So much for blood sisters.

She stood, went to the window; the sky leaden, the dawn twittering of birds broken by the overhead rumble of the first plane trekking to Heathrow. A track-suited man leaning against the cherry tree on the opposite side of the street flicked his fag butt across the pavement, a cascade of red sparks falling before it landed in the gutter. He glanced up, saw her watching and jogged away. A jogger, smoking? No way. Pierce had told her MI5 had been keeping an eye on the poll tax campaigners. The smoking jogger was a spook. Why was he tailing her? Because she had spoken to Anna? Or tried to speak to her, at least. She felt uneasy. She couldn't read Anna, couldn't understand why she had been blanked. A scritch, scritch below her feet distracted her. Mouse. Rat. There it was again. She examined the floorboard crack. A woodlouse skimmed the edge and flipped into the void. She had played woodlice racing with Anna in the Great North Wood above Dulwich, the day Jim took them both to visit his mate Harry at his allotment. Harry; perhaps he could help. He knew about Pierce, perhaps he would have some idea whether Anna was playing tricky games. She crossed to her desk, grabbed the Colman's Mustard tin hiding behind the rusty Anglepoise, emptied the contents: a Yale key, a black-and-white photo of Harry and the back of Jim's head, a scrap of paper with a number on it. She stuffed the paper in her pocket. She would use the phone box by the Vauxhall Tavern, see if she could meet him. The woodlouse emerged from the floorboard crack, antennae wavering. She left it alone, didn't want to traumatize it further.

CHAPTER 10

London, July 1976

YET ANOTHER SWELTERING Saturday, a couple of days after her Lewisham escapade with Anna. Sam had crept downstairs in the early-morning light because she was hungry but had stopped in the front room when she heard her parents arguing in the kitchen. She curled up in one of the dilapidated armchairs, tried to block the acrimonious exchange. Liz asking why Intelligence couldn't look after the families of its officers, Jim saying it wasn't straightforward and anyway Pierce was a... Liz had lost it before Jim had a chance to say what Pierce was, shouted the Force was just as fucking bad, expected her to be a welfare support service for their stupid secret missions. She slammed the door and left. Sam sauntered into the kitchen. Helen and Jess must have heard the argument too, because they came downstairs without speaking, divided the last of the Special K, chomped in silence. After they had cleared away their bowls Helen announced they were going to the King's Road and wouldn't be back until the evening. Anna appeared. Sam stuck some toast under the grill and was distracted by a fox running along the bottom of the garden carrying a plastic bag. Jim shouted at her because she let the toast burn. She mooched around the house all morning with Anna. Valerie drifted downstairs, lolled on the sofa, read a book then dozed. She hadn't bothered to eat any breakfast and her skin was waxy. Sam couldn't help thinking she looked like a corpse. At noon Jim announced he was going to see Harry at his allotment. He glanced at Valerie's clammy face and said he would take Sam and Anna with him, give Valerie a rest.

Jim was in a good mood, on an upswing because he was seeing Harry. He raced them up the path to the top of the hill. It was humid under the oaks of the Great North Wood. The earth was cracked and scaly, the dry clay puffed underfoot and the thick air smelled of petrol, barbecued meat and dog shit. The bottles in Jim's haversack clinked, but he reached the clearing first despite his heavy load. She came second. Beating Anna didn't give her any sense of satisfaction. Anna walked the last stretch and they stood together on the summit; the land falling away beneath them, the suburbs covered with a cloud of grey pollution. Jim gazed over south London and said god but it's a cess pit. Then he told them that during the Great Plague, when south London really was an open sewer, people had sought refuge from the epidemic in the woods, and had lived on nuts and berries, but when the trees were stripped, thousands had died of starvation under these very oaks. He was sweating as he spoke. He wiped his forehead. Everybody had to die somewhere, he added, and the Great North Wood was as good a place as any to meet your maker. Anna caught her eye and she flushed. What was wrong with her bloody father? Why did he always tell these stories that ended in death and disaster? Pronouncing doom like some sozzled nutter. He didn't notice her embarrassment, or if he did, he didn't care. He pointed down the south slope of the hill to the allotments and the sleeping giant lying flat on his back by a water butt, face covered with a newspaper. 'Lazy bloody bugger,' he said. 'Let's surprise him.'

They followed Jim as he zig-zagged downhill, dashing between the thirsty dahlias and wilting runner beans. He sprinted the last few yards and whipped the newspaper from Harry's face before he had a chance to work out what was going on. Sam reached the allotment as Harry was sitting up and spluttering. Jim stood legs planted apart, arms folded, looking down at Harry, pleased with himself.

'Caught you napping, you old lardy-arse,' Jim said. 'Thought they taught you to sleep with one eye open in Intelligence.'

Harry had recently moved from the Force to some part of Intelligence, according to Liz, who had mentioned it with a shake of her head and a wave of her hand because she couldn't be bothered, she said, to keep track of what was a state secret and what wasn't.

Harry said, 'There's nothing here worth keeping an eye on. It's all dead already.' His Welsh lilt added an extra note of melancholy to his doleful assessment. 'Water restrictions.'

'Can't you use a watering can?'

'They've turned the bloody stand pipe off.'

He rose grumpily to his feet. He was huge, shovel hands and boxer's nose. He looked like somebody you wouldn't mess with but Sam had always liked him; he'd always been nice to her. He retrieved his newspaper from Jim with a quick swipe, rolled it, whacked Jim over the head. 'To what do I owe this honour anyway?'

Jim nodded at Anna. 'This is Pierce's daughter. Anna.'

She smiled shyly, which annoyed Sam because if there was one thing Anna wasn't, it was shy.

'I can see the likeness.' He paused. 'Pierce.' He gave Jim a meaningful look, harrumphed. Jim inclined his head, the slightest gesture. They had known each other so long they could communicate with these odd nods and grunts. Jim lifted

112

the haversack off his back, fished inside, produced a black bottle. Guinness. He handed it to Harry then turned to Sam and Anna. 'Why don't you two go and play in the woods for a bit?' He rummaged in his haversack again, produced two red and silver cans of Coca-Cola – the proper stuff, not a Tesco's imitation. A bribe.

They trudged through the allotments, retraced their path up the hill. Sam tugged the ring-pull, swigged, the tepid bubbles fizzed in her mouth. She didn't mind being sent away, she was happy to hang out with Anna. Anna was more indignant. 'They're talking about my dad. I should know what they are saying.'

Sam thought sometimes it was better not to know. She decided not to say what she thought. Instead she told Anna about Margaret Finch, the queen of the gypsies, who lived in the wood and died at the age of a hundred and nine, and had to be buried upright because she always sat in one position and they couldn't straighten her corpse. Anna seemed to be interested in the story, which pleased Sam.

'Who told you about her anyway?'

'Jim.'

'He's always full of funny stories.' Anna gave her a quizzical look. 'Does it ever bother you that your dad tells so many stories?'

'I like the story about the gypsy queen. And the Fisher King.'

Anna dribbled a stone along the path, scuffed a dusty trail. Sam knew what Anna was getting at; she was asking about the secrecy, the fact that half the time they never knew where Jim was and they weren't supposed to ask and even if they did he would reply with some sort of riddle. She had been told she wasn't supposed to say anything about Jim's work to anybody because it could be dangerous. Although she was never entirely sure what the danger was – the threat was vague, a dark cloud hanging. She hadn't really thought before about whether she minded or not; it was the way it had always been with Jim. She only really thought about it when Liz got upset because Jim didn't come home and she had nobody to call, or he did come home and he was edgy – looking over his shoulder, peering into crowds, drinking too much. Shouting. Aggressive. Now she was thinking about it, had somebody she could talk to, she realized it did bother her. She gulped another mouthful of warm Coke and swallowed the wrong way. The bubbles exploded, she spluttered, sprayed droplets on the ground, where they sat for a moment like diamonds in the dirt before they evaporated. 'Doesn't your dad tell stories too?'

'Yes. But not like your dad. Not fairy stories. They're more like...' Anna left the sentence hanging in the sticky air.

'Does it bother you then?'

'Sometimes.'

'Why?'

'Because...'

Anna screwed up her face, her lovely mouth twisted. Sam was afraid she might cry. She had been jealous of Anna when she first met her, envied her confidence, her charm, thought she had everything she needed, everything Sam didn't have. But now she felt sorry for her. Her dad had disappeared, his life in danger, her pregnant mum poorly, and she had to stay in a stranger's house. A lump formed in Sam's throat; she stuck her hands in her pockets, tried to think of some way of cheering Anna up. A blackbird crashed through the branches, its feathers mangy, alarm call shrill. She suggested they find some woodlice and race them. The newspapers were full of stories about ladybird plagues – nobody seemed to have noticed that the woodlice were multiplying in the heatwave too, invading the scorched earth, crawling over desiccated leaves and carcases of frogs and birds.

'OK,' said Anna.

They collected the woodlice in their hands, watched them curl, flicked them along the ground, rolled them into the earth's cracks. When they were bored with racing them, they built a woodlouse city from the fallen twigs and half-formed acorns shed by the dehydrated oaks.

The shadows were lengthening and the midges were glimmering in slices of amber light as they wandered back through the ragged wood. They reached the line where the trees ended and the allotments began. Jim and Harry were in view, sitting on the ground. Harry was waving a bottle in the air, pontificating about something or other. 'Forget it. Don't go trying to sort it out. Ignore it. That's my opinion. Keep away.' Jim was holding a bottle too, but his shoulders were hunched and his head was drooping. A thrush announced their advance. Harry started, nudged Jim and he straightened. Not quickly enough to correct Sam's impression that there was something heavy weighing him down. He stood as they reached Harry's allotment.

'Been having fun?' Jim asked.

'Yep.'

'Time to go now anyway.'

He didn't want them hanging around with him and Harry, didn't want them joining in their conversation about Pierce. The tension was almost visible in the space between Harry and Jim, the way they didn't look at each other, Harry's tight smile, Jim's clenched jaw.

They trekked back through the wood in silence, the sun dropping over Brixton, everything purple and hazy under the canopy. A sudden snapping made Jim spin around, stop, stare through the trunks. Nothing. Dead branch falling. Fox.

Jim said, 'What a summer. We'll remember this one for years.'

CHAPTER 11

London, September 1989

JIM HAD BEEN right, she mused, as she climbed the wooded hill above Harry's allotment; everybody remembered the summer of '76. She wondered whether the drought had left physical marks on people too, whether a vertical cut would reveal a layer of parched flesh like a stratum of soil uncovered by an archaeological excavation or the growth rings of an axed tree trunk. This place had certainly looked different in the heat; the drought had coated everything with a sepia tinge. The wood had seemed wild that summer, an arid land where ghosts and gypsies wandered. Now there were signs of management. The lush undergrowth of brambles, ivy, dock leaves and long grass covered the dusty patches where they had searched for woodlice. Signposts offered directions to walkers. The oaks were vibrant, leaves bronze and gold in the early-autumn sun. The wood was healthier, but tamer. A place of Sunday strolls and picnics. Not dead people. She preferred it back then, she liked the wild edges.

The sight of Harry's bulky form hunched over a spade made her eyes brim. Harry had been a constant if sporadic presence in her life; since Jim's death he had always been there when she needed advice. She blinked, waved as he spotted her. The signs of wear were beginning to show on his face these days, she realized as she approached him; his pale hair not quite as thick as it had once been, his eyes more hidden behind the creases of his flesh, his always bulky outline now gravitating to a paunch. He straightened and smiled.

'So, you've bumped into Anna again, have you?' He never bothered much with chit chat. She hadn't told him about meeting Pierce on Hoy. Harry might be a friend, but he was still some sort of spook, still doing something or other for MI5. She had to watch what she gave away.

'Do you remember meeting her the summer of 1976? Anna came to stay at our place and Jim brought us over here so her mum could have a rest.'

'Yes, I remember.' His voice was wistful; remembering Jim, his old mucker. 'Seventy-six. Disastrous year for the veggies. The drought withered everything. I couldn't use the hose.' He surveyed his allotment, the ghosts of harvests past. 'I reckon something shifted in the earth that year – knocked it out of kilter. I don't think anything's been the same since.'

She would have scoffed at the idea if it had come from anybody else.

'What's changed?'

'Little things. I notice them, digging the same plot of ground, year in, year out. More foxes, fewer hedgehogs. Not so many thrushes.'

'I think you might be right. Do you remember I used to collect beetles?'

'That's right, you used to kill them with crushed laurel leaves.'

Everybody remembered that detail.

'Yes, but what I was going to say was, I haven't seen a dung beetle on a cowpat for years.'

'Antibiotics. Farmers give them to the cows, dung beetles get sick on their shit. And then there's the weather. What's going on? Summers hotter than before. Autumn doesn't start until mid-October. That hurricane we had a couple of years ago, it toppled some of the oldest oaks in the wood.' He swept his hand at the slope behind. 'I reckon the drought damaged them, weakened their roots, made them less able to resist when the wind whacked them.' He shook his head. 'That's what it was for the plants, the drought. A trauma.'

A tortoiseshell fluttered past her face.

'I remember playing up there, and the leaves had already turned brown, even though it was only July. Some of the oaks were dropping deformed acorns.' She paused. 'You sat here all afternoon and talked.'

Harry glanced away. 'That's right. So how come you met her again after all these years?'

'Chance. I went to a meeting with a friend.'

'Not one of your let's protest outside a top-secret nuclear weapons base type meetings, I hope.'

'No. Well...'

'I thought you'd given all that stuff up and were concentrating on the studying.'

'I am. A friend asked me to go with her. It was an anti-poll tax meeting.'

'Poll tax. Bloody stupid idea.'

'Exactly. And Anna was there.'

He pulled his mouth down at the ends. 'So?'

'It's just that...' She had to think of a reason. 'She pretended not to recognize me, and it unnerved me. My friend likes her, so I just wanted to find out whether there's... I mean, why didn't she say hello to me? Why did she insist her name was Hilary? Could she be an informer or something like that, a spy for somebody or other?'

'You mean like Pierce?'

'Yes, like her dad.'

'What do you know about Pierce?'

She reddened; he had caught her out.

'Anna told me he worked for the Firm.'

He shook his head. 'Spooks and their kids.'

Liz had once told her that Harry had been married, ages ago, but his wife had left him because she couldn't put up with his job. He had never remarried. It hadn't ever occurred to Sam that he might have had a child with his wife before they separated. Something about the sad way he said *kids* brought the possibility to her mind.

He scanned the ground when he sensed her scrutinizing his face, found a carrier bag. 'Here, you might as well have the last of the tomatoes.'

'Thanks.'

She poked among the drooping stems, delving for the ruby fruits, their ripe scent smothering. Harry leaned on his spade.

'Pierce,' he mused. 'Pierce the hero.'

Jim had once said he was a bit of a hero too.

'Why the hero?'

'The Freeman tape.'

Freeman. The name had a ring of familiarity but she couldn't pinpoint why – perhaps she had read it somewhere.

'What's the Freeman tape?'

'Well now, I don't see the harm in telling you that. Worst-kept secret in the history of spying, everybody was talking about it in the seventies. Especially Pierce.' His cynicism didn't mean much; Harry was cynical about most of his fellow spooks. 'Freeman was one of Pierce's covers in the early seventies. One of many. He was one of those operatives who seemed to be able to manage dozens of different identities at the same time. Have to hand it to him, it takes some doing. Anyway, he was working on arms shipments to Ireland, and he managed to tape some bigwig Libyan talking about Gaddafi's supplies to the Provos.'

Harry swatted a wasp away with the back of his hand.

'Big breakthrough. First solid piece of info on that supply line. Taped in a shared taxi apparently. The Libyan does all the talking. Freeman doesn't say a thing. He listens, lets the Libyan run. You wouldn't even know that anybody else was in the taxi except, right at the end of the conversation, the Libyan says his name. Freeman. Classic piece of tradecraft. It made Pierce. His reputation rests on it.'

Pierce hadn't told her about the Freeman tape; he didn't play the hero. Not to her at least. She decided she could risk another prompt.

'Then in '76, he had to go into hiding.'

'Yeah. That was the Czech.'

'The Czech was an arms dealer?'

'Arms dealer? The Czech? Not quite as simple as that.'

She could hear the tension in his voice.

'Oh? What was the complication?'

Harry sucked his lips, and she thought she had blown it, overstepped her quota. But he continued. 'The Czech wasn't quite what he seemed. Although beats me why anybody should be surprised that a dodgy Czech arms dealer wasn't quite what he seemed, but there you go. Reznik was his name.'

'Reznik?' Pierce hadn't mentioned his name.

'Yeah, Reznik. Do you know what Reznik means in Czech?'

'No.' Of course she didn't.

'Butcher.' He slashed the air with his hand. 'Lives up to his name. He's got this funny-looking left eye apparently – scar tissue eyelid and no lashes. The story is he used to catch cats in the village where he grew up, strangle and skin them, then sell them in the next village as rabbit meat. But one cat fought back, scratched his eye. He got an infection, his eyelashes fell out and never grew back.'

'God, he sounds evil. No wonder Pierce went into hiding.'

'Hmm. Pierce was playing the link man between Reznik and that terrorist group – the Red Army Faction. They weren't too nice either. Some of them are still on the loose.'

'What, they're still active?'

'They assassinated a couple of people in 1986. Siemens manager and his mate. They're fairly desperate these days. On the run and short of cash. Anyway, in '76 it was Reznik that was the main concern,' Harry continued. 'Pierce had to go into hiding when his cover was blown – to avoid being butchered.' He laughed. She blanched – Operation Fisher King was turning out to be riskier than she'd expected; she'd sent Tom off on the trail of the mad butcher. Still, it didn't matter. He was a hack. He could handle it. He wouldn't get anywhere with the lead anyway.

'What happened to Reznik?'

'He had to vanish too, because his credibility with his customers here had been blown. Rumour has it Reznik asked for a post in Moscow, but everybody there was scared of him, so they sent him across the pond. And our cousins over there eventually found out that he had connections with the KGB.'

'He was a spook?'

'You sound surprised.'

She was, but she couldn't tell him Pierce had said the Czech was working freelance.

'Not uncommon. Loads of arms dealers have connections with spies, security services. It's more a case of knowing who is working for whom.'

Perhaps Pierce didn't know about the Czech and the KGB. Perhaps Harry's information was wrong. It sounded like it was all just stories anyway. Nothing definite. She ducked and searched for the low hanging tomatoes.

'Is he still in the US?'

'Dunno.'

A two-spot ladybird landed on her arm, bumbled around for a moment then lifted its wings and fled.

'Although one thing I do know.' He turned and stared at her. 'These are dangerous times. The turf is changing. All those old Soviet state assets – oil, land, manufacturing – they're about to be sold off. Everybody's jostling for position, trying to get their nose in the trough. Men like Reznik, they'll be throwing their weight around. Nobody properly in control. He's a mad man without a handler. Anna's probably wise to be careful about revealing too much to anybody, keeping some other identity. Hilary, whatever; the name she's been using since she left your place, I would guess. Can't say I blame her for giving nothing away.'

'You think she might be in danger?'

He puffed his cheeks, surveyed the line of the hill.

'I'd rather be safe than sorry if I were her, even if he is still in the States. Families – always a weak spot. Everybody goes for the vulnerabilities.'

He nodded at the bag she was holding. 'You're a bit slow.'

She twisted another tomato from its stem, placed it in the bag.

'And you'd be wise,' he added, 'not to have too much to do with her. Anna or whatever she's calling herself now. Take a leaf out of her book; don't go digging.'

She opened her mouth, about to protest, decided it was pointless.

He shook his head. 'Not that you'll take any notice of what I tell you anyway.'

'I will.' She didn't sound very convincing, even to herself.

'Look,' he said. 'I can see it's going to bother you. This thing about Anna pretending not to recognize you. I don't want you playing detective. I'm not going anywhere for a few weeks. I'll ask some discreet questions, find out what I can about Anna. Check there's nothing dodgy going on that you should know about.'

'Thanks.'

'What's the best number to call you on?'

He dug around in a pocket, produced a notebook and pen. She scribbled the Vauxhall number down.

'Do you think it's safe to use my home phone?'

'Have you heard anything on the line?'

'No, but I've noticed people watching me a couple of times just recently.'

He frowned. 'What sort of people?'

'Joggers.'

'Joggers?'

'Well, they wear track-suits.'

He hesitated. 'It's always safer to use a phone box. I'll give you three rings, put the phone down, three more rings when I've got something and you can call me back. But don't expect too much, too soon. I've got to keep a low profile myself these days.'

'Why?'

'I'm on gardening leave.' He wrenched his spade from the soil.

She was shocked. She couldn't imagine anyone daring to give Harry the elbow. 'You've been sacked?'

'Not yet.' He lunged at the soil again. 'When they told me to go on gardening leave, I don't think they expected me to take it literally. Enjoying myself too much.'

'What did you do wrong?' She shouldn't have said that, it sounded like an accusation.

'Nothing. Nothing at all. Like I told you, these are dangerous times. The boundaries are changing. We've got a new boss, clean sweep and all that crap. She wants new blood. Yuppies.' He turned the soil. 'And she doesn't like me or my kind. Old school. I'm on the compost heap. Not like Pierce. The hero.'

'Is Pierce still working?' That wasn't what he'd told her.

Harry jiggled the earth from the spade. He'd cut an earthworm in two, both halves wriggling independently of each other.

'I've no idea what he's doing.' He gave her a stern look, which made her feel uncomfortable. Was she that transparent? 'But our lot – domestic – are certainly interested in him. It's his reputation, you see. The old Freeman tape; kept him protected all these years and now it's getting him noticed again.'

'Why now?'

'End of the Cold War, as I said. Everybody's looking for new agendas. It's all change.'

'What's that got to do with Pierce?'

'Intelligence are putting in a bid to take the lead on Ireland from the Force. The plods have always had the lead on Ireland up 'til now, but they're going to have trouble keeping hold of it when the Cold War comes to an end and there aren't any more commies for Intelligence to spy on. The Troubles. Terrorists. Plenty of demand still for information on that lot. Pierce's a useful name for MI5 to throw around. A reminder of past triumphs, gilding on the bid. That's probably why you've got joggers on your tail – they're keeping an eye on Anna because of Pierce, and now they've spotted you talking to her at this meeting, they are checking you out.'

She processed Harry's comments about Pierce, the watchers

guarding their asset. 'He didn't work for MI5. He worked for MI6.'

'Yeah, but the point is, he didn't work for the Force. He's not a plod. He worked for Intelligence and he produced the Freeman tape.'

Rivalries. Office politics. Pierce had hinted at that too; his comments about Jim, the Force's wisdom. *Fault*. She ventured one more question.

'How did Jim and Pierce meet? Were they working together?'

He didn't look at her when he replied. 'Something like that,' he said. 'Jim was… attached to some organization that was also in contact with Reznik, after weapons. Pierce insisted that Jim use him as a middle man with Reznik. So that's how they ended up working together. Pierce wanted to be Reznik's gatekeeper.'

Pierce's hints about Jim's involvement confirmed. She snapped. 'Oh god, so what did he do exactly?'

He turned, swiftly. 'You don't need to know that.'

She was taken aback by the fierceness of his response.

She persisted. 'Yes, but was his involvement… did it have anything to do with the Firm's sting going wrong, and Reznik's grudge against Pierce?'

Harry's face reddened, his lips folded in. She didn't care if she had annoyed him, she wanted to know whether Jim had harmed Pierce in some way.

Harry shouted suddenly, 'Don't do it, Sam.'

She was confused, uncertain what he meant.

'Don't chip away at your father's memory. Don't let anybody undermine him in your head.' He took a deep breath. 'Take the tomatoes. You look as if you could do with some extra vitamin C. What are you studying now anyway?'

She was relieved to be on safer territory again; his outburst had alarmed her.

'I'm doing an archaeology PhD.'

'Ha. Perpetual student. Well, if you've got the aptitude then good luck to you, that's what I say. Are you doing any excavating?'

'Sort of. I was in Orkney over the summer helping with a survey of a Norse site. I might use that as the basis for my thesis.'

'Orkney?'

'Yeah.'

'The place you used to go on holiday when you were a kid?'

'That's right.'

He thrust the spade into the ground, stood back, left it standing in the soil. 'Why are you going all the way up there? Scotland, overrated I reckon. What's wrong with Wales?'

He was joking, but she could detect a note of aggression which perturbed her.

'There's nothing wrong with Wales. I've always been interested in Norse history and Orkney is a good place to go for Viking ruins.'

'Do you know people up there?'

He knew she knew where Pierce was hiding.

'I've made a few friends.'

He crossed his arms, his belly sticking out below. 'You should think about Wales. I could introduce you to a few people there.'

'Harry, that's very kind. But the Vikings weren't big in Wales.'

'That's cos we fought them off.' He leaned on the handle of his spade, stared at her, pale eyes sharp in the folds of his skin. 'Maybe you should give Orkney a break. Think about going somewhere else. Wales is nearer.'

She laughed politely.

'I'm serious Sam. Leave it. Keep away.'

★

She rested on a fallen log when she reached the top of the hill. A gust rustled the leaves and drops of rain pattered above her head; a sudden shower from nowhere. She dipped her hand in the bag, selected a tomato, bit its flesh; pips squirted, juice dribbled down her chin. The tone of the conversation with Harry disturbed her. She suspected that his earlier note of scorn about Pierce's heroic reputation was sour grapes – Pierce was in favour and he was out on his ear. And the lecture about Jim – what was he on? Telling her what to think about her own father. She wondered, in retrospect, whether Harry was being upfront about Anna. Did he know something that he wasn't telling her? And then there was the warning not to go back to Orkney. He was overstepping the line. There was something threatening about his suggestions that she didn't like. Perhaps there was a good reason why he was on gardening leave, she mused, perhaps his new boss – a woman, she had noted – was fed up with all these ageing men who threw their weight around. No wonder she preferred the yuppies. *Leave it. Keep away.* That's what he had advised Jim too, all those years ago. Jim hadn't listened to him either. He hadn't been able to keep away from Orkney, whatever Harry's warnings. They'd gone there for a holiday in the August of '76, and that was when she glimpsed Pierce again. The second time that summer.

CHAPTER 12

Orkney, August 1976

THEY WENT TO Orkney later than usual that summer. They hadn't planned a holiday at all, because nobody seemed to know what Jim was doing. Was he lurking around the house for ever? Hoping for a transfer? Leaving the Force? Liz said she needed to get away; the heat, the water restrictions, the presence of Valerie and Anna were all fraying her nerves. Jim's behaviour too, she said one afternoon when she had taken Sam shopping for a pair of sandals. Everybody was on a short fuse because of the weather, but Jim's short fuse appeared to be attached to a grumbling volcano. His eruptions increasingly explosive. Drinking too much, even by his standards. She'd tried to talk to him about it, but he had refused to listen. He never was very good at confronting reality, she said; he had always preferred a good story to the hard truth. She sometimes worried what effect it all had on his daughters, she added. Sam didn't reply. The day after they had been to visit Harry, Liz announced she was going to find a cheap deal to Spain. The idea of a package holiday seemed to provoke Jim; he made a phone call, said he'd found a place for them to stay in Orkney and booked last-minute tickets on the motorail to Inverness. Liz, Sam suspected, was disappointed. She always wanted to go to the Med but deferred, every year, to Jim's desire for the north, distance from London. Away from people. He was weird like that; if you saw him in a crowd you would think he was sociable, chatting, having a laugh, always a drink in hand. But the fact was, he was more at home by himself, combing shores and mountains. Far out wasn't far enough for Jim.

Valerie and Anna had found another temporary home with a friend in a different part of south London, and she came round to pick them up a couple of days before Sam and her family were due to leave for Orkney. It was Valerie who gave Liz their next address and insisted Sam should come and visit. Anna was too busy trying to attract Jim's attention for anything other than a casual goodbye, let alone a thank you to Sam for letting her share her room all those weeks. She watched Anna give Jim her charming smile and heard her ask whether he could find a way of passing a small present to Pierce. Jim reacted strangely to the request, shuffling his feet like a naughty schoolboy, but eventually he said he might be able to fix something. She dug in her pocket and produced the two white mosaic tiles, and handed them to Jim. They are very precious, she said, quite seriously; magical stones that are supposed to protect the person who owns them. He looked at the tiles, perturbed, and Sam thought he had sussed their origin and would throw a wobbly, but he didn't say a word. They waved Anna and Valerie off and she watched Jim remove the tiles from his pocket, examine them again, stroll over to their Cortina and slip them in the glove compartment.

The croft was at the end of a track on the headland beyond Swanbister Bay, overlooking fields bleached by the sun. Even Orkney was suffering from the drought. According to *The Orcadian*, it was the driest August since records began and Orkney Council had issued a notice banning the use of hosepipes for watering gardens and washing cars. But Orkney's record-busting seventy degrees was a relief from the eighties and nineties of the south. The first day was cloudless, a scorcher. In the morning they swam in Waulkmill Bay. Helen and Jess sunbathed, which was, Helen pointed out, a new experience for them in Orkney because they usually spent their time sheltering from the wind and rain.

The price for their lazy morning came in the afternoon when Jim suggested a walk along the coast path. They ambled, sluggish in the heat. The path cut through the heather and past a dilapidated fisherman's hut, its drystone walls white with spindled lichen, before rounding the headland. Jim stopped abruptly, hand shading his eyes as he surveyed Scapa Flow. He stared at the dark island rising from the water on the far side.

'Is that Hoy over there?' Sam asked.

'Yes, that's Hoy,' Jim said. 'It makes me think of the island in *The Tempest*.'

'*The Tempest*?' Liz's attention grabbed by the mention of Shakespeare. 'That's an interesting comparison. Why the island in *The Tempest*?'

'Oh, I don't know.' Jim rubbed his cheek, as if some insect had bothered him. 'Let's keep moving.' He stomped off.

Liz stood for a minute, watching his back before she followed without a word. Helen and Jess dawdled behind. Sam tried to match Jim's pace. Skuas shadowed their path. She swiped the towering cow parsley, sent clouds of midges flying, stung her arm on a nettle, then searched fruitlessly for a dock leaf to soothe the lash of welts marking her skin. Orkney wasn't as much fun at this time of year. Not enough birds. Too hot.

The path turned inland along a harvested field, bales of hay awaiting collection on the hard-baked soil, and arrived at a wooden gate in a high wall. On the other side there was a graveyard, weathered limestone crosses marking grassy mounds. A dilapidated tower grew among the tombs, topped with a scalp of parched turf. A movement caught her eye; a face at the one small window, staring across the fields. She squinted. The face had vanished. She wondered whether she had been mistaken, but Jim had noticed it too. He frowned, strode across the graveyard. She caught up with him, examining the drop to the interior of the ruin. The window was about six feet off the ground; only a tall person could have hauled themselves up to look out. Jim was making the same calculation, she reckoned. His face clouded. He sensed her watching, and pulled himself together. Getagrip.

'The great drinking hall of the Vikings,' Jim said. He swept a hand in the air, indicating the shadows of buildings long gone, the ghosts of the departed. 'It's described in the *Orkneyinga Saga*. And this,' he pointed to the tower, the window at which the face had appeared, 'is the apse of the Round Church, built by Earl Hakon after a pilgrimage to Jerusalem. He was searching for redemption because he'd ordered the hit on Magnus.'

He was trying to behave as if nothing had happened, but she could tell he was edgy.

'St Magnus? The one who has a cathedral named after him in Kirkwall?'

'Yes. That's him. The sainted Magnus.' He examined the apse again. 'I suppose Earl Hakon had a lot to feel guilty about.'

Liz joined them and assessed the ruin. Jim put his arm around her. She pulled away from Jim's embrace, left him standing with his arm dangling at his side, a broken wing.

'I'll go and sort the picnic things out with Jess and Helen,' Liz said.

'Let's have a look around,' Jim said to Sam.

They moseyed about the tombs; Jim reading epitaphs, Sam

finding metallic weevils sheltering in the limestone cracks. A breeze blew up out of nowhere and swayed a canopy of trees beyond the graveyard wall. Jim froze, eyes narrowed. He had almost supernatural powers of seeing; he could identify a hawk high in the sky when she couldn't distinguish it from the sun spots dancing in her vision. She looked in the direction he was staring and glimpsed a flash in the shadows of the dancing branches. Was that the white of somebody's shirt? She looked again and saw a figure retreating. Jim set off, past the remains of the Norse drinking hall. She jogged behind, down a rutted track to a shady lane. A collie barked from behind a farm gate, leaped and rattled the bars. A car engine revved, then its bonnet emerged from behind the hedgerow. Jim stopped in the middle of the road, dappled light shining through the sycamores and falling on his face, revealing the tense line of his jaw. The car eased away, disappeared around the bend. Jim didn't move. The dog lost interest, ceased barking, trotted off in search of more exciting scents.

'Who was that?' Sam asked innocently.

'Dunno.' He said it without looking at her. 'Some bloke or other.'

Some bloke who drove a navy Volvo estate, she had noted. She looked at her feet and noticed the rock in the road at the same time as Jim. She leaned, but he was faster, kicked it with his boot, dropped and retrieved the piece of paper underneath, stuffed it in his back pocket.

They found Liz and Helen and Jess, sitting beyond the graveyard wall. The stray clouds had gathered, muffled the sun, casting the headland in a bleaker light.

'We waited for you,' Liz said. 'We haven't started eating yet.'

They sat on the grass and peeled the eggs that Liz had boiled, dipped them in a pot of salt. A hooded crow stalked the graveyard wall, waiting for leftovers. Nobody said much. Sam watched Liz fiddling about with plastic bags and tin foil, producing tomatoes, bread rolls. A packet of Penguin biscuits, the chocolate coating melted. Sam felt sorry for her then, always waiting for Jim to return.

In the evening, Sam wanted to play cards. For once she managed to persuade Helen and Jess it would be a good idea – there wasn't much else to do, Helen had noted grumpily. Liz never played cards. Jim loved a good game; anything except bridge, which he considered too middle class. But that night he wasn't interested. Restless, pacing the room, stopping to gaze through the window to Hoy. Liz suggested they should go for an evening stroll. He didn't want to do that either. He needed to make a phone call, he said. There wasn't a phone in the house so he had to drive up the road to the village.

The sisters played blackjack and poker and when they stopped playing she realized Jim hadn't returned. Liz was trying to read a book, but Sam could tell from the cast of her eyes and the lack of page movement that she was tracing the same line over and over again. It was near dark by the time Jim returned. Even in late August, after the night-long twilight of midsummer, the darkness was red tinged. He strode into the kitchen without greeting anybody, opened cupboards, rootled around, slapped doors shut, came back with a whisky tumbler in his hand, settled himself in an armchair. Helen and Jess had their eyes glued to the television, the idiot's lantern Jim called it, except when he wanted to watch a match. Liz observed him over the top of her book, noting the speed with which he knocked back his drink. Eventually he said, 'I want to go to Hoy tomorrow.'

'Hoy,' Liz repeated. She sounded resigned.

Helen lifted her head, howled. 'I don't want to go to Hoy.'

Jim said, 'I wasn't inviting anybody else.'

Helen turned her back on him and spoke to Liz. 'Can we go to Kirkwall?' She always gravitated towards towns and shops, even if they only sold Norwegian cardigans and fish.

'Will you be taking the car?' Liz asked Jim.

'Yes. There's a bus to Kirkwall from Orphir.'

Liz raised a resigned eyebrow. 'We'll go to Kirkwall then.'

Sam protested, 'I don't want to go shopping.'

'We all have to do things we don't want to do sometimes,' Liz said. 'That's what being in a family is all about.'

'Yes, that's what families are like,' Jim said.

She suspected he was thinking about a different kind of family – his shadow family of spooks and agents. Although, maybe the same rules applied.

'Can I go to Hoy with you?' Sam asked.

'No.'

'I want to look for the bloodstones at Pegal Bay.'

'No.'

'I don't want to go to Kirkwall,' she wailed.

Liz covered her face in her hands, which made Sam feel awful. She hadn't meant to provoke despair in her mother.

'Sorry.'

Liz tipped her head back as if she were consulting the heavens, removed her hands and looked at Sam. 'Don't apologize. You've got nothing to be sorry about.' She collected the dirty cups and plates scattered around the room, retreated to the kitchen. Water spurted; a tap turned angrily. Crockery clinked and banged. Jim leaned back in the chair, muttered to himself, pressed his palms down on the worn arms, levered himself to standing.

'OK, you can come with me if you are up early enough.' He shouted. He wanted Liz to hear. 'But you have to do exactly as I tell you and no whinging.'

'I don't whinge.'

'I don't whinge.' He mimicked her voice in a whiny way. She wanted to kick him.

'The ferry goes at eight from Stromness. I'm leaving at seven. If you're not ready I'm not waiting.'

He marched outside, his back to them, facing the sea, a black silhouette against the bloodshot sky.

'What's eating him?' Jess said.

Nobody answered. Sam wasn't sure why she was insisting on accompanying him to Hoy when he was in miserable git mode. She traipsed outside to tell him she wasn't going. He was standing, hands in pockets, staring at the heavens; Venus shining brightly in the twilight.

'I've only seen the Northern Lights once,' he said. 'Finland.' Finland? What was he doing there? 'We'd been drinking, there was snow on the ground so I was watching where I put my feet, and then something made me look up and I saw strange lights dancing across the sky. I thought at first I'd drunk too much vodka, but then I realized what they were. There's something uplifting about luminescence; the hand of God, the touch of grace. Unexpected lights in the darkness.' He sighed, turned to look at her then. 'I hope you see the Northern Lights one day.'

She watched the beams of a car's headlamps as they swept along the coast of Hoy, and decided she would go with Jim after all.

CHAPTER 13

London, October 1989

SHE SAT ON the dodgy flat roof of the Vauxhall house with Becky. They had signed a contract with the housing co-op promising they wouldn't use it because it was unsafe. They used it all the same; everybody in the square used the roof terraces on summer evenings, sitting out there smoking weed. Neighbours' candles flickered in the dark. The shadow of a Heathrow-bound plane crossed the waning moon. A police siren wailed. She rolled a spliff and puffed a few times, tilted the roach to Becky.

'Have you seen Anna since that meeting?'

'Hilary.'

'OK, Hilary.

'Look, I really like her and you're going to bug me if you keep going on about this Anna thing. And yes, we met for coffee.'

'Did she mention me?'

'I know this might be hard to believe, but you weren't the main topic of conversation.'

'Are you going to meet her again?'

'Yes.'

'Could I come with you?'

Becky spluttered, coughed, blasted smoke into the night air. 'Are you kidding?'

'I wouldn't stay. I just want to say hello and then I'll leave.'

'Piss off.'

Becky puffed, smoke and condensation from her warm breath mingling. Harry had told her to leave it, but she couldn't. She had to complete the task. Operation Fisher King. She was Ariel and her next move was to contact Miranda again, see if she could persuade her to admit that she was Anna, not Hilary. And then she would pass on the message from Pierce, ask her if she wanted to contact her exiled father. That was what she had told Pierce she would do, so that's what she would do.

'You're not going to let this rest, are you?'

'If you tell me to fuck off and leave it alone then of course I will. I'm worried, that's all. It's happened before, people I know being manipulated. By spooks. Police spies.'

Becky returned the spliff, knotted her fingers.

'You and your bloody dad and all this spies and the secret state stuff. Will you ever put it to bed?'

'I keep trying.'

Becky gave her a sympathetic glance, which made her feel guilty. Ashamed of the selfish part of her that wanted to sabotage Becky's budding romance with Anna, because she was scared of losing her best friend to lovey-dovey coupledom. Because she didn't want Anna to win.

'OK. Here's the deal. I'm going over to her place to see her next week. You can come with me to say hello – you're going to have to think of some excuse to explain why you're passing through Blackheath. And then that's the end of it. If she still says she's Hilary, you have to live with it.'

'OK. Blackheath. There's a big plague pit under the common.'

'God, I hope you're not going to use a plague pit as your excuse for turning up with me at her place.'

'I'll think of something better.'

*

Becky drove south-east from Vauxhall in her green two-door Morris Minor with red leather seats and a homely smell. She nudged the trafficator switch; the silver external arm flicked, the orange indicator light blinked and a car in the oncoming lane stopped and flashed to let her turn. Morris Minors had that effect on other drivers.

Becky gripped the wheel. 'It's a good job we're old friends.'

Sam wound the window down, cool air fresh on her face as they drove east along the Thames. She spotted the glass dome of the shaft descending to the Greenwich foot tunnel; she used to race along that tunnel under the river with Jim. Although now these ancient memories of her father seemed like hazy dreams. Perhaps he had always been fuzzy, part real, part imagined, a story she had told herself because she didn't know the truth.

Becky parked the car at the edge of the heath, the falling sun glinting on the double-deckers crawling across the plain.

'Number thirty-four.' Becky pointed to the top of the block. 'I think it's an old council block. Anna's bought her flat.'

'Blimey. Lucky her.' Only Anna could end up buying a cheap flat with the best view in south London: the heath, Greenwich park, the observatory, the glint of the river.

They puffed up the stairs. Becky rang the bell. Anna opened the door immediately; she must have watched them arrive. Becky hadn't warned Anna that Sam would be there, but she didn't seem surprised by her presence. Annoyed perhaps. Becky and Anna embraced, kissed. Sam hovered on the threshold. Anna avoided catching her eye.

'You remember my mate Sam.' Becky said it apologetically. 'She wanted a lift over to Blackheath to do some stargazing. There's a meteor shower tonight and Blackheath is a good place to watch the stars, apparently.' Becky was hopeless at lying. 'But she wondered if she could use your loo.'

Anna's eyes darted at Sam, crows' feet creasing and uncreasing as if she were about to laugh, then stopped herself. 'It's over there. There's a short hall and it's first on your right.'

'Thanks. I won't be long.'

She crossed the stripped floorboards, surveyed the spacious lounge. Empty in a stylish way, as opposed to empty in an empty way, which was Sam's approach to interior decoration. Battered leather sofa. Wing-backed armchair. White porcelain lamp that hovered over the coffee table like a spaceship waiting to land. No clutter. No personal knickknacks. One bookshelf in a far corner of the room; perhaps that had something on it. Sam stepped out of line to get a better view.

'You're going the wrong way.' Anna was monitoring her from behind. She twisted around, grinned. 'Sorry.' Spotted a tiny blue square on the shelf as her head swivelled back. She crowed silently. She reached the hall, found the toilet, sat there for a minute, devising her strategy. Flushed. Walked out. Anna was leaning against the wall, next to Becky who was radiating irritation.

'Thanks.'

'That's OK.'

'I'll make my own way home.'

The front door clicked behind her. She clattered down the stairs, out into the freshness of the night, giddy with triumph. The blue mosaic tile was sitting on the bookshelf. Proof, as if she needed it, that this was Anna. She glanced back at the glowing window of Anna's flat and was hit by a wave of self-pity; here she was wandering the streets of Blackheath alone while her best mate had fun with a woman who she had once thought was a friend and now pretended she didn't know her.

She had planned to head straight to the station and catch the train to Waterloo, but the heath drew her with its promise of open sky and solace.

She headed past the gorse and bracken – the only remnants of its former wildness – to a point which she calculated was furthest from the fast roads that slashed the heath, checked for dog shit, used the tip of her monkey boot to move the half-devoured corpse of a mouse and lay flat on her back. The last of the summer swallows dived and vanished. A breeze carried the sweetness of lime and rotting flesh. The sky curved around her, rimmed pink and orange by the city's glare but directly overhead the heavens were indigo, the bluest shade of night she had ever seen in London. The moon had not yet risen. Lights sparkled in the gloom and swirled around her head and she was not sure whether they were stars or the flickering candles that marked the plague pits of the heath and guided the corpse carrier to his night-time destination. She thought of all the deaths she had seen, all the people she had known who had passed away. Jim. Her ribs ached. She was not conscious of passing time or the figure approaching across the grass, although she was half expecting her; reckoned she would come and find her. Anna sat down cross-legged by Sam's side. Still, she did not move, waited for her to speak first.

'How is the meteorite shower?'

'I was lying. It was last month.'

Anna heaved a sigh and then she said, 'You saw the mosaic tile.'

'I knew it was you anyway, with or without the tile.'

Anna lay back on the grass. Sam could hear her breathing.

'I've not been out on the heath at night before.'

'Do you see that reddish light that isn't blinking?' She pointed. 'That's a planet.'

'Mars?'

'Yes. And then below it – Jupiter. When I see the sky like this, the constellations wheeling, it makes me long for nights without electricity and the light pollution of the city.'

'You haven't changed much. Do you still collect beetles?'

'No, but I search for them when I walk.'

'You were always such an odd bod; identifying the birds and the beetles and the flowers, all your stories about Celtic warriors and gypsy queens.'

Anna played along with the stories, she thought. Anna told stories too.

'I find it odd,' she said, 'when people don't know the names of the creatures and plants around them.'

'Ever the Druid. At one with nature but fairly awkward when it comes to relationships with real people.'

'Well, it is fairly awkward when you meet somebody you knew when you were a kid and not only have they changed their name, but they pretend they don't recognize you.'

'That's my right. I can do what I like with my name.' The snappish change of tone caught Sam off guard. She didn't reply.

'You came to my place, turned up on my doorstep, when I clearly didn't want to be recognized by you. Why?'

Sam plucked a blade of grass, twisted it around her fingers, taken aback by the harshness of Anna's attack. Perhaps it was fair.

'I was curious.' What else could she say? Pierce had told her that if she did find Anna, she shouldn't let Anna know she had met him. But now, confronted by Anna, it seemed like a tricky instruction. What games was Pierce playing? Was he hiding something from her? From Anna? Or was he simply being cautious, as he had said, in case Anna mingled with old Trots who had contacts with the other side? Spooks. They disrupted your life in strange ways, their shiftiness and suspicions were contagious. Anna was right; she was more comfortable with beetles and birds. They didn't encroach on her mind, try to bend her to their will. Too much contact with spies and you became one yourself; a chess-player, always searching for the killer move, second-guessing your opponent's strategy. A couple of joggers trotted past. Man and woman, deep in conversation.

'Do you think they're spies?' Anna asked, jokingly.

'Quite possibly.' Sam rolled on her side, leaned on her elbow, studied Anna.

'Why did you pretend you didn't know me?'

'I don't want anything to do with my father's past.'

'It's funny, isn't it, that in order to escape the shadow of a spy, you had to take on a false identity.'

'I've had this identity so long I don't think of it as false.'

'How long?'

'Thirteen years. Since we left your place, or thereabouts. I haven't seen Pierce since then.'

'You haven't contacted him at all?'

'No. It's easier not to have anything to do with him or his world. A relief in fact.'

The secret lives of their fathers, the dark clouds that threatened and yet tempted with the familiarity of their greyness, the excitement of the storm. She didn't think she could walk away so easily, deny the connection between herself and her father, but she often feared it was a mistake to chase the spectres of her past and so she could understand why Anna would make a different choice. Although Pierce had indicated that the break wasn't so clean, said he had spoken to Anna on the phone a couple of times.

'You didn't ever write or phone?'

'Nope.'

She wondered which of them was lying – Pierce or Anna – decided she wouldn't push Anna on this point because that would force Sam to reveal she had spoken to Pierce. God, she was as bad as either of them. She shifted on the grass, cold and damp. A church bell rang; she counted the chimes. Eleven. Later than she had expected. She'd suddenly had enough, didn't want to play these games.

'I'd better go, otherwise I'm going to miss the last train back to Waterloo.'

'You can stay at my place if you like. I've got a spare mattress.'

Just when she'd decided to walk away, avoid wading into treacherous waters. On the other hand… A tiny green pulse in the distance distracted her. She concentrated on the gloom. There it was again.

'Oh my god. Do you think that could be a glow worm?' She pointed at a dark clump of shrubs clinging to the edge of the heath. 'Over there by that tree?'

'You are still the same.' Anna laughed. 'A glow worm.'

Sam stood, brushed the grass from her overcoat. 'I'm going to investigate.'

Anna stood too. 'I'm coming with you. I didn't know there were glow worms here. Are they really worms?'

'No, they're beetles.' She strode towards the light. Anna kept pace with her. They reached a willow, drooping over a shallow pond. 'Oh, I'm being stupid. The females glow when they want to attract a mate. It's the wrong time of year. It was probably the moon's reflection in the water.'

'It's a lovely spot anyway. I haven't even been here in the daylight.' She sat on the grass. 'Or maybe I have. That's the Hare and Billet over there.'

A couple left the bar, arm in arm, swaying along the pavement. Chucking-out time. Sam suspected she had missed the last train. She would have to stay at Anna's flat and invent an explanation to assuage Becky's irritation. She didn't want to go home anyway. The whiff of bonfire was in the air and it felt like a proper autumn night. She didn't want to waste it. She plonked herself next to Anna.

'Do you want some puff?' Anna dug in a pocket for her Rizlas and gear.

'OK.' She was trying to cut down on the dope.

Anna rolled, lit. The reeds rustled, a heron stalked the pond edge, found a good fishing spot, lifted one leg, folded its neck. Sam pointed, 'Night fisher.'

'Do you remember the day at the river? Blackstone?'

'Yes of course.'

'You told me the story of the Fisher King and said that was why there was a drought; the king had been injured and the land was blighted.'

She passed Sam the spliff.

'The story stuck in my mind. You didn't say it, but I thought you meant that Pierce was the Fisher King. He had been compromised, something had gone wrong and he had to disappear.' She paused. 'We never did find out where he went. God knows where he is living now.'

Sam kept her eyes on the heron. Had Anna sussed her? Realized she had seen Pierce? Almost certainly. *Operation Fisher King.* It didn't matter; so long as she didn't confess. That would be wrong; Pierce had told her not to reveal the location of his hideaway to Anna and she didn't want to break his trust.

'Pierce told us it would be safer for us if we didn't go with him. We were scared that his enemies would come after us. We changed our identities – Intelligence didn't help us much. They got us some new documents, then we had to make our own way. Luckily my mum inherited some money so she bought a house in the West Country. It was a nice enough place, but it felt like an amputation – twelve years of my life removed. If you can't be open about your past, your memories, if you're always checking yourself, wondering whether you've slipped up, then you are incomplete. So it did feel to me as if Pierce's damage was our blight. Our curse. I got used to it in the end – Hilary Bird. But I'm not sure I ever quite recovered from the shock of that. That was why I pretended I didn't know you. You're part of a past I've discarded. I don't want to go through it all again.'

Sam didn't know how to respond; after all these years, her feelings about Anna were as raw and confused as they ever were.

'What about your mum? Is she OK?'

'She died.'

Sam winced. 'I'm sorry.'

Pierce certainly hadn't mentioned that; perhaps it was too difficult.

'Four years ago. Cancer.'

'That's awful.'

'The fifth of November 1985.'

'Guy Fawkes night.'

'Yes. She's buried at Norwood Cemetery. I find it hard to go there. I visit her once a year in the evening on the anniversary of her death.'

Sam didn't want to say something trite – time makes things better. She knew that was a lie in many ways. 'And what about the baby?' She didn't even know whether it was a boy or a girl. 'Well, I suppose it's not a baby any more.'

'Oh,' Anna said. 'She's been taken care of.'

She. A girl then, being looked after by relatives, Sam assumed.

'How about you?' Anna obviously didn't want to linger on Valerie's death. 'How is your mum?'

'Liz? She's OK. She's shacked up with a new man.'

'That's funny. They seemed to argue a lot, your parents. And Liz was quite rude about Jim. But I'm surprised they split.'

'They didn't split. Jim died too.'

'Shit. What happened?'

'He was killed. Eighty-four.'

She picked up a stone, chucked it in the pond. The heron flapped, beat the reeds with its wings, lifted its leg, skirted the water and flew away. Anna didn't question her assertion. Killed. She knew the score. Blood sister.

'Do you miss him?'

Not an easy question to answer.

'Yes and no. I miss his company, or at least his company when he was in a good mood. I don't miss the tension and fear and secrecy that went with his work. But I regret…'

She tipped her head back, let the heavens spin. The plough. Orion. Round and round.

'I regret that we didn't have more time… that I didn't know… I couldn't say…'

And still, she couldn't say.

'You'd better stay at my place.'

The first light crept over the horizon, the sky overcast, pavements dark with rain and pedestrians battling inside-out umbrellas. She lay there on the mattress, the lofty view of the heath below, wondering whether she should sneak away without waking Anna, avoid any further conversation. She had decided in the night that she had to step back from Anna's life. If Pierce wanted to contact Anna, it was his business, not Sam's. If Anna wanted to live her life as Hilary, that was her business too, and if Becky wanted to have a relationship with

Anna, or whatever identity Anna wanted to live by, then it would be selfish of Sam to interfere. She should be happy for her best mate, and happy for Anna because she deserved to have someone as lovely as Becky in her life. She stood and ambled over to the bookshelf she had eyed the previous evening. The blue mosaic tile had disappeared. She rubbed her finger over the spot it had occupied, a square of darker wood, the shadow of the tile in the sun-bleached pine. She twisted around. Anna was standing behind her; she had inherited the spooks' ability to materialize without warning.

'Did you sleep OK?'

'Fine thanks. You've got a lovely flat. The view is amazing.'

'I paid for it with the cash I inherited from Mum.'

'Money well spent. Did you go to university?'

'Yes. Cambridge.'

Of course, Pierce had mentioned.

'Isn't that where Pierce went?'

'Yes.'

Where half of Intelligence went.

'What are you doing now?'

'Campaigning against the poll tax.'

'What about Militant? Do you have anything to do with them?'

Anna laughed. 'Are you working for Special Branch?'

'Just asking.'

'No, I try not to have anything to do with Militant.'

'What about the Lenin-alike?'

'Goatee face? Yeah, he's definitely a mole, an informer of some kind or another. God knows who he is passing information to; he's so obvious it's laughable.'

'Aren't you worried?'

'About?'

'All the spooks tailing you.'

It was the nearest she could get to a warning.

Anna flicked Sam's arm. 'I'll outwit them.'

Anna; the fearless twelve-year-old who had stolen the Roman tiles from under the nose of the bearded custodian of Blackstone and had trailed her father's contact from his safehouse. The memory put her on guard again, reminded her that Anna had kept her plans well hidden, had always been keener on the spying games than her.

'What do you do for a day job?' She knew the answer because Pierce had told her, but she thought she'd ask anyway.

Anna stuck her hands in the pockets of her jeans. 'I do some acting here and there. The cash from one TV ad lasts quite a while. And how about you? Who pays your salary?'

Was that a dig?

'Research Council. I've got a grant for an archaeology PhD. UCL.'

'Becky said you'd been in Orkney all summer excavating some ruin.'

Awkward silence. She didn't want to talk about Orkney in case she gave Pierce's location away.

'Do you want some tea?'

'I'd better be going.'

'No, hang on please, I've been thinking. I've got something to ask you. Come with me.'

Sam followed her to the kitchen, all chrome and white shiny surfaces like something out of an interiors magazine; she must have inherited quite a chunk.

'Go on, have a cuppa.'

'Do you have any coffee?'

'I've got instant.'

She liked proper coffee, not instant.

'I'll have tea then.'

Anna filled the kettle.

'You know, thinking about you and your dad. What you were saying last night about regrets. I was wondering whether I should make an effort to find Pierce.'

Anna had her back to her, which was lucky because she couldn't see Sam flush. Anna knew all along why she was here, of course she did, Anna wasn't stupid. She studied the graceful lines of her white neck; like Anne Boleyn – a little neck and an irresistible manipulator. Anna stuck her hand in her pocket, removed something, held it in her closed fist.

'What do you think? Should I look for him?'

Anna opened her hand; the mosaic tile was lying there, blue and gleaming against the whiteness of her palm.

'I can help you find him if you like.' She should have stayed out of it; she'd made her mind up to back off. Too late now.

Anna said, 'If you can get a message to him, tell him I'd like to see him again.'

Sam nodded.

'And maybe you can find a way to give him this. From me.' Anna dropped the tile in Sam's coat pocket. 'I don't know what it is about these tiles,' she added. 'They mean a lot to me.'

Anna flashed her a smile, turned to attend the boiling kettle. Sam stuck her hand in her pocket, touched the tile, tried to decipher its secret meaning. Anna, as mysterious as ever.

'But what should I tell Becky?'

'What should you tell Becky about what?'

'About you.'

Anna handed her a mug. 'The truth, I suppose.'

'The truth?'

'That my real name is Anna and we met in the summer of 1976. My dad was a spook whose cover was blown and he went into hiding and we couldn't go with him, so we changed our names and I haven't seen him since.'

'OK. The truth.' She slurped her tea and wondered whether the truth was that simple.

'Actually,' Anna said, 'don't you tell her anything. I'll do it. I'm not sure I want her to know. Not yet anyway.'

'Right.'

Of course the truth wasn't that simple, because here she was lying to Anna, pretending she hadn't seen Pierce, just as she had pretended that she didn't know he was staying on Hoy in the summer of '76. The truth was what happened, and everything afterwards was a story.

CHAPTER 14

Orkney, August 1976

JIM DROVE LIKE a madman from the croft in Swanbister to Stromness, the sun already blistering despite the early hour. He parked on the quayside; the *Jessie Ellen* was waiting at the pier. 'The Cortina is staying here. I've arranged to pick up a car at Moaness. Come on, move it,' Jim ordered.

She stood by the clapped-out Cortina while he rummaged around in the glove compartment.

'Where are the fucking binoculars?'

He wasn't looking for the binoculars, she knew, because she could see that they were sitting right at the front of the compartment. He was searching for the two white tiles Anna had entrusted to him before she left with Valerie to their next temporary home. Anna had tasked him with handing them to Pierce, and he was taking his duty seriously. She watched him slip the small objects into his back pocket; the sacred treasures to be returned to the Fisher King so the curse could be lifted and the drought brought to an end. Everything and everybody happy ever after. Except not quite yet.

The Sound was glassy, barely a ripple, Hoy an enchanted island shimmering in the heat.

'In all the years we've been coming here,' Jim said, 'I don't remember a day as calm as this.'

The millpond flatness was more unsettling than a rough sea; everything was too bright. Unnaturally still. The ferryman said the tides and hidden currents were stronger in the calm. She hung over the side of the *Jessie Ellen* and scanned the horizon, searching for a tsunami or a tornado or anything that could explain the unusual serenity. Jim was edgy too. He clamped the binoculars to his eyes, swept the coast ahead, searching for something or somebody. A tiny bird flapped madly across the boat's wake; she caught a flash of red. Puffin? She thought they had all flown away to sea by August. Perhaps the heat had confused it. She nudged Jim's elbow, asked if she could borrow the bins. He ignored her, lenses glued to the coast of Hoy. He let the binoculars drop and dangle around his neck. 'I have to visit somebody.' She didn't bother asking who, because he wouldn't tell her, and anyway, she knew the answer already. Pierce.

'Rackwick Bay,' Jim said. 'It shouldn't take long to drive there. You're going to have to occupy yourself for a while, though.'

'OK.' She was used to entertaining herself; besides, she had her talisman with her and that would keep her company. She felt in the back pocket of her shorts, found the red tile Anna had given her, warm to the touch.

The titchy ferry chugged into Moaness. Pierce's navy Volvo estate was parked on the grassy verge beyond the jetty, a short, weather-beaten man wearing a fisherman's cap leaning against the bonnet. Jim strode over, exchanged a few words before the fisherman sauntered away to the jetty and boarded the *Jessie Ellen*.

'He lives at Rackwick Bay too,' Jim explained as she clambered on to the passenger seat. 'He's visiting Stromness for the day so we've got the car until he comes back on the ferry this afternoon.'

The Fisher King's car. She felt grand, sitting up front in such a large vehicle. The shore side of the coast road was fringed with sandy coves, lobster boats bobbing in blue seas.

'Pegal Bay is that way,' Jim said as they turned off the coast road. 'We can go there later.'

She wound the window down, stuck her head out, peered at the steep mountain slopes but she couldn't see their summits and felt claustrophobic, pinched between the rocks. She pulled her head inside. The scree fell away and they were driving through maroon bracken, past an enticing glen of tangled trees. Berriedale, according to Jim. The sky opened ahead of them and they reached a hollow in the sandstone cliffs. The tarmac road petered away and Jim parked the Volvo by a deserted croft. All the crofts here seemed to have been abandoned; wooden doors swinging on their hinges, caved-in roofs with crows nesting in their rafters. The only sign of habitation was a red telephone kiosk among the dilapidated buildings, the cables stretching back along the valley they had just travelled. She reckoned Pierce and the gnarled fisherman were the only people still living here.

Jim said, 'You can go and explore the beach.'

'OK.'

'Don't go in the sea.'

That was Jim's approach to parenting; he reckoned so long as his daughters were armed with a set of orders forbidding them from doing anything dangerous they would be safe. The law, and he had laid it down.

'I'll meet you back at the car in...' he flicked his hand,

checked his watch that he always wore with the face on the inside of his wrist, '... an hour. No, make that an hour and a half.'

She nodded.

'If I'm not back, wait for me here, don't come looking for me.'

'I won't.'

'Liz made some sandwiches, so we'll drive to Pegal Bay when I'm done and eat those there.'

He folded his arms and leaned back against the Volvo and she knew it was her signal to leave; he didn't want her watching him go.

'See you later then.' She set off along a stony track, past a roofless bothy, through the marram grass, leaping stepping stones across the trickling burn, heading to the sea. She stopped, glanced over her shoulder, saw Jim following a path along the far side of the bay, and right. She continued on her way; she had seen enough to work out where he was heading – there weren't many crofts from which to choose. She clambered over the ridge of the dune, the bay curving away below, a fingernail of sand. She sat among the sea-ringed boulders, the sun radiating on the shingle. So quiet, so still, she could hear the crack and pop of the incoming tide, filling the spaces between the pebbles. The cry of a solitary oyster catcher broke her concentration. She watched it paddling along the shore with its funny red legs and orange beak dipping in the water. It waddled towards the cliff and disappeared. Where had it gone? She stood, clambered over the rocky fingers slanting into the sea, and jumped down to a sandy inlet, wet and channelled by the ebbing tide, followed it along to a narrow cave mouth between the folds of sandstone, invisible from the beach. She passed through the entrance, deeper into the rock. The jagged lips obscured the sunlight; for a moment she could see nothing in the gloom and then, as her eyes adjusted, she spotted glittering creatures – barnacles, anemones, mussels – studding the rough walls like jewels. Entranced by the beauty of the cave, she followed the rocky floor upwards until it joined the sloping roof. The far end was littered with treasures deposited by the ocean: feathers, bones, sea glass, a kelp-entwined creel, fading buoys, salt-rusted metal scraps. A secret Aladdin's cave. She wondered whether the water would reach the roof at high tide. She dug the toe of her plimsoll into the triangle of sand at the very back of the cave and saw that it was dry; a safe place in the heart of the sandstone. She lodged herself there for a while, listening to the distant lapping of the water and the clamour of the gulls.

After a while she walked back to the shore, blinking in the sunshine. She thought she had been inside the cave for ages, but only ten minutes had passed. Another hour before she was supposed to meet Jim back at the car. She glanced at the croft above the bay, bit her lip. It wasn't far. She could get there and back in under twenty minutes and Jim would be none the wiser. And anyway, it looked as if Pierce's place was to the side of the path that wound its way up the cliff and she wanted to follow it because she was sure the view would be spectacular. There was no harm in it. He said don't go in the sea, he didn't say don't walk up the cliff path. She retraced her trail across the boulders to the dunes, over the burn.

She skipped along the path, past deserted homes with the relics of their former inhabitants still visible through their glassless windows – smashed paraffin lamps, broken crockery, an armchair with the springs in its seat painfully exposed.

Ghost town. What was it like living here, she wondered, in the long nights and storms of winter? Did Pierce have electricity? Water? Where did he buy his food? The croft into which Jim had disappeared looked well maintained with its whitewashed walls. At least it had a roof, even if it was made of turf. The windows were open. The path was hidden from view, she hoped, by its banks and the long grass and cow parsley growing on either side. She reached a bend, the croft to her right. If she took a couple of steps off the path through a gap in the bank, she would be within earshot of the open windows. Her pulse thumped in her neck and she couldn't work out why she was even considering doing this; the possibility of information which she could use when she got home and saw Anna again, perhaps. A reckless streak. She took the steps. Too late now. If Jim looked out the window at the wrong moment, she would be in for it. She could hear Pierce's voice – not the soft low tone, but the harsher clipped syllables that had startled her, and taken Jim by surprise, that afternoon when he dropped Anna off outside their house. *Water... fault*. And, she could hear now, they seemed to be repeating the same conversation. Except this time Pierce sounded angrier.

'The fucking water... betrayed.'

Betrayed. Traitor, Anna had called her when she wanted to return the stolen tiles to Blackstone, and now here was Pierce accusing Jim of the same crime.

Jim replied, his voice strange and tense, 'I would never betray...'

She didn't like what she was hearing. She wished she hadn't done this, peered through this crack, the open window, a glimpse into another place, a much darker place, she didn't want to see. Where her father wasn't reliable, where he did bad things. *Betrayed*. She'd had enough. She couldn't bear it,

transferring it from pocket to pocket, convinced that it was keeping her safe from harm. Her talisman. She removed it, held it in the crease of her left palm, brushed it with one finger of her right, its warmth tingling her skin. And suddenly she wanted rid of it. She didn't want anything to do with this strange family which had been dumped on their doorstep. Her blood sister Anna. This man Pierce. These odd relatives who came to stay and drew her into their orbit in ways which intrigued her but also scared her because she felt she was losing control. Hearing things she didn't want to hear. She'd had enough. She raised her arm and aimed; if she chucked it, the tile would fall down and down the face of the sandstone cliff until it made the tiniest splash in the Atlantic and she would never have to see it again. Maybe it would be washed by the tide to the small triangle of sand at the back of her Aladdin's cave and found by some other girl in some other time, many years from now when whatever Jim had done would be buried and forgotten and nobody would ever, ever know. She lowered her arm. She couldn't do it. She was scared she might harm herself, lose the magic protection of the tile. Hurt Anna. She cast her eyes around for a suitable spot, identified a fissure in the head of the whale stone, a mouth-shaped crack, wide enough for her to wiggle her hand between the two layers of rock. She reached in, fiddled around, feeling the hidden space and found a hollow where earth and moss had gathered, a natural cubbyhole. Her fingers touched hardness, a sharp point, she scrabbled, drew the object out. A bird's skull. She examined it in her palm, distracted from her anxieties for a moment by the curve of its black-tipped beak, the fragile roundness of the bleached cranium. What kind of bird was it? A crow perhaps. A deep rasp made her look up – a vast black corvid circled overhead. She could tell it was a raven by the diamond shape of its tail.

'Is this your friend?'

The raven cawed, scolding her, swooped close.

'I'll put it back, don't worry.'

She turned the skull on its side, eased the tile inside the eye socket, squeezed her arm inside the rock's crevice and gently deposited the raven's skull back in its hidden grave. She withdrew her hand, stood quickly before she had a chance to change her mind, half expecting a bolt of lightning to strike her dead now that she had been parted from the protection of her talisman. Nothing happened. She turned and spotted another path she hadn't seen before that cut a diagonal across the slope and ended at the back of the village nearer to the car. She ran and skipped, gaining speed on the slope, reached the Volvo. She looked back over her shoulder and saw Jim leaving the croft. She'd made it just in time.

She thought he might have guessed she had been spying on him, almost anticipated a bollocking. But he seemed subdued; the meeting with Pierce had left him more sad than mad. They sat in the car. He turned the ignition, did a three-point turn, crawled along the track.

'Don't tell Anna you've been to Hoy,' he said as they passed through the barren, scorched valley. 'It would be safer for her if she didn't know.'

She nodded and she felt that she shared some of the burden of his sadness, some of the blame and the guilt.

CHAPTER 15

Orkney, October 1989

Prospero: Hast thou, spirit,
Performed to point the tempest that I bade thee?
Ariel: To every article.

See you October 3rd

SHE HAD BEEN quite pleased with her coded note to Pierce. Although having written it, posted it to the PO Box number he had given her, battled train cancellations because of lines blocked by fallen trees and braved a gut-churning ferry crossing to Stromness, she was beginning to wonder whether too much time scouring *The Tempest* for suitable quotes had morphed her into Ariel, her cipher, complete with storm-inciting powers. She collected the archaeologist's Honda 50 – he'd kindly told her she was welcome to it if she was mad enough to ride it in this weather. He always left the key in the ignition, he said. She could use it whenever she wanted. She had ridden through the deluge to a cheap and damp B and B in Kirkwall.

Waves of rain sliding over grey paving stones. Water trickling down her neck every time she ventured to the library archive. She spent two days reading old excavation reports from the Earl's Bu, searching for evidence of the Norse settlement below the surface. There were hints of older ruins – a pictish stone with a carved crescent moon had been found – and strange accounts of hundreds of small cat bones sifted from the soil. The animals had been butchered, knife cuts visible on the bones. Why would anybody butcher a cat? Ritual. Or something more practical – pelts. Bred to be skinned. She thought of Reznik the cat strangler then; butcher by name and butcher by nature. Harry's reaction confirmed Pierce's assessment of him as a ruthless operator; a dangerous arms dealer who would pursue his enemies to the grave. She tried to concentrate on the excavation records – but her mind was drifting, sifting memories, washing away the dirt and debris until all that was left were shards of scarred bone. Fears about Jim. She closed her notebook, wandered to the window, watched sheets of rain falling. The apse of the Round Church at Orphir was so badly built it should have collapsed, she had learned, and the only reason the circular stone wall remained standing was the strength of the mortar that glued it together. Earl Hakon's guilt for murdering Magnus had been mixed in with the putty, she reckoned. Guilt had a habit of persisting. When she turned up at Pierce's croft in Hoy earlier in the summer, he had asked her whether she was at the Round Church because she was a penitent and, of course, she was; remorse for past errors and fears about her father's sins the force driving her from one end of the country to the other in an autumnal storm.

The rain stopped on the 3rd, chased away by a howling wind that sped her along the road to Houton. Greylag geese combed the sodden fields in straight lines, like policemen searching for a body. Gusts stripped the leaves from the sycamores and whisked them around in golden flurries. The Houton ferryman in his yellow oilskins laughed when she asked whether the crossing might be cancelled because of the wind. He said this was nothing. This wasn't even a gale. If they cancelled the ferries every time there was a gust of wind in Orkney, nobody would ever go anywhere. Don't go climbing the cliff paths, though, he warned. Play it safe.

Waves rolled the ferry as it crossed Scapa Flow in the thin dawn light. Gusts rocked the bike along the coast road past Pegal Bay. She tried to quell the wind in her mind without much success. The inland road between the scree slopes was calmer than the coast, but still she was relieved to part company with the Honda when she reached Rackwick Bay.

Pierce was leaning against the doorframe of his croft, watching her climb the path. He looked more like an ageing Prospero, she thought, in the mysterious low light of Orkney's autumn; more unkempt than the last time she had seen him, windblown strands of brown hair striping his forehead.

He straightened as she approached, raised a hand dramatically. 'What, Ariel! My industrious servant, Ariel!'

A performer – like Anna. There was something in his rendition of Prospero's lines that unnerved her; even in those few words he reminded her how much she had disliked the character the first time she had read *The Tempest* for her English A-level. Prospero was cruel to both his slaves, Ariel and Caliban, but it was the way he treated his daughter Miranda that hacked her off the most. Mind control. Complete psychological suppression. She had decided that *The Tempest* was a play about abusive patriarchy. Her teacher had corrected her assertion; it was Shakespeare's final work, his farewell to the stage. A play about reconciliation with the inevitability of death as well as with one's enemies, he said. She had never been entirely convinced.

She smiled awkwardly at Pierce, uncertain how to react to his disconcerting theatrical greeting.

'Good to see you.' He said it with a genuine warmth that dispelled the peculiar twinge produced by his brief Prospero performance.

'Good to see you too.' She meant it. He wasn't straightforward – he was a spy after all – but he was interesting. And, give him his due, he was trying to do the right thing. Resolve the discords in his life, reconstruct his relationship with Anna. A blast of wind ruffled the edge of the turf roof.

'You arrived with the first proper tempest of the autumn. Very appropriate.'

'The ferryman said it wasn't a gale.'

'Hah. The ferryman. Let me guess, you're talking about the large ginger whiskered bloke on the Houton to Lyness crossing.'

'Yep.'

'He grew up on Hoy. He's used to the conditions here.'

'Don't you ever get scared here alone?'

'The weather doesn't scare me.'

She thought that was probably true. He had the air of a man who wasn't easily scared, someone you could rely on in difficult circumstances; military coup in a far-flung country, broken-down car on a motorway hard shoulder, knife-wielding maniac advancing. The one thing that rattled him was the Czech. Reznik the Butcher.

'Let's not stand on the doorstep. Come in.'

She could barely see inside the croft, it was so gloomy. The hurricane lamp guttered on the kitchen table. Why didn't he buy another? Surely he could afford more than one. She watched him fill the kettle, place it on the hob. She could imagine Pierce commanding a room full of strangers with his presence and his stories hinting at bravery and insider knowledge of state secrets. And yet here he was, living the life of a hermit, a castaway in Hoy. Hardly anybody knew he was here apart from her and a few of his contacts in Intelligence. And probably Harry. Her conversation with Harry was bugging her. She was sure he had known Pierce's location all along – Jim must have told him in '76 when they met at his allotment. Pierce handed her a cup of tea, sat in the chair next to her.

'I gather from your postcard that you've met Anna?'

'Yes.'

'How is she?'

'Very well. She hasn't changed much.'

His face cracked and wrinkled. 'Well, that's fantastic. Debrief me on your meeting.'

Debrief. She hesitated, she hadn't prepared herself, decided what she should or shouldn't say. Pierce was watching her expectantly.

'I went along to a poll tax meeting and saw her there. It was in a crypt in Brixton.'

He tutted, eyes rolled to the rafters and back.

'But I really don't think you have to worry about her mates. She doesn't have anything to do with Militant, so I doubt whether there's any security risk to her knowing where you are.'

'You didn't tell her where I was living, did you?'

He leaned forward, face hardened, fist clenched in palm. She flinched, instinctively dodging a potential blow, the threat in his voice catching her off guard.

'No, I didn't tell her where you were living.' She replied calmly, but she could hear the defensiveness in her voice, made wary by the glimpse of a darker shadow behind Pierce's jovial façade. He stretched back on his chair, hands behind his head, relaxing again, and she dismissed the moment; she was on edge and had probably overreacted. Just the tone of a man who expected his orders to be obeyed.

'Well, maybe she isn't anything to do with Militant, but my informants are pretty clear that there are some funny old Trots in that group and we can't be sure of who they know, so I think my caution is justified.'

She watched him curiously; she couldn't get her head around the surveillance of Anna. Here was Pierce, using the secret state to spy on his daughter from whom he had become estranged because of his job. Nuts.

Pierce must have sensed her reaction to his comment. He changed tack. 'I'm sure it's a phase. I wish she would find herself a proper job, though.'

'She's an actress.'

'Yes, but is she on the stage? Or in a film?'

'She's done some TV ads.'

'Quite. That's hardly... Why can't she be more like you?' he asked. 'Do something with her brain. A postgraduate course. Take the civil service fast stream exam. Train to be a barrister. I don't know – there are a thousand more productive ways of changing things than sitting in a darkened room in south London with a huddle of conspiracy theorists plotting the overthrow of the state.'

'They're not plotting the overthrow of the state,' she said. 'They are protesting against the poll tax.'

'I know. I know. Sorry. I'm the frustrated father, trying to help his daughter from a distance. I mustn't let it get to me. The most important thing is – do you think she would like to see me again?'

His eagerness was touching, exposed his vulnerability. She dug in her pocket, found the blue tile, removed it and held it in the flat of her palm for Pierce to see. 'She wants to see you. She asked me to give you this tile.'

'Ah.' He pulled a curious expression which she couldn't

interpret. Surprised? Touched? Pained? 'Now that brings back some memories. Jim handed me two similar tiles in the summer of 1976, except they were white.' She wanted to ask what had happened to them, but decided it was better not to interrupt his flow. 'Yes. Marble. Jim was bemused by them; he told me he had no idea where Anna had found them. Although I suspect he did.'

She suspected he did as well.

'Jim said they were a gift from Anna, and I took them, a token of something or other. Love, I like to think, but maybe I was fooling myself.'

'I don't think so.' Sam placed the tile on the coffee table, edged it in his direction. He didn't touch it. 'The tiles mean a lot to her, because...' She felt foolish trying to explain the tiles – the Fisher King's treasures – their magical powers and significance.

'Of course.' He left the tile on the table, as if there were something awkward about it. Maybe he had realized, after all, that Anna had nicked them from an ancient monument. Or was he interpreting Anna's secret code in a way she could not decipher?

'So I suppose the next move is mine.'

She nodded.

He smiled. 'Great. Good stuff. Well done.' He dug in his pocket and produced a folded wodge of notes, flicked through them. 'I've got five hundred here for you. Will that cover your expenses for this trip?'

More than. 'Yes. Thank you.'

She was taken aback by his generosity.

'Let me make a note.' He stood, handed her the cash. Five hundred in twenties. He went to his desk, took out his notebook, jotted something down. *Ariel, five hundred 3rd*

October, she guessed. He really was oddly anal about money. Everybody had their quirks.

'Operation Fisher King completed,' she said.

'Almost. One more thing.'

She baulked.

'It's nothing much.'

She glanced at the notes in her hand, neatly squared, twenty-five heads of William Shakespeare all facing the same way.

'Could you tell her that I'm here in Hoy and she can contact me via the PO Box number I gave you? Would that be OK?'

Churlish to refuse, after he'd given her five hundred quid. Eight hundred, counting the three hundred he'd given her in September.

'I want to make sure the ball is in her court. I don't want her to feel forced into seeing me. If you could give her my contact details, it's all up to her. Is that OK with you? Would you mind doing that for me?'

'That's fine. And then I'll be free. Like Ariel.'

'Yes, and I can lay aside Prospero's magic books, drop the dark arts of the secret state, the spells and tradecraft, and return to the real world of ordinary mortals.'

She thought Harry suspected differently; he believed Pierce was planning a comeback with MI5.

'You don't ever think about returning to the Intelligence services then?'

'Good god no. Not at all.'

He wouldn't tell her, even if it were true.

'My plan is to do something completely different. I've got a friend who is running an ethical public relations company.'

'Ethical PR?' She couldn't keep the scorn from her voice. 'Isn't that an oxymoron?'

'I can see why you and Anna get on.' He chuckled. 'This

company only takes on clients whose objectives meet the company's human rights policy. No South African investors. No users of child labour. Do you think Anna would approve of my proposed career?'

'I imagine she would think it was better than spying.'

Perhaps Harry had got himself worked up about nothing. She puffed her cheeks; believing Pierce meant doubting Harry.

'Are you OK?'

'Yes, I'm fine.' Dismissing Harry made her uneasy. The wind howled down the chimney. 'When we met in September, you told me you had come to Hoy because of the Czech.'

'Yes.' There was a tightness to his voice and she noticed his Adam's apple bobbing. Maybe she shouldn't be pursuing this, but she'd started so she might as well finish.

'Do you think the Czech ever worked for the KGB?'

'Now where would you have got that idea from?'

He was regarding her sternly and she felt dumb. Her amateurish attempt to wrangle some information from Pierce, the professional. She glanced out the window; scaly clouds like dead fish passing, the angry spume of breakers crashing on the shore. What was she doing here, making herself vulnerable, exposing herself to these elements she didn't understand and couldn't control?

'Look. We're family.' He said it in a kindly way, which made her feel better. 'When I talk about the family, I mean all the intelligence and security services. MI5, MI6.' He gestured with his hand, indicating there might be others he wasn't going to mention. 'And of course, I have to include the Force and all their units, like the one your father worked for, because sometimes we collaborated with them.' He ambled over to the window, stood with his back to her, hands linked at his tailbone. 'And in all families,' he continued, more to the bay than her, 'there are loyalties and disagreements. Not just between the Force and Intelligence. MI6 has, historically, looked down on MI5 because we tend to think it's full of ex-cops. They're often in minor roles. Not necessarily at the centre of things. They're good at what they do, of course. Like your friend Harry…'

He left the name hanging in the air. She got the message. Harry talks out his arse. Ex-cops in MI5 were at the bottom of the family tree, the lowest branches. Apart from the police spies. The black sheep, who got in the way and worse. That summer's day in '76, she had heard Pierce bellowing through the open window. *Fucking tortured.* She had understood the words literally because the pain made it clear he was being literal; he had been tortured. And now she had pulled the fragments together, she suspected that a fanatic from the Red Army Faction had taken Pierce when the operation was blown and tortured him to try to find out who he was working for and what he knew about the Czech. *I dealt with them*, he had told her. Whatever had happened, somehow he had survived, although not without injury. The wounded Fisher King. And she was left with the nagging question about her father – was Jim to blame for Pierce's suffering? Had he somehow given away the information that endangered his colleague? She heard Jim's voice small and tight. *I would never betray…* Perhaps it was better not to know, she would regret hearing a dark tale about Jim. She needed to know. She had to face the ghosts if she wanted to exorcize them. She decided she could risk a confession.

'You know I came here with Jim, that August when he gave you the two white tiles?'

Pierce nodded slowly, steepled his fingers. 'I gathered.'

'Jim left me down on the beach. I got bored, wandered up the path to look for him, and I overheard a conversation.'

Pierce raised an eyebrow.

'What did you overhear?'

'You mentioned...' She wasn't sure she could say it now. Perhaps she'd got it all wrong, her youthful imagination over-dramatizing. 'I heard you mention torture.'

He winced.

She flustered. 'I didn't know whether you were referring to real...'

He looked pained. She shouldn't have mentioned it. She was so stupid. Clumsy. 'I mean...'

He ran his tongue around the corner of his mouth, closed his eyes. She didn't know what to say. The silence ran on. Eventually he opened his eyes, stared straight at her. 'You did hear me talking about torture.' His voice was quiet. 'Did you hear Jim say anything?'

I wouldn't betray. She couldn't repeat his words.

'No. I only heard you. I was upset, worried that Jim had done something wrong. You know what it's like when you're a child and you hear adults talking and you pick up the vibe even if you don't understand what they are saying. I remember being scared and I ran away along the cliff path. To the rock that's shaped like a whale.'

'Ah. I know the spot. The Raven's Nest, that's what I call it. Apparently there used to be a pair of young ravens that nested there for a couple of years, but then one died and its partner kept hanging around. Grieving, so the locals said.'

'Oh, I saw a raven there that day.'

Pierce leaned to one side, rubbed his lame leg, as if even the mention of that difficult summer was stirring old wounds.

'I'm sorry if it's painful for you to... I just wanted to know whether Jim...'

'No. Don't apologize. It's not...' He glanced away and back.

'Look, it wasn't all Jim's fault. I don't want to go into it now. Let sleeping dogs lie.'

He wiped his mouth with the back of his hand and half smiled at her in a way which was obviously supposed to be reassuring, but it made her stomach sink. *It wasn't all Jim's fault.* There was no escaping the implication – Jim fucked up. Big time. Dumped him in it. She wanted to run. Disappear. A creeping sense of shame, inadequacy, coming over her in his presence. She was conscious of Pierce scrutinizing her reactions. He leaned forward.

'The conversation you overheard…'

She nodded.

'I don't suppose… Jim didn't say anything afterwards to you about an envelope, did he?'

He was surveying her with an intensity which made her feel uncomfortable.

'An envelope?' She tried not to redden. Her mind raced to her hollowed-out book *The Secret Island*. The envelope she had hidden there. Why was he asking her about the envelope now? It seemed odd, a minor detail, given the seriousness of the conversation. *Fucking tortured.* Maybe he was searching for a diversion. Fair enough, but she didn't want to tell him about the envelope. Instinct; keep something back for another time. Or maybe it was just the possessiveness she felt for the photo of Anna.

'No, Jim didn't mention an envelope.' It was true – he hadn't mentioned it. She'd learned that trick from Jim. Don't lie; craft your answer to avoid telling the whole truth. Did she look guilty?

'Well, not to worry. It doesn't matter.' He grimaced, as if it did matter. 'I suppose what does really matter,' he raised one eyebrow, 'is letting Anna know that she can contact me via the PO Box number I gave you.'

She was relieved that he was steering the conversation away from tricky subjects now – Jim's actions, the envelope she had treasured all these years.

'I'll pass the message on to Miranda,' she said. 'I mean Anna.'

'Great. That would be fantastic. Could you bear to drop me another note when you've done it?'

'No problem.'

He patted her on the shoulder. 'You'll go far. You're smart. You've got a huge amount of integrity.'

His words of praise made her feel peculiarly happy; he had the kind of charisma that made you want to please him, earn his praise. Avoid the sharpness of his disapproval.

'Just don't,' he added, 'ever think of taking up spying as a profession.'

'Don't worry, I won't.'

'Although, I have to say, I think you would be pretty good at it. I think you could make the grade. A proper spy. Which reminds me.' He tapped the side of his head with his finger. 'Have you read Graham Greene, *Our Man in Havana*?'

She nodded.

'You remember Lamb's code?'

'Vaguely.'

'We agree on a book to use and send each other page and line numbers as a starting point for encoding and decoding the alphabet.' He laughed. 'It can be quite useful sometimes. I was just thinking, why don't you use Lamb's code when you drop me that note? Make an onerous task more exciting.'

She grinned, joining in with his obvious delight at playing spy games. 'OK.'

He waved his hand at the bookshelf. 'Do we have any books in common?'

She could see the backs of several le Carrés – but it was a white spine that caught her eye.

'*The Collected Poems of T. S. Eliot.*' Another of her English A-level texts.

He eased the book from the shelf, handed it to her. 'Do you have the same edition?'

She flipped through the familiar pages and confirmed their copies were identical.

'Good. T. S. Eliot it is. Very appropriate given his references to the Fisher King and *The Tempest* in *The Waste Land*. "The Fire Sermon", if I remember correctly.'

'Right.'

The confidence of his detailed literary references made her feel slightly inadequate; she couldn't quite keep up. A reminder – as if she needed one – that she was an amateur at this game. That was the difference between proper spies and police spies, she decided as she stood to leave. Proper spies could reference T. S. Eliot. Although, how could she forget, Jim's favourite book was *Ulysses*, which was hardly less demanding than T. S. Eliot; he kept it by his bed for solace during sleepless nights – though not, as far as she knew, for decoding secret messages. Pierce held the door open for her, the wind rushing in, and she was reminded again of Prospero, the ageing magus.

Through the rocky valley, right along the coast road. The bike battled with the gradient. She reached a bend, spotted the solitary marker of Betty Corrigall's grave among the browning heather and remembered driving back from Rackwick Bay with Jim, that August day in '76; they had reached this same bend and Sam had glimpsed the white headstone. She wanted to find out who was buried on such a lonely spot, although she wasn't sure why she had suggested it because Jim was in a grim mood and examining a tombstone was hardly going to cheer him; it would have been better to head straight to Pegal Bay. Jim parked on the verge anyway, and they had trudged across the moorland. Even in the sunshine, it was bleak. No human settlement in view, endless heather in front, black lochan water behind, chilling gusts blowing in from the sea and making her shiver.

She read the words on the tomb. 'Here lies Betty Corrigall.'

'It's made of fibreglass,' Jim said. 'I suppose that's to stop it from sinking in the bog. It must be quite recent – look, the ground around its base is still disturbed.'

The fibreglass tombstone might have been new, but the body it marked was not. A small plaque explained that Betty Corrigall was a young woman of twenty-seven who had lived in Hoy in the eighteenth century. She had become pregnant and then tried to drown herself when the father ran away to sea. She had been rescued, but the shame was too much for her and she had hanged herself. None of Hoy's churchyards was prepared to take her body and so she had been buried in unconsecrated ground on the boundary between two parishes. Her bog-preserved body had been found by two peat cutters in 1933. The noose with which she had hanged herself lay by her side, but disintegrated as soon as it was exposed to the air.

She said to Jim that it was unfair; the girl had done nothing wrong. It was the father of the child who was at fault. Jim didn't reply, his eyes on the far horizon, his face tense and grey. She had felt an urge to break his trance. She couldn't imagine what it was like to be so unhappy you would want to end your life, she said. Eventually he replied, 'Sometimes when you're really unhappy, or scared, it helps to go somewhere else in your mind for a while.'

She asked him what he meant, although, at some level, she understood exactly what he was saying.

'Think of a safe place, a calm place, and imagine you are there. That's what I do. Retreat.'

She had conjured up the places she considered safe – her bedroom, the school, the library. None of them seemed quite right, and then a thought had struck her.

'Oh. I found a cave at Rackwick and when I walked to the back of it, there was a patch of dry sand that wasn't touched by the sea. That felt like a safe place to me.'

Jim had locked his hands behind his head, grimaced as if he was in agony. She had panicked, scared he was having a heart attack.

'Are you OK?'

'I'm fine. I was thinking, that was all. If you felt the cave was safe, then it's a good place to go in your mind.' His mouth twisted. 'But you shouldn't have been playing in a cave.'

'The tide didn't reach the back, that was the...'

He raised his fist, held it above her in the air and she ducked. 'You have to be careful around water. Don't take the sea for granted.'

He lowered his arm, but his face was still red with anger, his voice sharp. She had wanted to cry; his sudden temper had scared her. It didn't make sense. It was all so weird; Pierce hiding here, Jim and her pretending neither of them knew. The shouting. *Fucking tortured*. All this stuff about safe places. The trip to Hoy had been a big mistake. She really wished she hadn't tagged along with Jim.

She braked, eyes on Betty Corrigall's burial place. Remembering that strange conversation with Jim now made her want to revisit the grave again, re-tread the old ground, see if any of it made more sense second time around. What was it with Jim? She sometimes suspected he had suffered from manic depression – all those highs and lows. She parked the Honda on the verge, followed the sodden path from the road, boots sinking in the sphagnum moss. She reached the picket fence surrounding the grave, stood silently, head bowed; poor Betty so lonely all these years out on the cold slopes of Hoy. A V of honking geese flew overhead.

She scanned the ground for something she could leave on the tomb, and decided she would have to make do with a sprig of heather. Somebody had left a jam jar at the foot of the headstone; she could use that for her offering. She leaned over the fence, lifted the jar, removed the wilting stems and spotted an object she thought she recognized. Surely she must be mistaken. She held the jar up and peered through the bottom of the glass; it was definitely there. A small white square. She tipped the jar, let the water dribble out, caught the tile in her hand. How extraordinary. Grimy, but unmistakable. One of the white Roman tiles from Blackstone. The Fisher King's magic treasure. Pierce had deposited one of the two tiles that Anna had sent him via Jim, in this jar on the grave of Betty Corrigall. She didn't know what to make of it. Perhaps it was a casual gesture; he was passing, like her, and had been moved to leave something personal on the tomb. But spies never made casual gestures. A spy's empty milk bottle was never simply an empty milk bottle; it was a signal. Their daughters were just as bad; Anna's tiles were not randomly distributed, she was sure. The red, white and blue carefully assigned to their chosen recipients. Pierce had left the tile on Betty Corrigall's grave for a reason. What was it? She brushed the tile clean; the white definitely felt colder than the blue. She dropped it in her pocket.

She squelched across the moor, reached the Honda, swung her leg over, twisted the key in the ignition and sat there for a moment with the bike still on its stand, staring across the water, comparing Pierce and Jim. There had been times when Jim's behaviour had been turbulent, difficult. On the surface, Pierce seemed more genial and in control, and yet he had odd undercurrents. Religiously noting all the cash he handed over in his notebook. The flash of threat when he thought she had given away his address to Anna. The sudden question about the envelope. She still liked him – he was interesting and generous – but you could never take a spy at face value. She would have to take another look at the contents of that envelope when she returned to Vauxhall, she decided as she kicked the Honda's start pedal and the bike leaped across the heather.

CHAPTER 16

London, September 1976

SHE FOUND THE envelope shortly after they returned from their summer holiday in Orkney. The heatwave had dissipated, the dusty streets of south London made strangely unfamiliar with the lick of rain. Sam was glad to have her room to herself again, but she missed Anna. Valerie had left the number of their latest residence. Sam called, but nobody picked up the phone. She tried again an hour later, still no answer. She didn't want to waste the last weekend of the school holiday sitting at home calling somebody who wasn't in. She decided to visit Bridget. That was the reason she gave herself for returning to the street where she and Anna had located Pierce's safehouse. They mooched around the Riverdale Shopping Centre. Sam was bored. She missed Anna. They went back to Bridget's house and played Mouse Trap for a while before Sam got irritated with Bridget's hysterical laughter every time the plastic diving man landed head first in the tub. She had to leave.

She walked the wrong way down the road, not back to the bus stop, but towards Pierce's safehouse where they had spied on the blonde woman only a few weeks previously. Just checking, that was all. She strolled past the bomb hole, spotted a fox dozing in a far corner, reached the house and looked for signs of life. The curtains were drawn. Maybe she could double-check. She glanced around. The street was empty.

She couldn't see the harm; she scraped the gate on the path, ran up the steps to the front door, rang the door bell. Distant chimes echoed. She rang again. More chimes but no footsteps. She glanced over her shoulder; the street still empty. She skipped down the steps, into the long grass of the garden, dodged the branches of an apple tree. She jumped at the hum of a wasp hovering around her ear and, in her head, Anna egged her on, teasing her for being a scaredy cat.

The far side of the garden was a dump. Tangled clumps of straw and hogweed, nettles sprouting between piles of bricks, a coil of rope, discarded tyres, planks, tarpaulins. What had Pierce used this place for, she wondered. Anna had found the address on a gas bill in the name of Davenport. His safehouse, she had said, paid for by MI6; the Firm, Anna had called them. And yet, it seemed they hadn't reclaimed the house since Pierce had done a flit to Hoy. Left it to rot. She reached the back steps to the kitchen door. Oddly, there was an empty milk bottle on the top step, which was the wrong place to leave it; the milkman wouldn't see it there. Perhaps it was a secret message – empty milk bottle; nobody at home. She was beginning to enjoy herself, playing the detective. Shame Anna wasn't here too. She stooped to examine the bottle. The sound of a car drawing up on the road and a door slamming made her freeze, her mind blank for a second before she jumped from the top step, darted into the long grass, headed for the densest corner of the wilderness, ignored the nettle stings. Curled up small. She listened, expecting to hear footsteps disappearing as whoever was in the car walked along the street but, to her dismay, the garden gate scraped on the path. She pushed herself further into the undergrowth. She thought for a moment that it might be Anna and Valerie, but she realized from the thud of the footsteps on the path that these were men, not a twelve-year-old girl and her titchy mum. She should have walked straight to the bus stop. God only knew who these men were and what they were after. She tried to calm herself. Getagrip, Getagrip. Even if they did find her, they wouldn't harm her. They were probably from the Firm, coming to tidy up their property.

She could hear their voices, harsh, spitting words that weren't English. What language was it? Russian? She didn't think so; she'd heard Russian before when Jim had brought his KGB drinking mates from Tilbury docks around to their house for a late-night vodka, and this didn't sound like Russian. Similar, though. Was it Czech? She was starting to panic; anything could happen. What if she was found? Abducted. *Fucking tortured.* Her throat was scratchy and her eyes were full of tears. She tried not to look at the intruders but she couldn't help peeping at the two men in leather jackets, bulky backs visible as they ascended the steps to the kitchen door. Dark-haired. Swarthy men, Bridget's mum had said, with a tone of distrust. Taking over the street. The taller man lifted the milk bottle, examined it, then turned and chucked it up in the air, sent it twisting in a high arc. She thought it might drop on her head, but it fell short, landed on the grass with a thud.

She sensed the gaze of the men following the path of the bottle and hardly dared to breathe, hoping her brown tee shirt would camouflage her, fox-like in her den. A guttural shout made her think she had been discovered, but the men weren't looking in her direction any more – they were banging the door, kicking it, yelling. They conferred on the top step for what seemed like hours before they descended and strode off, their thick legs barely ten feet away from her hiding place. The car engine revved and wheels squealed. Still, she didn't dare move, worried they might return. She dug in her back pocket, removed the packet of Smarties she'd stashed there, pinged the lid off, emptied the sweets into her cupped palm, the food dye staining her clammy skin tangerine, dropped a Smartie in her mouth and chewed. If she got to the end of the packet and the men still hadn't returned, it was safe to move.

She placed the last sweet in her mouth, crunched the hard sugar shell between her molars. Nothing. She stood, about to make her way to the front of the house when her eye was caught by a green glint; a glorious emerald, flat-nosed rose chafer, scurrying along a jagged plank lying in the grass. The chafer wiggled its antennae, searching for a route to the dank underside. She couldn't quite let it disappear. She shifted the splintery wood; the chafer had vanished but lying on the flattened white grass underneath was a tartan tin of Crawford's assorted shortbread. She prodded the tin; it wasn't rusty, it didn't look as if it had been there long. She gripped the lid and prised it open, found an envelope inside. She removed it, stuck it in her back pocket and scarpered.

She didn't open the envelope until she was sitting safely at the front of the double-decker bus. It didn't seem to contain much. A used chequebook. She flicked through the stubs. Boring. She replaced it in the envelope and removed what looked like a photo. A picture of Anna in school uniform staring nonchalantly at the camera. Only Anna could manage to look cool in a school photo. She had no idea how the envelope might have ended up in a biscuit tin in the back garden of Pierce's deserted house. She half wondered whether Anna had left it there herself in the hope that Pierce might find it if he returned. Another of Anna's strange designs perhaps, like the mosaic tiles, except this time she had left a trail of pictures of herself across south London in places she thought her father might visit. The possibility made her sad; the idea

CHAPTER 17

London, October 1989

SHE WAS KNACKERED after a sleepless night on the train from Inverness. She pushed the front door of the Vauxhall house and listened. Becky snoring, still asleep. She was desperate for coffee, but it had to wait. She went straight upstairs to her room, removed *The Secret Island* from the bookshelf, placed the Bryant & May matchbox gently on her desk, dug out the envelope she had found in the garden of Pierce's safehouse at the tail end of the summer of '76. She opened the envelope and grabbed the chequebook, weighed it in her hand; she hadn't taken much notice of it before, more interested in the picture of Anna. The cover was dirty cream, imitation vellum – *Gaillard & Cie* embossed in gold cursive letters. *Cie*, French for Company. The first page revealed an address in the City, the small print indicated the bank was registered in Lausanne. Swiss bank account. All the cheques had been used. There were no credit slips in the book, but at the back there was a printed calendar, a hole punch marking cash withdrawals. The holes made her smile, the dissonance of somebody with enough dosh to merit a Swiss bank account being subjected to such a menial process of recording transactions. The name printed at the bottom of the calendar provided an explanation, she suspected, for the attention to boring detail. Mr H. Davenport Esq. Henry was Pierce's first name, Anna had once told her, although everybody who knew the real him called him by his surname. Perhaps he used his real first name as part of his fake identity, as spies sometimes did. Davenport was the surname on the gas bill that Anna had found, which had led them to the safehouse in Lewisham, where she had found the envelope.

Pierce had obviously been concerned about the envelope – and she assumed it was this one. Harry had said he was a man of many identities – but it seemed likely that Davenport was the alias Pierce was using in 1976 when his cover was blown. She flicked through the cheque stubs. He had dutifully written details on each one: name, date, amount. He had confessed to his habit of noting every penny spent as if it was a weakness. Funny that he could change his outward identity so easily, but the ingrained habits remained, whatever his name. He probably insisted that the bank clerk made the hole punches in the calendar. She held the chequebook upside down, waggled it, half expecting a coded message on a Rizla paper to fall out. Nothing, but she could feel the tension in her hand, sensed there was something important there which she couldn't quite discern. She replaced the book of stubs in the envelope.

Becky stirred, stomped downstairs. Sam followed her to the kitchen.

'Oh wotcha.' Becky opened a cupboard, removed a corn-flakes box, shook, reached for a bowl from the dirty pile in the sink, gave it a cursory rinse, filled it with cereal. 'I didn't hear you come home.'

'I got back early this morning.' Sam yawned. 'What's been happening?'

'This and that.'

The tension between her and Becky seemed to have evaporated in her absence – what a relief.

'Want some coffee?'

'Please.'

Becky messed with some filter papers and a plastic funnel, reached for the kettle.

'It's official.'

'What, you and…?'

'Yep. We're an item. Anna and me.'

Anna had reverted to her original name, which quite surprised Sam – she must be serious about Becky.

'Great.' She managed to sound as if she meant it.

'Anna said you were right, she did meet you in 1976.'

Sam wavered, about to say told you so, before she decided smugness would not go down well here. 'It doesn't bother you then?'

'Why should it? Your father was a police spy and I've never let that affect our friendship. Why should I care if Anna's father was a spy and his work necessitated a name change? I don't judge people by their father's occupation. Or their names.'

Anna had come clean, it seemed. The percolator bubbled. Becky poured and handed her a mug of coffee, settled down to eat her cornflakes.

'Anna said you were a bit of a weirdo when she first met you.'

'Weirdo?'

'She said you collected beetles.'

'What's weird about that? Darwin did it too.'

'She said you trapped them in jam jars and suffocated them with crushed laurel leaves.'

Kind of Anna to reveal that detail.

'You're the Eichmann of the insect world.'

'I only had about ten beetles in my collection.' In a

matchbox morgue under her bed. She was a weirdo. She'd given up collecting them – after Anna had mocked her, in fact. Decided she had to observe and respect, not collect. 'Darwin had hundreds.'

'I always suspected you had a dark side. That must be what attracts your war-junkie friend Tom.'

'What's he got to do with anything?'

'He called while you were away.'

She sipped her coffee.

'I'm going into town in a bit. Do you want to come?' Becky asked.

'Thanks, but no. I'm too tired.'

Becky lifted the bowl to her face, slurped the mush at the bottom, chucked it back in the sink. 'I'm seeing Anna tomorrow.'

She lay in the bath, watched a spider weaving a web in a corner, listened to Becky schlepping around her bedroom, The Cowboy Junkies playing. 'Sweet Jane'. Sam stuck her toe up the hot tap, wiggled it. Becky clicked the cassette player. The music stopped.

'Bye.'

Footsteps running down the stairs, front door slamming. Sam was irritated, with herself as much as anything. Anna hadn't given Sam her phone number – don't call me, I'll call you. And yet she was canoodling with her best mate, hanging out with Becky and mocking Sam behind her back. The story about the beetles. Sod that. She removed her toe from the tap, climbed out of the bath, dried and dressed, checked through the window to make sure Becky's Moggie Minor had definitely gone, and tip-toed into her bedroom. Why was she tip-toeing?

There wasn't anybody in the house to hear her. Guilt. She knew she was abusing her friend, invading her privacy, reverting to bad habits, well-worn techniques of the spying trade. Becky's address book was lying on her desk, open at the A page. Anna's name and number in red ink. Sam memorized the number, backed out the room. Once she had passed Pierce's details on to Anna, she would go straight, never again resort to the tradecraft she had absorbed from her father. She ran to the phone box by the Royal Vauxhall Tavern.

'Anna. It's Sam.'

'I might have guessed. Where did you get my number from?'

Sam ignored the question. 'Can I come over and see you?'

'OK.'

She didn't sound that enthusiastic.

'When?'

'Now?'

'Later. Eight.'

'Your flat?'

'No. The heath. The pond where we were the other night.'

'OK. See you later.'

The year was skidding away. Soon the clocks would be going back and it would be dark by five. The gloomy evenings never used to bother her, but now they felt oppressive. The pavements were covered in slushy leaves and dog shit. The undimmed headlights of a car coming up behind her on the hill made her turn. She shielded her eyes, a silver Beemer accelerated past. The seventies semis gave way to grander Georgian terraces as she neared the top of the hill. Was that a universal rule in London?

The slummiest houses were always at the bottom, the lowest-lying land. She turned in to Hare and Billet Road, the expansive heath beyond. She passed the pub, glowing windows revealing men sharing a pint and the latest match scores. She sensed a car crawling behind her – searching for a parking spot? No – it drew alongside. Silver Beemer. Again. The window of the passenger seat lowered and a man in a green bomber jacket leaned out.

'What are you doing here? I thought you lived in Dick Street?'

The plain-clothes copper from the poll tax meeting. What a jerk. Hadn't they got anything better to do than intimidate women?

'Why don't you fuck off?' she said.

He grinned and waved and wound the window back up, satisfied that he had managed to annoy her, she presumed. The car sped away. Tosser. But he left her feeling jittery, out here on the heath alone at night. She surveyed the clump of birches by the water's edge; an amber flame leaped, hovered, flickered and vanished. Was that Anna rolling a spliff? She set off across the grass, its dampness slippery underfoot, dingy clouds shrouding the moon and making it difficult to see where she was treading. She reached the reedy edge of the pond, the water lapping gently. No sign of Anna. Perhaps she had imagined the flare. She edged around the pond, reached the trees, stood there in the shadows, listening for footsteps, watching the water. A ripple and a splash – a fish leaping for insects. An owl hooted. She searched for the bird among the branches and saw a ghostly figure emerging from the grey trunks. Anna.

'Why do we have to meet out here?'

'I think my flat is bugged.'

'God, I'm not sure it's any safer out here – I just saw the bouncer from your anti-poll tax meeting driving by in a silver Beemer.'

'Oh, a bloody plod. I'm not worried about them.' A plop of rain dimpled the surface of the pond. 'Let's get back under the trees. I'll roll a spliff.'

They huddled in the birch thicket; the last of the leaves provided some dripping cover.

'You got a message to Pierce?'

'Yes.'

Anna had her head bent over the Rizla papers, her black curls flopping forward. Sam couldn't see her face, found it hard to gauge her reactions.

'Are you going to tell me where he is?'

'Not exactly. I've got a PO Box number. You can write to him, fix up a meeting place. You have to use the name Steven Hill.'

She lifted her head. 'Steven Hill? Seriously. Why can't you just tell me where he is?'

'I swore I wouldn't. I can't.'

'For fuck's sake. Spies. Bloody spies. I thought I was done with spies.' Anna swiped a branch, sending leaves and raindrops flying.

'Why do you think he's been hiding all these years? Do you think somebody is still after him?'

Reznik the Butcher. But he had fled to the States. She briefly wondered whether Tom had unearthed any more details. Probably not.

'He implied it had almost become a habit – hiding. He's become used to living in exile.'

As soon as she said it, she realized she'd given away the fact that she hadn't just passed a message on to Pierce via some third party – she'd met him. But Anna knew that anyway. Too bad.

'He's had enough of being a hermit. I think he wants to move back to London.'

'And do what?'

'Work for an ethical PR company.'

Anna handed her the spliff.

'What's an ethical PR company when it's at home?'

'You'll have to ask him that.'

'Didn't you ever want to completely disown Jim?'

She wrinkled up her face, tugged on the roach. She had been caught up in one of Jim's old grudges a couple of years back. A difficult period she had tried to forget. She had seriously considered adopting a new identity so there was no chance that anybody else from Jim's shady past could track her down; the idea had seemed too extreme at the time, adopting a false identity so she could cut free from Jim's life as a spy. Better to face the demons. So she kept telling herself.

'There have been times when I've not wanted to have anything to do with him because of his work.'

'And what about the way Jim behaved at home? He was a bit of a drinker, wasn't he, your dad.'

'Yep. A bit of a drinker.' Understatement.

'Didn't Liz ever get fed up with him?'

'Of course she did.'

Liz didn't shout much, she was more likely to go for a sharp retort before she got in the car and drove away to one of her departmental meetings, but there had been unexpected outbursts. Crockery thrown, windows smashed, times when it was best to duck and run. The autumn after the heatwave had been particularly stormy, she recalled; arguments about Jim's job, Liz yelling she'd had enough of his bloody secret operations, Jim saying he had to see it through. She gave the spliff a final toke, handed it back to Anna.

'Every family has its disagreements.'

'Sure.'

Anna was getting cold feet about contacting Pierce.

'I gave him the tile,' Sam said.

'What did he say?'

'He was... he didn't say a lot.'

'Has he still got the white ones?' Anna blew a stream of smoke in Sam's face. 'Tell me. Did you see the white tiles? The Fisher King's magic treasures?'

Pierce had asked her not to tell Anna his address, he didn't instruct her to keep quiet about the tiles. And, anyway, she wanted to crack Anna's code; she was certain their movements and locations contained a hidden history of which she was part, yet she still couldn't decipher their meaning.

'I did find one of the white ones, in fact.'

'In his house?'

'No. On a grave. Betty Corrigall.'

'Betty Corrigall?'

'She was a young woman who committed suicide in the eighteenth century. She got pregnant out of wedlock and the father ran away to sea. She's buried on a hill above the sea between two parishes. Unconsecrated ground.'

Anna drew on the roach, tipped her head back. Was that a smile at the edge of her mouth or was it just the way she was puffing the smoke?

'Wedlock.' She couldn't have been smiling, because there was definite anger in her voice. 'That just about sums it up, doesn't it, the institution of marriage. Wed bloody lock. A prison.'

'Sure.' Sam agreed. 'The grave is very touching, though. Somebody from the island put a headstone there in 1976.'

Anna blew more smoke. 'So you found one of Pierce's white tiles on this grave?'

'Yes. I stopped off to pay my respects and spotted the tile lying in the bottom of a jam jar.'

'Are you sure it was one of the tiles from Blackstone?'

'Yes.'

She could have pulled it out from her pocket and shown her, but she sensed if she handed the tile back to Anna, she would never find out what it meant. Anna hadn't asked for it anyway. She was kicking the ground, stirring the saturated leaves.

'Fuck him. Fuck, fuck, fuck him.'

Sam had seen Anna upset before, but not agitated like this. She didn't know whether to try to soothe her or let her rant. Perhaps she was upset because Pierce hadn't cared for the tile she had given him, relinquished it, left it on a stranger's grave.

'This isn't going to work,' Anna said.

'What?'

'Me seeing Pierce again.'

'Why not?'

'I've got my own life and he's got his. We've gone our different ways. I'm not sure I want to explain myself to him, suffer his disapproval for the choices I've made.'

'I'm sure he won't disapprove of anything you've done.'

'Really? You think he'll be proud of my acting, the political protests? My girlfriends?'

She examined the dead, mushy leaves carpeting the ground.

'I don't think he'll mind that you're gay.'

'What do you know?'

'I...'

'Did you tell him?'

'About you and Becky? No, of course not.'

'He hasn't been in touch for thirteen bloody years and now, just as I feel like I'm getting my shit together, he's in the mix again. I'm not sure I want to know. Fuck it.'

'He'll be really disappointed if you don't get in touch.'

'Tough.' She jabbed the glowing end of the spliff at Sam. 'What about you? Has he done some kind of a deal with you?

Is he twisting your arm in some way, to make you play the go-between?'

Anna was difficult to deceive. She gave it a go. 'No. I just think you should try and make amends with your dad while you can. You don't know how much longer he'll be around.'

'The dead dad card.'

'It's a good reason. If your dad suddenly died and you hadn't seen him, you'd feel terrible.'

'He's not going to die suddenly.'

'My dad did.'

Anna stared at her. 'Well, maybe that was because he was stupid.'

'Stupid?'

'Yeah, stupid. Fools rush in...'

She'd heard Anna use that phrase about Jim before. 'What are you saying?'

Anna mashed the spliff on the ground. 'I've had enough of hanging out here. I'm going home.'

She turned and strode away.

'Wait a minute, Anna.'

'No. I'll call you if I want to talk to you again. Don't call me.'

'Anna...'

'Bye.'

There was nothing she could do. She watched Anna disappear, then returned down the hill to the station, rain hitting harder now, passing cars spraying dirty gutter water, brake lights, traffic lights, street lights, blurring and refracting in the damp night air. Her mind on Anna. It wasn't the first time they had argued and Anna had disappeared. She was replaying the summer of '76 in their relationship; she'd thought she could change the ending second time around, but now it seemed she was wrong. She couldn't.

CHAPTER 18

London, September 1976

SAM HAD BEEN back at school for nearly three weeks and still she hadn't been able to get hold of Anna. She was fed up with everything. School. Friends. Family. Nothing was any fun. The last weekend in September and she thought she'd give the number Valerie had left them another try. It rang and rang and rang. Where was she? Somebody picked up. Anna. Cool and dismissive. Yeah, they'd been there all along. Maybe they had all been out. Shopping or something. Sam tried not to reveal how pleased she was to hear Anna's voice. They arranged to meet in Crystal Palace Park – the mid-point on their bus routes. By the dinosaurs. She'd got it all worked out. She had the envelope from Lewisham in the back pocket of her cords. She and Anna were blood sisters, they shared their secrets. They were in an exclusive club of two: the daughters of spies. And she had some very important intelligence to hand over. She'd decided she would tell Anna all about her dangerous escapade in Lewisham with the shouting Czech men, give Anna the envelope and say she *thought* Pierce was living on Hoy. *Thought*, she had concluded, meant she wasn't actually breaking her promise to Jim; she wasn't telling Anna she *knew* where Pierce was staying, she was just saying what she *thought*. And she might have *thought* that Pierce was in Hoy even if she hadn't been there with Jim and heard him shouting through the window. She'd pick her moment, though; she didn't want to waste her precious nuggets of information.

Anna was sitting on the brontosaurus. She slipped off the strange Victorian beast when she saw Sam approaching, cart-wheeled across the brown grass, hugged Sam, said how much she had missed her. Sam was overwhelmed.

'How was Orkney?' Anna demanded. 'Did you do anything interesting?'

Sam stroked the flank of the dinosaur; what was it made of? Clay? Wood?

'It was OK. It's better in July. More puffins. What have you been doing?'

'I've been bored. I don't have anyone to hang out with. I hope we don't stay in that house much longer.'

'Do you think you'll move back to your old house eventually?'

'No. Mum says we can't go back.'

Her eyes were teary. Sam searched for a way of distracting her.

'There's an old underground station buried below Crystal Palace Park.'

'Is there?'

'Yes. They built it during the Second World War, but there was a crash, a train ran into the platform and everybody was killed, and they couldn't get the bodies out. So they buried the train and the station, filled in the tunnel. It's still down there.'

'Is that a true story?'

'Helen said you can hear voices underground, people in the train screaming. She's been here at night and she saw a ghost; a girl. A teenager. She was wandering around crying. That's what Helen said anyway.'

'I've got a good story too.'

'Have you?'

'Yes.'

'Tell me then.'

Anna's eyes glinted. 'It's about Jim.'

'Jim?' She wasn't expecting that. 'What do you know about Jim?'

'My mum told me something.'

'What did she tell you?'

'I promised not to say anything. It's a secret.'

'Tell me.' Sam was furious; the conversation had taken a wrong turn, flipped around. Anna had somehow managed to get an advantage over Sam as she always did, made her feel stupid. Inferior.

'I can't tell you.'

'It's about my dad. You have to tell me.' She wondered whether Anna had guessed she knew something about Pierce and was trying to worm it out of her.

'Fools rush in, that's what my mum said about Jim.'

'What does that mean? Fools rush in?'

Anna pouted. 'Don't shout at me like that.'

She hadn't shouted. But she was furious. If Anna wasn't going to tell her what she knew about Jim, she certainly wasn't going to tell her about Pierce.

'I'm going to buy an ice cream.'

'I don't want one.'

'I wasn't offering you one.'

'I'm not coming with you.'

'Good.'

'See you around then.'

'No,' Anna said. 'Don't call me again. You're not my friend.'

Anna stormed off, up the hill.

'Anna, come back.'

She didn't turn around. Sam started to cry. She didn't want to argue with Anna. She wanted a friend.

'Anna, wait.'

Anna shouted, 'Leave me alone, you bloody traitor.'

She tramped back to the bus stop, a burning feeling in her chest.

Sam had waited for a couple of days after the argument in Crystal Palace Park before she phoned. She was desperate to talk to Anna now, no longer cared about any promises of secrecy she'd made to Jim. She would give Anna the envelope, tell her what she had discovered in Hoy and she hoped, in return, Anna would tell her the story she had heard from Valerie about Jim. *Fools rush in.* Although, she still wasn't certain whether the secret really existed or was just something Anna had concocted to annoy her; tit for tat. Bait. Anna was good at baiting Sam. She didn't care. She dialled the number. Valerie's friend answered and Sam asked if she could speak to Anna. Valerie and Anna had moved on to a new address, the nameless woman on the other end said warily. She was sorry she couldn't help but she had no idea where they had gone.

'Oh.' Sam was desperate to prolong the conversation. 'If you see her, could you tell her that Jim managed to deliver the white tiles, please?'

'White tiles?'

'The Fisher King's treasures.'

'Of course. I see. The Fisher King's treasures.' She said it in the patronizing voice of an adult who has just twigged that the child they are talking to is playing imaginary games and has decided they'll join in with the fun. 'I'll tell her that.'

She put the receiver down. She wanted to cry. She was regretting leaving the red tile at the Raven's Nest in Hoy now; perhaps if she'd kept hold of it she wouldn't have lost Anna. At least she still had the photo.

CHAPTER 19

London, October 1989

SAM WAS FIDDLING with the icy white tile she'd found on Betty Corrigall's grave when the phone rang. She grabbed the receiver.

'Hello.'

'Sam, it's Tom.' He sounded excited. 'Have you been away again?'

What was he after?

'I've had my head down.' Vague answer.

'Can we meet?'

He was after more information, more leads. She could keep her distance, but that wouldn't stop him if he was on to a story. She knew what he was like; better to humour him, keep him on her side, and anyway, she wanted to know if he'd discovered anything about Reznik.

'Sure. Where and when?'

'This evening.' He was keen. 'The usual place.'

'Where's the usual place?'

'You know.' God, he was being cryptic, behaving like a spy.

'You mean the place where we met last time?'

'Yep. Eight?'

'Great. See you there.'

She replaced the receiver. She peeked out the front window. A woman in trackies and headphones was leaning against a lamp post at the end of the road, pulling her foot up and backwards, as if she had cramp. She had seen her before, jogging along the embankment. Yuppies, Harry had said. MI5 was employing loads of yuppies, getting rid of all the saddo cops with their paunches and belief that the most critical intelligence work took place down the pub. The woman fitted the bill: young, female and fit. She drew the curtains, veiled the last dregs of daylight.

She left an hour early because she didn't want to take the direct route. Six thirty and already the light had faded from grey to the phosphorescent dusk of south London. She headed east to the Oval; dirty water in the potholes and paving stone cracks, drains clogged with polystyrene burger boxes and Tennent's cans. Not much traffic; everybody staying at home to watch TV. She checked over her shoulder, spotted a humungous figure in a black windcheater and jeans lumbering some distance behind. Heading to the pub, perhaps. She reached the Oval, jumped on the first double-decker heading the wrong way, sat on the sideways bench by the back platform. The bus was accelerating when the man in the windcheater rounded the corner, sprinted, grabbed the pole, yanked himself aboard; lighter on his feet than his waddle down the road had suggested. He made his way to a seat behind her. She caught him watching her in the window reflection, small eyes and fat cheeks. The bus pulled into a stop, a woman with a toddler got on, sat next to her. The conductor pinged the bell. She leaped to her feet, jumped from the back of the bus, danced across the road, dodging a black taxi and a cyclist and sprinted the short stretch to the bus stop on the other side, grabbed the pole of the bus pulling away, ran up the stairs and sat at the front. The bus stuttered along Kennington Road, past the Mecca Bingo Hall. She laughed at herself, her madness and overreactions and paranoia. She wiped her nose on her sleeve. Actually, she was crying.

Tom was the only person sitting outside the National Film Theatre café; everybody else had the sense to go inside because it was cold and damp. He was wearing a dark overcoat over a suit. The lights of the embankment were shining on his scalp, revealing the thinning hair around his forehead. She panicked momentarily, wanted to run; she didn't want to be with this ageing version of the teenager she had first known when they were young and idealistic and believed they could change the world if they joined arms and shouted loudly enough. Ban the bomb. And now the Cold War and the years of mutually assured destruction were coming to an end, and the free world was triumphing, except it didn't feel much like a victory. More like succumbing, to what she wasn't sure. The bloody suits perhaps. He smiled as she approached, but it was a polite smile which made her wonder whether their relationship had finally tipped over the line of friendship into something else – contact. Informer. Any affection that might have existed leeched away leaving only an addiction she couldn't quite give up: the need to talk about her secret history to somebody who would listen. Somebody who was happy to prod around in the shadowy past of her father. It wasn't healthy. He didn't care. He was only interested in himself, his story, his career.

'Let's walk along the river,' he suggested.

She heard a laugh, swivelled. A couple swayed past, his arm wrapped around her waist, her face nuzzling his neck, dragon's breath in the nippy air.

'God, you're jumpy. You're not as fearless as you were when you were a teenager.'

It irritated her that he was doing mental comparisons to her younger self, even if she had been doing the same to him.

'Is anybody as fearless as they were when they were a teenager?'

'Well, I suppose you've got an excuse, what with your dad and all.'

Blimey, Tom showing signs of empathy. What was that all about? She might as well milk it anyway.

'I suppose his death has made me more cautious. I didn't take death seriously until Jim copped it. He was always announcing he was about to die and we just laughed it off, assumed he was being maudlin.'

'He told you he was about to die?'

'Yes. Regularly. All through my childhood. Oh, hang on, though… was it all through my childhood?'

'And it didn't bother you?'

'Like I said, we didn't take it seriously. None of us did. We joked about it; Jim and his pronouncements of doom. A coping mechanism, I suppose.'

'But why did he say he was about to die?'

'Maybe he thought he was. And eventually he was right. Of course. But then again, eventually he would have been.'

They strolled upstream. She'd forgotten how tall Tom was: six foot at least. She had to crane her neck to look at his face, which was annoying. He tapped a fag out of a soft-top packet of Kent, offered her one.

'No thanks. You know I don't smoke fags.'

'Thought I'd offer. Do you still smoke as much dope as you used to?'

'I never smoked that much.'

'You did.'

'OK, maybe I did, but I don't smoke as much as I used to. So what anyway?'

He didn't answer. She wasn't sure why she was going at him;

perhaps she was trying to push him away because she knew it was stupid being here in the first place. He lit his fag with a Bic, held it between his thumb and finger, sucked, like an old man in a boozer. The Fleet Street veneer of hard living, tough choices, been there, seen that, don't believe a word of it. And yet all they did was sit at a bloody typewriter and tap, tap, tap. It wasn't exactly life-threatening work. The only reason hacks got such a good press was because they were the ones who were doing the fucking write-ups. She was being unfair.

'What did you call me up about then?'

'Arms dealers. Spooks.'

A black cab zooming across Westminster Bridge clipped the gutter, sprayed black water. He'd been following up on the story she'd given him about the Czech. Reznik the Butcher. She had given him the lead after all. Why did she do this? Why did she leak information to Tom of all people? Because she knew he'd be good at following the trail. Tom the gutter crawler, the gongfermor, as Jim would have said. Perhaps she had been hoping he would prove her wrong, show her friendship meant more to him than her information, that he simply wanted to see her. At least she now knew the game she was playing, couldn't kid herself he was after anything other than a story. Somewhere deep inside she discerned the spark of disappointment, rejection. She smothered it. She had to deal with the reality; they were in a mutually exploitative relationship.

'So. Karina Hersche,' Tom said.

They had reached her home stretch, the embankment path between Westminster and Vauxhall. The Houses of Parliament on the north bank and behind them a wall separating the path from St Thomas' Hospital.

'What about her?'

She headed for a bench, parked herself on the wet slats between the Victorian wrought-iron swan heads that served as arm rests. He sat down beside her.

'OK then. Tell me what you found out.'

'It's an interesting story.'

'Oh god.'

'Although, I'm not sure it's going anywhere. It's all old stuff. No juice. I need some more details. Other sources.'

Which was why he had phoned her.

'Don't tell me you found Karina at the address in Lewisham?'

'Not quite. She'd moved. But only once. It wasn't too difficult to trace her.'

'Where does she live now then?'

He lit another fag, dragged. 'I can't reveal her address.'

'Oh come on, Tom.'

'Confidentiality. A basic rule of journalism. Protect your source. It would be unethical to tell you.'

'Since when were you so big on ethics?'

He ignored her question.

'I have to say, though, the place she's moved to is pretty cool.'

'Oh?'

'Not your usual bricks and mortar.'

Cool. Not bricks and mortar. What did that mean? She lived in an igloo? A tent? He sucked hard on his fag, avoided eye contact. A starling sidled along the embankment wall, probed the cracked concrete with its yellow bill, jabbed at some unseen insect, realized Sam was watching and fluttered away across the river. Water. Perhaps Karina lived on the Thames.

'Was she scared when you contacted her?'

'Surprised perhaps. Not scared. In fact, when I told her I was after info about a Czech ex-StB agent turned arms dealer, she seemed quite eager to talk.'

'I hope you told her you were a hack.'

'I'm not a spook. I'm not like your dad. There's no trickery involved. It's all done in good faith.'

Good faith? What did that mean? Why should anybody have faith in a hack?

'Did you tell her how you'd found her?'

'No. Like I said, I always protect my sources.'

He smiled at her expectantly, as if he was waiting for him to thank her. Well, he could get stuffed if he expected her to be grateful he hadn't given her name away.

'Although I did, er, mention your friend's name.'

'What? Which friend?' Panic. She couldn't remember whose name she had given him. Pierce? Harry?

'Anna.'

'Anna?' Of course, she'd let Anna's name slip, didn't think it mattered; she couldn't have been on her guard.

'Yes, Anna. I had to tell her something. I had to gain her trust.'

'I thought you said there was no trickery involved?'

'That's not trickery, it's... All I said was that I'd heard something via a friend who was a friend of a girl called Anna.'

'And did the name mean anything to her?'

'Funnily enough, it did.'

'Really? How come?'

She was perturbed.

'She said Anna was the name of the daughter of her one-time boyfriend.'

Boyfriend. She pictured the young, pretty, blonde woman Anna and she had trailed across Lewisham that sticky day in August 1976. Anna had been convinced that this woman, Karina, who had turned up at Pierce's safehouse, was one of his contacts. Not her father's bloody girlfriend. Perhaps Karina was lying to Tom, making up a story to cover her own back. Perhaps she wasn't. Pierce was a spook. And that's what spooks did after all – shagged their way to secrets.

'What did Karina say about this boyfriend of hers then?'

He stared over his shoulder in an exaggerated sweep of his head, searching for figures in the dark.

'There's nobody there. I've looked.'

'I forgot, you're an old hand at this game.'

A drift of mushy leaves from the overhanging planes had caught around the iron legs of the bench; she spread the mulch around with her foot.

'She said he was an arms dealer called Henry Davenport.'

Jesus. Henry Davenport. Tom had unearthed the cover name Pierce was using in '76.

'I assume Davenport isn't his real name,' Tom said. 'The father of your friend Anna. The guy who was involved in the Intelligence sting.'

She nudged one of the plane's fallen fruit, spiky like an underwater mine, rolled it under the sole of her monkey boot.

'How did Karina know about Anna?'

'Davenport told her he was divorced, but he had a daughter called Anna who he saw occasionally, but not as much as he would like.'

Bloody spies. They wove their legends from truths and half-truths and, it turned out, their daughters' names.

'She said she'd seen a photo of her in his house, a really pretty girl.'

The photo; it had to be the one she found in the envelope along with the chequebook.

'She even thought she'd seen her once in the street after he'd disappeared in '76 – Anna and a friend.'

Sam flushed; so much for their surveillance skills.

'She hasn't seen him since. She said he had to go into hiding because the Czech arms dealer was after him. She said Davenport's life was in danger, he mentioned something about torture, apparently.'

She twitched. *Fucking tortured.* Change the subject.

'So what's Karina's story?'

'She was born in Prague in 1957.'

'Fifty-seven?'

'Yep.'

'That means she was nineteen...'

She had realized Karina was young when she saw her in '76, but she hadn't guessed she was only nineteen. Still a teenager. The revelation gave her an uneasy feeling. Best not to dwell on the details.

Tom nodded. 'Her father had some bureaucratic job with the StB, working for Omnipol, back office support for arms sales, something like that.'

Like Reznik, she noted.

'Then in 1970 he was sent to be a functionary in the Czech Embassy in London.'

'Was he still working for the spooks?'

'Possibly. Karina wasn't sure. Or she didn't want to say. Either way, her mother had an affair with some English diplomat she met at one of these vol-au-vent parties embassies always seem to have, and in the space of two years she managed to ditch her first husband, shack up with this other bloke, marry him and finesse the paperwork so that Karina and she could become British citizens. But they kept in contact with all these Czech émigrés and, although she tried to avoid them, she also moved in the same circles as some dodgier characters her birth father knew. Which was how she ended up at a party held by this Czech man called Pavel, who she was told was an arms dealer.'

'Pavel?'

'Yeah. She said he had a fearsome reputation and she guessed that wasn't his real name.'

'It isn't. His real name is Reznik. Which is Czech for butcher.'

'Oh great. You didn't tell me that earlier.'

'I forgot.' She didn't want to bring Harry into the conversation.

'I asked her whether this Pavel could have been an ex-StB agent. She said it was possible because almost any Czech arms dealer would have links with Omnipol and would almost certainly have been working with the StB. But she didn't know for sure.'

'Well, it sounds like a bit of a dead-end story to me.'

She said it with some relief.

'That wasn't the interesting part.'

'Oh?'

'The interesting part was Davenport.'

'What about him?'

'Karina met him at the same party. Pavel's party.' He took a drag, squeezing the filter again in that same old geezer way which was starting to annoy her. He stuck his hand in his overcoat pocket, pulled out an envelope, removed a photo. 'She gave me this.' A snap of two people smiling at a restaurant with a bottle of bubbly in an ice bucket in the foreground, chandelier overhead. 'It was taken in Paris in 1975.'

She gawped, the faces as she remembered them from her snatched glimpses in the summer of '76: Karina and Pierce.

'You have met him then?'

She stalled, working out how much to give away. 'Yes, I saw him once very briefly at our house. When he dropped Anna off.'

Sam kicked the spiky ball of the plane fruit, sent it flying into the embankment wall.

'Davenport was Karina's boyfriend,' Tom said. 'Lover, as she put it.'

Lover. She had a fleeting image of the pretty blonde girl, sad and desperate, hanging around outside Pierce's deserted house in Lewisham.

'The photo was taken in Paris. He was always whisking her off on glamorous holidays, apparently. She said he was the first and greatest love of her life.'

Sam placed her face in her hands, elbows on knees, stared at the muddy puddle beneath her feet. Spies had a knack of making themselves the love of the lives of the women they were using. She didn't want to think about it, didn't want to know.

'According to Karina, Davenport was an ex-big game hunter from Zimbabwe.'

'A what?'

'A big game hunter. He told her he organized tours for rich tourists so they could shoot wild animals. You know, lions, tigers.'

'There aren't any tigers in Zimbabwe.'

'I know. I was just...' Tom waved the photo. 'Anyway, Davenport told her he'd given up the game hunting because there wasn't enough money in it, and had become an arms dealer. A legitimate arms dealer – rifles to hunters, that kind of thing. But he had contacts in the illegal arms dealing trade – I get the impression there's no real dividing line between the two – which was why he was hanging around at Pavel's party.'

The puddle rippled; concentric circles spreading. Raining again. She'd sent Tom on the trail of Reznik, but he'd ended up finding out more about Pierce.

'Do you think that's why he targeted Karina for a relationship? Because she was Czech, a known name in the crowd, a useful addition to his cover?'

'Quite likely. Well, she said he sometimes asked her to translate Czech documents for him, but she is very attractive so maybe Davenport just liked demonstrating his pulling power. Obviously, that's not the way she saw it. She reckoned they had this amazing relationship and they were going to get married and walk off into the sunset together.'

'Did you tell Karina anything about Davenport?'

'Of course I didn't tell her anything about Davenport. I don't know anything apart from the vague hints you've given me. As I said, she already knew he had a daughter called Anna because he told her himself. What is Davenport's real name anyway?'

So that was what he was after – a name. Well, he could fuck off; he wasn't going to get it from her. 'I don't remember the details.'

He flicked his fag butt; it sizzled as it hit the ground.

'Anyway, whatever Karina believed about her relationship with Davenport, or whatever his name is, they didn't run off into the sunset together. One day in '76 he disappeared without warning. And shortly after that, she was visited by these two Czech guys who wanted to find out what she knew about him.'

'Oh my god. Did they hurt her?'

He lit another fag, dragged and coughed. 'They roughed her up. Threatened her with rape.'

'Shit.'

'She kept her cool. She was well enough connected in the Czech community to drop a few names that put the wind up them and obviously made them think twice about pushing it too far.'

'Sounds like they did push it too far to me.'

'She's smart, knows how to deal with this sort of stuff.'

Tom fancied Karina, she reckoned; attractive older woman, good backstory.

'And anyway, she didn't have anything to tell them – she didn't know where he had gone. She didn't have any information so she didn't have to pretend. She seems to have got more information out of it than they did. These heavies told her Pavel was looking for him because he was involved with this arms deal with the Red Army Faction which turned out to be a trap.'

'She had no idea Davenport was an agent?'

'No.' He jabbed his fag in the air. 'In fact she was convinced it was a total mistake. She said Davenport would never knowingly have anything to do with stupid terrorists, he was far too ethical for that. She said all his clients were legit. She's not naïve but she seems to have been completely conned by him. I think somehow coming from the Eastern Bloc made her suspicious of anybody from behind the Iron Curtain, and wide-eyed about the freedoms of the West. She was desperate when he disappeared, totally out of her mind with worry. That was why she kept going back to the place where she reckoned she spotted Anna – his house in Lewisham. She wanted to warn him he was in trouble. She wondered whether she should go to the police, but she didn't in the end, because she didn't trust them. And then one day about a month after he had vanished, she got a letter from him. Posted from Harare.'

'Zimbabwe?'

'Maybe he really did have connections in Zimbabwe and retreated there.'

Or persuaded somebody to post the letter for him from Harare so it had a Zimbabwean postmark.

'What did the letter say?'

He stroked his chin; he hadn't shaved. Men often let their chins bristle, she had noticed, when their hair started receding.

'The letter said that he'd had to leave the country because he believed his life might be in danger. He said he was incredibly sorry to leave her like this, he would come back when he thought it was safe, but he had been badly scared.'

Tradecraft. The letter didn't give anything away, but at least part of it was true, she reckoned; Reznik's men were after him. The only false details were his name and his hideaway. He had ended up in Rackwick Bay. Not Harare. She wasn't going to tell Tom that. She picked at her thumbnail with her teeth. He wasn't telling her everything he knew either. What details was he hiding? Karina's address and what else? He was on guard, as much as she was. Big Ben's chimes startled her. Ten thirty. Too late for more talking now.

'I'd better get moving,' she said.

'Do you want me to walk back with you?'

He was staring at the river, arms folded. Was that a straight-forward offer, or was he asking her if she wanted to sleep with him? Which she didn't, and never had done. Not much anyway. They were just friends, of sorts. She fretted the back of her front teeth with the tip of her tongue. She didn't fancy him, but on the other hand she did want more information: the details about Karina he was holding back. She glanced sideways at Tom again, let her eyes linger on his face. She couldn't believe she was doing this.

'Yeah. It would be nice if you could walk me home.'

She said it in a kittenish voice that she didn't even realize she possessed. It produced an easy smile from Tom. Not his cynical, sly journalist smile. Men were so predictable, so easily led.

Thankfully Becky was out for the night. The house was silent, except for his breathing next to her. Duvet on the floor. She leaned down, grabbed it, yanked it over their bodies. Lay there, feeling pleased with herself. Interestingly, her ulterior motive had added a frisson that wouldn't have existed otherwise. Her determination to sleep with him because she wanted to get to the pillow talk had made what would have been a mediocre shag into something more exciting. She was in control, and it gave her a shiver of satisfaction. What's more, it was making the post-fuck chat less excruciating. They both knew this was going nowhere. She didn't have to test his reactions and intentions. She didn't care. What she did care about was how much information she could extract from him now he had let his guard down and they were lying there together in her bed. She didn't want to push it – he might begin to suspect. She stared into the amber darkness. A greenish light glowed in the corner of the room.

'I forgot to switch my computer off.'

'Amstrad?'

'Sounds like a jumbo jet warming up when I switch it on.'

'I've got one too.'

'Do you do everything on your computer now, or do you still use a typewriter?'

'I have a notebook and pen.' He'd always carried those. 'And I write my notes up every evening on the computer.'

'Disciplined.'

He put his arm around her; he smelled of sweat. Sticky. She almost pulled away, but caught herself in time, rolled into him.

'You've not been to my new place, have you?'

'No. Where is it?'

'The Barrier Block.'

She spluttered. 'The Barrier Block? In Brixton?'

'Yep.'

'Why did you move there?'

'It was cheap.'

'How much?'

'Thirty quid a week.'

'That's probably thirty quid more than anybody else pays – I thought most of the flats were squatted.'

'I'm subletting from a council tenant.'

'Well, they saw you coming.'

'The flat's quite nice. The view's not bad. There's a courtyard out the back with some trees in it.'

'Isn't that where all the junkies shoot up?'

'I don't know. I don't really care.'

He lit a fag.

'I hope you've got a good deadlock on your door.'

'Actually I haven't. The bloke I rented it off said somebody kicked the door in and smashed the frame. He'd replaced the Yale, but he hadn't managed to refit the mortice. I suppose I should do it. But I haven't had any trouble.'

'Lucky. What's the number of your flat anyway?'

'Fifty-eight. Second floor. Look, I'd better try and get some kip. I've got to work in the morning.'

She'd riled him with her onslaught on his new home, his lack of south London nous.

'It's Saturday tomorrow.'

'I work for the *Sunday Correspondent*, remember?'

He touched her arm. She rolled away. She couldn't sleep with him so close. Was there a polite way of telling somebody you didn't want them in your bed? No. She would feel mean making him walk home in the middle of the night. She lay there, listening to his breath. Slower. Slower. He twisted around.

'There was one more thing Karina said, by the way.'

'Oh?'

'I asked her whether she had any ideas about what made this Czech arms dealer think Davenport had set him up.'

Tension cranking; he was about to drop something heavy

on her, she just knew. She was ready for it, features set in impassive mode.

'What did she say?'

'There wasn't anything definite, but Davenport mentioned this name a couple of times that she could tell made him edgy.'

'Right.'

She didn't want to ask. He was going to tell her anyway. He put his hand on her shoulder.

'Jim,' he said.

She didn't move. Sweat running down her chest, between her legs.

'That's a pretty common name.' Her voice was calm. That was why he wanted to sleep with her, he just wanted to catch her in an unguarded moment, drop Jim's name and test her reactions. See if she burst into tears and blabbed. Well, she was one step ahead.

'You don't think it was your dad? Involved in some way when he was working undercover?'

'No.' She had spoken too emphatically; she should have left room for doubt to show she wasn't bothered by the possibility. 'Apart from anything else, he wouldn't have used his first name as a cover.'

'Wouldn't he?'

'Nope.' Was it obvious she was lying through her teeth?

'As you say, it's a common name. Jim.'

He caressed her neck. She tried not to flinch.

'The reason Karina wanted to talk to me was because she thought I might be able to help her find out what happened to Davenport.'

'Well, that's too bad. Because you can't.'

She rolled over, turned her back on him.

'Sam, she still worries about him.'

As if he really cared about Karina's feelings and wasn't trying to nail his story.

'Tough.'

'You don't think there's any way of finding out where he is or whether he's safe?'

'No.'

'God, you've got a really hard streak.'

That was why she was still alive. She said nothing.

CHAPTER 20

London, October 1989

WIND SHOOK THE sash windows. She was awake already, but the rattling woke Tom.

'What's that noise?'

'Winter approaching.'

'What's the time?'

'About five.'

She had felt confident about asking him home the previous night, revelling in her emotional detachment, but in the coldness of the morning she felt awkward.

'I have to go to the office. I know the security guard. He'll let me in.'

'Why do you have to go to work so early?'

'I want to follow up on something.'

She clenched her fist, dug her nails in her palm.

'Karina?'

'Yeah. I just want to see if she'll talk to me again, see whether the story has legs or not.' He placed one hand behind his head, scratched his armpit.

'I'm not going to mention Jim.'

As if she would take his word on that. 'Are you going straight to the office?'

'Yes. But look, we should talk.'

'Sure.' She had done enough talking with Tom.

defensive arrow slits but were actually designed to protect the inhabitants from the noise of a proposed bypass. The bypass never materialized. The forbidding estate remained, squatted by dealers and psychos drawn to its dystopian atmosphere. Tom was mad not to have made more effort to secure his front door. And even madder to have revealed his lack of locks to her.

A concrete tower marked the nearest entrance. Second floor, he had said. She wouldn't have taken the lift even if it had been working. Legend had it that somebody had been trapped inside for three days because the fire brigade refused to enter the building. She climbed the steps, peered through the cracks at a leafless sapling below; a crow loitered on the top branches, cawed its welcome to the day. First floor, second floor. A graffiti sprayed sign – *Class War, all pigs are bastards* – pointed to the flats. Through the first fire door, the second, third, fourth, strip-lights flickering, the thud, thud, thud of somebody's bass vibrating through the walls. She looked over her shoulder. The exterior door had closed, cutting any natural light. She had better do this quickly because she was starting to feel claustrophobic. She reached number 58, knocked on the door. No answer. The letterbox was higher than she had expected; she had to stand on tip-toes to push her hand through. Good thing, she thought as she wriggled her arm around on the inside searching for the latch, that Tom didn't have a dog. She stretched, strained, found the latch, twisted and entered.

Tom's flat was actually a maisonette. Beyond the darkened entrance the front room was spacious and light with vast sliding glass doors to a balcony and beyond a clump of naked silver birches shivering in the breeze. The flat would have been fine if Tom had bothered to do anything with it, but he hadn't. The room was a mess: scattered paperbacks, crumpled clothes, piles of dirty crockery, a slice of half-eaten toast and a trail of squashed baked beans leading to the kitchen. He might have donned a suit but he hadn't dropped his teenage habits. She wasn't sure whether that was reassuring or not, finding the last remains of her old mate Tom scattered across a carpet in a south London no-go estate. The room whiffed of Tom's sweat, which Sam found distracting. She didn't want to be reminded right now that she had slept with him.

The Amstrad was on a desk in the corner, the only ordered part of the room. She switched it on, stared at the humming machine willing it to hurry. She didn't like being here, a trespasser. She felt sneaky, spying on her mates again. Even though he had asked for it. A grey light appeared, flickered, broadened. The cursor flashed. She typed and scrolled, scanned the list of files, picked two that looked promising: *Karina*; *Spies and stuff*. He really should be more security conscious, she thought as she saved the files to her floppy disk. She switched the computer off, checked she had left everything as she had found it and made sure his front door was firmly closed behind her as she left.

She skipped home. The tramp had already relocated to his daytime residence by the derelict employment office. She waved, ran on, reached the square – no joggers lurking – shoved the front door, straight to her bedroom, fired up her computer and jammed the disk in the slot. *Karina*. A transcript of the conversation Tom had relayed: Prague, London, Paris, how much she had loved Davenport. Sam cringed. She didn't want to read it all again right now. The detail she needed was at the top: an address. *Greenwitch*. And then Downings – she knew it; water. Downings was the name of a mooring on the Thames near Tower Bridge. She'd walked past it a couple of times, attracted by the collection of brightly painted barges tied to the embankment, and noticed the sign. *Greenwitch* must be the name of a houseboat. Cool place to live, Tom had said. He was easily impressed, she decided, and then she realized she was feeling jealous, but she couldn't quite identify whether it was because Karina lived in a houseboat on the Thames, or because Tom had obviously fallen for her.

She opened the second file she had copied: *Spies and stuff.* First heading – *Eastern Bloc*, and underneath brief notes on the Russian KGB and then a paragraph on its sometimes fraught relations with the satellite states and their secret services – the Czech StB and the East German Stasi. Boring background research. Her eyes drifted over the paragraphs and caught another heading – *Torture*. Her finger jammed the scroll key, panicking. Had Karina told Tom more than he was letting on? *Fucking tortured.* All he had was a few lines on interrogation techniques favoured by secret services everywhere. God, she didn't need Tom to tell her about torture methods. She knew all this stuff anyway: sleep deprivation, noise, drive the victim nuts, and when they are reduced to quivering pulp, be nice to them. Offer them their favourite drink. The old good cop, bad cop routine. And finally, water torture. Underlined. She wiped her forehead, felt a headache building. Had Karina mentioned water torture? She forced herself to look at what he'd found out about water torture. One sentence underneath the heading. *Water torture is a favoured method because its scars are as much psychological as physical.* Nothing specific then. She breathed a sigh of relief, carried on scanning.

Right at the end of the file she spotted a heading that caught her interest. *Red Army Faction.* What had he managed to dig up about them? *Ultra-left terror organization, use assassination, kidnapping and bombing to protest against what they see as the fascist foundations of West German state. Have killed thirty people including industrialists, judges, policemen and military. It is rumoured that members of the Red Army Faction have been sheltered and trained by the East German Stasi.* She read the last sentence twice, processed it. A gang of West German anti-fascist terrorists were trained by the torture-using East German secret police. The Cold War was fought with smoke and mirrors; the battle-lines never clear. Then she remembered what Pierce had said about the Red Army Faction. *I dealt with them.* She sat with her head in her hands for a moment before she switched the computer off.

CHAPTER 21

London, October 1989

SHE WAITED UNTIL the evening and decided to risk the direct route, hoping the dusk would provide her with some cover. She thought about Tom as she walked towards Vauxhall, the air bone-achingly cold. Why had she confided in him? Bitter experience had shown her it was foolhardy to believe that anybody could be trusted. And yet she had revealed details about her father's past to Tom, a bloody journo. She had given him a lead to follow. But she had wanted him to find out about Reznik. She didn't want him disinterring Jim.

She reached the Vauxhall Tavern, passed the phone box, red and comforting. The sight of it made her want to talk to Harry. She had reasons to doubt some of the things he had told her, but she needed his help to stop Tom. She checked around; nobody apart from two men lounging on the grass behind the pub, smoking, despite the brass monkey weather. She heaved the door open, entered the kiosk, stared at the hookers' cards stuck above the phone. Some things never changed. The two oldest professions in the world. Sex and spying. And both relied on public phone boxes, anonymous spaces of communication where the caller could not be identified or traced. She lifted the receiver, dialled Harry's number. The phone rang and rang. He'd probably gone for a pint. She waited for the answering machine to click, pushed the coins in the slot and listened to new boss and now here was a spook from MI5 – Harry's own organization – telling her not to trust him. She felt dizzy with uncertainty. If she couldn't trust Harry, Jim's closest mate, who could she trust? She lurched to the nearest bench, flopped down, stared at the scribbled writing again, still feeling dazed. *Don't trust Harry.* And then she felt angry. She had her own reasons for questioning Harry's opinions, but she was hardly going to trust the judgement of some jogging spook who barged her against a wall and dropped a note in her pocket. She ripped the paper, dropped the pieces in the nearest rubbish bin.

She passed her usual meeting place with Tom at the South Bank. The lights of the embankment cast her shadow against the concrete walls, creeping along behind her. She reached the once grungy Gabriel's Wharf, now inviting with its bustling cafés, and wondered whether she was overreacting to Tom. Who cared about the activities of a bunch of spies in the seventies anyway? History. Cold War all but over. Maggie's power waning. The state, secret or otherwise, hardly existed any more. It was all big business and private finance these days; buying futures, selling services, property development. Even the old meat factory, the OXO tower, looked as if it was about to have a makeover; fenced off, gaping skips waiting. She reached Rotherhithe Street, a darkened canyon between brick cliffs, iron walkways spanning the narrow gap between the wharves, newly scrubbed cobbles underfoot. A pseudo-French restaurant boasting foie gras on its menu was just stirring for its evening sittings, and next door, a shop selling parmesan in expensive lumps was shutting for the night. It made her grumpy, this fake Mediterranean of south London; made her feel like a grubby outsider in her own backyard with her pen-stained overcoat and monkey boots. Not glamorous enough. The daughter of a spy. Not even a James Bond MI6 kind of spy, but a squalid police spy with her own dodgy track record of hanging out with potheads and protestors. She felt more at home in the underbelly of London, strolling the dirty mud banks of the Thames, and no, she didn't care if the city was changing all around her – stuff the suits, the free market, the end of the Cold War – she didn't want to change her ways, she wanted to stick to the old rules. Say nothing. Tom's investigative skills had been useful, but she was right to spike his story.

The London Docklands Development Corporation, a sign announced, had constructed a bridge across the inlet at Butler's Wharf. She clanked over the steel grids. Halfway across she caught sight of the sloshing gorge below and was hit by an unexpected dizziness, vertigo, tugging her down and under the river, dirty water filling her mouth and nose. Drowning. Getagrip. Getagrip. Breathe. She lifted her eyes, fixed her gaze on the bricks of the wharf on the far side, shuffled across the bridge, leaped the last few feet and leaned, panting, against the bricks. She rested there for five minutes or so, unsure what had hit her, the trigger for the panic. *Water torture.* She shouldn't have read Tom's file. She shook her head, ducked under a stone lintel leading to an unlit narrow alley between the river's wall and a derelict warehouse. The outer rim of the redevelopment mania. She followed the alley around and reached the gated jetty, peered through the iron bars at the huddle of houseboats moored along the shore, hung with bunting and flags, shrubs and trees in tubs on their long flat decks. The mooring looked like a waterborne version of the square in which she lived with Becky – down-at-heel and alternative, not a trace of buffed stainless steel in sight. She pushed the gate. Locked. She could climb over it, she reckoned. She checked behind, searching the recesses of the alley, couldn't see anybody, and was about to grip the iron bars when she heard laughter and spotted a couple anxieties than disguise them. 'My name is Sam.' Tradecraft for beginners: use your real first name and fake the last. As Pierce had done and, she supposed, as Jim had done too. 'I wanted to talk to you about Henry Davenport.'

'Henry? Henry Davenport?' A note of alarm in her voice.

'I'm sorry, I didn't mean to startle you.'

Silence, apart from the lapping of the Thames and the squawk of a gull. And then her voice again. 'You're on your own?'

'Yes.'

She felt eyes scrutinizing her but couldn't see a face. The cabin door opened a crack.

'Come in.'

Karina was more attractive, less artificial, than Sam remembered from those brief glimpses all those years ago; blonde side-swept hair and curving cheekbones like a character from *Doctor Zhivago*. Scruffy jeans and jumper, nothing fancy. Thirty-two, if she was born in 1957, as she had told Tom. Her eyes had a hardness to them, which made Sam wonder whether she was quite what she seemed. She had a sudden doubt about Karina's story – what if Karina had lied to Tom? Perhaps she had been working with Reznik all along, and she was the one who had betrayed Pierce. Perhaps she was working for the StB or the KGB, and had passed information back across the Iron Curtain. She didn't look like a spy. Or maybe she did.

The interior of the barge was dark, lit by a hanging storm lamp, that swayed with the motion of the boat and washed a tawny pool across the wooden floor. The room was long and low, window benches along one side slung with silver mirrored cushions, and on the other, a stack of canvases against the kitchen cupboards. Karina was a painter. She gestured at the window bench. Sam made a space among the cushions and calculated the angles of her story again, wondering whether

227

she needed to adjust her lines for the possibility that Karina was a spook.

Karina had her back to a window on the far side of the barge, Tower Bridge glinting behind her head.

'What's your name?'

'Sam.'

'So you know about Davenport?' Her voice was eager.

Sam nodded. 'You called him Davenport, not Henry?'

'He didn't like Henry.'

'Oh. I see.'

'And why did you come here?'

She said, 'I know Tom, the journalist who talked to you.'

'How did you find me? How did you know my name?'

'I was the person who gave him the information about Davenport.'

'Ah.' She had figured out her identity, Sam could tell; dragged her face from the blurry memories of the summer of '76, two girls dogging her around Lewisham. Anna's sidekick.

'Tom told me he was researching a story about the fall of the Soviet regime and the fate of their spooks. We were just having a casual conversation. I'd had a bit too much to drink. And I told him about my friend Anna – Anna Davenport. She stayed with me in the summer of '76 with her...' She stumbled. What should she say about Anna's parents – their marriage? It didn't matter what she said because she was lying anyway. 'Her parents were divorced. She told me she thought her father had gone on the run because some deal with some Czech ex-secret-police arms dealer went wrong.'

She paused for breath, wondered whether this sounded too much like a prepared story, but she needn't have worried because Karina was drinking her words, fixated on her mouth. Sam fidgeted on the seat. She had to continue now anyway.

'He had a house in Lewisham.'

Karina said nothing, just watched. Sam searched for some connection.

'On a street near a restaurant my dad used to take us to when we were kids. Cominetti's I think it was called.'

Karina smiled then. 'Casa Cominetti. Yes, I know it well. Davenport used to take me there sometimes.'

'I used to love the pudding trolley. I always wanted the profiteroles.'

Karina plucked at a silver chain running across her collar bone.

'Yes, I remember the profiteroles too.'

'They seemed so sophisticated to me when I was ten, profiteroles.'

'Yes.' She laughed. 'Profiteroles. Very continental for England in the seventies.' Sam laughed with her, caught by a sudden memory of her childhood and Jim.

'So we went to look at the house one day after Davenport had disappeared, to see if we could find him there. And we saw you, followed you back to your flat. We were mucking about. The front door was open. Anna wanted to see if she could find your flat and talk to you; she guessed you must know something about her dad. She saw an envelope with the name Karina Hersche, and she thought that it might be you. I remembered the address.'

Did that sound plausible? It was more or less the truth anyway.

'How did you know Anna?'

'Her father knew my dad.' Christ, that was a slip.

'Did they work together?'

'I'm not sure. Maybe. He said he was a friend.'

'What did your father do?'

'He was a merchant seaman.' Wild invention; the type of person a Zimbabwean arms dealer might know, she reckoned.

'Is you father still alive?'

'No. He died in 1984.' She could almost understand, as she fabricated, why spies ended up mixing facts with total fictions.

'I'm sorry about your dad.'

She sounded as if she meant it. Sam fumbled for a response. 'Everybody dies eventually.' What was she doing, extracting sympathy for the death of a non-existent merchant seaman? Tying herself in knots with all these false identities. 'I wanted to apologize to you, because I was over at Tom's place last night, and he said something about running with the story. I couldn't believe it. I mean there can hardly be anything to run with anyway. I was so annoyed with him. I had no idea he would use some tiny piece of information from a casual conversation as a basis for one of his stupid bloody investigations. And then I saw a piece of paper on his desk – and it had your name and this address on it. Or, at least, it had the name of a boat and this mooring. I wanted to come and apologize, and warn you not to say anything else to him.'

Karina was fiddling with the chain around her neck. 'Is he going to publish something? He told me he wouldn't publish anything. He said he might be able to help me locate Davenport.'

'Did he?'

'Yes, he said he thought he might have a contact who knew where he was living.'

'I think he was making that up.' She said it vehemently. Bloody Tom. 'The only information he's got about Davenport came from me, I'm sure. And I have no idea where he is living now. He was baiting you.'

Karina's face dropped. 'Oh, I probably told him more than I should have done because he said he might be able to help me.'

'That's the way hacks work. They butter you up, try and make you think they are on the same side as you. But all they're after is information. It's always an exploitative relationship.'

'Oh my god, I wasn't thinking.' Her eyes were watering, losing any hardness they might have had, and Sam suddenly felt appalled; with herself, with Tom, with Pierce. All of them manipulating this woman. 'I shouldn't have told him anything. I really only did it because I was desperate to find out what had happened to Davenport. Now I'm worried that I might have endangered him.'

She wasn't bluffing. Definitely not. She was a woman who had been duped, fallen in love with a spy. Sam felt gutted; she hadn't expected this, didn't know quite how to respond, found herself looking for an explanation which could make Pierce's behaviour seem more reasonable. It was what spies did after all, betray people. For the greater good. Collective security. People sleeping soundly in their beds at night.

'Please don't worry, I'm sure you haven't done any harm at all. I doubt whether Tom has enough information to publish anything. I just wanted to warn you, in case he came back to talk to you again. If he does, tell him to shove off.'

'Yes. Of course. That's what I should do.'

She looked doubtful, vulnerable, and Sam was reminded of the young woman she and Anna had trailed in 1976: distraught, searching for her lost boyfriend.

'Here. Can I give you my address in case you want to contact me for any reason? If Tom comes back, let me know. I'll sort him out.'

She'd knee him in the bollocks if she had to, incapacitate him for a couple of weeks.

'Yes, that would be very kind. It would be great if I could have your address, it's nice for me to be in contact with somebody who knew Davenport, even if only indirectly. Perhaps one day you might bump into his daughter again; I'd like to meet her.'

Oh god, she was so stupid. She swung from cunning trickster to dope in the flit of a moth's wing; she shouldn't have offered to give Karina her address. A step too far – taken because she felt sorry for her, falling for a ghost. It didn't do to allow your emotions to enter into these kind of exchanges – she should remain more distant. She would have to lie again and give Karina a completely false address, because she couldn't reveal where she actually lived. She wasn't sure she could face lying again. She'd try diversion instead.

'That's all I wanted to do. Apologize and warn you.'

'That's very kind of you.' Karina was still fiddling with the chain, held it up, revealed a small white object that twisted and caught the light in a peculiar way. Sam leaned forward, couldn't help herself, reached across. The Fisher King's treasure, crystalline surface glittering in the lantern light.

'That's an unusual pendant.'

'The tile was a present from Davenport.'

Pierce had given the second white tile to Karina and she still wore it around her neck. Jesus. She really was smitten. First love. Or maybe it was the sudden disappearance that kept her dangling, unable to let him go.

'He posted it to me after he vanished. He went to Harare. He sent me a postcard, and then a week later, this tile in an envelope. There was a note inside that said it was an ancient magic object that would keep me safe from harm.'

He'd used the Fisher King treasure line on Karina.

'I knew a silversmith and I asked her to make it into a pendant.'

What was Pierce doing, sending Karina, his girlfriend-contact, one of the tiles that Anna had given him? Maybe it was an indication that he had genuine feelings for her, that she really meant something to him. But he had lied to her, told her he was divorced, pretended he was somebody else. Sam couldn't work it out, confused, not entirely sure with whom she felt angry and why, which side she was on. She was overwhelmed by a sudden surge of rage. A blast of wind swung the paraffin lamp, thwacked a wave against the barge, rocked it sideways, brought her attention back to Karina.

'Are you OK?'

Karina had been watching her with some concern, she realized.

'I thought you were going to faint.'

'I'm fine. Sorry. It's the motion of the boat.'

'Yes, it does roll quite a bit.' She furrowed her brow. 'Especially when the wind whips the water.'

Sam nodded at the tile dangling around Karina's neck.

'It's a lovely pendant. It does have a magical glitter.'

'I used to believe it felt colder when I was in danger – a warning – but I'm sure I just imagined it.'

'I don't know,' Sam said. 'Maybe some objects do have magical powers to protect us.'

'It felt cold when you called out just now. That's why I hesitated to answer the door.'

'Oh, I'm sorry.' She couldn't think of anything else to say, how to extricate herself from the awkward turn of the conversation.

'But obviously it was nothing. You couldn't possibly be harmful to me, a young woman like you. You have such an open face.'

Sam flushed. 'Look. I'd better leave you now. I don't want to take up any more of your evening.'

'It's fine. You were helpful. Thank you for coming.'

Karina held the cabin door open. The Chinese lantern hung motionless; the gust that had rocked the boat an aberration in the calmness of the night. 'Oh, your address, wait please.' She dug in her pocket, pulled out a receipt from Sainsbury's and a pen. 'Write it on the back of this.'

Sam's brain blanked; caught off guard, she couldn't think of an address that wouldn't look obviously false to somebody who knew London, as Karina must. She didn't want to deceive her any more than she had already. Sod it. She wrote her real address. And immediately had second thoughts. How stupid was she?

'Please do contact me if you like.' She'd really messed that up. Given away more than she had intended. 'There's one more thing…' She shouldn't be asking this, but she couldn't help it. She needed to know and she had concluded it was safer to ask out here in the open, where the noises of the river might mask their conversation, than in the confines of the cabin. 'Do you have any idea how this Czech arms dealer…'

'Pavel.'

'Pavel,' Sam repeated.

Her neck prickled, goose bumps forming on her skin; she glanced around the barge, along the river, a sudden feeling that she was being watched. But there was nothing to see apart from the lights of the traffic crossing Tower Bridge.

'Do you have any idea what made Pavel turn on Davenport?'

Karina clasped the pendant at her neck, gripped the tile in her fingers, her face drawn in pain, and Sam thought for a moment she was about to shriek at her and accuse her of being a traitor. 'I never entirely understood what happened.' She glanced around the deck. 'I grew up in that world. That's how I met Davenport; I was at a grand party at Pavel's house. Before we came to London, we lived in Prague and my father worked for Omnipol – they make guns. I always assumed he was employed by the Czech secret police.'

She frowned, peered east along the far riverbank, focused on the dark warehouses of Wapping, shook her head, turned to face Sam again.

'That trade – arms dealing – it's full of informers and spies and double dealers. I always suspected Pavel was one of these men. He was known to be, as you said, an ex-member of the StB. There was something cruel about him, sadistic.'

The Butcher; everybody was wary of Reznik, even if they didn't know his real name.

'Davenport was the only dealer I ever trusted. He didn't really want to sell guns, but he turned to it when the visitors stopped going to Zimbabwe because of the unrest there. He was brave and honest.'

Sam held her features steady, willed herself not to react in any way.

'I tried to warn him about Pavel, but he judged other people by himself. He had high moral standards, and he assumed others did too.'

High moral standards. She was standing face to face with one of the victims of Pierce's deceptions, a woman who believed he was called Davenport and had once been a big game hunter in Zimbabwe. And yet, she could understand why Karina had fallen for him. Pierce oozed old-fashioned decency and charm; he lied for a living, but when you were with him it was hard to doubt his conscience, he weighed the damage carefully against the outcomes of his actions. He suffered guilt for his deceptions.

'But there was one name he did mention a couple of times, shortly before he disappeared, and I wouldn't have remembered the name if there wasn't something odd in the way Davenport talked about him.'

'Odd?'

'As if... I don't know... he was worried about him. He told me once that the problem with Pavel was that he had too many deals going on and the more deals he was doing, the less able he was to check their backgrounds, and that made everybody vulnerable. And then he said the name of a man who unnerved him in some way. Maybe he was worried he couldn't trust him.'

She didn't know why she was pursuing this; unearthing the truth in order to rebury it. She had to be careful she wasn't digging her own grave at the same time.

'What was the name?'

'Oh, it was a passing mention. Jim.'

She was ready for it, able to brush it off lightly.

'Jim,' Sam repeated. 'That's a common name.'

'Yes, of course.'

'Well thank you for telling me all this.' Thanking Karina seemed completely inappropriate, but she couldn't think of any other way of ending the conversation and leaving quickly. 'I'd better go now.'

'It was nice meeting you. Let's stay in touch.'

Sam nodded, glanced over her shoulder as she stepped on to the walkway, waved at Karina standing against the door-frame, the warm glow of the cabin behind, and she reckoned she'd dealt with that situation quite well. She looked down. The water churned beneath her feet and a wave of terror surged through her mind.

CHAPTER 22

London, October 1989

SHE PACED THE cobbles of Rotherhithe Street, keeping close to the walls, hands in pockets to keep them warm. The conversation with Karina had put her on edge. She had trampled on Tom's investigation, but she had given away her first name and address and had come close to revealing the identity of her own father. She decided to return to Vauxhall by a different route. She cut down to grotty Tooley Street, turned left beyond London Bridge Station, clambered aboard a double-decker heading south along Borough High Street, sat and stared out the window. Two boozers taking swings at each other outside a pub. A swaggering dealer, shoulders hunched, sweatshirt hood up, heading north with his faithful Staffie trotting at his heel. The bus pulled into a stop; a briefcase clutcher in a grey suit and homburg climbed on and parked himself in front of her. She examined the back of his neck, the neat line where hair met flesh, decided he looked too much like a spy to actually be one. Although he was glancing at the window, watching her reflection in the glass. The bus reached Westminster Bridge. Nobody got on. Nobody got off. The conductor pinged the bell. Snap decision; she stood, skipped and leaped for the pavement before the double-decker had time to pick up speed. She glanced back at the departing bus and caught the man in the suit swivelling to watch her. A black Merc speeding too close to the kerb made her step back. A late-night runner paced the pavement, checked her up and down, crossed the traffic lanes, jogged north across Westminster Bridge. What was he after? She looked left and right. The streets were empty. Too empty. Perhaps she'd made the wrong call, jumping off in this no-man's land of deserted offices and shuttered greasy spoons. She decided to head down Westminster Bridge Road, and catch a bus back to Vauxhall from there.

Under the iron girders of the railway bridge, the wheels of a train grinding on the track overhead. In the corner of her eye she caught the runner who had passed her earlier on the other side of the road. Damn. She had been stupid. Too cocky in her home territory, wandering around in the middle of the night in the dark and deserted streets of south London. She quickened her pace. The jogger matched her speed. Neck and neck, heading south. She wanted to lose him. She glanced right; she was passing the gaping mouth of the old Necropolis Station, the hellish entrance to the railway line that once carried corpses to the suburbs. She could dart in there, wait for the jogger to pass. She sidestepped into the shadows of the walled yard, looked back, caught the jogger standing and gawping, felt a fleshy hand over her mouth, hardly had time to react before her right arm was grabbed and twisted painfully behind her back and she was forced forward towards a black saloon with the backseat door open, parked out of sight from the road at the rear of the yard. The Merc that had passed her five minutes earlier. Shit, she had walked into this one.

'Move.'

She tried to squirm around, resist, shout for help, but his hand was still muzzling her mouth. She bit his thumb.

'You bitch.'

He shoved her neck down, forcing her towards the rear of the car.

'Get the fuck in.'

He grabbed her legs. She kicked him. He caught her monkey boots, tipped her on to the backseat. She kicked again, caught him in the balls.

'You little fucking...'

He slammed the door. His accent wasn't English – European she guessed, but not eastern European. He lumbered into the driver's seat. The engine revved.

'Let me out.' She pulled at the handle. 'Let me out now.'

'Central locking.'

She twisted in the direction of the whiny mosquito voice. A skinny man in a badly fitting suit was hunched on the other side of the passenger seat, hair combed over, trousers shiny as if he spent too much time stroking his thighs.

'Let me out.'

He ignored her, lit a fag.

Tyres squealed as the Merc left the cover of Necropolis Station and swerved into Westminster Bridge Road. She looked back through the darkened rear window; the runner was staring at the car's number plate, scribbling on his palm. She banged on the window.

'Forget it.'

'He was following me under the bridge. He's taken your number plate.' Jesus, it came to something when she was glad that a spook was taking notes about her. 'MI5,' she added.

He scoffed, smoke puffing out his nose.

'MI5. They won't do anything. Don't kid yourself, you're not that important.'

'I have friends waiting for me at home.'

'Tell us your address and we'll give them a call, let them

know you've been held up.' He released a whinnying snigger, amused by his own humour, didn't seem to realize he had dropped the fact that he didn't know where she lived. Unless he was bluffing. She suspected he wasn't. They couldn't have been shadowing her for long, they must have spotted her entering and leaving Karina's. She had sensed she was being watched.

'Who are you?'

'The solicitor.'

He looked like he could be a solicitor, but not the kind you'd feel relieved to see if you were banged up in a police cell. A bent brief. The car was picking up speed, heading east.

'Who do you work for?'

He opened his mouth. A phone rang, green light flashing between the front seats. The solicitor, if that's what he was, leaned, retrieved the handset attached to the car with a curly wire, held it close to his face.

The electronic crackling made it difficult to decipher the words of the caller.

'Yes. Ten minutes.'

He replaced the receiver in its cradle.

'You're expected.'

'By whom?'

He tapped his ash on the car floor, stared out the window. Fuck this, fuck this. What was going on? She wanted to scream but she had to keep calm. Getagrip. She'd been in worse situations. The solicitor wasn't holding a gun to her head. There was no edge of hot menace to him, just a tepid indifference. He was somebody's fixer. A factotum. Doing his job. She had to outwit him. Them. Whoever they were. She couldn't escape from this car so she had to use her brain. Who was she dealing with? Not MI5; the lurking presence of the Merc had shocked the jogger as much as her. The Merc didn't belong to Intelligence then, or at least not the part that had been trailing her. Another part of Intelligence? MI6? The Firm wanting to find out what she had said to whom about Pierce? Perhaps Harry had passed her phone message on to somebody, let them know she'd been leaking details about their agents to the press. Jesus. She hoped not. She had doubts about Harry, but she couldn't believe he would betray her in that way. She was certain this was something to do with Pierce, but perhaps her abductors were nothing to do with the secret state. She stared at the back of the driver's head visible through the head rest; cropped mousey hair, thick neck. Silent. His hand dropped to the gear stick, gripped it, white scars slashed his knuckles. Thuggish. What kind of thug had a solicitor? Kidnapped people off the street? Her stomach lurched.

Racing through the Borough streets she had walked earlier that evening, heading across London Bridge. South of the river was home, north was uncharted territory. The dome of St Paul's flat and grey against the rusty clouds, swerving around the City's narrow streets, dark walls looming. Then east along the river again. Past the Tower of London to Docklands; streets lined with the ruins of half-demolished wharves, insides hanging out, the Merc's tyres bumping over Wapping High Street's cobbles.

'Where are we going?'

The solicitor twitched his head at a boarded warehouse, the gallows frame of a winch silhouetted against the sky.

'Execution Wharf.' He sniggered. There was an edge of nervousness to his laugh.

The Merc swerved right and she had a split-second sense they were about to ram the wall before she heard the metallic scrape of heavy doors and the car descended a ramp to an underground car park, headlights swinging around the emptiness, veering, braking, reversing into a bay.

The solicitor's voice whined. 'I wouldn't try anything funny with him.' He nodded at the driver. He turned around and stared at her – hard grey eyes, square jaw, thin cracked lips – before he lumbered out of the driver's seat and opened the passenger door. He was huge. She clambered into the cavernous darkness and her eyes fixed on his scar-slashed knuckles gripping the door handle.

'What's your problem?'

She jumped, shook her head, unable to reply; she'd pinpointed his accent. He'd said v instead of w. German. Her panicked brain went into overdrive, making dangerous connections. German. Kidnapped. Red Army Faction. Fanatics. Trigger-happy. *I've dealt with them*, Pierce had said. They had questioned him in '76, she guessed, but he had survived and thought that was the end of it. They shot a couple of people in '86, according to Harry. On the run, desperate for cash. Her mouth was dry. Was it possible they were chasing Pierce again for some reason? After the money Pierce had extracted from them in his arms dealing sting all those years ago? And she was their hostage.

'This way.'

No chance of making a dash for it with the enforcer behind her. Across the empty underground car park; damp walls, steel jacks holding the roof, water on the floor, the reek of the river in the air. Right on the shore, she reckoned, the Thames lapping at the foundations come high tide. Through a heavy door, round and up a dingy stairwell. Numbers tapped into a key pad, a click, door swinging into a narrow corridor, plastic sheeting on the floor, dangling wires from the ceiling. No source of external light, stark fluorescent strips overhead.

'What is this place?' She wanted to sound confident, but her voice wavered.

'Luxury apartments. Or at least they will be when they are finished.'

The solicitor scrabbled for something in his pocket, produced a bunch of keys, selected one, grabbed the handle of the first door on the left, pushed it, ushered her towards the pitch dark.

'I thought you said somebody wanted to speak to me.'

'You have to wait.'

The solicitor handed the keys to the driver, shuffled away.

'Hang on…' She didn't want to be left alone with him. He shoved her forward, caught her off guard with his aggression. She stumbled. The door slammed, key clicked in the lock.

She shouted through the door. 'Where's the light?'

'Shut your fucking mouth.'

She stepped away from the door. Shivering. Eyes damp. Getagrip. Assess the surroundings. She could tell from the closeness of the air and the lack of echo that she was in a tiny space. Definitely not a luxury apartment. A broom cupboard more like. Fuck. Hot tears ran down her cheek. Incarcerated in a darkened cell in the middle of a deserted wharf by a gang of desperate terrorists and nobody even knew she'd been kidnapped. Apart from a useless MI5 shadow who had done nothing to help. Serve her right for messing in things she didn't understand. She had no idea how long she would be stuck here. What if they didn't let her go? She grabbed the door handle, pushed; it didn't give. She banged.

'Let me out. Let me out now.'

No response. Waste of breath. She had to stay calm. Think. They wouldn't keep her captive here for long – what would be the point? They were trying to mess with her head. She wasn't going to let them scare her. Maybe she could reason with them. She was being dumb. They killed people. She had to escape. She stood for a moment, waiting for her eyes to adjust, and spotted a faint line of light hovering in the dark. She stumbled towards the glimmer – a few paces – ran her fingers along the source, rough and faintly warm, a plywood boarded window. No glass in the frame. She couldn't be much above ground level; they had driven down a ramp and climbed one set of stairs. The room was on the left of the corridor, which meant it must be above the street not the foreshore of the river. She pushed at one corner of the boarding. It budged. The key in the door behind her turned; she jumped away from the window.

'What's that noise?' His towering bulk filled the frame.

'I didn't hear anything.'

He stepped into the room; the door swung shut behind him.

'Don't fuck with me.'

She could smell his beery sweat. He lunged, shoved her against the wall, and for a moment she thought he was about to assault her, but he stepped away. Slammed the door. She waited to see if he would return, still slumped against the wall, hardly daring to breathe. The lock clicked. Footsteps retreated. Blood pounding in her head. She had to get out. Now. She edged back to the window, dug in her pocket and removed the penknife she always carried, opened the longest blade, slipped it down the crack between boarding and frame, levered – there was some give. She wiggled the penknife, focused on the covering of the window, willing it to move. She levered again. The board creaked. Too intent on loosening the board to listen to what was going on behind. The door burst open.

'Move away from the window.'

He strode across the room. She managed to slip the penknife up the coat sleeve of her left arm before he grabbed her by the right, yanked her to the door.

'You come with me now. You have to answer some questions. Or else...'

He pulled her into the corridor and left the sentence hanging. She could work the ending out for herself. The Red Army Faction, terrorists trained by the East German Ministry of State Security. She didn't need Tom's notes to tell her about their methods because she'd found out when she was ten.

CHAPTER 23

London, October 1976

THE SPLATTER OF rain on the windows broke the silence of the library. The long hot summer was well and truly over, but still it played on her mind. Since Anna's disappearance she had nobody to talk to, nobody who would understand her fears. In the absence of Anna, she reverted to her old routines. Trying to join in with her sisters' latest occult endeavour. Cycling up the long hill. Freewheeling back. The rain had driven her to the local library to return her overdue books. She wandered the fiction stacks, remembering the day in Hoy. Pierce shouting in his croft. *Fucking tortured.* Jim's scary behaviour. *Water. Fault.* In the end, nothing terrible had happened, and yet she felt the threat lingering, the cracks beneath her feet.

'Hello.'

She jumped, startled by the voice behind her, then smiled when she saw it was her friend Ed, stacking the shelves. Well, he wasn't exactly her friend – he was too old to be her friend, but she liked him. He was large, black and wore National Health blue plastic glasses held together with Sellotape. He worked at the library most days, but he wasn't allowed to sit at the desk and stamp the books because the other staff thought he was slow. He wasn't slow. At least not slow in the head. He was quite slow at reshelving the books, but Sam reckoned this was because he liked to align the spines. He had one of those brains that remembered things. She could ask him for books about a particular object or a place, and he could give her a list. He didn't go by content, or even meaning – just the words in the title. In some ways, he was better than the other librarians because he never tried to guide her to books he thought she should read; he told her what she wanted to know.

'Ed. You made me jump.'

He pushed his glasses up his nose. 'Are you looking for something?'

She paused. Maybe she was looking for something. She could trust Ed not to ask questions. 'Are there any books on torture in the library?'

He didn't blink. '*Torture Methods Used in the Spanish Inquisition*. Burquist and Havell. 1976. Oxford University Press. It's just come in.'

That wasn't what she wanted. 'Is that all?'

He removed his glasses, fiddled with the Sellotaped arm hinge.

'Amnesty International. *Report on Torture*. Revised Edition. 1975. It's in the reference section. It's got a red cover.'

'Thank you.'

She scuttled off to locate the document, shelved in a corner above the phone directories, took it to an empty table. She looked at the contents page. A long list of countries, including the United Kingdom. She was shocked. Did they all use torture? She flicked to the index. *Beating. Electric shock. Forced feeding. Fourth degree.* She felt odd reading these things, but she persisted and she found the word she wanted: *water. Immersion in water.* She turned to the relevant pages.

'Placing themselves on either side of me two soldiers took me by the legs and submerged me into a barrel of water which covered my head and chest up to my middle. I nearly drowned.

They questioned me again. The next day they submerged me in the barrel four or five times before they pulled me out nearly drowned.'

She read the paragraph twice. It made her queasy. Why would anybody do that kind of thing to somebody else? In the silence of the library, she could hear her heart thumping. Now she'd found what she was looking for, she wished she hadn't. *Fucking tortured. Water.* She didn't want to think about it. She shouldn't have bothered.

Ed was standing behind her.

'You found the Amnesty International report on torture?'

'Yes.'

He leaned over her shoulder, read the words aloud.

'*Submerged me into a barrel of water which covered my head and chest up to my middle.*'

'Ssh.' She looked around wildly, checking nobody could overhear them.

He pushed his glasses up his nose again. 'The *Guardian* had something on the front page about water and torture last week.'

'Did it?'

'Yes. *East German political prisoner tells of cold water torture.*'

'Cold water?'

'Yes. I'll get it for you.'

He ambled over to the newspaper stacks. She could hear the soles of his shoes slapping the lino as he returned. 'There.'

It was a short report and she scanned it quickly: East German political prisoner escapes across Berlin Wall and tells of torture at the hands of the Ministry of State Security. They tortured him while he was in prison, he said. The worst was the water torture. They pushed him into a bath of cold water, until he was ready to confess to anything. He made up some story because he thought he was going to drown. She stared at the article, words replaying in her mind. *Tortured. Water. Tortured. Water. Tortured. Water. Fault.* She was shivering, rocking on the edge of a precipice, dark water sloshing below. She needed a way out, an escape route, a place to hide. She remembered Jim's advice that day at Betty Corrigall's grave: go somewhere safe in your mind. She traced the path across the dunes, along the round boulders, over the red rocks, followed the sandy inlet to the opening in the sandstone cliff, headed to the triangle of dry sand right at the back of the cave among the skeletons of gannets and seaweed and fraying blue polypropylene rope. A safe place where the sea couldn't take her, above the high tide mark. She stayed there for a while, the sea creatures that spangled the cave walls gleaming in the last of the afternoon sunshine.

She was aware that somebody was standing behind her.

'I've found another book on torture,' Ed said.

'Thanks, Ed. I think I've read enough.'

CHAPTER 24

London, October 1989

HE CHIVVIED HER along the corridor, stark in the strip-light glare. The blade of her penknife jabbed the fleshy base of her thumb; she had to curl her fingers and grip her coat sleeve to stop it from dropping. One door stood open at the far end of the passageway. He shoved her through. She stumbled, found her footing, surveyed her surroundings. A vast double height space, broken by concrete pillars, brick walls unplastered, copper pipes exposed, red, green, black wires dangling, empty apart from two chairs and a desk with two mugs and three thermos flasks lined neatly along one side. Beyond the desk, sliding glass doors through which she could see the darkness of the river and the lights of the south side twinkling. The solicitor was hovering shiftily by the glass and next to him the back of a broad-shouldered man with thick wavy hair cut short, check shirt, faded jeans and trainers. He had his hands in his pockets and at first glance she thought he looked too casual to be dangerous, but there was something – the subservience of even the hefty enforcer perhaps – that tripped an alarm bell in her head. Her inquisitor turned around to face her. Square chin accentuated by short-cut beard and moustache, olive skin, sharp nose and steel-rimmed spectacles partially hiding his eyes. But not entirely. The rays from a bare lightbulb caught his left eyelid, peculiarly creased and red as if he suffered from eczema, its rawness drawing attention to his lack of lashes. Reznik the Butcher.

'Pleased to meet you.' Monotone voice, syllables propelled from his thin-lipped mouth like bullets. He held out his hand. She ignored it.

'I hope Wolf has behaved himself.' He gestured at his thick-necked enforcer. Wolf. 'The company he used to keep before he was employed by me wasn't known for its politeness.'

He removed his spectacles, wiped the lenses on his sleeve, replaced them.

'These are interesting times. The men who used to guard the Wall are now jumping over it themselves.'

Wolf wasn't a terrorist after all. Worse. He was a state killer. An Iron Curtain guard; a cog in the ruthless East German security machine. He must have realized which way the wind was blowing and decided to do a runner before the next regime turned on him. Palled up with Reznik. She realized her legs were shaking.

'I've tried to get him to improve his ways, take up nice hobbies. He likes to go fishing at weekends, don't you, Wolf?' The guard grunted. 'Unfortunately he tends to drop more bodies than he catches. You can't teach an old dog new tricks is the saying, I think.'

The solicitor sniggered. Fuck off, creep.

'I need the toilet,' she said. She had to find a better place to stash her penknife before it dropped on the floor.

'Of course.' He indicated a door on one side of the room. 'I bought this property quite recently. It's one of a number I have in my portfolio. It will eventually be converted into apartments. As you will have noticed, we haven't got very far with the wiring. But there's no problem with the plumbing. Plenty of water.'

He smirked, nodded his head when she jumped at the mention of *water*. She hesitated, her throat dry. Was she about to walk into a trap?

'Please. Be my guest.'

She edged across the room, conscious of three men staring as she opened the door, pushed it shut behind her. There was no key in the lock. The room was white tiled, windowless but large. Toilet in one corner, bath and sink on the far side. She sat on the toilet, peed, the splash echoing around the room, let the penknife slip out from her arm into her hand, closed the blade, and jammed it down the side of her monkey boot. It dug into the flesh of her foot, but at least it was secure and not immediately visible. She stood, hoiked her pants and trousers.

'Get a move on.' Wolf; standing right outside.

She crossed to the sink, twisted the tap and washed her hands. She glanced at the bath. Full to the brim. She shook her hands, stepped over to the bath, stuck her finger in the water. Cold. *East German political prisoner tells of cold water torture.* Her brain whirred, unable to get any traction. She had to stay calm. Getagrip. The door handle moved down. Wolf swung in, grabbed her by the arm, twisted it behind her back, thrust her over the bath.

'You know why that's there?'

She didn't reply.

'I will show you then.'

He was spitting in her ear, his other hand on the back of her head, yanking her hair, ripping the roots. She shrieked. He tightened his hold, shoved her head forward. She waited for the force of water in her nose. It didn't come. He released his grip on her hair, his hand now searching her coat pockets. Tissues, bus tickets, chucked on the floor. Thank fuck she'd hidden her penknife. He dragged her across the tiles, hurled her through the door, sent her skidding across the room. She smashed into the desk, sent a thermos flying. The Czech reached and caught the green metal tube, replaced it on the desk. She staggered to her feet, pain in her ribs, her shins, her head.

He gestured at the glass doors. 'Come.' He nudged the handle, pushed on the frame; the rank smell of the river blew in through the opening. She had no choice, and anyway, she wanted to take her bearings. In the night air, standing on a small balcony hanging over the Thames, alone with Reznik. Directly beneath, a narrow band of foreshore, glistening in the ambient light of the city. The tide had reached its high point and turned, the brown edge of the water slipping down the muddy bank. The golden crown of Tower Bridge's north turret visible above the dark line of the wharves.

'A lovely view, yes?'

'Yes.'

The buzzing of a helicopter flying low along the river interrupted the conversation. She watched it heading east – City Airport perhaps.

'You recognize this place?' He pointed at the far shore. Rotherhithe; a jigsaw of wharves and wooden steps and greening jetties, a string of fairy lights waving in the breeze, the faint red glow of the Chinese lantern. She tried not to react. She had sensed she was being watched when she was standing on the deck of Karina's barge. She was right; the balcony was diagonally opposite the Downside mooring; she had been picked up because she had been seen visiting Karina. But surely Reznik didn't abduct all her guests. What was it about Sam that had roused the Czech's suspicions? Perhaps he had clocked Tom visiting the *Greenwitch*, checked him out and discovered he was a journo, then spotted her with him. He could just be fishing – she was a young woman alone, easy to intimidate.

Or was it possible, after all, that Karina was working with the Czech and had sent him a coded message across the water as soon as she had visited? She suspected not. She had given Karina her address and her abductors didn't know it. Karina was unwitting bait.

He repeated his question. 'You know this place?'

She shrugged.

He clicked his tongue impatiently.

'Perhaps you need something to clear your head.' He gripped her arm and shoved her back into the room.

'Take a seat.'

She sat and he sat opposite. He leaned forward, elbows on the desk. Up close she could see his unyielding grey eyes through the lenses of his spectacles, his scarred, lashless eyelid intensifying the harshness of his gaze.

'You know in my country at this moment, the people are rising,' he said. 'The writers, the intelligentsia, the students. It's 1968 again, another Prague Spring. Freedom, that's what they are demanding. Freedom. Down with the men in Moscow, the KGB, the puppet rulers, the secret police. Freedom. What do you make of that?'

'As you said – interesting times.' She hadn't expected to be engaged in a debate about the crumbling Soviet Union. 'Regimes change.'

'Do you think these protestors will find the freedom they crave in the West?'

'I don't know.'

'You don't know? I think you do. I think you know that the freedom here is illusionary, that the politicians here are as likely to lie to you as over there, that the freedom to choose doesn't mean much when you can't afford to buy the goods on offer.'

He pressed his chin with his index finger.

'But you are benefiting from that freedom,' she said.

'You think so?'

'Well, you've bought all this.' She nodded at the room, the view. 'You told me you've got a whole portfolio of properties.'

'Indeed, I have. But you know, it's not so easy for me because, at the moment, I have to do everything through intermediaries. I have all sorts of middle men to help cover my tracks. And even the best of middle men don't always live up to expectations.' He laughed and nodded in the direction of the solicitor, who made a weird snuffling noise. Sam almost felt sorry for him.

'What is that saying? If you want something doing... Of course, some people, some institutions, don't care who you are, where you are coming from, so long as the cash is there. But there would be so many more possibilities, so many more opportunities if I could be sure my record was clear. All those assets the state will have to sell. Škoda. Omnipol. But for that, I need the help of a few old friends.'

Pierce, he meant of course. Was that the reason Reznik was after him? To clear his slate so he could deal more openly on the markets? Harry had warned her that now was a dangerous moment to be dealing with Eastern Bloc spooks, ex or otherwise.

'I don't see what any of that has got to do with me.'

'I think some of these old friends, maybe they work for the British secret state.'

'I don't know anything about the British secret state.'

He gave her a hammed-up quizzical stare. 'So you've never watched a James Bond film?'

She laughed. 'Yes, but those are films. They aren't... they're not true.'

'How do you know that?'

'Everybody knows that.'

'The books were written by a spy.'

'That doesn't make them factual.' She couldn't see where this argument was going.

'Secretly every British spy likes to think that he is James Bond. Don't you agree?'

'I don't know.'

'What, you don't know any British spies or you don't know what they like to think?'

His eyes locked hers, scrutinizing her reactions. He didn't know anything about her, he was testing her with his jokey conversation, trying to force a trip. She hid her thoughts somewhere inside her mind, retreated to the small triangle of dry sand at the back of the cave, kept her sight on the glittering sea creatures decorating the rocky walls. A bluebottle buzzed. He fiddled with a drawer in the desk, removed a rubber band, swirled it around his index finger, searched for the fly, took aim at the sliding doors, flicked. Direct hit. The band and fly plummeted to the floor, leaving an apricot splodge on the plate glass. He pushed himself back in his seat, locked his hands behind his head, smiled. His teeth were surprisingly jagged; they made her think of the pike she had found with Anna in the dried-up river at Blackstone.

'In my country, the children of the security services are recruited before they leave school.'

'I doubt that happens over here.'

'Oh? You know something about the way the security services treat their children here?'

She stopped. Had he caught her out, or had he given something away? Did he have any solid information about her or was he revealing his suspicions, testing them? He was watching Karina because he knew she had a connection with Pierce. He had guessed Sam had a connection too; perhaps he had discovered that Pierce had a daughter and he had put two and two together and come up with the wrong answer. He thought she was Anna. The supposition unexpectedly cheered her; the idea that anybody could think she was related to Pierce felt like a compliment. He'd mistaken her for the daughter of a proper spy, able to play the mind games, outwit her opponent.

'No, I don't know anything about the way the security services treat their children,' she said. 'Just what I've read in books and heard in the news. I don't think the secret state is quite as ruthless here as it is behind the Iron Curtain.'

'Well, it is true the British like to wring their hands after they've killed somebody.' He sounded irritated. 'But I didn't bring you here to discuss the merits of our different systems.'

'So what am I doing here?'

He ignored her question. 'Do you want a drink?' He gestured at the flasks. 'Tea, coffee, milk.'

She assessed the three thermos flasks sitting on the desk; it made her think of the three-card trick Jim had been taught by one of his mates from his days on the beat in London's East End – could she identify the one thermos that didn't contain any poison?

'None of them are drugged.' He smiled, pleased with himself for guessing her thoughts. 'Of course, I can't expect you to trust me on that. I'm happy to have whatever you have. Tea or coffee?' She hadn't had anything to drink all evening, she was thirsty. Perhaps she could risk it.

'Coffee, please.'

'You're a coffee drinker. I thought English ladies liked their tea.' He was mocking her in some way; she wasn't exactly sure how or why. 'Luckily I prefer coffee too.' He unscrewed the lid of the thermos, poured the black liquid into the two cups.

'Milk?'

'No thanks.'

'Black coffee. That is unusual. I don't know so many English black coffee drinkers.' He leered as he spoke, revealed his pike-like teeth, made her feel that he had somehow trapped her in his sharp jaw. 'I'm afraid we have no sugar.'

'I don't take sugar.'

'Good.' He lifted the cup, took a mouthful, then another, placed his empty mug on the table. She reached for her cup, gulped the liquid down.

'Now, perhaps you can tell me what you were doing visiting Karina Hersche on her lovely boat.' He waved his hand at the river. 'The *Greenwitch*.'

'I've no idea what you are talking about.'

He whacked the table with a suddenness that made her jump, scattered the thermoses. 'Don't lie to me.' She edged the chair back, felt resistance, turned and found her face smack against the brick wall of Wolf. She twisted back. The Czech was on his feet, leaning over the desk, his weight on his hands, his face up against hers, blasting her with his shotgun syllables. 'Don't be stupid. I thought you were smart, but maybe you're not so smart after all. Maybe you're a stupid girl who can't see the shit she's in, who can't work out what Wolf enjoys doing with his tub of water.'

Her eyes were watering.

'Now tell me – why were you visiting Karina Hersche?'

She tried to kill the fear coiling in her gut. She had to give him a fragment of truth.

'I have a friend who is a journo. I went out for a drink with him the other night and he mentioned he was doing a story about the situation in Czechoslovakia, the resistance to the Soviet regime, so he'd been going around talking to Czech exiles in London and he said he'd visited this woman who lived on a houseboat, whose parents had fled in '68. He said she was really interesting, but she'd asked him not to use her details in the piece. But when I went round to his place later, I saw a draft of the article, and it mentioned the name of her boat and said it was moored near Tower Bridge. I had an argument with him about it. He didn't think it mattered because he hadn't given her exact location. But there's only one place to moor a houseboat near Tower Bridge. He can be really arrogant sometimes. He refused to budge. I went to warn her, and tell her what he was planning to do.'

He sat down, swung in his chair, balancing on the back legs, smiling mockingly.

'Very inventive,' he said. 'I won't bother to ask you for the name of your journalist friend, or what paper he works for. Wolf.' He beckoned to his enforcer. She froze. He stuck his hands under her armpits, yanked her up from her seat. He was going to stick her head in the water. Half drown her. She couldn't take it. This was stupid. She knew what Reznik was after – he wanted Pierce. She should let him have the information. Pierce could look after himself. Why was she defending him?

'Take her away,' the Czech said. 'Give her a chance to come up with a better story. She's a coffee drinker, after all. I have a soft spot for people who share my tastes.'

CHAPTER 25

London, October 1989

THE KEY CLUNKED in the lock. The room dark apart from the faint glow along the bottom of the window boards. A shout from the corridor made her freeze, the whiny voice of the solicitor.

'You're wanted.'

'Yeah. OK. Coming.'

She waited. Wolf's heavy footsteps diminishing. Silence. The enforcer had clumped away, returned along the corridor to Reznik. Now or never. She edged across the floor to the window, pushed the bottom of the board with her fingertips. It shifted an inch; loosely attached to the wooden frame. She squinted at the slither of light. The board stopped short on one side and she could see now that it was held in place by a batten nailed against the exterior frame. She wiggled her fingers down the side of her monkey boot, eased the Swiss Army knife out, pulled the blade, slid it in the gap between batten and brick wall and levered. The batten shifted with the pressure. Whoever had fixed the boarding over the glassless window hadn't expected this room to be used as a cell. She yanked, street light flooding as the fixing loosened. She paused. If she pushed too hard and the batten and board fell off together, the whole lot would crash to the ground and bring Wolf back. She turned her attention to the board, pushed gently at the bottom corner, managed to ease it far enough away from the outside wall to slip her hand into the gap and around the edge. She pushed; the nails holding the batten creaked. She almost toppled with the momentum of her own force, regained her balance, and peered at the ground, a good fifteen feet below. But the sill was wide – and there was a drainpipe attached to the wall near the window with brackets at regular intervals. An old-fashioned solid lead drainpipe. She could climb down that, if she could reach it.

She waggled the plywood covering. It was still held in place by the second batten nailed more securely on the other side of the frame. She released her grip. The board swung, pivoting on its one point of attachment. She would have to exit backwards. She gripped the jamb, lifted herself on to the sill, twisted, edged to the far corner, stretched her right foot across the drainpipe, slid her foot down until her toe touched a bracket, swung one arm over, gripped the bracket above her head. Point of no return. She had to move quickly, no time for fear. She swung her left leg over and then her arm and half crawled, half slid down the drainpipe, ignoring the burning sensation in her hands and legs as her limbs scraped rusty metal. Her boots touched the ground. She glanced along the curving cobbled street. Derelict wharf buildings. Skips. Scaffolding. Nobody in sight. The river behind her. She turned left, heading west along the street, past a darkened pub. A shout behind, coming from above. Wolf. He'd already discovered she had escaped. Shit. The precariousness of her situation almost paralysed her. Getagrip. She dived down a narrow alley, engulfed by the shadows of its high walls, the smell of dank water filling her nostrils before she reached the steep flight of steps to the Thames. She descended the slippery stones and lingered in the shadows, assessing her path. The tide was ebbing fast, revealing the grey foreshore, but the walls of the wharf on her right jutted beyond the river's edge. Was the water shallow enough for her to escape this way? Behind her, the metal clank of the garage door opening, the Merc engine throbbing. If they were in the car, they wouldn't see her down here. She made a dash for the wharf wall and headed out to its far boundary. The Thames lapped at her feet. She paddled, hand on the rough bricks, fearful in the darkness of straying too deep. She rounded the end of the derelict building and found, to her relief, a stretch of bank exposed on the far side.

She traipsed west, feet sinking in the wet mud. Up above, lights here and there in converted warehouses, Marvin Gaye drifting through an open window, laughter, glasses chinking. Down below, rats scurried around the tidemark of the city's rubbish. Over a rotting jetty, past a huddle of barges stranded as the river retreated. She reached a deep gulley, a stream running into the Thames, its banks steep and muddy. A flight of steps ran alongside, ascending the embankment wall to a gate in a fence. She couldn't go back or cross the gulley. She had to climb. Over the gate at the top, into the backyard of a pub, closed for the night. A dog snarled. She ran at the far fence, leaped, hauled herself up, legs scrabbling as the Alsatian lurched at her feet, dropped to the other side and darted across a bend in the road into a red-brick housing estate.

The headlights of a car swept around the corner. She dived behind an unkempt privet hedge. Close shave. The Merc sped past, tyres kissing wet cobbles. She ran again, heart pounding, leaving the estate, along the road, swerved into an alley. She stopped to take her bearings. The prow of a ghostly cruise ship cut across the far end of the narrow passage. St Katherine's Dock. She had walked around here with Jim at the tail end of the seventies; they had been gobsmacked by the massive yachts and tanned men in white suits which, back then, had seemed like something dropped on London from Hollywood. These days the excesses of the hugely wealthy were a more common sight in the capital. She could cut across the quayside to Tower Bridge. If she could make it over Tower Bridge without being spotted she could walk along the south bank to Vauxhall. Was it safe to go home? Reznik didn't have much information on her, she reckoned. He had assumed she was Pierce's daughter. He didn't know where she lived. If she managed to get back without being spotted, she was probably safe for a couple of days; time enough to work out her next move.

She reached the end of the alley, confronted the ranks of yachts nosing the walkway, pale reflections rippling in the water. Directly ahead, the swing bridge dividing the inner and outer marinas. Nobody in sight; St Katherine's Dock had a strangely deserted feel as if it had all been bought up, but nobody actually lived here. She emerged from the alley, charged across the bridge, half expecting Wolf to appear from the shadows, and headed for the cover of a colonnade. Her nervous reflection followed her in the windows of the dark and silent cafés. She found the slip road to Tower Bridge, halted and watched the intermittent line of traffic heading south over the river. She would be too exposed on the bridge. She needed another route. The thump of bass music distracted her; she searched for its source: the river. A disco boat. She scanned the dock, identified her path across the walkways to the Thames and ran, clanking over metal gangplanks, past a concrete tower of luxury apartments, tilting along the pier. Two figures staggered in the opposite direction, the more upright woman only slightly less inebriated than the one she was supporting. She sprinted to the brightly lit boat at the far end, a wizened boatman unlooping a rope, weather-beaten skin furrowed, slick black hair receding, fag dangling from the corner of his mouth.

'Wait.'

He looked up.

'What, luv?' Impatient and tired rather than unfriendly.

'Could you take me across the river?'

'Look, luv, this isn't a flippin' taxi. We only pulled up here to let those two off cos they was chuckin' up all over the shop. Hen parties are the worst.'

She looked at him pleadingly. 'I'm being chased by somebody.'

'What is it with you girls these days? You're always getting into some drama or other.'

She fished in her back pocket, found a tenner, waved it at him.

'Oh put it away, luv. I don't want your money. I just want an easy life. Come on. Mind the gap if you don't want to get wet. I'll go and ask the guvnor if he minds doing an extra stop.'

She clambered aboard. The engine chugged. He pushed the boat away from the jetty.

'I'll sit here.' She plonked herself on a bench by the railings, watched the raucous crowd of screaming women, pink deely boppers bouncing as they floundered. The boat nosed its way into the Thames.

The boatman returned, gave her the thumbs up.

'You're in luck, the skipper's feeling generous.'

He sat next to her. They passed below Tower Bridge, the vast underside of iron girders arching above her head. The boatman didn't bother looking up; seen it all before. He eyed the drunken hen partiers flashing their boobs. A woman in stilettos lurched, tripped and brought a clutch of her mates down with her; a squealing heap on the deck.

'London, it's one giant madhouse these days.'

'Does anybody ever fall overboard?'

'We've had one or two. I'm surprised there haven't been more, to be honest. I mean, look at the state of them.'

'Do you rescue them?'

'Of course we rescue them.' He fished a packet of Number Six from his jacket, tapped the carton, removed a fag, offered her one.

'No thanks.'

He flicked a Bic, the flame accentuating the lines around his mouth.

'Nobody's ever fallen overboard and drowned?'

'Only one. The coroner reckoned it was misadventure. But I think it was suicide because it seems he went out of his way to find a spot on the boat where he was alone.' He lifted his hand to his mouth, fag between index and middle finger, puffed. 'Nobody spotted him in the water. Drowning. Not a great exit.'

She glanced over the railing, the thick grey Thames churning in the boat's wake, and she sensed herself going under, water closing over, descending, light fading.

'So this man who is chasing you.'

She jumped. 'Yes?'

'You know him?'

'No. Somebody I met in a bar. He bought me a drink, then I couldn't get rid of him.'

The boatman puffed. 'You don't look like the kind of girl who hangs out in bars taking drinks off strangers.'

'Everybody ends up doing odd things sometimes.'

He leaned back, observed the southern shore of the river.

'Where do you live?'

'Up by Vauxhall.'

'There's a jetty just past Hungerford Bridge. I can see if the skipper minds dropping you there if you like.'

'Thanks.'

Rain splashed as she stalked along the embankment. Big Ben clanged three. By the time she reached Lambeth Bridge, the wind had risen and the drops were hitting her at an angle, stinging her face. She hadn't consciously called up this storm, but perhaps it was helpful; blurring the view, deterring all but the most determined late-night joggers. She crossed the road away from the river, darted down an unlit street of garages and brickies' yards, past a joy-ridden BMW, doors akimbo, radio blaring – Soul II Soul, 'Keep on Movin''. She fixed her sight on the skeleton of the Oval gasholder, clung to the pavement beside the railway arches. A fox loped across her path, barked and slunk away. She turned right into the square, checked over her shoulder, made a dash, key in her hand. She twisted, stumbled through the door, stood dripping in the hall and listened; the sound of Becky's long, slow snores. She went to her room, set the alarm, and crashed.

The jangling bell woke her. She reached over, fumbled, jammed her finger on the button to stop it ringing.

'Is that you?' Becky's sleepy voice from down the hall.

'Yeah.'

She rolled out of bed. She had to warn Anna that she might be in danger; Reznik could be on to her. She needed to warn Karina too, although if Reznik had wanted to question Karina, he would have done it by now. He was aware, she suspected, that Karina knew nothing about Pierce's whereabouts; she was more useful as innocent bait.

She stuck her sockless feet in her monkey boots. Still soaking. The soles peeling away from the uppers; she needed a new pair. Perhaps it was time to graduate from monkey boots to proper shoes. Stop paddling in murky water. She squelched across the room, drew the curtain an inch and peered from behind its folds. The rain had stopped, grey light filtered through a wall of clouds, autumn dwindling. Starlings twittered. The street empty. She stomped down the stairs and into the street, reached the telephone box, dialled and jammed the coins in the slot when Anna answered.

'Anna.'

'I thought it might be you.'

'Why?'

'Dunno. Intuition. What is it?'

'You're in danger.'

'Sure.'

'No, really. It turns out the Czech arms dealer that was after Pierce in '76 is still at large. He's here. In London.'

Anna's response was offhand.

'What's that got to do with me?'

'He's called Reznik. He doesn't know where Pierce is, but he's searching for him. He picked me up and questioned me.'

She took a breath. She didn't want to tell Anna about Karina; that would complicate matters.

'I was cornered last night when I was walking home. This Merc appeared, a heavy grabbed me. I ended up in Execution Wharf in Wapping.'

'You sound like one of those Americans who thinks they've been abducted by aliens.'

'I'm serious. They questioned me. I didn't give anything away. There was a tub of cold water, which scared me shitless. But then I managed to escape without being seen.'

'What's the tub of cold water got to do with anything?'

'Torture. They hold your head under so you feel like you're drowning.'

'Sam, you always were prone to overreaction. Storytelling.'

Fuck her. 'I'm trying to help. I think they mistook me for you.'

'It sounds like a bit of a mess to me.' She said it coldly, a note of accusation in her voice.

'Maybe you should go to the police.'

'And say…?'

'That you're in trouble.'

'Because I think a Czech arms dealer is after me?'

'Yes. You're the daughter of an ex-MI6 agent. You've had to change your name. They'll understand that. They'll believe you.'

'I'm surprised you have so much faith in the integrity of the police.'

She had a point.

'What did you say this Czech guy's name was anyway?'

'Reznik.'

'And where did you say you were taken?'

'Execution Wharf in Wapping. It's a building he owns, he's doing it up, just beyond the bend in the river. You need to get protection.'

'Get protection.' She scoffed. 'When has anybody ever given me any protection? I'm collateral. You'll be collateral too if you're not careful. Maybe I'll just disappear.'

'Disappear?'

The phone beeped. Sam fed more coins in the slot.

'Go somewhere else. Sell up. Move on. I can change my name again.'

'Don't you get fed up with running away?'

'No. I like it.'

Said with a heavy dose of sarcasm.

'And how about you? How are you going to make sure Reznik doesn't find you again and dunk your head in a bathtub?'

'I don't know. I haven't worked that one out yet.'

'Don't you have a number you can call?'

She did, but it was Harry's and she wasn't sure how reliable he was any more.

'No, I don't have a number.'

'So you'd better drop all this stuff.'

'All what stuff?'

'All this escaping from wharves in the dead of night and calling people from phone boxes. Don't you think you should go dig up a few pottery shards somewhere instead?'

'That's what I was trying to do.'

'You didn't try hard enough.'

'What are you saying?'

'I'm saying thanks for trying to sort it out between Pierce and me, thanks for letting me know his enemies are on my trail, but drop it. Mind your own business. Leave it alone. It's been nice knowing you, now fuck off.'

Anna slammed the receiver. 'You fuck off too,' Sam said into the dead line. 'Blood fucking sisters. Any time you want me to risk my neck for you, just let me know.'

She trudged back from the phone box, limbs and ribs aching, reached her front door and stopped. Becky was talking on the phone in the hall.

'Look, I don't think you've given it a chance.'

Anna hadn't wasted any time; she must have called Becky as soon as she'd put the phone down on her. She was obviously serious about cutting her ties and disappearing.

'Look, I don't want to...'

Sam didn't want to barge in on the break-up conversation.

'Think about it. Give it a few days. Maybe we could go for a cup of coffee, talk it over.'

On the other hand, she couldn't drag herself away.

'Well, if you're sure, what can I say?'

Silence.

'OK. Never mind…'

'OK.'

More silence.

'Hello… Anna, are you there?'

She'd put the phone down on Becky too. Sam willed her not to call Anna back. She heard footsteps retreating along the hall. Sam decided to stroll around the block, pick up some coffee from the Italian deli on the corner of Vauxhall Park, give Becky a chance to recover.

Becky was pottering around the kitchen when she returned.

'Where've you been?'

'Here and there.'

'You've missed the drama.'

'Oh? What's happened?'

'I've been dumped.'

Becky didn't sound that upset about it.

'Anna dumped you?'

'Just now.'

'This early?'

Becky twisted her wrist, checked her watch. 'Yep.'

'She called you at eight a.m. to dump you?'

'Sam, you keep asking about the time which, to me, seems to be the least significant detail in the story.'

Sam's mouth drooped. 'You're right. Sorry. You don't seem that upset.'

'I'm not.'

Perhaps she'd have a delayed reaction. On the other hand,

Becky was resilient. She could deal with rejection. She suspected, though, in this case Becky was bluffing.

'I thought you'd fallen for her, big time.'

'You're disappointed I'm not rolling around on the floor howling?'

'No, of course not.' She wasn't. The selfish side of her was relieved to have her best friend back again. 'I'm glad you're not heartbroken.'

'She is incredibly fanciable. But I was beginning to feel myself that it wasn't quite working.'

'Why not?'

'Dunno.' She padded to the sink, filled the kettle, dropped it on the hob, lit the gas ring. 'That's not true. I do know. Do you remember that conversation we had a while back about your inner and outer self?'

'Oh yeah.'

'You said you thought your inner self was very different from your outer self and I said I don't know what you're going on about. My inner and outer selves are one and the same thing.'

'Yep. I remember.'

'Anna was too much like that – there was the outer surface but I suspected she had a whole inner person that was completely different. It probably didn't help to find out that her real name wasn't the one she originally used to introduce herself. She said she couldn't get used to being Anna again. It freaked me out a bit.'

Becky was perceptive, as well as resilient.

'I don't freak you out, though.'

Becky laughed. 'No. I've known you too long. You've always been Sam. And whatever you say, I suspect your inner and outer selves aren't as different as you make out.'

She re-ran her night with Tom, how easily she'd disguised

her feelings, pretended she had fallen for him when all along she was merely interested in extracting information.

'Maybe I'm better at maintaining a cover than Anna.'

'No, you're useless at maintaining a cover.' Becky paused. 'What you're good at is living in your head. Fantasy land. You've always got some story on the go. Plague pits at Blackheath. Vikings in Orkney. Your dad and some conspiracy or other.'

'I'm not sure that's fair. I mean those aren't stories...'

She trailed off, too tired to explain, opened a cupboard, found a packet of pittas, removed one and took a bite, became conscious of Becky watching her, a smile twitching at the corner of her mouth.

'What's so funny?' She sounded grumpier than she intended.

'Tom phoned.'

Tom. It was all his bloody fault anyway. If he hadn't gone chasing after Karina, she wouldn't have had to locate her on the *Greenwitch*, and then she wouldn't have been picked up by Reznik.

'When?'

'Late last night.'

'What did he want?'

'Dunno.' Pause. 'I knew you were seeing Tom.'

'I'm not seeing Tom.'

'That's not what he said.'

'I don't care what he said.'

'Why are you so coy about it? He's not that bad.'

'I'm not being coy. I'm telling you, we are not an item.'

'Suit yourself.' Becky raised a knowing eyebrow. 'But he sounded pretty desperate to speak to you.'

'Well, he can fuck off.' Maybe Karina had phoned him after her visit and told him she didn't want him to do anything with her story.

*

She traipsed back to her bedroom, lay on her bed and covered her face with her hands, suddenly overwhelmed. Fed up. Exhausted. Scared. What was she supposed to do now? Wait for Reznik to come and find her and have another go at drowning her? The memory of Wolf's hand gripping the back of her head, her face an inch away from the water, made her shudder. She pulled her knees into her chest; foetal position. She wondered whether she'd ever have a bath again. Enjoy swimming. She was quite a strong swimmer, but she never had liked going underwater, preferred to swim on her back. Although she'd only ever had one bad experience and that was in Orkney at the end of the summer holiday of '76 – memorable for all the wrong reasons. Waulkmill Bay. A couple of days after they had been to Hoy. Jim had gone off his rocker, lost it when she'd drifted too far out to sea. Not drowning but waving. Or was it the other way around? She yanked the duvet over her body. He'd lost it again the year after Waulkmill Bay as well. July '77; their last ever family holiday in Orkney. And now she came to think about it, that second moment of holiday madness had been water related too.

CHAPTER 26

Orkney, July 1977

THE SUMMER OF '77 wasn't as blistering as the summer of '76, but it was still hot. Nobody fancied the beach, despite the sunshine. The annual trip to Orkney seemed to have triggered their collective family memory of the previous year's Waulkmill Bay incident – Jim going apeshit because Sam had swum out of her depth. Oddly, the episode seemed to have affected Liz more than anybody. She kept referring to 'that afternoon at Waulkmill Bay last year', and muttering that Jim still needed to sort himself out. She had spent the first week of the '77 holiday saying she wanted to be alone. Even Helen's suggestion of a trip to Stromness with her and Jess wasn't enough to entice her; all she wanted to do was sit in the garden of the croft and read a book. Everybody else was getting restless. They had spent days moping around, the sisters playing card games. Jim huffing around the house, going for long walks by himself.

Five days before they were due to head back to London, Jim announced he thought they should all go on a trip somewhere together. Liz pointed out that it was raining and reached for her book. By the late afternoon the rain had started to ease, and blue sky had appeared on the horizon. He suggested Maeshowe; it was years since he'd last been. Sam said yes please immediately. Liz said no thanks. Much to Sam's surprise both Helen and Jess said they'd like to go too; cabin fever, so desperate to get out they'd even jump at the chance of visiting a Neolithic tomb. They piled in the Cortina and left Liz in peace.

It was still spitting when they arrived. There were guided tours, but Jim didn't want to go on the tour because he hated being organized and hated going with the crowd. They paid for their tickets at the mill, collected a torch and waited for the gap between two tours when the gate was left open. There wasn't anybody else in sight. From the west as they approached across the fields, Maeshowe looked like an oversized mole hill. When Sam turned around and looked back, though, she could see the line that ran from the cairn's long, low tunnel entrance through the solitary giant Barnhouse stone to the dip in the hills of Hoy. Even if she hadn't known this gap was where the sun set on the day of the winter solstice – slicing the top of the Barnhouse stone, shining along the cairn's passage to the far wall of the tomb's interior – she would have found the alignment moving. Neolithic. Stone Age. She thought these were inaccurate names for people who, she sensed, were in some ways more sophisticated than them.

She pointed at the Barnhouse stone as they trekked through the sodden grass to the cairn. 'See that standing stone over there. See how it lines up with the…' Helen yawned.

'Look, please don't make the mistake of thinking that just because I'm here, I'm actually interested in any of this history shit.'

Jess said, 'I see what you mean, though – it's a ley line, isn't it?'

Helen jabbed Jess sharply in the ribs with her elbow, unable to tolerate her sister's rebellion against the hierarchy.

'Ow.' Jess knocked Helen's arm away. Helen whacked her back.

Jim, striding ahead, stopped and bellowed, 'Will you lot stop faffing around.'

He was worse than all of them put together, Sam thought.

He waved the torch. 'I'm going in.' He ducked and disappeared. Sam ran to catch up, dropped and bent double as she edged along the tunnel, the floor wet beneath, the huge, damp stones pressing down above, guided by the dim light ahead. It wasn't as claustrophobic as Cuween Hill, where the entrance passage was longer and lower, but it wasn't far off; the smell of wet earth cloying. Jim was standing in the centre of the tomb, shining the torch around the vast, long slabs of rock, stacked and layered so neatly.

'Corbelling,' he said. 'How did they manage it?'

Jess and Helen joined them. He pointed the beam at the four upright corner stones with their angled tops.

'I've never taken much notice of those before, but they remind me of the stones at Stenness.'

'Oh, you're right. The tomb is a bit like a house built around a miniature stone circle.'

'A home for dead people,' Jess said. 'Lovely.'

'Here, hold this a minute.' Jim handed the torch to Helen. 'Shine it on that lintel. I think that's where the Viking dragon is carved.'

Helen obeyed. Jim went to have a closer look.

'Welcome to the House of Darkness.' Helen said it dramatically. It was a while since she'd performed the House of Levitation chant. Sam was amused by this version, customized for Maeshowe. Helen pulled Sam's sleeve, drew her closer. The three sisters huddled in the middle, while Jim inspected the tomb's walls.

'What's that dripping noise?' Jim asked, eyes still searching the stones for Norse runes.

'Water,' Helen observed. 'Dripping.'

'I know it's water dripping,' Jim said testily. 'Where's it coming from?'

'There's a leak in the roof,' Jess said. The drip, drip echoed around the chamber. 'It's like Chinese water torture.'

'Belt up,' Jim said.

Sam felt Helen's arm tense.

Jess seemed oblivious to Jim's mood, chattering almost nervously. 'Oh god, wouldn't it be awful if we were trapped in here and it filled with water?'

'I said shut it.'

'This House looks dark,' Helen said.

The water dripped.

'This House is dark.' She flipped the torch switch, plunged them into immediate and total blackness.

Jim shouted, 'I told you. Stop fucking about. Switch the torch on.'

Helen continued, unperturbed.

'This man looks ill.'

'Turn it on.'

'This man is ill.'

Jim issued a strangled noise, half man, half beast, alarming in the pitch black. Sam's head pulsed, she couldn't catch her breath. What was wrong with him? What was wrong with Helen? In command of the torch and refusing to switch it on. She could hear shuffling, feet moving, hands on surfaces – Jim, huffing and muttering. Fuck. Fuck. Get me out.

'What's going on?' Jess said.

Silence. Apart from the drip, drip, drip of the water.

'This man looks dead.' Helen seemed determined to complete her chant. 'This man is dead.'

'I think he's gone,' Jess said.

Helen illuminated the torch.

'I think he's gone mad. What's got into him anyway?'

She said it quite calmly.

'I don't think you should have done that,' Sam said.

'I didn't do anything he didn't ask for. He behaves like a jerk half the time, so why shouldn't I?'

She shone the torch on Sam's face. 'What are you upset about anyway? He might be a psycho, but I doubt whether it's genetic.'

'Why do you have to be so horrible about him?'

'Why do you have to be such a daddy's girl?'

Jess said, 'We'd better go and see if he's OK.'

They squeezed through the puddled tunnel to the daylight. Jim was a megalith standing in the field, his back to the cairn, ahead of him the Barnhouse stone, and beyond, the dark mountains of Hoy. Part of the ancient alignment. Out here, he seemed sturdy. Dependable. And yet he had just flipped, for no apparent reason. She regarded him, outlined against the dark slope of Hoy, remembered his Waulkmill Bay eruption, and thought she could guess what was eating him. *Water... fault.* She wondered whether either of them, Jim or her, would ever be able to feel quite so at ease in Orkney again after the events of the previous summer. The year of the heatwave had left its mark.

CHAPTER 27

London, October 1989

BLACKNESS THICKENING AS the water closed over her head. She wanted to breathe but she couldn't open her mouth. Pain in her lungs. Head. Fingers twisted her hair, forced her under. A light glinted in the dark. She couldn't tell whether it was above or below and she thought it was the end. She wanted the pain to be over. She tried to swim but she couldn't reach the brightness. She heard a shout and she broke the surface, spluttering, gasping for air.

'Sam, are you OK?'

Becky's voice. She was standing by the door, hand on light switch. Sam wheezed. No oxygen in her lungs. An iron weight on her chest. What had woken her? She knew this sensation. It had happened before when she was a kid, hearing somebody shouting, waking, spluttering. A man's voice yelling.

Becky sat beside her, arm around her shoulder.

'Breathe through your nose.'

She inhaled. The wheezing subsided, eyes still weeping.

'I didn't know you suffered from asthma.'

'I don't.'

'What happened? Did you choke on something?'

'No. I dreamt I was drowning.'

'Did your life flash before your eyes?' Becky sounded more curious than sympathetic.

'No. I wanted to open my mouth to breathe but I couldn't, and everything was black.'

She rubbed Sam's back.

'Yeah, the life flashing before your eyes is a bit of a myth. Drowning is actually a form of asphyxiation – the body's reflex keeps the mouth shut to prevent water entering, but then the brain doesn't get any oxygen and ends up smothered with carbon dioxide.'

'Thanks for telling me.'

'You're OK now?'

'Yes, I think so. What time is it?'

'Five.'

The night-time escape from Execution Wharf had left her knackered, bruised and sniffling. She had spent two days dozing and drifting, the room dim, dawn, noon and dusk blurring in London's overcast autumn haze.

'Listen, somebody knocked on the door and asked if they could come in and talk to you.'

Sam inhaled, coughed, face reddened. Reznik. His enforcer. Had they found her? Becky patted her on the back again.

'God, what is wrong with you?'

'Who?' She managed to push the words out between breaths. 'Who knocked on the door?'

'A woman. She's got blonde hair. She says she lives on a houseboat.'

Karina. Her trachea narrowed. She wheezed.

'Sounds like asthma to me.'

Sam swung her legs over, perched on the side of the bed, hands either side, head hanging, deep breaths. The floorboards bucked beneath her feet. 'Did you let her in?'

'She's in the kitchen. Was that a mistake?'

'No. No, it's fine.'

'You seem a bit better now.'

Sam nodded.

'I'll leave you to it. I'm going out.'

'Where are you going?'

She didn't want Becky to leave; she needed her friend's normality, her refusal to be intimidated by the shadows and secrets that haunted Sam.

'I'm on the prowl. It's the best cure for a dumping. I'm going to meet a friend in Brixton then we're going to the Fridge.'

'Venus Rising?'

'Yup.'

Becky headed for the door. 'Come and find me if you fancy a dance later.'

'I don't know...'

'Don't tell me, you're meeting Tom.'

'No, it's not...'

'You don't have to make excuses.' Becky clumped down the stairs. 'See you.' The front door banged.

Sam made her way to the kitchen. The back door open, cigarette smoke wafting in, Karina leaning against the trunk of the rowan. A sparrow hopped among the leafless branches, striking at dangling red berries. She smiled nervously.

'I'm sorry, I had to come.'

Piled blonde hair glinting, lines across her brow softened in the darkness. One of those women who would skip middle age, remain girlish until old age caught her and made her brittle.

'It's OK. Don't worry.' Sam found herself reassuring Karina, as if she were a child. 'Do you think anybody followed you here?'

'No. I took evasive measures.'

'Evasive measures?' Sam was relieved Karina had been careful, but perturbed by her professional language. 'Are you trained?'

Karina laughed nervously. 'No. I know that life because

of my father, even if I'm not part of it.' She held a cigarette delicately between two fingers, smoke curling around her face. 'I wish I didn't know about it, but I do. People tell me things.'

Sam edged down across the yard, closer to Karina.

'I can't always be sure why they are telling me things, or whether the things they tell me are true.' Karina cupped her right elbow in her left hand, the red tip of her cigarette dangerously close to her hair. 'But in this case I believed them and I had to do something.'

Her left hand flitted from her elbow to her neck, fiddling with the chain of her pendant, the white edge of the mosaic tile visible above the dip in her shirt.

'I have been told that Pavel has returned to London. Of course, Pavel wasn't his real name.'

'Oh?' Sam tried to sound surprised.

'No. I always thought he was untrustworthy. His real name is Reznik.' She puffed, eyed Sam through the cloud of smoke. 'And he knows where Davenport is living.'

'That's not possible.' Sam's reaction was immediate. Defensive. She hadn't revealed Pierce's hideaway. She had said nothing. She had a sudden sense this was a trap; Reznik didn't know where Pierce was hiding, she had been allowed to escape from Execution Wharf and Karina had been primed to follow her. Karina sensed her scepticism and her face crumpled, eyes brimming.

'You have to believe me, please. I don't know anybody else who can help.'

Such intense feelings for somebody she hadn't seen for thirteen years. She didn't even know his real name; in love with a spectre. Sam lifted a hand to comfort her, retracted it, confused.

Karina said, 'I wish it wasn't true, but I am scared that Reznik will hunt and kill him.'

'How do you know all this?'

'I told you, I grew up with people from this world. I still have contacts. Sometimes they are reliable. Sometimes not. But in this case, I am sure the information is correct. I am told it is from Reznik's solicitor. He let it slip to somebody who knew my father – a family friend, I suppose. A Czech. I don't think the solicitor was aware of the connection.'

A bad slip for the solicitor to make; she didn't fancy his chances of survival if Karina's information was correct and Reznik discovered the source of the leak. Unless, of course, he'd realized his number was already up and was playing games to undermine Reznik and save his own skin.

'My father's friend is a property dealer and was supposed to be signing a contract on a place Reznik is buying. He's been chasing him for weeks, but Reznik has been evasive. He managed to corner his solicitor this morning at one of his other developments – Execution Wharf. Reznik wasn't there. The solicitor allowed him to look around the place, and when he went out on the balcony, he found a pair of binoculars on the table and saw my houseboat in full view across the river.'

Sam didn't say anything; unwilling to reveal how much she already knew. She had instantly liked Karina and judged she was genuine, but her history was complicated, her loyalties not straightforward. Perhaps she was being used, her strings pulled in ways she herself could not discern.

'This contact said he couldn't put his finger on it, but he thought I ought to know. Instinct for danger, I suppose, after so many years living behind the Iron Curtain. So this friend came and told me straight away. I was unsure at first that it was anything serious. But then he told me Reznik used to operate under the name Pavel, when he was in London last, in the seventies, and then I felt scared.'

'But did the solicitor tell your friend that Reznik was after Davenport?'

'He made a joke about an ex-big game hunter becoming the hunted. That has to be Davenport.'

'Oh.' A movement in the ivy fringe of the fence caught her eye; a rat emerged, assessed the courtyard and slunk back to the undergrowth. 'What else did you hear?'

'The solicitor said Reznik might be away a couple of days, because he has to find this man.'

'Find him? I thought you said Reznik knew his location.'

'Not exactly. Apparently Reznik has gone to some island off the north coast of Scotland.'

How had Reznik discovered Pierce was in Orkney? Pierce had told her that only a small handful of people had ever known where he was living; a couple of trusted colleagues in Intelligence, Jim and herself. Jim was dead. She hadn't given the information to Reznik. If he had been betrayed by one of his Intelligence colleagues, they would have given him the precise details of his hideaway. There was one other person who knew he was in Orkney and might have a motive for betraying him, she suspected. Harry. He didn't have much time for Pierce, although he had been vague about his reasons. She thought about the note slipped in her pocket. *Don't trust Harry.* Was it possible that Harry had found Reznik and told him the location of Pierce's hideaway? Sam poked a mound of leaves with her toe, recoiled when a worm slithered away.

'Sam, please take this.'

She looked up. Karina had removed her necklace and was holding it in the air. The Fisher King's treasure twisted, ghostly white.

'Take it.'

Sam caught the tile in her hand; its coldness burned her skin.

'Maybe you can find where Davenport is hiding?'

Sam didn't dispute Karina's suggestion; her voice was so pleading.

'It's urgent.'

Sam dangled the tile by its chain, let it twizzle.

'Please, take the necklace to him and warn him he is in danger.'

Karina had that strange mixture of knowingness and naïveté she recognized in herself; a child of the shadow state.

'If I take this to Davenport, then I might also lead Reznik to him. Perhaps that's the point. Maybe the solicitor is setting you up. Setting us both up to lead them to Davenport.'

'It's too late to worry about that. Reznik has set off anyway, he will find him whether you look for him or not. If you are quick, you can reach him first. You, I think, know these islands better than Reznik.' She gave her a sly glance. 'I saw a book about the Orkney Islands on the kitchen table when I walked in. Please, if not for me and Davenport, then for your friend Anna. She would be unhappy if anything happened to her father, I am sure. Whatever you do, please do it quickly.'

She smiled sadly, paced away through the kitchen without saying goodbye, let herself out the front door, left Sam standing amid the rowan's decaying leaves.

Too late to do anything that evening anyway. She clasped the pendant around her neck and toyed with Karina's plea. Her head told her it was best to take Anna's advice and mind her own business. Her gut told her it was her own business. Her past, her fate, her future, was tied up with Pierce's. She had turned to face the shadows and she had to see it through. Karina was right: whatever Anna said about her father, she wouldn't want to be an orphan. If she reached Pierce in time,

285

he could persuade his Intelligence friends to deal with Reznik, and then they would all be safe – her, Anna, Pierce, Karina. And anyway, if Pierce was killed, she would never find out exactly what Jim had done, in the long summer of '76.

She hadn't flown to Orkney before. A first time for everything. It was the quickest way to get there and, she figured, the easiest way to throw off any watchers. Becky had a Debbie Harry wig which she had bought for some student union bash. Sam jammed it on her head, examined herself in the mirror, startled by her own reflection – a more glamorous version of herself. She ferreted for her baker boy cap and perched it on the artificial hair, grunged the look down a notch. It would have to do. She bolted along South Lambeth Road, head down, to the Portuguese tourist agent, always open at the crack of dawn. The woman sitting behind a computer, lacquered nails and false eyelashes, gave Sam's bouffant wig an approving nod, asked what she was after, tapped the computer keyboard. A return to Kirkwall, flying north today, returning south tomorrow. Kirkwall? Where was Kirkwall? Orkney. Scotland. Pained face. Wasn't it cold and wet? Could she make a flight that left Heathrow at twelve thirty? She would need to be there an hour before, that gave her three hours to cross London. She could do it, but she would have to run. She paid in cash – twenties from Pierce's stash.

She stopped at a phone box on the way home, called the archaeologist, checked whether she could use the Honda. He said he was going to Kirkwall that morning. He'd drop it off at the airport car park, key in ignition, helmet by the wheel. Nobody would take it, not unless they were mad.

*

Becky returned home bleary-eyed as she was about to leave.

'Why are you wearing that wig?'

'Got to run. Might not be back tonight. Tell you later.'

She slouched into the airport with her cap over one eye, avoiding the focus of the security camera, checked in, made her way through the metal detector and went straight to the ladies'. She locked herself in a cubicle, put the toilet lid down and sat. The smell of crap was overwhelming, but she was prepared to put up with it if it meant she was less likely to be seen. She waited until her flight was called, exited the cubicle, straightened her wig in the mirror. She looked like a madwoman. Too bad. She bought the *Guardian* from a newsagent and headed to the departure gate.

The plane was half empty. She had a window seat and nobody sat next to her. She peered through the porthole at the receding ground, transfixed by the autumnal spread of London below, the silver Thames looping through the gilded city. She unfolded the *Guardian* as they reached the clouds, thumbed the pages searching for the cryptic crossword. She was in luck. Araucaria; her favourite setter. Her eye caught the date at the top of the paper – 31 October. Halloween – it had almost slipped by without her noticing. She smiled, remembering Halloween parties past; dressing up as witches, carving jack o' lanterns from gnarly turnips, parading around the block while their neighbours eyed them with suspicion and the local boys jeered. Not that they cared what the wankers at the end of the road thought of them, not then. Jim joined in the party games if he was around, playing the old hag in grandmother's footsteps, bobbing for apples, hamming up his part in murder in the dark. Samhain, he called it. The feast of the dead. The end of harvest and the beginning of the darkness. Even when they were teenagers, the sisters had insisted on having a Halloween party. Although by then they had graduated from bobbing apples to the Ouija board, Helen doing her tarot readings. Liz joined in, after a fashion. *Fear death by water*, she had said when Helen handed her the Hanged Man from the tarot pack. It's a quote, she had added when Helen had pulled a puzzled face. *The Waste Land*. Jim's participation had dwindled. Maybe that was the pattern in all families – the increasing distance between father and children as they aged. Perhaps it would have happened that way anyway, even if he hadn't worked as a police spy, preoccupied by the dangers of his job. Perhaps it wouldn't. She folded the paper in half, cast her eye over the list of clues and picked out an anagram, rearranged the letters in her head. Cryptic crosswords were much simpler than relationships and in some ways more satisfying. At least they were resolvable.

Her head was itching by the time they landed at Glasgow. She bought two cheese sandwiches, three bottles of water, two bars of Cadbury's Dairy Milk, shoved them all in her backpack and headed to the toilet. She removed the wig in the privacy of a cubicle, wondered whether she really needed to wear it as she stared at the gap under the door and watched feet passing. High-heeled courts. Tasselled brogues. Adidas trainers hovering. The door clattered as the trainer wearer tested the lock.

'This one's free,' somebody shouted further down the line of cubicles.

'Zank you.' East European accent.

Her heart thumped. The trainers moved away. Sam jammed her wig and cap on her head, opened the cubicle door, dashed

288

to the departure lounge, saw the boarding light flashing for Kirkwall, ran to the gate, straight on the titchy plane. She huddled in her seat, unfolded the *Guardian* and used it as a screen to mask her face. She watched the shoes boarding below the paper. No Adidas trainers. The air hostesses closed the doors. The plane trundled along the runway, propellers blurring, stomach surging as it tilted, grey and green below.

They dropped below the clouds over the Pentland Firth, the sun sinking into the sea, burnishing the sky as they landed. A battalion of geese flew overhead – winter arrivals she assumed, like her. She made a beeline for the toilets, removed the wig, stuffed it in her rucksack. She checked her watch. Four fifty. She had shouted goodbye to Becky at ten. Six hours and fifty minutes to travel from one end of Britain to the other. She now had forty minutes to reach Houton and the ferry to Lyness.

She trotted to the car park, located the Honda, helmet waiting by the front wheel. She twisted the key, kicked the starter pedal. Nothing happened. She froze. Until this point she had been carried along by the momentum of the journey. A leaf on the wind. Her plan was simply to find Pierce and warn him about Reznik. She hadn't thought beyond reaching the ferry at Houton on time. She patted her coat pocket, comforted by the torch and penknife. Once she got to Rackwick she'd be fine anyway; she had her doubts about Pierce's relationship with Karina, but they didn't detract from her view of him as the type of man you could rely on in a crisis. He knew how to stay calm in dangerous situations; that had been his job before he'd gone to ground in Hoy. He'd dealt with terrorists. Arms dealers. She kicked the starter pedal again. The bike chugged and shook.

Beyond Kirkwall the houses thinned, and the comforting glow of the street lamps evaporated. She knew this road but the darkness transformed the landscape. She focused on the tarmac, ignored the menacing shadows and movements in the corner of her eye. Headlights of passing cars came and went. A short-eared owl swooped too close and she swerved, almost lost control. She followed the lane past the Earl's Bu. The filigree branches of the coppiced sycamores were black against the sky and Jim was standing in the shadow of the hedgerow. She took a second look. Nothing. Ghosts of the past. She remembered him standing in that same spot in the summer of '76 as if it were yesterday, not thirteen years ago. She could recall the details – the jeans, the boots, the shirt he was wearing, the tightness in her stomach as she watched Pierce's retreating Volvo. What had Pierce been doing there that day? Jim had never said whether the meeting happened by chance, although she had sensed Jim's surprise when he saw Pierce watching through the window of the Round Church. Perhaps he was alarmed, not surprised. Pierce had located her in exactly the same place thirteen years later. He was always careful, Pierce had told her, when he visited Stromness; he didn't want his face well known. And yet he visited the Earl's Bu regularly. He found solace in the place, he had said. Or perhaps he was drawn back to those events in the summer of '76 that wouldn't let either of them go.

The ferry was waiting at Houton pier. A curlew flew along the coast, its haunting song hanging in the air. The wind had dropped, the clouds cleared, the night sky darkening from crimson to violet, the first stars glinting. She boarded the ferry, parked the Honda, sat on the passenger walkway, ate one of her sandwiches. The ferryman wandered over; she recognized him from her previous journey to Hoy in September and was comforted by the familiar face even if he wasn't somebody she knew. She dug in her pocket for her wallet.

'You're going to Lyness?'

'Yes.'

'There isn't a return ferry tonight.'

'I know.'

'Are you going to stay in the hostel?' Concerned, rather than nosey.

She nodded.

He took her money.

'Don't you miss the sun here in the winter?' she asked.

'There are compensations.' He pointed to Orion. 'On a clear winter's night, the Milky Way stretches from horizon to horizon. That makes the darkness worthwhile. Mind you, there are plenty of nights when it's wild and wet and all you can do is pray for the dawn to come.'

'Do you think it will be a wild and wet Halloween tonight?'

'Not a chance. Somebody's been to see Bessie Millie.'

'Bessie Millie?'

'The witch of Stromness who tamed the winds if you gave her enough money.'

'A night of Samhain supernatural calm then.'

'Aye. Supernatural, that's for sure. The ghosts will be out tonight. Samhain,' he repeated thoughtfully. 'That's a Gaelic word. Are you a Scot?'

'No, but my father was.'

'Not from here.'

'Glasgow, or thereabouts.'

'You don't sound very certain.'

'I'm not.'

He handed her a ticket. 'Families are funny things.'

Especially when they live in the shadow of the secret state. He ambled away, left her staring at the black and glassy water.

CHAPTER 28

Orkney, 31 October 1989

THE WALLS OF Lyness harbour solidified in the dark. She clanked on to the harbour road, glanced behind for a last sight of the ferryman, waved as she passed the derelict army barracks. A dog howled. The grizzled head of a Halloween turnip lantern glimmered on a front step. Halloween. She had enjoyed the spooky games with her sisters, but here, alone in the darkness, Samhain was not so much fun. Unnatural calm the ferryman had said, and there was something too still, too expectant about the air, as if the restless souls were waiting for the wall between here and eternity to crumble so they could cross over to the land of the living for this one night. She conjured the faces of the dead people she had known, chanted their names in her head. They were reaching out to her, she couldn't hold them back. Not tonight. She headed north along the coast, the bleak slopes of Hoy on one side and on the other, the ocean. The road was wide but in the dark she had a continual sense she was too close to the edge, in danger of falling.

The road dipped to Pegal Bay, the scrubby willows and stunted ashes hunched like witches in the gulley, the burn gurgling and frothing. A bird of prey screeched and the bike's headlight caught the bleak emptiness of the moor ahead. Flickering lights in the distance took her by surprise; she couldn't recall a settlement along this part of the road. She instinctively clutched the brake, peered ahead as the beam caught the white marker of Betty Corrigall's grave. Stooped figures, candles blazing in the stillness of the air. Halloween ritual, she supposed, locals remembering the dead. The scene made her think of Pierce, leaving one of the white tiles that Anna had given him in the jam jar on the grave. Why had he placed it there? Was he recalling his own dead in some muted way, remembering those he had lost? She twisted the throttle, urged the small bike to go faster as she descended the hill, keen to put some distance between herself and the grave. She glanced behind but could no longer see people or flames – some trick of the landscape. She flicked her eyes forward and caught a figure in the beam, running along the verge. A woman. Small. Perhaps it was a girl. Where had she appeared from? She swerved, glimpsed a long white dress and bare feet in the periphery of her vision. She veered again, heart beating. Panicking. The girl was in trouble, fleeing from the graveside mourners. Betty Corrigall. She looked in the wing mirror, spotted the white dress, except it wasn't white, it was dirty, smeared with gunk, dark bloody gunk, the woman's pale face with its delicate bird-like features locked in a scream. Valerie. Anna's mother. She gripped the front wheel brake too hard, almost sent herself flying. Came to a halt. Dismounted. Stood in the road. Deserted. She yelled.

'Valerie, where are you? Are you OK?'

Words eaten up in the gloom. No answer. She fumbled in her pocket for her torch, directed it along the road – empty blackness. No sound. Not even a gust of wind rustling the heather. She must have been mistaken. Jumpy. Her panicky brain churning, calling up the dead, making subconscious connections between Valerie and Betty Corrigall because she'd found Pierce's white tile on the grave. Two young dead women. She was imagining things, telling herself Samhain ghost stories.

She remounted the bike, set off again. Confused and shaken. She almost missed the turning for Rackwick Bay, swung at the last moment, headed inland, heart still hammering. She hated this part of the journey, trapped between the mountains, the sheer walls enclosing her in their rocky hold. Everything worse at night. She glanced at her watch. It was only seven p.m. It felt much later. Her tormented mind was playing tricks. She concentrated on the road. Past the path to the Dwarfie Stane, the strange tomb carved out of a huge sandstone block; the only human landmarks in this desolate stretch of Hoy commemorated death. Gravestones. Tombs. No place for the living. A ghostly creature sprang down the slope below the ancient cairn, darted in front of the bike – a mountain hare, fur white in the beam. The hare flipped away, engulfed by the heather. She caught her breath, drove on. The black peaty water of a burn gleamed; she must be close to Rackwick. She stopped, listened. Gulls mewing. An owl's hoot. The distant thrum of an engine. Not a car. What was it? A generator perhaps. She decided to push the bike the rest of the way. The darkness was almost total with the headlight extinguished. She didn't want to use her torch, not yet anyway. It might help her to see but it would also give away her presence if anybody was watching Pierce's place. She tipped her head back, found the crescent moon, Orion's belt and then the brilliant yellow of Capella, the seafarer's guide. The atmosphere was so clear and sharp it magnified the light, made the stars seem brighter, closer. Time and space collapsing.

She rounded the bend to the hollow of the bay. Only one croft with windows glowing. What had Pierce said about his neighbours? A couple of old fishermen who couldn't bear to leave and some artistic types – a photographer and a musician – who rocked up in the summer months. They wouldn't be here this late in the year. She pushed the bike into a field at the inland end of the near deserted settlement, leaned it against a crumbling stone wall, placed the helmet on the grass by the front wheel. She decided to leave her rucksack too – cumbersome to carry – and took her bearings. The bay facing west, Pierce's croft halfway up the slope to the north. Dark. Her stomach rose to her gullet. His paraffin light was never very bright anyway; maybe he had curtained his windows. She shivered. She wasn't sure which was scaring her more: the possibility that something had happened to Pierce or the prospect of being out here alone at night. She'd been banking on Pierce to take over once she had reached him – she wanted him to deal with Reznik. And now it seemed as if he'd already vanished. If Pierce wasn't there, she would go straight back to Lyness and find the hostel. Maybe she should do that anyway, turn around right now. No, she had come this far, she had to see it through.

She stumbled on the uneven path, but by the time she had reached the slope her eyes had adjusted to the dark. First curve. Second curve. The ridge of the hill clear against the pale glow of the northern sky, lighter than she had expected. It couldn't be the moon – that was behind. Perhaps it was Stromness, or a lighthouse. Either way, it cast the hill in relief. Her eye travelled down and she could just make out the white of the croft against the purple of the hill. Definitely no light inside. No sign of the Volvo in its usual spot either. She craned over the path's bank, assessed the house again as best she could in the dark, searching for movements, faces in the window, gleams from the paraffin lamp. Nothing. Pierce was not there. She looked back at the bay; the one croft that had been illuminated was now dark. All she could see was the faint golden crescent of sand and white foam of breaking waves. She was the only visitor here tonight, there was nobody else about. She might as well go and check through Pierce's windows, make sure he wasn't at home, lights dimmed. And then she would ride back to Lyness and stay the night at the hostel.

She trod the path to the croft's entrance, knocked. No answer. She depressed the squeaky handle – it needed oiling – pushed her shoulder against the door. Locked. She sidled around to the valley side of the croft, the window overlooking the bay, squinted through the pane, leaned back to see if she could find a better angle. Pointless exercise because it was too dark to see inside anyway. A crunch startled her. She froze. Listened. Waves pounding. Fulmar's guttural call. Heart thumping. Another crunch. Shoes on gravel. Somebody was walking down the cliff path, towards the croft. Perhaps it was one of the old fishermen out for a night stroll. She ducked below the window, crept to the corner, feet silent on the grass, pressed herself against the wall. Waited, hoping to see a figure below her on the path. Nobody. The night stroller hadn't gone past – he had taken the path to Pierce's croft and was heading for the door. A neighbour hoping for a Halloween hot toddy? She waited for a knock, an enquiring hello. The door handle squeaked. A thud and another, louder. Harder. Whoever it was, they were trying to force the door. Her mind raced, searching for a plan, the safest path. The sharp crack of a kick and wood splintering shattered the night air. Shit.

Getagrip. Return to the Honda. Head start. Drive to Lyness. Safety. She had to move now while the intruder was in the house. Intruder? Reznik or his enforcer Wolf. Whichever, he would be armed. She had to run. The downhill path was hidden from view by its banks. She could make it to the bottom without being seen but she had left the Honda, stupidly she now realized, on the far edge of the hamlet – she would have

hard, the safe place was in her mind. She just had to reach it. He wouldn't find her there, not in the dark. He would search the stoved-in crofts but he wouldn't think anybody would hide on the beach. She wormed along the ground to the doorframe, eyed the far wall of the fold. Beyond, the slope of a grassy dune and beyond that, the boulders and sand of the beach. If she made it that far without being seen, she would be out of view, out of earshot. Out of gunshot. She inhaled, sprinted, clambered over the dilapidated wall, foot sinking in the soft sand on the other side. She beat a diagonal path across the marram grass towards the icy sheen of the sea. The burn broke her path – much broader and faster than when she had last seen it in the summer of the drought. She waded, the water flooding her monkey boots. She glanced behind; no sign of any pursuer. The cliff loomed dark. She slithered down the boulders to the shore. Was the tide ebbing or flowing? The sand gleamed wet beyond the pebbles; the ocean was retreating. She kept away from the sea's edge; she didn't want to leave a trail, stumbled across the slippery rocks, reached the base of the cliff, edged past the sandstone outcrop, found the mouth of her cave. Safety. She retreated away from the lip, fumbled for her torch in the engulfing darkness and headed to the dry sand at the far end. The torch beam caught a ledge at the very back. She climbed and perched, spine against jagged rock, chin on her knees, rotting kelp and sweet dead flesh of seabirds in her nose. The swish of distant waves gently lapping calmed her.

The cave mouth framed her view. A ribbon of sea-sorted rocks; large boulders diminishing to pebbles then grains of sand. Beyond the shore the Pentland Firth shimmered, bright with diamonds of starlight. The sandstone outcrop obstructed sight of the hamlet. She wouldn't be able to see if Reznik was approaching across the bay unless she returned to the entrance of her hideaway. But he wouldn't find her here, even if he reached the beach. This was her safehouse. She hugged her legs. Shivered. Damp and tired. Scared. She should never have let herself be drawn into this mess. Pierce must have got wind of Reznik and managed to slip away. And now she was here, trapped in Rackwick with the ruthless butcher.

She wondered whether she should check the beach. She'd been here twenty minutes. No, she'd wait a little longer before she did that. She extinguished her torch and eyed the cave mouth. The band of sand was narrower than it had been ten minutes earlier, the white froth inching closer. The tide was coming in, not going out. Jesus. That gave her less time than she had thought before the entrance was cut off by the sea. She switched the torch on again, cast the light behind her head, caught barnacle rings and kelp in crevices above the flat ledge on which she was precariously balanced. She'd got it wrong, this wasn't a safe place. The high tide would reach her chin, drag her out to sea. She checked the cave mouth again. The sand had disappeared. The water had reached the pebbles. What was she playing at? She had to leave now, find another hiding place before she drowned.

She eased off the ledge, edged her way down the slope to the barrier of sandstone between the cave and bay. Waves scraped pebbles. A curlew called. She inched closer to the lip, scrabbled the wall, the rock digging into her hand as she hauled herself up and squinted over the barrier. A beam of light swung across the boulders. Reznik was searching the beach beyond the barrier of sandstone rocks that she hoped would provide her with protection. She released her hand from the rock, dropped backwards, landed badly, the pain shooting up her spine. She limped to the rear of the cave, clambered back on the ledge, hand bleeding, back aching, foamy water nibbling the cave lip, waves stronger than before. She didn't want to drown. But on the other hand, if she left the cave, Reznik would see her and god only knew what he would do to her.

She huddled, gripping her knees, arms shaking, watching the waves invading. Twenty minutes and she would have no choice; the sea would block her exit. Her eyes welled, the water glistened through the film of tears, and as she watched, the ocean's glint changed from white to green, sparkling with an unearthly luminescence. She blinked, the greenish glow remained. What was it? Strange creatures of the deep rising to the surface in the moonlight, perhaps. The sheen was enchanting. Magical. Perhaps it wouldn't be so bad to drift away with the light embracing her, comforted by the creatures of the deep. She wasn't thinking clearly. *Fear death by water*, Liz had said. Jim had warned her too, fist raised, face red with anger. *Don't take the sea for granted. Find a safe place in your mind*, he had said, *but don't go in the cave*. Jim. He had lost it, that afternoon when they were standing by Betty Corrigall's grave. She had been scared of him then, when she was ten and felt powerless in the face of her father's temper; she could see now as she watched the shimmering water that he was more worried than angry. Unable to explain the dangers he perceived, the web of deceptions and silences which had entangled him. Trapped, him and her. Waiting for the end. *It's a terrible death*, Becky reminded her; asphyxiation, carbon dioxide kills your mind. She was right, anything had to be better than certain death by drowning. She was being stupid. She had to take her chances. Reznik wouldn't shoot her on sight; he wanted information. She could talk her way out of it. She glanced at the advancing tide. At least if he shot her, it would be quick.

She slid down from the ledge, ran the length of the cave, halted at the entrance, momentarily bewitched by the green waves. Time to leave. She scrambled up the sandstone barricade, grazing hands and knees, reached the top, surveyed the bay. Reznik was standing ten feet from the rocks with his back to her, gazing at the sky. She looked up too and saw the flames dancing above the ridge of hills. She gaped. Not bio-luminescence after all but the Northern Lights, emerald rays throwing reflections on the water. *The touch of grace*, Jim had said and she felt it too, the ethereal light filling her with wonder; almost enough to calm her fear. Everybody had to die sometime, and reach the light. Reznik sensed her presence and swivelled. She ducked. Too late.

'Sam.'

He knew her name. How had he found out who she was? Had he spoken to Harry? She didn't reply, hung on below the level of the ridge, hiding behind her sandstone barrier, trying not to dwell on the possibility of Harry's betrayal.

'Sam. We need to talk.'

She didn't budge.

'Come and look at the Northern Lights. The work of God.'

She tried to interpret what he was saying, analyse his tone of voice. His awe in the presence of natural wonders reminded her of Jim. Some things transcended ideological divides, individuals' beliefs. She had learned to deal with Jim so she could cope with Reznik. Perhaps his reputation was overblown. The Butcher. The cat killer. He'd given her a chance when he had questioned her in Execution Wharf. She glanced back at the sea swirling, engulfing the cave floor. She had no choice anyway. She poked her head above the parapet. He waved at her, gestured at the glow in the sky. Both his hands, she noted, empty. Perhaps he wasn't bluffing, perhaps he did just want to talk.

'Have you ever seen anything like this before?'

'No.' Her voice was faint. 'No.' She repeated herself more confidently. 'I haven't.'

She eyed him carefully; impossible to tell whether he was carrying a gun under his jacket.

'Come down. I won't harm you.'

She clambered on top of the outcrop, sidled along, aware of her vulnerability, exposed on this ridge. He strode towards her as she jumped and landed on the sand. He smiled, revealed his uneven teeth, needle sharp. She took a step back. He grabbed her arm.

'Well, my friend, let's walk by the water.'

'I'd rather stay here.'

'You are like your father, a little stubborn.'

'You don't know my father.'

'No? He's a coffee drinker, I believe. A man after my own heart.'

Reznik was right, her father was a coffee drinker. No gnat's piss tea for him. But what did that have to do with anything? How did he know anyway? Reznik was blindsiding her with his cryptic references to Jim. Trying to trip her. Or was he confirming that it was Jim who blew Pierce's cover all those years ago? He hadn't merely made a slip, dropped Pierce's details to the wrong person, he had deliberately sabotaged the Firm's operation, betrayed Pierce directly to Reznik. A traitor. Her legs buckled. Getagrip, getagrip.

'I don't know what you're going on about.'

She yanked her arm, trying to escape his grasp. He released her, and almost instantaneously his hand went for his jacket. He pulled a pistol and held it to her head.

'I think you know more than you pretend.' The cold metal of the barrel burned her scalp. 'You'll do what I say now.'

She shuddered uncontrollably. She didn't want to waste her life for this. A feud between an arms dealer and an old spook. She heard a click. The safety catch. The tears clouded her eyes, blurred the emerald spangled ocean. But what could she tell Reznik anyway? He'd already located Pierce's hideaway. She had no other information to give him.

'This way.'

He nudged her towards the water. He'd shoot her for the hell of it. She stumbled; hard to walk in the darkness with a pistol aimed at her skull. They reached the edge, luminescent waves breaking around their feet.

'What do you want from me?'

'You know why I'm here.' He jabbed the barrel. 'I'm looking for Pierce.'

'Pierce?' She was expecting Reznik to call him Davenport; that was the identity by which he had known him in '76, after all. He must have discovered his real name in the intervening years; it probably wasn't that difficult to unearth.

Reznik continued. 'Pierce the hero. That's his reputation. Yes?'

She didn't feel inclined to comment.

'Where's he gone?'

He sounded more desperate than angry.

'I don't know.'

He spat at the sea. 'I told you why I need to find him – I want to see what information he holds on me and clear my name, and I thought you could help me.'

'I don't see how.'

'Don't you? I think you and I may be on the same side,' he said.

She scowled.

'Yes. We build these walls, these boundaries – East and West, life and death – but they can't stop people crossing.'

The Northern Lights danced on the edge of her sight. She said nothing.

'You know,' Reznik went on, 'the strangest thing about Pierce is that I always believed we were both on the same side as well and I think, in some ways, I once loved him.'

She was perturbed; he sounded as if he meant it. 'Loved?'

'Yes, it's odd, isn't it? But why not? Not in a sexual way. No, not at all. In a deeper way than that; I saw him as my soul mate, the only person in this world who understood me.'

'Blood brothers,' she suggested.

'Exactly. That is Pierce's gift, don't you think? People fall for him, his upper-class English charm. And why should I be any more immune than any of his doting girlfriends? Hmm?'

'I… I don't know.'

She was confused by this conversation, no idea where it sprang from or where it was leading.

'And when you love somebody, betrayal is harder to take. Institutions, you expect betrayal from them. Only a fool would be surprised when a regime – East or West – betrays its spies. When the tide turns. When the gutless politicians want to wipe their bloody hands. Yes. But men and women you have built a relationship with – a friendship? No. Then the betrayal is bitter. You don't forget it.'

'But how did Pierce betray you?' She didn't understand; she thought Jim had betrayed Pierce.

'Isn't it obvious? Pierce wanted me dead. Pierce was the one who betrayed me to the…'

She heard the crack and was blasted sideways in the same moment. She was in the sea, gulping salt, gasping. She twisted, inhaled brine. Crack again. On her back in the water. Reznik spinning and spinning and falling, bone and flesh confetti raining on the water. Splashing. Silence. His face next to hers, except half of it was missing, needle teeth bared like the dead pike she had seen with Anna, water lapping crimson, lights dancing green on the remnants of his skin. One eye, staring upwards. Lashless. Unblinking. A sharp pain jabbed her side. Had she been shot too? A breaker crashed over her head, filled her ears and eyes and mouth with water. She spluttered, lurched to her hands and knees, wriggled backwards, coughing, waiting for... for what? The sting of a bullet. The end.

Nothing happened. It must have been Pierce who shot Reznik. He had been there all along, hiding somewhere. He had spotted Reznik, stalked him around the hamlet, waited for the right moment to attack. Pierce had saved her life. She lay on the beach, winded, glad to be alive, the whiff of cordite hanging in the air, emerald rays sparking. She twisted her head, slowly, painfully, searched through the darkness, spotted the figure standing on the rocks behind her, revolver pointing in her direction. It wasn't Pierce.

CHAPTER 29

Orkney, 31 October 1989

'LUCKY.' HARRY WIPED his revolver on a cotton handkerchief, wrapped and stashed it in the inside pocket of his leather jacket.

'Lucky?' She glanced at Reznik's corpse, buffeted by the waves.

'Not him. You. Lucky I found you in time and my aim isn't too rusty.' He nodded, a gesture of self-approval.

She stepped back from the ocean, shook and flapped her arms, attempting to dry her drenched and salt-encrusted coat.

'Not a bad shot, if I say so myself.'

She should be feeling relieved, but the shock of the encounter with Harry's firepower had been way too much for rational reactions.

'You killed him.' She didn't bother to hide the tone of accusation.

'You think I should have politely asked him to stop pointing a pistol at your head, do you?'

The waves rasped Reznik's corpse over the pebbles, scoured the jagged edges of his skull. If Harry had waited before blasting Reznik's brains, she could have discovered more about Reznik and Pierce. The betrayal. Jim. Her life had been saved, but her chances of resolving the fears that plagued her were sinking in the Pentland Firth.

'What are you going to do with the body?'

'Leave it.'

'What, here?'

'The tide will claim him anyway.'

'Won't the police find him?'

'They'll think it's suicide.'

'With three shots in his head?'

'Stop worrying about details, will you?' He sounded exasperated. 'Give the skuas a couple of hours, then nobody will be able to count the holes. And he's got a pistol in his hand.'

Harry gestured at Reznik's fist, gripping the gun he had been pointing at her head. She was lucky, she could see now, Reznik hadn't squeezed the trigger in his death convulsions, otherwise she would be lying in the water next to him. She glanced at Harry and felt a belated surge of gratitude. He had saved her life.

'You are a good shot, Harry.'

He beamed.

'But there won't be any bullets missing from his pistol.'

He tutted, waded into the brine, stooped, oblivious to the breakers, fiddled with Reznik's hand, inserted his own fingers around his, aimed the pistol at the sea and pulled the trigger. The gun flashed and cracked as Harry discharged the bullets, the addictive perfume of gunpowder peppering the air.

'There. Nobody will be asking too many questions about him anyway. Not if they've got any sense.'

He searched Reznik's pockets, gave the corpse a prod with a plank of driftwood and launched him beyond the breaking point of the waves. He waded back.

'What about his car?' she asked.

'He doesn't have a car. He arrived by boat. Look.'

He pointed to the far side of the bay, the Noust – the landing spot once regularly used by fishermen, the rusting winch the only reminder of their laborious life. She could just discern the outline of a small dinghy. That explained the distant thrum of an engine as she approached the bay earlier that evening – outboard motor. A vast, lumbering figure was pushing the boat over the shingle to the water.

'Oh shit. That looks like his enforcer, Wolf.'

Harry shrugged. 'He didn't try to help Reznik, did he?'

'No.'

'Leave him. More trouble than he's worth. Don't want two bodies floating around. Anyway, with any luck, he'll wait until we've gone then pick up his ex-boss and dump him somewhere out at sea. He won't want to leave a trail that might lead back to him.'

Reznik had joked about Wolf's fishing skills – dropping more bodies than he caught. Too bad, she thought as she watched the dinghy skulking on the far side of the bay, that the joke turned out to be on him.

'How did you find me anyway?'

'I've had a busy couple of days. I got your phone message, couldn't contact you, heard Reznik was back, got wind he was on his way to Orkney, so I thought I'd better head north too. I knew Pierce was on Hoy – I've known that all along, in case you hadn't worked that out.'

She had.

'I took the ferry from Stromness this morning, managed to rustle up a car at Moaness, but drove the wrong way – headed south to Lyness. Fortunately for you, I went to the bar this evening and heard a ferryman talking about a young woman heading north along the coast road on a Honda 50. Not scared of Halloween ghosts, he said. I thought it might be you. I suppose that's the good and the bad thing about small islands – nothing goes unnoticed. I'd already ruled out Moaness, so that left the road to Rackwick Bay and I took it. Spotted the bike behind a wall. Honda 50.' He grinned. 'Where's your noodles then?'

'What?'

'Noodles. The Japanese made Honda 50s for noodle carriers. Semi-automatic. No clutch, see, so the takeaway drivers could carry a bowl of noodles.' He curved his arm to demonstrate.

She smiled – why had she ever doubted Harry? 'Did you have a Honda 50 then?'

'No, I was more of a BSA man myself, back in the day – the old beezer. British classic. To me a bike's not a bike if it doesn't leak oil on your trousers.'

He dug in his pocket, removed a torch, shone the beam on a sodden piece of paper he had fished out of Reznik's pocket. A driver's licence.

'That's odd.'

'What?'

He shook the document dry, inserted it in his jacket pocket. 'Never you mind.'

She knew better than to persist. Instead she asked, 'Were you going to warn Pierce about Reznik?'

'No. I was going to warn Pierce to stop playing his stupid bloody games.'

'What stupid games?'

'These stupid games he's playing with you – asking you to contact Anna for him. Playing the go-between. Jerk.'

'How did you know he asked me to contact Anna?'

'Because I wasn't born yesterday. I know what he's like. And I know what you're like too.'

'Somebody must have warned Pierce about Reznik, because he's disappeared.'

'MI5, and I suspect they were warning him about me not

Reznik. Because that's how far up their own arses they are.'

She decided not to mention the note the jogger had stuffed in her pocket. *Don't trust Harry.*

'Where does Pierce live then?'

She pointed. 'The white croft.'

His eyes didn't follow the direction of her finger; he tilted his head, gaped at the heavens. The intensity of the glow behind the hills had dimmed, but the green haze was still visible, a mysterious light in the dark. They both gazed for a while, held by the beauty of the swirling rays. Eventually she said, 'Harry, do you have any children?' She wasn't quite sure what had made her ask, and she thought as soon as she had said it that he would take offence. He didn't.

'Yes. A daughter, your age or thereabouts. I don't see her these days, though. Her mother, my ex, moved to Australia.'

She said nothing. They watched in silence until the emerald gleams had died.

The doorframe was splintered, the latch kicked clean away.

'There's no electricity.'

Harry found the paraffin lamp, fiddled with the wick, lit it with a Bic.

'Blimey. You've managed to make that lamp shine brightly. Pierce kept it dimmed.'

'You don't say. Sums him up if you ask me; keeps people in the dark.'

He held the lamp high, illuminated the chaos on the floor. Papers, envelopes, books, pens, photos. Reznik had taken the desk drawers, emptied them, kicked everything around as if he were having a tantrum.

'What do you think he was searching for?'

'Pierce's next hiding place possibly.' He nodded at the mess. 'He was pretty desperate to find him, it seems. Get shot of him. Wipe his slate clean.'

'Don't you think there might be more to it than that?'

Harry scooped up some of the papers, flicked through them. 'Hmm.' He dumped the papers on the kitchen table, tucked his hand in his jacket and removed the document he had retrieved from Reznik's corpse.

'See this driver's licence? It's fake ID, in the name of Freeman.'

She scrunched her face. 'The Freeman tape.'

'Exactly. Freeman was Pierce's cover name. According to Pierce.'

According to Pierce, said with a sneer.

'Why would Pierce and Reznik both use the same cover name?'

He plodded over to the window, the top of his head silhouetted against the star-splattered sky.

'Maybe they didn't.'

'What do you mean?'

'I mean, I'm not sure Pierce did use Freeman as a cover name. I think he just told his handlers he did.'

Sam shivered; the croft was freezing with its door kicked in and without the heat of the wood burner. She rubbed her hands, tried to concentrate.

'So if Freeman was Reznik's cover name, who taped the Libyan gun dealer?'

'Reznik, I would assume.'

'How did Pierce get the tape then?'

'He must have acquired it from Reznik somehow, passed it on to his handler, claimed he had taped the conversation and took the credit for exposing the Libyan arms link to the

Republicans.'

What else had Pierce lied about, she wondered.

'When I was with Reznik before you… well anyway, he was talking about the bond he had with Pierce.'

Harry raised an eyebrow.

'It sounded as if they had some sort of, I don't know, relationship going back ages.'

'There we go. They had a deal – information, cash. Both of them freewheeling, making extra dosh on the side, keeping their bosses happy with juicy snippets they'd got from each other. The Freeman tape would have been more valuable to our side than Reznik's, so he sold it.'

'And Reznik's side was…'

'The Soviets. I told you there was a rumour that Reznik went to the KGB after he left the StB.'

She had doubted him when he first told her and Pierce had dismissed the idea. She wasn't about to question Harry's word now.

'Reznik's real masters have always been in Moscow, if you ask me. Doubt whether he ever managed to cut that rope. No such thing as an ex-KGB agent.'

No such thing as an ex-spook full stop, she reckoned.

'Might be the end of the Cold War,' Harry ruminated, 'but I doubt that means the end of the Soviet secret state. Moscow – they'll play the long game. Patience. They can sit out the winter, enjoy the thaw, take their time to plan the spring offensive.'

A shooting star crossed the sky behind Harry's head. Or perhaps it was a satellite. She stuck her hands in her pockets.

'If Pierce and Reznik were exchanging information, doesn't that make them both some sort of double agent?'

'Possibly. Although in Pierce's case, I think the word double agent is too glamorous. Too ideologically motivated. Bit of a shit, I would say. Treacherous twerp. Does anything to advance his own interests and protect his reputation.'

'Oh god.' She had risked her neck for him.

'I did warn you.'

She felt ashamed that she had doubted Harry.

'What happened to Pierce in '76 then?'

'What do you mean?'

'I thought somebody – the Red Army Faction – found Pierce, roughed him up, questioned him and let him go. Or he escaped.'

'Pierce wasn't picked up by anybody. Where did you get that idea from?'

'I heard him talking about it with Jim – when Pierce dropped Anna off at our place and then here in Hoy. Fucking tortured, Pierce said. I asked Pierce about it earlier this summer and he as good as confirmed he had been tortured and questioned.'

'Then he was lying through his fucking teeth.'

Harry wasn't making sense.

'Well, what were Jim and Pierce talking about?'

'Jim, I would have thought.'

'My dad?'

'Yeah. Your bloody father. Reznik and his mates picked him up in June 1976, held him for fuck knows how long, gave him the cold bath treatment.'

'Jim? Questioned by Reznik?'

Of course, Reznik had told her as much when they were standing together on the shore; he had guessed she was Jim's daughter because she liked coffee. He had picked them both up – thirteen years apart – played the same favourite drink game with her as he had with Jim.

'How many times do I have to tell you?'

'Well, you've never told me before.'

'You didn't ask. And anyway, you know too much. Or not enough. A little knowledge, as you seem to have discovered, can be a very dangerous thing.'

She continued, undeterred. 'But when Jim was interrogated, do you think he give them any information about Pierce?'

'No. He said nothing about Pierce. He might have mentioned Davenport, but that was because he was sticking to his cover story, which was what he had been trained to do. He told them he was part of this...' Harry waved his hand, 'other organization who were trying to buy weapons. Davenport was their middle man. He had disappeared and he was searching for Davenport too because he wanted to find out what had happened to their money. And in the end, Reznik believed him and let him go.'

She rubbed her arms trying to generate some heat, remembered that endless sweaty summer; Jim had been absent for months before he reappeared without announcement in July.

'But then the rumour mill started churning,' Harry continued. 'Drip-feeding stories. Jim had been loose-tongued, handed over details about Pierce and his family to Reznik. All total bollocks. I talked to Jim about it that day you visited me in the allotment, told him I thought Pierce was the two-faced gob-shite source of all the crap and he would do best to steer clear.' He sighed. 'Jim didn't take my advice.'

And now she realized that she'd got it wrong too. She'd overheard Jim confronting Pierce about the rumours, but had misunderstood the fragments of conversation. *Fucking tortured. Water. Fault.* She had sensed the tension and she'd been scared. Her child's imagination had created a story to account for Jim's peculiar behaviour and the strange events of that difficult summer, a story that she'd buried deep, left to fester. When she talked to Pierce he'd drawn it out, picked it up, encouraged her to believe that her father was a traitor, the treacherous brother Antonio who betrayed Prospero and had him exiled to this island. What a jerk.

'Pierce is full of bullshit,' Harry said. 'Always was. Spins his stories to protect his own back. Deflect attention.'

Was that what he had been doing all along – pointing his finger in the wrong direction to cover his own actions? *Pierce was the one who betrayed me*, Reznik had said in the moment before he was shot.

'Do you think it was Pierce who let the Red Army Faction know that Reznik wasn't a straight arms dealer?'

'I would say so.'

'Why would Pierce betray his own informant when they had a good deal going?'

'Maybe he was worried he was about to be uncovered as a double dealer by Reznik, wanted to get rid of him. Dropped some information that he hoped would be a death sentence, one way or another.'

'What a shit.'

'Spies often are, I'm afraid.'

She sniffed, searched her pockets for a tissue, found a damp rag.

'One more thing, Harry...'

'Yes?'

'What was the organization Jim was monitoring, the other one that wanted to buy arms from Reznik?'

Harry's reply was sharp. 'You don't need to know that.'

'But why...'

'Look.' He put his hands in his pockets. 'I know it's difficult, but sometimes it's better not to know. Let it go.'

Perhaps he was right; she'd found out what she wanted to know. Jim hadn't betrayed and injured Pierce. Maybe she should listen to Harry this time.

She swooped, lifted a photo she'd spotted among the papers: Pierce somewhere exotic, palm tree behind him, white cotton shirt unbuttoned, arm wrapped around a young woman. What nationality was she? South-east Asian. Thai perhaps? Malaysian? She held the picture closer. The girl was very beautiful. Very young. It made her queasy looking at it. She stood, crossed to the kitchen bin, pressed the foot pedal, ripped the photo, let the pieces drop.

'What did you do that for?'

'Felt like it.' She didn't want to explain. She wasn't sure she could. Gut feeling, and not a good one. She returned to the mess Reznik had created on the floor, scuffed the papers with her boot. 'Perhaps Reznik was worried that Pierce was holding on to some incriminating evidence that he had paid him for information. Pierce told me he always kept records of payments. He admitted it was something of an obsession.'

Harry gave her a sidelong look. 'What a stupid bloody game this is. Egos. Office politics. All disguised as something more honourable. Defence of the realm. National security. What's the point of it all?' He gestured at the bay. 'Why would anybody bother with all that stupidity when they could have the sea and the cliffs? The Milky Way. Wouldn't mind living somewhere like this myself. Grow a few vegetables – plenty of seaweed for fertilizer. Fix up a wind turbine.'

'You could move here, now Pierce has deserted the place. Or do you think he will come back?'

Harry pursed his lips, sucked in air. 'Interesting question. The thing is, Reznik might be dead, but Pierce still has enemies lurking out there somewhere.'

'How do you know?'

'Somebody told Reznik where he would find Pierce. It

wasn't me. It wasn't you. It wasn't anybody in MI5 or the Firm. So there's somebody else who wants him out the way. Did you tell anybody where he was living?'

'No.' She hadn't told Tom or Karina.

She wandered over to the kitchen, filled the kettle, searched for tea bags – better than nothing – and spotted a small, familiar object: the blue mosaic tile she'd passed on to Pierce from Anna at the beginning of October. Pierce had left it abandoned in a corner when he fled. Didn't he realize how much these tiles, the Fisher King's treasures, had meant to Anna? Couldn't he even show some loyalty to his own daughter? She reached for Karina's pendant dangling around her neck, thought of the tile she'd found on Betty Corrigall's grave and her spectral apparition of Valerie running in the dark. Three tiles, three deserted women. She scooped the tile from the kitchen table and jammed it in her back pocket. She was a bit slow off the mark. She had given away Pierce's location to the person who wanted him dead; she just hadn't clocked she was doing it at the time.

CHAPTER 30

London, November 1989

THE RETURN FLIGHT from Kirkwall had been uneventful. She had slept through both legs of it, glad to be in the warmth of a plane even if it was delayed on the runway before takeoff. Becky had hardly noticed her absence, she'd only been away one night.

'Was the party any good?' she asked.

'What party?'

'You were wearing the Debbie Harry wig. I assumed you were going to a Halloween party.'

'Oh. Yes. Of course.'

She ran upstairs to her room, located *The Secret Island*. Removed the used chequebook from the envelope. She knew what she was looking for this time. She flicked through the stubs. Three of them, Pierce had carefully noted, were hefty cash withdrawals for payment to Freeman, all made in '74. That was why the name Freeman rang a bell when Harry first told her about the tape – she must have seen the name on the cheque stubs, registered it in some dusty memory file. Pierce had told her, back in September when he handed her three hundred pounds and noted it in a book as money for Ariel, that he had slipped up once with his records of cash paid to informers.

It was important to give your contact a unique code name, he had said – because he'd made that mistake with Freeman. If he was handing cash to Freeman, it raised the suspicion that Freeman was somebody else, not him. Pierce the hero. What a jerk. She replaced the envelope, removed the white tile she had found on Betty Corrigall's grave and dropped it in her pocket.

She slept and then she trudged to the phone box and called Anna's number. The phone rang and rang. She waited a day and tried again. No answer. She took the train to Blackheath, puffed up the hill to Anna's flat, rang on the door, banged and shouted. A neighbour appeared and said that Hilary had moved out suddenly and hadn't left any contact details. Anna had vanished again. She paced across the heath, brown in the violet light of dusk; reached the pond where she had met Anna the last time she saw her, watched the clouds gathering in the water. The heron landed, raised one foot and dipped its beak in the reflections. She re-ran their conversations, looking for something, anything that might give her a lead. She blew on her hands to warm them, and when that failed, jammed them in her pockets and felt the white tile she had found on Betty Corrigall's grave. Its marble iciness jolted her – and she remembered that Anna said she went to Valerie's grave in Norwood Cemetery on the evening of the anniversary of her death. Guy Fawkes night.

Sunday 5th November. A cold fog muffled south London, chilled her bones. She took the bus to West Norwood; located the side street to the cemetery's entrance. The gothic stone arch that once admitted black-plumed horse-drawn hearses dominated the end of the road. The left side of the arch was buttressed with a line of towering railings, erected by the Victorians to deter body snatchers. On the near side, two teenage girls – fifteen or sixteen – were puffing fags, leaning against the wall.

'Gate shuts at four today.'

'Thanks.' One hour until closing.

'Penny for the guy.' The girl nodded at a pile of rags propped up against the cemetery wall, dressed in a smiley tee shirt and clutching a bottle of Lucozade. She dug in her pocket for some loose change. The girl stuck out her mitt to take the coins.

Sam's hand hovered in the air.

'I don't suppose you know whether there's another way in to the cemetery do you?'

'What, you mean another gate?'

'Whatever. Just a way of getting in when the main gate is locked.' She wondered whether she needed to give them an explanation. 'I want somewhere to go for a spliff.' Spliff. They weren't into dope. They were into Es and rave parties. The girls exchanged a glance and she thought they were about to start giggling, but then one answered.

'Yeah. If you go back along this road, take the first left, walk to the end and there's a gap between the wall and the railing which is easy to get through. Everybody uses it.'

'OK. Thanks.'

She dropped the coins in the girl's hand. They ambled off, left the guy lying on the ground.

A magpie chattered and vanished in the mist as she walked under the arch. The twisted branches of oaks loomed like some old smoker's lungs, clotted with the black remains of discarded crows' nests. Norwood was once part of the Great North Wood, the stretch of forest that covered the hills of south London and north Kent. If the mist cleared, she reckoned she would be able to see Harry's allotment on the slopes of Gypsy Hill from here. But the fog wasn't clearing and the light was rapidly dwindling. She glanced at the stone mausoleums, the grass around their plinths severely trimmed. The regimented order of the tombs gave the cemetery an unsettled atmosphere, not at peace with death and encroaching nature. Norwood Cemetery had been created by the Victorians to accommodate the corpses that could no longer be buried in the overflowing city graveyards. Lambeth Council had taken ownership in the sixties and had started digging up the graves, chucking out the corpses and selling off the plots to raise some quick cash. In south London, nothing was sacred. The disinterred wraiths haunted every corner, moping around the monuments of the residents who had been too grand to be removed, resentfully watching the new bodies being motored in to take their graves. Even in death there was a hierarchy. Especially in death. The rich got to keep their resting places. The poor had been evicted.

Valerie had to be a resident of one of the recycled plots. She should be easy to find on the far side of the cemetery among the rows of shiny marble arranged more or less in date order. She ambled down the hill and was about to check the epitaphs on the first row when she heard footsteps behind. A jogger padded past; the whites of his swanky trainer soles vanished in the mizzle. She kept walking, not daring to stop until she could be sure she wasn't being watched.

A rocket shrieked – the first firework of the evening – a yellow flash dissolving in the watery vapour. The runner hadn't reappeared. She retraced her steps, eyes on graves, reading dates. She caught sight of a 5, stooped. Peter Grey. Loving father and grandfather. Born 1906. Died 31 September 1985. Right row. She edged along. Six graves in from the path she spotted a stone with the name *Valerie Archer* etched in the smooth surface. Archer must have been her maiden name. Born 3 July 1946. Died 5 November 1985. Christ, she was only thirty-nine when she died. How old was Anna? Two years older than her, born 1964. Valerie was only eighteen when Anna was born. She really was young. A girl. Like the phantom woman running down the road that night in Hoy. She wiped her forehead, sweaty, woozy. Getagrip.

She returned to the path, scanned the ground, spotted a rock lying against the neatly trimmed grass and shoved it with her foot until it was in line with Valerie's grave, marched on, headed for the main gate, left the cemetery behind and turned in to the High Street, spotted the jogger with the flash trainers in the distance, running north. Good riddance. A crack made her jump. She whipped around, caught the whiff of gunpowder and spotted two boys scarpering, lobbing bangers as they retreated. Another whoosh – pink, yellow, green artificial Northern Lights exploded in the grizzle.

She grabbed a coffee from a deli to warm herself, checked the High Street again. No joggers. Past four already – the main gate would be closed. She crossed the road, followed the directions she had been given, found the gap in the railings and slipped inside the cemetery. She was in among the grander mausoleums and Victorian angels with broken noses. She trod carefully around the graves, avoiding the uneasy spirits, made her way down the slope and found her marker stone, scanned her surroundings for a suitable hiding place, spotted a house-shaped tomb decorated with praying angels and barley twists. That would do – set back from Valerie's grave but close enough to see what was going on. She slumped behind the salmon granite plinth, tested the view, adjusted her position and waited, bum on damp soil, spider crawling over her leg, bangs and flashes blazing smudgy trails in the damp night sky. Hard to tell now whether the vapour hanging in the air was drizzle or smoke. A bat flitted past. Disappeared among some cedars then reappeared, swooped close to her head. Shouldn't it be hibernating? Maybe it had been woken by the fireworks. She tipped on to her hands and knees, crawled a few feet to get a better look, stretched and spotted a familiar figure. She retreated to the shadow of the tomb, heart thumping, watched as Anna approached, lit a candle in a glass jar, knelt and placed it on her mother's grave. Between the cracks of fireworks she heard a sob. Anna was crying. A lump formed in Sam's throat. She was wretched, spying on Anna. What was she playing at? She hugged her knees, regarded the sky, a silver shower raining, and wondered whether she should crawl away, leave Anna to her own devices.

A voice disturbed her. 'You can come out now.'

She didn't move.

'Sam, you fucker. I know you're there.'

That made her mind up for her anyway. She stood, made her way over to Anna, hands in pockets like a naughty schoolgirl.

'I thought you might be here. What do you want anyway?'

'I wanted to talk to you.'

'So you thought you'd hang around in a dark graveyard and leap out at me from behind a tomb?'

A rocket exploded.

'You didn't tell me how to contact you.'

'Well, perhaps there's a message there that most normal people would have absorbed.'

'Well, perhaps most normal people wouldn't send their mate

off on dangerous errands to see their ex-spy of a father who is being trailed by an arms dealer called the Butcher.'

'I didn't send you. You sent yourself.'

A scream broke their argument. A gang of kids ran down the cemetery path waving sparklers in the air.

'I'm sorry. I shouldn't have disturbed you at your mum's grave.' She glanced at Valerie's tombstone, the tea light flickering in its jam jar, and spotted another jar next to it, half buried with something darkish sitting in the bottom. She leaned over, squinted, swooped and stuck her fingers in – rainwater, woodlice, and then the smooth surface. Anna's eyes bored her back, but she didn't try to stop her. She scooped the tile out, realized there was another below and fished that one out too. The two red tiles Anna had given to Valerie.

'Two. Why two? I thought one was for your mum and the other one was for...'

Anna lunged forward, snuffed the tea light with her finger. 'Back.'

She indicated with her head, a beam sweeping the path in the distance, swirls of mist and smoke in its arc. Sam dropped the tiles in her pocket, and they retreated behind the barley twist tomb, watched the figure in a hooded windcheater descending the hill. He halted by Valerie's row, sidled across the grass, stopped by her headstone, inspected the grave with his torch, returned to the main path, and headed back up the hill.

'MI5,' Sam said.

'I know.'

'Do you think he came in through the gap in the railings?'

'Probably. Everybody does. Perhaps we should talk,' she added.

'We should leave before the spook comes back.'

'Yeah. This way.'

Sam trailed after Anna, the smoke making her wheeze. Up ahead, Anna had stopped at the far edge of the cedars, waving her hand frantically. Sam drew level, peered through the needles and saw the spook guarding the gap in the railing. They retraced their steps.

Out of earshot, Sam whispered, 'Do you think he knows you are here, or is he waiting to see if you turn up?'

'The latter, I suspect. If we wait long enough, he might go.'

'What if he comes creeping around the cemetery again?'

'We'll have to find somewhere where we won't be seen.'

'I know a good place. Although you might find it somewhat gloomy.'

The back entrance to the catacombs was in a corner of the rose garden on the site of the old chapel. She had been shown it by a mate who was employed by a Youth Opportunities Scheme to collect litter from the cemetery lawns. The catacomb entrance had been blocked for years, but the debris had been cleared when the council had been awarded a grant to build a café in the garden despite the fact, her friend had told her conspiratorially, that some of the corpses below contained anthrax. The entrance to the steps was taped off, a *Danger Keep Out. Falling masonry* sign the main deterrent to would-be explorers. A rickety wall shielded a plank-covered hole in the ground. It didn't take much effort to remove the planks and find the flight of steps descending to the darkness. Replacing the makeshift cover above their head was a more difficult task, but between them they managed, Sam shining her torch while Anna edged the boards back.

'Do you think he'll follow us down here?' Sam asked.

'Nope.'

'Mind, there's a puddle at the bottom.'

She jumped over it, stood for a moment, the whines of fireworks dimly audible through the walls. The air was damp and mouldy and held an odd metallic whiff, like dried blood on a childhood scrape, but still it was something of a relief to be away from the choking smoke of bonfires. She shone the torch around; white arches, cast-iron gates, the shelves and shelves of dilapidated coffins. Yellow eyes fizzled and vanished. Rats. A fox perhaps. She edged along the aisle, Anna behind her, directing the torch into the dark caverns on either side.

'Oh my god, are those all coffins on those shelves?'

'Yes.'

'They're rotting.'

'Only the outer cases.'

She swung the beam around a vault, illuminated wooden caskets decomposing, jet-black beetles scurrying from the light. 'They're all lead lined.' She swept the light along a shelf to demonstrate, caught a grey viscous goo oozing from the corner of a mouldering wooden shell. 'Or at least they are supposed to be.'

Anna gagged. Sam decided it was best not to mention the anthrax, shifted the light to the central aisle.

'What's that?'

Anna pointed to a large platform on a pole.

'A catafalque. Hydraulically powered. It's a lift. Services were held upstairs in the chapel and then the coffins were lowered down here on the catafalque.'

'How do you know all this?'

'I have a friend who works here.'

'You're obsessed with death.'

'I'm not.'

'You went on about plague pits when you stayed the night at my flat in Blackheath.'

She was about to defend herself, but Anna had a point; death played on her mind.

'I don't want to argue.'

'What do you want then?'

'I want to know why you told Reznik where to find Pierce.'

Anna sighed. 'There's no pulling the wool over your eyes.' Sam shone the torch in her face. 'Don't do that, you fuckwit.'

'Sorry.'

Their relationship still followed the contours laid down when they first met. Anna the leader, the scornful commanding officer. Sam, the subordinate, seesawing between attempts to win Anna's approval and trying to gain the upper hand.

'Is there anywhere safe to sit down in here? Can we sit near this...'

'Catafalque.'

'Yeah, that thing.'

They huddled, the cold rising from the earth below. Anna dug in the canvas bag she had slung across her chest, produced a bottle of water and a packet of raisins. 'Lucky I brought some provisions. We could be here a while.'

A rocket squealed.

'I'd better switch the torch off to preserve the battery.'

'OK.'

Faint shafts of light fell through the gaps in the boards covering the entrance. Something brushed her cheek. She yelped.

'It's me,' Anna said. 'I wanted to know where you are.'

'I'm here, right next to you.'

'Good.' She sounded scared. The darkness made it harder for Anna to lie, Sam thought. Or maybe it made her less likely to be misled by Anna's sparkling blue eyes, the generous smile.

Sam nudged her. 'Reznik.'

Anna said, 'You and me. Do you think we should start up our own intelligence business? Private eyes?'

'That's a terrible idea.'

'We couldn't make a worse job of it than the wankers who are employed as spooks by the state.'

Anna was trying to distract her.

'Reznik. Why did you tell...'

Anna interrupted. 'Why didn't you tell me in '76 that you'd seen Pierce in Orkney?'

'Because Jim told me not to say anything.'

'So why did you come and look for me thirteen years later? What's your game?'

'I bumped into Pierce in September when I was working at an archaeological site in Orkney. He told me he wanted to see you again. He wanted contact, reconciliation...'

'Reconciliation?' Anna shouted. Her voice echoed around the vaults. 'Are you dumb? I can't believe you believed that shit. What's wrong with you? He didn't want reconciliation.'

Her voice echoed around the crypt.

'What do you think he wanted then?'

'He wanted to control me, like he always did. He wanted to make sure I wasn't about to say anything bad about him to anybody, give him away. My guess is he knew that I was his biggest enemy, I was the person most likely to betray him, so he was trying to draw me in, find out what I was doing and thinking, bind me to his side. I wouldn't be surprised if he had a plan to fucking well kill me if he thought I was a risk to his bloody life.'

Part of her wondered whether Anna had lost it, raving down here in the dark about her father wanting to kill her, but she also recognized the truth of her assessment. Pierce was a controller, she had belatedly realized, a coercive manipulator who used people without a second thought about the risks to them. Prospero, master of the dark arts, lying through his teeth when he said he was about to put his books of sorcery aside. The man who always kept his paraffin lamps dimmed so you could never quite see what was going on.

'But why do you hate him so much?'

'Why do you think?'

'I don't know... I...'

'What have you got in your pocket?'

Sam fumbled. Her penknife. Something else. The two tiles she had found on Valerie's grave. Two. Anna had said she would give Valerie two of the red tiles, one for herself and one for her unborn child. Anna had placed them both on the grave. She squeezed them against her palm, their warmth comforting.

'You told me your sister had been taken care of.'

'I didn't want to talk about it.'

'Talk about what? What happened to your sister?'

'Nothing. There was no baby. My mum had a miscarriage when she was six months pregnant.'

Valerie had been about five months pregnant when she turned up at their house in '76; they had pitched up in July and the baby was due in November. She had seemed ill – frail – at the time. Forever lying down, wanting to rest, pallid, the sweaty sheen on her face. Sam had assumed that all pregnant women were like that: sickly. Anna had been worried. The two tiles must have been her prayer for protection; talismans to ward off disaster.

'I'm so sorry.' She didn't want to ask too many questions, although she could sense Anna was waiting for her to dig. 'Did something go wrong with the pregnancy?'

'Pierce.' Anna spat his name. 'That's what went wrong with the pregnancy. Fucking Pierce. He was a violent fucking bastard.'

The hairs on her arms stiffened; as soon as Anna said it, she could see the signs. Valerie's bullied and fearful demeanour, Anna's protectiveness of her mother. Sam had felt physically threatened by him as well and then dismissed her instinct. She felt stupid for not twigging earlier – she had worked in a women's refuge after all. She'd always thought the mosaic tiles, the Fisher King's treasure, told Anna's story, and perhaps her subconscious mind had recognized the pattern of abused women, screamed at her while she was riding past Betty Corrigall's grave. But her conscious mind had dismissed the obvious.

'Pierce was a wife-beater. A domestic abuser.'

'Yeah.' Anna gulped, swallowing her tears. 'He always was a domineering shit. But Mum thought he was having an affair and confronted him. He said it wasn't an affair, it was work related. He couldn't tell her about it because it was a state secret. And she couldn't say anything about it to anybody because that would put him in danger.'

'Bastard.'

'I hate the way the fucking spooks use their state secret bollocks to control their own bloody family. Step out of line and something nasty will happen. You can't say anything to anybody. What kind of crap is that?'

'It's total shit.'

Anna sniffed. Sam dug for a tissue, passed it to her.

'Anyway, she got pregnant. I suppose Pierce thought having a baby would shut her up. Except then she found a plane ticket for Paris and a photo of this woman and the gas bill for his supposed bloody safehouse. She asked him about it again. He flipped. Really flipped. He can't stand people challenging him.'

She remembered the strange tension of the conversations between Pierce and Jim that had left her feeling scared.

'He called her a slag and a whore and punched her in the belly. Told her she should get an abortion. Kicked her some more for good measure.'

'Why didn't she do anything? Leave? Call the police?'

'For fuck's sake, Sam. You know it isn't that easy. Even less so then. I mean, can you imagine what would have happened if she'd called the police in the seventies? If a plod had bothered to turn up at all, Pierce would just have had to tell him everything was OK and they would have listened to his accent, tugged their forelocks and backed away.'

Anna was right, of course.

'That day in Lewisham, when we went to the safehouse and the woman we followed, well, girl really...'

'I knew that was his girlfriend.' She sniffed again. 'We were always given this Pierce is a hero bullshit. You must have heard the story about how Pierce saved the whole of Western civilization by stopping this gun-running route between Libya and Ireland.'

'Yes, I had heard that story.'

'That added to the sense that somehow whatever Pierce did at home had to be excused, forgiven, because he was this big fucking hero, risked his life and all that crap...'

Sam felt gutted. She had fallen for the Pierce myth too, believed that he was the Fisher King, the wounded hero who needed help. Pierce, the brave spy.

'Valerie was relieved when he said he had to disappear,' Anna said. 'So was I. We were both glad to have a chance to get away from him, set up a new life by ourselves. But by then it was too late, the violence and the stress had already damaged her. You saw what she was like when she was staying with you. Not eating properly. Not sleeping. Scared.'

'And then she had a miscarriage.'

'Yes. Shortly after we left your place. And that really fucked her up. Not just the immediate effect. It did her head in and I think in some ways in the end it killed her, because she gave up caring about herself. Pierce had eaten away at her, made her feel she was worthless, deserved to be treated like shit. She knew she was ill, she knew something was wrong, but she didn't do anything about it. She let it go. It was almost as if she wanted to die.'

Anna was crying. Sam reached over, found her hand in the dark, wrapped her fingers around hers, said nothing; some comfort being among the dead, a reminder that nothing is permanent. The pain as well as the joy will end.

'Did Pierce know about the miscarriage?' she asked eventually.

'Somebody told him.'

'Do you think he realized it was his fault?'

'Of course he did.'

'Did he try to make contact?'

'No. Thank Christ. At least not then. Later.'

'He phoned you?'

'Yes. That's right. Eighty-five. After he heard Valerie died. He must have got my number from somebody in Intelligence. He phoned me, told me how much he regretted what had happened between him and Valerie, tried to tell me how much he missed me, how much he'd like to make amends.'

Sam thought of Pierce leaving the white tile on Betty Corrigall's grave; a tile for the woman who had been destroyed by the cowardly father of her baby. A community that judged her, not him.

'Maybe he really did feel some remorse. Guilt.'

She knew it was a stupid comment. *Once a bastard always a bastard.*

'Pierce feel remorse? He mopes around feeling guilty, but

332

it's all about him, isn't it? Poor Pierce and his awful burden. He doesn't give a toss about anybody else. He's a total self-indulgent control freak. Haven't you noticed?'

She had; she had seen his dark shadow – Prospero the manipulator – unnerved by the fleeting moments of threat. He had managed to control her, warp her thoughts about Jim, twist her arm into doing his bidding.

'Everything he ever said,' Anna continued, 'was a ploy, a way of roping us into his way of seeing things, doing what he wanted you to do. He couldn't cope with anybody who acted independently, thought for themselves.'

Sam couldn't let it go. 'Don't you want to have it out with him, though? Face your demons and sort it out?'

'Oh please, don't give me all that closure stuff. It's not what I want. You're projecting your own feelings on to me. Just because you're desperate to forgive your father doesn't mean to say that I should find a way to forgive mine.'

Sam stared into the dark. Her eyes had adjusted now and she could discern the outline of the vault in front of her, lime-flaked walls glowing faintly, the dull grey of the lead containers stacked. Was she desperate to forgive her father?

'Maybe Jim was never violent like Pierce,' Anna said. There was an uplift at the end of her sentence, more of a question than a statement. *Maybe*. Sam kept her eye on the vault, took a deep breath.

'Why are you sighing?'

'I don't know. It's just...' How old was she then? Fifteen. Standing in the kitchen, minding her own business one evening, conscious of his presence behind her. She had picked a glass up and it had slipped out of her fingers, fallen, splintered on the ground. An accident. She was about to bend down and collect the pieces but before she could move Jim was right there, behind her, fist in the air. 'You clumsy fucking...' She had raised her arm and blocked his blow.

'You've got no right to do that.' She had said it calmly. She had no idea where the words came from. One of the feminist books she had been reading maybe, fuck knows. But she said it as if she meant it, because she did. It was what she believed, and it worked. For her at least. Her words had an effect on him, she could see it in his face. Shame possibly. He knew when he was crossing the boundary. He had lowered his arm and walked away. The event had created a distance between them – or cemented the distance that was already there. But he hadn't done it again. Three years later she had ended up working in a women's refuge, seen women with black eyes and swollen face and it had put her own experience into perspective. Jim had his moments of aggression, but he wasn't that bad. And anyway, as she had discovered from Harry, perhaps there was a reason for his behaviour; the interrogation, the violence, near death by drowning. Perhaps it was wrong of her to make excuses for him. It didn't make his behaviour right, but it made it more comprehensible. She wasn't exactly forgiving him. Reconciling herself with his memory, drawing some kind of a line, searching for some peace with his legacy.

'Jim could be aggressive, but I don't think he was a total bastard. He was a bit of a tosser sometimes though.'

'You're right. He was a bit of a tosser.'

She could see the outline of Anna's face, her pale skin, her square jaw, and she remembered the last time they met in '76, by the dinosaurs in Crystal Palace Park, when Anna had taunted her with a secret about Jim, which she had refused to tell.

'What do you know about Jim?' she asked.

'Valerie told me about it. She said that Pierce had put some bits and pieces in an envelope in the safehouse that he meant to take with him when he left – including a photo of me and some details that revealed all sorts of stuff about his identity. He forgot to remove it. After he found out his cover was blown, he ran off to Paris, scared to go back because he knew the place was being watched. So, typical Pierce, he asked Jim to go and find the envelope. And Jim said yes. My mum always said she thought Jim was reckless, but brave. And kind.'

Sam had been irritated by Jim's attentiveness to Valerie when they stayed at their place but she could see, in retrospect, that he was right to be concerned – he must have recognized her vulnerability.

'But you told me Valerie said fools rush in when she was talking about Jim.'

'No, that was me being mean. Pierce told my mum that Jim wasn't careful and he got caught and handed the envelope over to this Czech and that was why he had to go into hiding and keep quiet about everything – because Reznik had a photo of me.'

Sam wheezed, a sharp intake of breath accompanied by mould spores and firework smoke. She started to cough. Anna patted her on the back.

'I'm OK. I'm OK.'

She wheezed again, tried to catch her breath.

'Here, have some water.'

She swallowed the cold liquid greedily.

'Pierce was lying.' She wheezed again. 'Jim didn't hand the envelope over.'

'How do you know?'

'I found it in '76. I went looking for you after our argument in Crystal Palace. I went back to the safehouse and found it in the garden.'

'Seriously?'

'I've still got it.' Sam gulped some more water. 'What a bastard.' If Pierce was Prospero the master of the dark arts then Jim was Caliban, she thought now, Prospero's abused and maligned slave.

'That's why I didn't care if he died,' Anna said. 'Because he's a bastard. I certainly didn't want some psychotic arms dealer coming after me because he thought I might know where Pierce was hiding. I dropped a note through the door at Execution Wharf – straight after you'd told me Reznik was there, in fact. You told me where Pierce was hiding, more or less.'

'I know. The tile on Betty Corrigall's grave.'

'Exactly. I guessed Orkney and looked it up in the *Rough Guide*. Collateral,' she added. 'That's what we are. Collateral. Pierce the bloody hero and their stupid operations, that's all Intelligence care about. They follow me around, but they're not protecting me, they're watching me to protect their precious bloody asset. So fuck that for a laugh. I wanted him dead.'

'Death doesn't resolve anything.' Sam waved her hand at the vaults, the shelves of decaying coffins. 'The dead are always with us. The arguments you had with them, the bad feelings, the unexplained memories – they don't disappear. They live on with you. It's better to deal with it now while he's still alive so at least when he goes you'll have some answers; you won't be left wondering or wishing you'd told him exactly what you thought.'

She felt Anna's hand on her arm. 'You know, when he phoned me after he had heard about Valerie's death and tried to engineer some great reconciliation between us I told him what I thought of him. I said as far as I was concerned, he'd murdered my mother and her baby and I'd left two tiles on her grave as a reminder of his crimes and I wouldn't be happy until he was dead. I haven't changed my mind.'

Sam screwed the lid on the water bottle, handed it back to Anna.

'Unfortunately your note to Reznik didn't work. Pierce got away.'

'So I gathered. Did you warn him?'

'No. He was gone before I got there.'

'Who was it then?'

'Some part of MI5.'

'Wankers.'

'Do you think that one guarding the gap in the railings has gone yet?'

'We could go and look. What can he do to us if he sees us anyway?' She said it with a hint of aggression. 'Why are they still watching me? Reznik is dead. Their precious asset Pierce is safe to do what he wants to do. Stay. Go.'

'Maybe Pierce told them that you said you wouldn't be happy until he's dead.'

'That would be typical Pierce. Keep an eye on my daughter. She's got issues. A bee in her bonnet. He's probably told them I've got Soviet connections.'

She was right, Sam thought, he probably had.

'They've given up watching me.'

'Have they?'

'I think so.'

'Well, that proves how stupid they are, because you were always far more dangerous than me. It was you who killed beetles in jam jars with crushed laurel leaves, after all.'

'Oh, not that again.'

'I was joking. What I meant was – I reckon you've got a ruthless streak.'

'Thanks.'

'I meant it as a compliment.'

Neither of them spoke for a moment. No more fireworks whizzing, only the drip drip of a dreary south London night. Guy Fawkes over for another year. Sam dug in her pocket, scooped out the two red tiles she'd picked up from Valerie's grave.

'Here, you'd better take these back.'

'No. You keep them. Do something with them.'

'What?'

'Dunno. You decide. What happened to the blue one? Did you give it to Pierce in the end?'

'I did, but he left it in his kitchen and I took it back.'

Anna laughed. 'When I was a kid he told me that he used coloured drawing pins to communicate with his contacts.'

'Reznik?'

'Probably. He said when they wanted to pass a secret message on, they stuck the pins in special places near escalators in underground stations. London. Paris. Prague. The colours all had different meanings.'

She knew it, Anna's mysterious code.

'What did they mean?'

'Red meant danger, be careful. Look after yourself. Blue meant all clear. Go ahead as planned. And guess what white meant.'

'I can't.'

'There's a traitor in the house.'

Anna cackled wildly. Sam joined in, their laughter echoing around the vaults. No wonder Pierce had tried to get rid of the two white tiles Anna had sent him in '76. And had been reluctant to take Anna's blue tile when she gave it to him in the summer. He must have always wondered what games his daughter was playing with him, whether she would outwit him in the end.

Anna stopped laughing. 'Have you still got the red one I gave you?'

'I left it in a secret place on Hoy in '76.'

Sam could hear Anna's brain whirring. 'Perhaps you should go and get it then.'

Sam sighed. She hated Pierce for manipulating her and Jim, but she still couldn't help being pleased when Anna gave her a part in one of her plots. Maybe she was looking for an excuse. 'I don't suppose you know where I can find a hand gun, do you?'

'Actually, I do. Why, do you need one?'

'I don't know yet. I haven't worked it out.'

She felt Anna's hand in her pocket. 'If you do, that's my new number. Give me a call.'

CHAPTER 31

London, 7 November 1989

SHE WAS TRYING to concentrate on her research proposal. She had a title, but little else. *The Earl's Bu: seeing below the surface*. The ringing of the phone startled her. She ran down the stairs but Becky had beaten her to it.

'Tom,' she mouthed, smirked and passed her the receiver.

He wanted to meet and talk. There was a heaviness in the way he asked that made her fear he was going to have some kind of conversation about relationships, which she didn't want. On the other hand, she did want to find out what he had been doing. She agreed to meet him at their usual place.

'I knew you had something going with Tom,' Becky shouted from the kitchen.

'I don't.'

She wrapped herself in her overcoat, pulled a woollen beanie down to her brow. The wind had cleared the mist that had hung around for days. Rain slanted through the street lamp's arc. She lowered her head against the gusts, lumbered along the railway viaduct, choosing the darker path beside the boarded arches; squatted nightclubs and raves over for the summer, the muddy patch behind the Vauxhall Tavern furred with fag butts and plastic beakers. There was an end-of-year sadness in the air.

End of decade. End of era. She cut through the furthest arch, opposite the chainlink fence that guarded the wasteland below Vauxhall Bridge. Dumper trucks and cranes visible behind the crosshatch wire; signs of serious construction. Vauxhall, Jim's favourite bridge, the place where he had died. In her head, the wasteland and foreshore were his memorial garden, and now it was being concreted. She was being stupid. Sentimental. She should let it go. Life, like the river, flows on. The tide was high. The loops of embankment lights were shining, but the muddiness of the water dulled their reflections. Everything was drab this evening. A jogger brushed past her as she climbed the steps to Westminster Bridge. Sam stared at her sweaty back, but she didn't turn. As she had told Anna, Intelligence had given up following her.

Tom was sitting outside the café with a cappuccino in front of him. Seeing him there made her laugh; who else but Tom would sit outside in the wind and rain? Well, who else apart from Tom and her? They were similar in their odd habits. She sat at the bench opposite him across the table.

'Why are you sitting out here?'

'I prefer it to being inside.'

'So do I.'

Silence. Sam didn't usually mind silences – she often instigated them – but this one was awkward. 'I'll go and get a coffee.'

She returned with her espresso. A firework exploded over the river; its whizz and bang dampened by the rain. Tom jumped anyway, the coffee cup in his hand jiggling, foam and liquid spilling down his coat.

'Shit.'

'It's only a rocket. Some kids must have had one left over from Guy Fawkes.'

'I know that.' He sounded defensive. 'You'd jump every

time you heard a rocket going off if you'd spent six months in Afghanistan.'

'I wasn't mocking you.' She folded her arms, felt bad. She usually did mock Tom about his time in Afghanistan, tended to dismiss his stories as showing off. It wasn't as if he was a soldier risking his life. All he did was take a few notes. 'Do you think your stint in Afghanistan affected you badly in some ways?'

He raised an eyebrow; it wasn't usually her who asked the personal questions. 'Yeah. My mum was having a go at me the other day. She said I should go and talk to somebody. She came to visit me in my flat and she wanted to know why I'd chosen to live in a war zone.'

The fluorescent strip-lights of the Barrier Block flickered in her mind. 'She's got a point.'

'Post-Traumatic Stress Disorder.'

'What about it?'

'My mum thinks I might have it.' He wiped his coat with a paper napkin. 'You know what it is then?'

'Yeah. I read something about it the other day in some journal or other I was leafing through in the college library. It's when you experience some kind of shock, isn't it? A near-death experience and can't deal with it.'

'That's right.'

'Did you have a near-death experience in Afghanistan then?'

'Not exactly. But it was six months of constant stress and fear about my safety. Not to mention a high death rate among the Afghans I was staying with. PTSD can be caused by prolonged exposure to stress, apparently, as well as one specific event.'

'What are your symptoms?'

'Flashbacks. Nightmares. Irritability. Some people deal with the trauma by distancing themselves emotionally from everybody around them.'

He gave her a meaningful stare which she wasn't sure how to interpret.

'Do you think you've got it then?'

'Possibly.'

A mangy pigeon hopped on to their table; she shooed it away.

'Do you have flashbacks?'

'Yes, sometimes. And I do some wacky things when it comes to relationships.' He gave her another meaningful stare. 'You know. Sleep with people without really connecting with what I'm doing.'

Oh, now she understood the funny looks – he wanted her to know he only slept with her because he was emotionally fucked up. If he didn't have Post-Traumatic Stress Disorder he wouldn't have bothered. Charming. PTSD, a licence to behave like a dick. Sod him. Although, of course, she had only slept with him because she wanted to prise some information out of him, but that wasn't the point.

'I'm sorry,' he said.

'For?'

'Well, you know, the other night. I wanted to clear the air earlier, but you didn't seem to be around.'

'No need to apologize. I only slept with you because I've got Post-Traumatic Stress Disorder as well.'

He pulled his baffled face.

'Yes. Prolonged exposure to stress when I was a kid, growing up with a wacko dad who did a mad job. I can see, now you list the symptoms, it's what I've got. It explains everything. I only ever sleep with people I have no emotional connection with whatsoever.' She swigged a mouthful of coffee. 'Like you.'

He seemed momentarily stumped, and then he smiled, realized she was joking, sort of. 'You're not bothered then?'

He sounded disappointed.

'No.'

'Good.' He leaned forward on the table. 'You know, there might be some truth in you and the PTSD.'

She glared.

'Seriously. Perhaps Jim's job did have a lasting impact on you. Emotional numbing, that's what it's called. When you try and distance yourself emotionally from people and events.'

It was true, Jim's job had put pressure on all of them – at the time and later, in the aftermath of his death. But she wasn't sure she had a psychological disorder. She thought about her evening in the catacombs with Anna; Sam hadn't tried to distance herself from Anna, she wanted to talk. That was why she had followed Pierce in the first place. She wasn't running away or numbing herself. She was doing her best to deal with her father's legacy in her own peculiar way.

'I don't think I've got PTSD. I can see that when I was a teenager I dealt with a lot of painful stuff, including my dad's death, by cauterizing it. I probably came across as emotionally detached. You know what, though, I didn't really have much choice – it was a survival strategy.' Getagrip. 'I'm not sure how else I could have dealt with it. Now it's not necessary, I don't do it.'

Not much anyway.

He squished his mouth from side to side as if he was considering her answer, which she found irritating. In Tom's case, she reckoned, it wasn't that she was playing at being detached, more that she was aware that their relationship wasn't particularly healthy, even if she did like him.

'Let's go for a walk,' he said.

They strolled along the Albert Embankment, crossed Westminster Bridge. Big Ben struck nine.

'I've dropped the story about Davenport and the Czech arms dealer.'

'Your editor wasn't interested?'

'Well, it never was much of a story, but it wasn't that. I was paid a visit.'

'Oh?'

'Welsh bloke.'

She coughed, patted herself on the chest. 'A Welshman? What was his name?'

'He didn't tell me.'

Harry wouldn't.

'What did he say then?'

'He said he worked for Intelligence and he'd heard I was pursuing a story about some old MI6 sting involving a Czech arms dealer and a bunch of terrorists.'

She didn't dare look at Tom, although there was nothing in his voice to suggest he suspected her of ratting on him, that Harry's appearance was anything to do with something she might have said. He had to be a bit dim if he couldn't guess, though – who else could it have been?

'I think Karina got scared because she'd given away too much,' he said. 'She must have had a contact somewhere.'

'Yes, that sounds plausible.' Even if it wasn't true.

'This Welsh bloke said there was no way I could run the story.'

'Did he threaten you?'

'Not exactly. He said I was out of my depth – being naïve. He said it wasn't the way it worked – not with the press and the secret services. Too many people in high-up places in Fleet Street have too many friends in Intelligence. He's right, of course, they all went to school and college together. It's an Old Boys' club, isn't it. The Establishment. Class loyalty. The press is as much part of it as...' he waved his hand in the direction of the Houses of Parliament, 'that lot. He was quite nice about it actually.'

Good old Harry.

'Although he looked like a bruiser. Broken nose. Hefty build. Not somebody you'd like to meet in an alley on a dark night.'

No.

'He was right, of course. It was a bit optimistic to think I could run with a story about the Firm. It was never going to get very far. It's not even my brief. The security correspondent would have done his nut.'

Tom didn't seem too upset.

'He gave me a good snippet of info, though, which I think I can use.'

'What's that then?'

They had reached Lambeth Palace. Tom crossed to the embankment wall, leaned, peered upstream to Vauxhall.

'You know that derelict piece of land up there by the bridge, the one you told me about?'

'By the mouth of the Effra run-off? Near where Jim died?'

'Yes. Guess who has bought it.'

'I can't.'

'MI6.'

She spluttered. 'MI6? The Firm?'

'Yes. Apparently they've called in all these big-name architects and they're planning some huge edifice. Changing times. They're coming out of the shadows. New era of transparency... Well, the building's not going to be discreet, put it that way.'

The news annoyed her. Jim would have been irritated. MI6 – bunch of public school boys – building on his grave?

Tom straightened himself. Scratched the back of his head. He was about to say something awkward.

'I suppose I'd better say goodbye then.'

'Yes.' She certainly wasn't inviting him back to her place again.

'No. I mean I'm going. I'm leaving the country.'

'I didn't think it was that bad.'

'Not because of you.'

'I was joking.'

'Oh, OK.'

'Where are you going?'

'The States.'

'What about the *Sunday Correspondent*?'

'What about it? It's a new paper. It might float, it might not. I'm not sure I can be bothered to hang around and find out. Anyway, I've been offered a job on the *Miami Herald*.'

'Miami? Isn't that another war zone? All those drugs and mobsters.'

'Possibly. But there was a vacancy for a crime correspondent. The last one left because he got fed up with writing reports about toddlers drowning in jacuzzis while their parents were snorting coke.'

'Great.'

'You know, I think the best way to deal with your fears is to face them. It's no good hiding.'

She decided not to reply, watched the clouds scudding across the moon.

'I'd better go now,' he said.

'Me too.'

A polite kiss and they parted. She was glad they had left each other on good terms. She paced on, turned away from the river, down a side street. She didn't want to pass the building site, not now she knew it was owned by the Firm. And she didn't want to watch Tom walk away, didn't want to look over her shoulder and see he wasn't turning to watch her go. A drop of water trickled down her cheek. Raining again. No. She was crying.

CHAPTER 32

London, November 1989

'WELL, GOODBYE TO the Cold War,' Sam said as they watched the BBC report of the Berlin Wall being dismantled by the crowds. The end of the German Democratic Republic, the Stasi, the StB, the Iron Curtain, the ideological East–West wars and counter-wars. Although possibly not, according to Harry, the end of the Soviet secret police, the KGB. They would wait it out one way or another, hang on through the thaw.

'Goodbye and good riddance. Something positive to celebrate,' she added.

'The anniversary of Kristallnacht,' Becky said.

'Oh, is it?'

'Yep. The ninth of November 1938. The beginning of the end. If you were Jewish and you weren't out by then, you'd probably never get out.'

Becky opened a bottle of San Miguel with her teeth, necked its contents.

'Do you think the protestors planned to do it today, on the anniversary?'

'I don't know.'

'I wonder whether it's a good or a bad omen.'

'It feels quite ominous to me. Spooky. God knows exactly what that wall was holding back – on both sides. Anti-semitism doesn't just evaporate, it runs too deep.'

She thought of the Red Army Faction, their attempts to root out fascism in the West sliding into violence and support of the totalitarian East. They stared at the screen in silence, the ebullient tone of the reporter suddenly sounding off-key.

Sam arranged to meet Liz at Jim's grave, 12th November. Their wedding anniversary. Liz was busy – autumn term and she had been made Head of the Department. Roger, the former head and Liz's partner after Jim's death, had run off with one of his students and found himself some well-paid professorship on the West Coast of the States. Not Ivy League, Liz had pointed out scathingly. She had applied for his vacated post and yes, she added, she would jump in his grave just as quickly. It was a Sunday and Liz had said they could meet in the afternoon, but then she realized she had to prepare some paper so she phoned and they postponed it until the evening. Sam drove south to the periphery of London in Becky's Moggie Minor, arrived before Liz.

Dark already, the evening clear, she strolled through the familiar graveyard, the grass and fallen leaves on its shaded side still embalmed in an icy coating from the previous night's deep freeze. Jim's headstone was to the south. The bony trunks of the birches beyond the churchyard gleamed. The silver disc of the moon shone through the tangled branches, rising so fast she could almost see it moving. By the time Liz arrived, it was swinging above the canopy of the small copse.

'Full moon,' Sam said.

'Jim would have liked that.' Liz remembered Jim more kindly with the passing years, Sam reckoned. Or perhaps Roger doing a bunk with a younger woman had given her a different perspective on her late husband. Liz was carrying a carved turnip head, dried and shrivelled, its gaping mouth grotesquely twisted.

'Jess gave it to me to put on the grave. She turned up for Halloween and Helen came down for the day as well. They carved it together before going off to the pub.'

'They had a Halloween celebration without me?' The injustices of being the younger sister excluded from her older sisters' activities still rankled.

'Jess said she phoned you in the morning to see if you wanted to come over, but Becky said you weren't there.'

Of course; that was the morning she was running around buying a plane ticket to Kirkwall. She had spent Halloween on Hoy – she had already shoved that night as far down in her memory as possible.

Liz stooped, placed the gnarled lantern in front of the headstone.

'Have you got a light?'

Sam jiggled in her pocket, produced a box of Swan Vestas, squatted and lit the tea light Jess had left inside the lantern. The candle spluttered and, when she placed the lid on top, burned black smoke that filled the air with the sourness of mouldy turnip.

'Did you bring the tile?' Sam asked.

Liz nodded.

Sam fiddled in her coat pocket again, removed the tiles she had collected, held them in her left palm and counted them off one by one into her right. The two white tiles Anna had given to Pierce – one on a pendant from Karina, the other found on Betty Corrigall's grave. The blue tile that Sam had retrieved from Pierce's kitchen. The two red tiles that Anna had placed on Valerie's grave – one for her mother and one for the baby that was never born. Five tiles. Liz rummaged in her bag and removed the sixth, the red tile Anna had given her because she thought Liz was cool. Only one missing – the red tile Sam had buried at the Raven's Nest behind Pierce's croft. The summer of the heatwave. Anna's instruction to Sam to deal with the tiles had felt like a challenge, a fulfilment of the bond they had sealed in '76 when they had cut their thumbs with her rusty penknife and become blood sisters. Miranda charging Ariel with a final task. Sam had decided it was fitting to leave them on Jim's grave. She had brought an empty Marmite pot with her to hold them.

'Where does this come from anyway?' Liz lifted her glasses and examined her tile. 'I've never looked at it properly before. I dumped it in a drawer and forgot about it.'

Liz's question made Sam feel sheepish. She had long ago ceased thinking about the tiles as stolen ancient artefacts – in her mind they were the Fisher King's treasures. Anna's colour-coded grand design which told the story of her and Pierce, Valerie and Karina, Sam and Liz. And Jim who was, Sam reckoned, the ghost in the machine. Sam wasn't prepared to confess their true origin to Liz.

'How extraordinary. It looks just like the Roman mosaic tiles I saw when I went on a Mediterranean trip with Roger.'

Sam remembered Liz going on that trip – '86. She had always hated Roger and she had been annoyed with Liz for bunking off with him and enjoying herself when she was still dealing with the emotional aftermath of Jim's death.

'Yes. We were in Corinth, and I wanted to visit a Roman villa, but Roger was being ridiculously snotty and said he didn't come to Greece to visit Roman villas, so I went on my own, left him sulking in the hotel. It was probably the best day of the holiday. There was an incredibly interesting tour, and I was given a Roman mosaic tile to hold. There's something about the weight and density...'

She held the tile in the air and the moon cast a silvery light on it, made it glisten in the dark.

'Something… magical,' Liz added.

A crow landed on Jim's gravestone, caught Sam's eye, winked and flew away.

'You're right, they are Roman tiles actually.'

Liz lowered her arm. 'Really?'

Sam stuck her boot in a tussock of grass, nudged it with her toe.

'They come from Blackstone Villa.'

'Sam. I hope you didn't steal them.'

Were you ever old enough not to feel like a naughty child when your mother told you off?

'It wasn't me.' She was about to blame Anna. What a cowardly thing to do. She had to take her share of responsibility.

'It was both of us. Anna and me in '76.'

'Anna. That poor girl, and her mother who didn't look much older than her daughter and was pregnant, poorly and having to deal with her husband's… issues.'

'That's right. And Anna and I were left to our own devices.'

'You never took kindly to being told what to do…'

'It wasn't a criticism. I was just saying, we were doing our own thing and we cycled over to Blackstone…' She smiled when she remembered that day. 'We were acting out the Fisher King.'

'The Fisher King? Chrétien de Troyes? *Perceval*?'

'If you say so.'

Sam could see she was on to a winning line here – Liz was likely to judge a crime less harshly if she thought the act had some literary merit.

'I was going by Jim's version, which he claimed came from the Celts – the wounded king who is supposed to be guarding a precious object, the holy grail, but it gets stolen from him. So we were pretending to be Celtic warriors – well, I was a Druid with magical powers and Anna was Boadicea, and we decided the tiles were the stolen treasure, the sacred objects of the Celts that the Fisher King was guarding, so we had to reclaim them. It was the year of the drought – do you remember? And I reckoned if we reclaimed the sacred objects, we would heal the Fisher King and it would rain. And, in fact, as soon as we had pocketed the tiles, there was a thunderstorm. Well, actually there wasn't; in the end the storm didn't break. It was all rumble and no rain.'

'Yes, but that's not how the story is resolved anyway.'

'Oh?'

'In Chrétien's version, the king can be cured if Perceval, the young knight, asks the right question, but he never does.'

'What's the question?'

'The healing question? It's, who does the grail serve? To me it's a myth about wounded masculinity and...'

Sam dropped the tiles into the Marmite pot which she had removed from her coat pocket.

'Sam, you can't leave those on Jim's grave. You have to take them back to Blackstone.'

Sam swirled the tiles around the pot.

'Jim wouldn't want you to leave them on his grave, I'm sure. I'll say one thing about your father: he always had the greatest respect for ancient monuments.'

Sam couldn't help laughing. 'Well, I suppose he wasn't all bad then.'

'I didn't mean it like that. Of course he wasn't all bad. Your father had some very impressive qualities, even if in his later years they were...' She trailed off, shook her head. 'I don't know what happened; he wasn't always that difficult. He didn't always drink that much.'

'Do you think he might have suffered from Post-Traumatic Stress Disorder?'

'Post-Traumatic Stress Disorder? What's that?'

'It's when you suffer from some sort of physical or emotional shock and it traumatizes you, and you have flashbacks and get angry and think you're about to die all over again.'

She could see Liz frowning, the moonlight highlighting the deepening lines on her face. She sighed, said nothing.

'Didn't he have nightmares?' Sam persisted.

'Yes, he did. He used to wake up thinking he was drowning, fighting for air...'

She remembered. Her recurring dream – waking up and hearing somebody shouting, not knowing whether it was real or in her head.

'Why didn't he do anything about it? Why didn't he get help?'

'I don't know, Sam.' Her voice had an edge to it. 'Nobody offered him any help. We didn't think about things like that at the time. Post-Traumatic Stress Disorder. It's life, isn't it, and you have to get on with it. People deal with things in different ways. I suppose I dealt with it by getting on with my job and trying to jolly you lot along and looking for comfort in literature. Jim dealt with it by drinking and going for long walks and, I suppose, telling his stories...'

'The Fisher King.'

'Yes, the Fisher King. Or his version of it.'

Sam wiped her eye. 'When he told me that story I thought he was talking about somebody else, but now I think the Fisher King was him. He was saying he was wounded and I didn't realize it.'

'Of course you didn't. You were only a child. And maybe he wasn't talking about himself, maybe he was trying to amuse you with an interesting story.'

'What was the healing question again?'

'Who does the grail serve?'

She tipped the tiles out of the Marmite pot, replaced them in her pocket. 'I'll take them back to Blackstone.'

'Good. Look at the moon. It's so bright, and the craters are so clear.'

'It's a perigee moon.'

'A what?'

'Perigee. The moon looks bigger when it's at its closest point to the earth – and tonight the perigee has coincided with the full moon.'

'Perigee moon. That's the kind of thing Jim would have known.' Her voice cracked. 'People aren't perfect. People get things wrong and make mistakes. Of course they do. Sometimes you just have to let these things go.'

She leaned, lifted the turnip lantern's lid, snuffed the candle with her fingers. 'Let's leave the lantern here. The squirrels can eat it.'

'Do you think the squirrels have given up hibernating?'

Liz stood. 'I'm not sure they ever did hibernate. Maybe I've forgotten the details.' She smiled, started back along the path and glanced at the moon, high in the indigo sky, as she left.

One of her tutors had the name and number of the Blackstone site director, which she had given Sam after she had made up some story to account for her sudden, desperate interest in Roman villas. The director was called Lucy. The site was closed to the public from October through to March, but after Sam had explained the issue, Lucy agreed to meet her there on the fifteenth. Sam drove to the site. She thought she'd be able to find it on autopilot, but they had built a new bypass – a feeder road for the M25 – and it confused her. Eventually she found the lane which she used to cycle along. It had been tamed; overbearing privet hedges cut down to size, newer, blander houses sprawling up the hill. Creeping urbanization, the periphery seeping south. The site of the villa was more orderly too – the straggling riverbanks cut back, the golf course swallowing the land which had once been wild. Men in Rupert Bear trousers dragging caddies over the places where she had once played, built dens, pretended to be a Celtic rebel with Anna.

And the site itself had been tarted up, made into a more appealing tourist attraction with a shop selling crap Roman-style jewellery and Airfix models of centurions. It was a positive change, though, that it was a woman who came to greet her, not some leering bearded man. Lucy, she said, and offered Sam her hand to shake. Mid-thirties Sam reckoned, in DMs, jeans, with a pierced nose and cropped hair. She wasn't judgemental or too inquisitive, although Sam still wasn't inclined to tell her the whole truth. She said she had a friend who had a brother, and the friend had found the tiles in his bedroom and he had boasted about taking them from a mosaic at Blackstone.

As soon as Lucy saw the tiles, she identified the part of the mosaic where they belonged. She laughed, more concerned about getting them back than creating a fuss about how they had gone missing. Very sensible. Sam followed her around the walkways to the mosaic; the rampant bull running off with a passive naked woman on its back, some diaphanous wisps of cloth across her stomach. The sea was blue, the bull was white and the woman was outlined in red, a gap of bare earth where the woman's butt joined the bull's back.

Lucy removed her boots, lowered herself, trod lightly around the edge of the mosaic, then across to the bare patch. She ducked and arranged the tiles Sam had handed her. They filled the space exactly, apart from one missing square in the woman's outline.

'There.' She stood back, hands on hips. 'What do you think?'

'Good fit.' She didn't say anything about the missing piece, neither did Lucy.

Lucy retraced her steps, joined Sam on the walkway.

'To be honest,' Sam said, 'I've never been entirely sure about this mosaic.'

'Why not?'

'It gives me the creeps. What's happening to that poor woman on the back of the bull? Who is she?'

'The woman is Europa.'

A gust of wind howled under the eaves of the building, rattling the roof.

'The bull is Jupiter. It's a Greek myth that the Romans adapted. I suppose it's a foundation story, an origin myth of sorts. It was originally Zeus and Europa, but the Romans changed Zeus to Jupiter. The gist is the same, though – Jupiter saw Europa, fancied the pants off her, turned himself into a bull, abducted her, carried her away on his back and raped her. Then made her queen of Crete.'

Sam frowned. 'And they wanted to celebrate that story in a mosaic?'

'It's not a particularly enchanting tale, I grant you. But there haven't been many societies where violence against women isn't the norm, and women aren't regarded as second-class citizens.'

She half wished she hadn't brought the pieces back, kept Europa's backside forever safe from Jupiter in a Marmite pot on Jim's grave. Anna, Sam remembered, had insisted the tiles were loose at the edge of the mosaic, which wasn't quite true. She suspected Anna had deliberately taken the tiles marking Europa's private parts, trying to protect her from the violence of Jupiter.

Lucy dusted her hands. 'Well, thank you for returning the tiles.'

Sam departed the villa and wandered along the riverbank. The water level was much higher than it had been in the drought of '76, but everything else seemed diminished. Less magical. Perhaps it was because she was older. Or maybe it was simply because the year was dwindling and the grotto of overarching green leaves was now a ribcage of bare branches. Or maybe it was because she didn't have Anna by her side. She found a gap between the trunks of an ash and a willow, slid down the bank to the river's edge, the swollen brook carrying twigs and fag packets from the wood at the top of the hill. This was where they had played that summer, Anna and her, the defenders of the Fisher King, recovering his lost treasures from Blackstone. What was it Liz had said about the story's resolution? The young knight was supposed to ask the healing question – who did the grail serve? Anna had always known that whoever the grail served, it wasn't her. Or Valerie. Or Sam, or Liz. Or Karina. They were all collateral. She crouched by the water's edge, dabbled a finger in the brook, swirled it around, withdrew it when she spotted the serpentine body of a pike, hanging in the shallows. Still, Anna had nearly got her revenge. After all, it was Sam's account of the tile on Betty Corrigall's grave that had helped Anna deduce Pierce's location. The thought cheered her; Miranda had almost upended the story with the tiles she had stolen and distributed, used Ariel to disarm Prospero and rid him of his sorcerer's dark powers. A fat rain drop pocked the river's surface. Then another, and another, the brook a mass of bubbles and ripples. Time to go.

CHAPTER 33

London and Orkney, December 1989

SHE PULLED HER edition of *The Collected Poems of T. S. Eliot* from the shelf and found the page and line she was after. *The Waste Land*, the verse about the Fisher King, the one Pierce had pointed out to her when he was explaining Lamb's code. The king fishing in the dull canal with the arid plain behind him and the shipwreck of the king's brother ahead. He liked those lines, he said, which joined the myth of the wounded Fisher King with Prospero, the patriarch exiled on his island. He liked them so he could have them back. She would chuck them in his face. Lamb's code. She wrote the alphabet and each of the corresponding letters taken from the lines of *The Waste Land* underneath, and then used the key to send Pierce the message. She wanted to let him know she had something that might interest him – an envelope she had found. It contained a photo and a used chequebook in the name of Davenport. She didn't add that on three of the stubs somebody had written *cash for Freeman*, that all the payments were made in 1974 and, in total, they amounted to a hundred thousand pounds. He didn't need her to fill in the details: that Freeman was Reznik's code name and that Pierce had paid him cash for his information. And probably sold him some of his own secrets too.

Spies. They were all the bloody same. Seriously. Who would trust a spook? He wasn't even competent – he'd lectured her about the superiority of Intelligence tradecraft, scoffed about police spies and then he'd left the envelope with the crucial evidence that revealed his duplicity and a photo of his daughter in his own safehouse. He'd sent a police spy to retrieve the envelope. And then she, the copper's daughter, had found it when she lifted a plank in the back garden because she wanted to be Charles Darwin and liked looking for beetles. But his main weakness, his Shakespearean flaw, was not incompetence. It was cowardice. According to Pierce, he was a hero. As far as she was concerned, he was a coward and a violent bully.

She slipped the coded note in an envelope, addressed it to his PO Box number, dropped it in the gaping red mouth of a letterbox, hoped that nobody would intercept it or, if they did, wouldn't be able to decode the message and would pass it on anyway. All she could do now was wait. Not quite all she could do. She called Anna, collected the revolver and five rounds. Pierce's parting gift to Valerie in case she ever needed to defend herself. Bit late, Anna had said, given that the person who caused her the most harm was him, and he was leaving.

The days were getting shorter, the light seeping away. The dead leaves had all been swept away from the gutters, Vauxhall Park bald and cracked from frost and rain. Still no response. Perhaps he hadn't taken the bait. She bought an Advent Calendar; she managed to find one with no Christian imagery at all – woodland creatures sprinkled with glitter – and had checked with the shop assistant that none of the pictures behind the doors contained a baby Jesus. No, it was all fluffy animals. She pinned it to the kitchen wall and draped a string of fairy lights around the shelves. Becky objected – her family had celebrated Christmas along with everybody else, but she wasn't entirely comfortable with overt signs of Christianity in the house. Neither was Sam. She said that Advent was a pagan ritual, an ancient urge to mark the dwindling of the light, count the days one by one until the darkest day of the year. The winter solstice. Becky bought her line.

She had almost given up on Pierce. Almost decided it was probably for the best if nothing happened. She was opening the first window of her Advent Calendar – robin with a sprig of mistletoe – when she heard the flap as the postman dropped something through the letter box. She sauntered down the hall. Plain white envelope. Postmark Ripley – a place she'd never heard of – but she recognized the writing. She retreated to her room with the letter, located her copy of T. S. Eliot's *Collected Poems*. The numbers at the beginning of the note referred her to page 77, line 359. *The Waste Land*, 'What the Thunder Said'. She wrote the alphabet on a piece of card, found the equivalent letters starting from the line he had given her, completed her key. And then she decoded his message.

Meet me at the croft. December 21st. I will be there all day. Will reimburse. Keep this between you and me.

December 21st. The shortest day. Six hours of light. At least he was offering to reimburse her expenses. *Keep this between you and me.* What did that mean – don't tell Anna? Don't tell Harry? She couldn't think of anybody else who would give a toss or believe her anyway. She wondered whether he had told anybody about it, passed the decoded message on to his mates in Intelligence. No. He was trying to keep the information she had from them, not reveal that the daughter of a police spy had a piece of paper which might confirm he wasn't quite the hero he would have them believe. The real danger for her wasn't his colleagues, it was him. Now Pierce knew she had the cheque stubs with Freeman's name on them, she was a threat to his reputation. Which was his life. And she already knew he used violence in order to control. She felt safer with the revolver. He wouldn't expect her to have a gun, still less be capable of using it, which she was, because she'd learned how to fire one from an expert.

She removed the envelope from *The Secret Island*. She hesitated, and decided to take the matchbox with her treasured dung beetle in it as well; it reminded her of Jim and she wanted him by her side. She didn't want to catch the plane – the revolver might alarm the metal detector. She went by train to Thurso, the Cairngorms white with snow, the birches skeletal in the cold dawn light.

The sky was inky by the time she boarded the ferry and the wind was strengthening. The purser had announced that the crossing could be rough. Pitching and rolling as they headed north. She clung to the railing, fixed her eyes on a distant light – star? lighthouse? – and tried to calculate how many times she had made this journey. All those wet and windy summer holidays; sandcastles, cairns, puffins, stone circles, skuas, Vikings, seals. The years blurred. Seventy-six stood out. The only summer it didn't rain. The year they went to Hoy. The drought that shook the earth and the summer that changed Jim, marked a downward shift in his behaviour. And then there was the summer of '84; that one stood out too. The midsummer trip to Orkney with Tom and Jim. She'd never forget that holiday in Orkney because Jim had been killed on the journey home. Her last conversation with him had been on the train from Inverness, the evening not yet dark. She had asked him then why he had invited her to go with him, fearful he was manipulating her in some way. He had looked surprised at the question, replied it was because he thought she might enjoy the trip. She had trouble taking his comments at face value then, when she was eighteen. And now? And now five years on, she could return to the conversation in her mind and believe him. He had been trying to bridge the gap that had grown between them she realized now. And, belatedly – posthumously – she felt she was moving closer to him as well, more able to understand his behaviour. Less quick to judge. She leaned over the ferry's railing, watched the water foaming and white as the brow of the ferry cut through the waves, the cross-currents of the Pentland Firth tugging below the surface.

The green numbers on the digital bedside clock glowed: six fifteen. 21st December. She had booked the hotel room for two nights using Pierce's cash. She had to get moving. She retrieved the Honda 50 from the archaeologist's garage, while he stood and shook his head. 'In this wind?' But he hadn't tried to stop her. 'Oh, the grant came through,' he shouted as she walked the bike to the road. 'We've got enough for another survey of the Bu next summer.' She gave him a thumbs up and headed east to Houton. Still dark; everything draped in brown; the hills, the heather, the houses.

The horizon lightened as she headed towards the jetty. Eight thirty and the ferry was waiting. She wondered whether the wind was too strong to make the crossing. The swell of the waves was ominous. The boat lurched and yawed as it pulled away from the coast. The ferryman appeared.

'There's a passenger lounge down below.'

She didn't want to be below the deck. She wanted to keep her eyes on Hoy.

'What time will the ferry do the return crossing today?'

'Two o'clock.'

She had five hours on Hoy.

'So long as the wind doesn't get too much stronger,' he added. 'Where are you going today then?'

'Moaness.' Did everybody lie as easily as her?

'I was worried you were thinking of going to Rackwick and hiking to the Old Man.'

'No.'

'Good thing too. I wouldn't go near the cliffs today. You think the wind is bad here, we're in the shelter here. I had an aunt who lived near Rackwick,' he said. 'My brother and I stayed with her when my mother had to go and work in Thurso. We used to climb the cliffs in the wind. We liked to pretend we could fly. One of us would lie on the grass, crawl to the edge and peer over to watch the waves crashing below, but the one who wasn't looking had to keep hold of the wave-watcher's ankles in case the wind took us away. Or the sea – the sight of it can pull you over if you're not careful.'

She flinched, felt the waves crashing over her head, her lungs filling with water.

'We must have been mad.' He chortled, shook his head.

She pulled her backpack closer to her chest, felt the hard outline of the revolver.

'Aye,' he continued. 'There's hardly anybody living in Rackwick these days, apart from a couple of old fishermen.'

'Oh, I thought there was a writer there, I can't remember his name. Somebody mentioned him once.'

'Steven Hill?'

'Maybe.'

'He's not there all the year. He leaves in the winter months.'

'Really?' Pierce, the lying toad. 'Where does he go then?'

'Somewhere hot, Thailand I think.'

The photo. Pierce with an arm around a young Thai girl. Loathsome.

The ferryman peered at the sky. 'At least it's not raining. Not yet anyway.'

She rode slowly, the Honda wobbling in the wind, worried that one strong blast could carry away her like Dorothy. She reached Pegal Bay; the burn no longer an enticing trickle but a wild torrent gushing to the sea. Up on the moor, only a thin band of light visible between the charcoal of the hills and the steel of the clouds. Ahead, Betty Corrigall's headstone, alone in the endless heather. She gripped the throttle; the Honda leaped and shuddered. She had to stay calm. She couldn't afford to lose it now, too much at stake. Including her own life.

Through the valley of death, the cracks and paths sharply etched in the grey winter mountains. Past the Dwarfie Stane, across the burn. The bike skittered in the headwinds blowing in from Rackwick Bay. She dismounted, wheeled the bike along the road, edged around the deserted crofts and left it lying on the mat of dead rosebay willow herb in the bothy ruin. A raven alighted in the sheep fold, struggling to maintain its balance, cawed and took flight again, carried inland by the gusts. She glanced at Pierce's croft. The windows had the blankness of an empty house. Had he dragged her all the way here for nothing?

Flown off to Thailand already? Was he just messing around, calling her to his hideaway because he wanted to demonstrate he could still pull her strings? Bastard. The Volvo was parked by the side of the croft, so maybe he was at home. He'd better be there. She delved into her backpack, clasped the revolver, swung the cylinder out, checked the loaded rounds. Five. Pushed the cylinder back, cocked her finger through the trigger, tweaked, felt the resistance, jammed it in the inside pocket of her overcoat. Maybe she wouldn't have to use it, but it was there if she needed it. And if she needed it she would use it.

The wind whipped her breath away as she climbed the path, its iciness stung her face. She fixed her sight on the croft, eyes watering. Still no sign of Pierce. She reached the door – a replacement for the one Reznik had kicked in – knocked and waited. No answer. She knocked again, called his name. Nothing except the howl of the wind. She pressed the door latch, felt it give, pushed and the door swung open. She crossed the threshold. Pierce wasn't at home. His gloomy room was much as it was the last time she met him here in early October, shelves neat, saucepans stacked, floor clear and swept. A book was lying open on his desk. She edged over. *The Collected Poems of T. S. Eliot.* Page 75. Section IV of *The Waste Land*. 'Death by Water'. A handwritten note lay on top of the verse.

Dear Sam,
I've gone for a stroll. I'm at the Raven's Nest. I'm waiting for you.
Yours faithfully, Pierce.

She stared at his words. *I've gone for a stroll.* A stroll.

What was he playing at, luring her up on to the cliffs in this wind? Her gut dropped, palms sweaty. *Fear death by water.* She should have known this wouldn't be straightforward. She thought she'd cornered him, but Pierce was a master of manipulation. She could hear his voice, always the edge of irony, the mocking banter of the upper classes. *Yours faithfully.* The only person he was faithful to was himself. She should turn around, walk back down the path, and drive away. He was playing games and she shouldn't be drawn. She put her hand against her coat, pressed the revolver against her rib. Still, she had her self-defence. She wondered whether she could manage the wind.

There were two paths to the Raven's Nest. That summer afternoon in '76 she had walked up one, and run down the other. The coastal path went along the cliff-edge. The other path curved inland before cutting back to the top of the hill and down to the Raven's Nest from above. The view from the Raven's Nest was over the sea and the bay. Pierce's croft and the bottom of the cliff path were hidden by the spur of the hill. He must have thought he didn't need to watch her climb – he would know what time the ferry arrived, how long it would take her to ride from Lyness and climb the cliff path to the Raven's Nest. *I'm waiting for you...* He wouldn't expect her to take the inland path, he would assume she didn't know it existed. So that was the path she had to choose.

She followed the track along the hillside contour, reached a V and then started the serious ascent in a diagonal back towards the sea. The cliff path and the Raven's Nest followed a ridge below the brow. She would remain hidden until she reached the ridge, and then she would emerge above him. She glanced up and saw grey-fingered clouds like owls' wings scudding above her head and a blast of wind hit her full force in the face, raced around her mind, possessed her. She paused, tried to catch her breath, collect herself. She had no plan. No script. All she had was the envelope and her revolver and the wind. That would have to do.

She kept her eye on the skyline for Pierce's figure looming above. He did not appear. Perhaps he wasn't waiting after all. She wasn't about to take any chances. She dropped to the ground, wormed the last few feet of hillside, peered over the brow. Above, the bank of clouds smothering the sun. Below, ranks of breakers marching across the Pentland Firth. The top of Pierce's head a few feet away, facing towards the bay, waiting to see her emerge around the final bend of the coast path. She dropped back below the brow, heart thumping. Could she do this? Could she pull it off? She felt for the revolver, removed it from her coat, gripped it in her right hand and stood, the gale yowling in her ears.

He turned around the moment she appeared above him, wavering on the brow. She aimed the barrel at his head and caught the split second of surprise, the sheer fury before he smiled, his blue eyes crinkling at the edges. He tilted his head to one side, as if he were about to address somebody who was a tiny bit dim. God, he was a patronizing jerk, she could see that now.

'Sam, there's no need for...'

That. She could barely hear him in the wind, her mind completing his sentence. She edged along the ridge, keeping the revolver aimed at his head, watching his hands to make sure he didn't reach for his own weapon. She was right above him now. It wouldn't require quite so much effort to make herself heard.

'Put it away, Sam, and then we can tal...'

'Put your hands in the air.'

He pulled a *really, Sam, is that necessary* grimace, facial expressions as effective as words in the gale. She gestured with the barrel. 'Up.'

'OK, Sam, if that's how you want to play it.' She could hear the bored weariness, the dismissal of the silly little girl with her gun. Or maybe she inferred the tone of his voice from his face. He raised his hands, stumbled, momentarily losing his balance, the wind wrong-footing him.

'I've brought the envelope.'

'Where did you find it?'

'Where Jim dropped it. In the back garden of your safehouse. You sent him there to collect it. Correct?'

She was keeping her sentences short, to the point. She wanted him to hear all her words.

'Yes, Sam. Correct.' He rolled his eyes as he said it. Sam, the tedious daughter of a useless police spy.

'Why did you ask Jim to look for it?'

He didn't respond.

She answered for him. 'Because you're a coward.'

He pulled his mouth back some more, dropped his hands.

'Don't move,' she shouted.

He lifted his hands again. 'Calm down, Sam, there's no need for this.'

'Why was the envelope important?'

'You know why, Sam. Because it had a picture of Anna in it. She would have been endangered if they found it.'

'You don't give a stuff about Anna.'

'That's not true.'

'You are a violent bully.'

'Sam. That's Anna making things up. She's angry with me because I had to leave her. She likes to think she's a victim. She tells stories.'

She kept her eyes on his face, assessed how far his feet were from the cliff-edge. Not quite his body's length away, she reckoned.

'You kicked Valerie when she was pregnant. She had a miscarriage because of you.'

'That's another exaggeration.'

'You're a wife-beater. You murdered her baby.'

'Let's not get hysterical.'

'Why did you leave one of the tiles Anna gave you on Betty Corrigall's grave?'

He pulled a puzzled frown. 'Say that again, Sam, I didn't quite catch it. The wind…'

She took a step forward. He inched back. She had to be careful, she was right on the edge of the ridge now, aiming the gun down at his face. She didn't want to trip and blow it.

'And what about Jim? Were you hanging around Earl's Bu because you wanted to do penance for Jim? A life you ruined to save your own skin?'

He gave her his *don't be stupid* look.

'Or is it less about guilt and repentance, and more about fears that your crimes will come back to bite you? Do you give a fuck about anybody else? Can you stand anybody else if they don't serve you? If you don't control them?'

'Sam, perhaps we should go back to the croft and talk about this, out of the wind.'

'I'm fine out here, thanks.'

She glanced at the sky, the clouds thickening, the gale losing some of its strength. 'The wind's dropping anyway. Tell me why you lied about the torture.'

'Torture?'

'You made me believe you had been tortured, when it was Jim who was half drowned because of you.'

'Oh, Sam. Is that what this is all about? Some misunderstanding about Jim?'

'Misunderstanding?'

'I didn't say I was tortured. You read that…'

'You wanted me to believe that my father had betrayed you.'

'I can't control what you think.'

'You try. You spread false rumours.'

'Sam, you believe what you…'

'Why did you pick on him?'

'He got in the way.'

'He helped you.'

'Sure.'

'It haunted him. It fucked up his head. Fucked up my family.'

'You and Anna have clearly been comparing notes,' he said. 'Two young women, looking for a story to justify their shared victimhood.'

'A story? You're the storyteller.'

He tipped his head to one side again. Jesus, he was loathsome. His smile hardened.

'Sam, you have the envelope. Why don't you give it to me and we can both get on with our lives.'

'What do I get in exchange for the envelope?'

He snapped. 'I've given you plenty of cash. I've got some more if that's what you're after.'

'I don't want cash. I want you to admit that you're a bullying coward.'

'Yes, yes, yes. I agree to all that. Of course.' He said it so dismissively. 'Now please hand me the envelope.'

She stuck her left hand in her pocket, grasped the corner of the envelope. 'OK then,' she said. 'Have your fucking envelope.'

She tossed it in the air above his head, he leaned back to grab it, reached and missed. A gust caught the paper. Pierce reached again, snatched, grabbed the envelope, regained his balance, five inches closer to the cliff-edge than he was before.

'There. If your precious reputation means so much to you, take it. Now nobody need ever know your dirty secret. Apart from me. And Anna, who knows exactly what you're like.'

He raised a supercilious eyebrow.

'And Jim,' she added.

'Jim?'

'Yeah, Jim. I'm sure he suspected in his gut that you were a total fucking coward who made up stories to cover his own arse.'

Pierce smiled again. 'Well, we all make up stories, don't we.' He stared at her sternly, the headmaster ticking off the recalcitrant pupil. 'And what Jim thinks doesn't really matter now because he's dead.'

'No, he's not.'

Pierce smirked. 'Don't be silly.'

'He's here. He hasn't gone.'

The wind whipped again.

'I can hear his voice. He's waiting for you.'

She frowned, straining to hear. Pierce caught her look, or perhaps he even heard Jim's voice, because he frowned too and he turned to follow her gaze, just over his shoulder, behind him.

'Jim.' She waved her left hand.

He turned again, twisted his body, she called the wind in her mind and it blasted him, caught him off guard and he stepped back to right himself, but he stumbled, and the wind blew again and punched him in the gut. He thrust his arms out sideways to steady himself and gain his balance, but he couldn't find his centre of gravity. He looked straight at her. He wasn't smiling, face locked in panic, but she smiled at him and waved goodbye as the gust took him over the edge. The other side. She wondered whether she would hear a splash.

Was that a scream? Or was it the wind? Perhaps it was Jim laughing. A skua fluttered past her feet along the cliff's edge, watching the rocks below.

'Oh, I nearly forgot,' she shouted. 'Miranda said fuck off, Prospero. And Ariel says thank god she's finally free.'

She replaced the revolver in her pocket. Self-defence only. All she'd done was tell a couple of stories. *We all make up stories, don't we.* Yes, Pierce, we do all make up stories. And she was better at it than him. She glanced at her feet, checking her foothold, well back from the edge of the cliff. Her toes were resting against the smooth rock humped like the back of a whale. She lowered herself on to the grass, edged her hand along the crevice, inside the whale's mouth, and searched the hidden hollow. Her fingertips touched a small object, smooth surfaces, sharp points. She eased it into the daylight. The raven's skull, the tile still lodged in the eye socket, the red one Anna had given to her and she had left here in the summer of '76. She removed the tile, squashed it in her palm, felt its warm corners pressing her skin, then dropped it in her pocket. The last of the Fisher King's treasures. A raven fluttered overhead. Ravens were loyal birds; once they found a partner they stuck with them through life. And death too.

She reached into her pocket and removed the Bryant & May matchbox, pushed the drawer, removed the carcase of the beetle, the one she had found on a summer's day when she was seven or eight. She had been rambling with Jim across a field and he had stopped, pointed in wonder at the emerald creature sparkling on the cowpat. She wanted to take it home. He said the beetle was part of the natural cycle, breaking down the cow shit, fertilizing the grass for the cows to eat, so maybe she should leave it. But she said Charles Darwin collected beetles and she wanted to be a naturalist like him and he had said that's a good ambition. You know, he said, if you try hard enough at school you can be anything you want to be. He had found a matchbox in his pocket, emptied it and taken it home for her and she had kept it all these years. She placed the beetle in the eye socket of the raven's skull, eased it back inside the crevice. That was how she wanted to remember him; Jim, her father. Rest in peace. Dust to dust.

CHAPTER 34

Orkney, 21 December 1989

'How was Moaness?' the ferryman asked.

'Windy,' she said.

'Aye.' He walked away.

She headed west from Houton, followed the road to Stromness. She stopped at a telephone box. She called Anna's number, stuck her coins in the slot when Anna answered.

'Hello.'

'Oh, it's you.'

'I've recovered the last of the tiles. I've dealt with it.'

There was a pause, Anna digesting her message. And then she asked, 'What's that noise?'

'It's the wind.'

'Oh, OK.' She laughed. Not maliciously. There was a joy to it. 'Thank you.' Another pause. 'Blood sister,' Anna said, and replaced the receiver.

Sam thought for a moment, then dialled the Vauxhall number.

'Hello.' Becky.

She jammed her last coin in. 'It's me, Sam.'

'Where've you got to? You didn't say you were going away.'

'I know. I was just phoning in case you were worried. I'll be back first thing the day after tomorrow.'

She would get the night train from Inverness.

'I've got a surprise for you,' Becky said.

'What?'

'I've bought a Christmas tree.'

'Why?'

'They were selling them cheap outside the petrol station. I fancied one. I'm an adult. I don't have to be bound by my upbringing. If I want a Christmas tree, I'll have one.'

'You're right,' Sam said. 'See you soon.'

The wind was dropping now, and she twisted the throttle as she headed north towards Stenness. She had time, she hoped. She reached Maeshowe. There were two cars parked by the mill.

'I don't think you'll be in luck today,' the woman said. 'Too cloudy.'

'I'll have a ticket anyway. I'll give it a go.'

'There's a couple of people in there already with the guide. The gate is unlocked, just push it open and join them. Here.' She offered her a torch.

'I've got my own.'

A curlew sang its sad lament. She turned around, gazed back at Hoy and thought of Jim, that day in '77 when he had fled the cairn, the dripping water and Helen's House of Darkness chant too much for him, and they had found him out here, standing and staring at the mountains. Then the sky had been bright after a summer rainstorm, but now the silhouette of the dark isle was deep purple against the leaden sky. The woman in the mill was right, she reckoned, there wasn't much chance of the sun appearing today. Never mind. She stooped as she reached the gate, shouted hello to announce her arrival, lit her torch to illuminate her way along the low entrance to the chambered cairn. She reached the centre, caught the damp layers of corbelled stone, the calm faces of the people waiting. The archaeologist was there, near one of the side chambers. Of course, he would be here. He wouldn't miss this. She went and stood by him. Extinguished her torch.

'In the darkness,' he whispered, 'there is light.'

They waited in silence. The darkness complete. She fumbled in her pocket, felt the tile that Anna had given her, removed it and dropped it gently into the side chamber, the ancient resting place of the dead. Let it go. The tale of the Fisher King, over. A tear dribbled down her cheek. The shortest day and the sun was sinking, moving west, dropping below the clouds, between the slopes of Hoy's hills. And the last rays of the setting sun shone across the water, over the meadow, through the tomb's long tunnel, and illuminated the grey stone of the furthest wall.

AUTHOR'S NOTE

THANK YOU TO Laura and Maddy and everybody at Head of Zeus for suggestions and support. Thank you to Oli for advice and encouragement at the right moments. Thanks to Mark for suggesting the Earl's Bu, and Guy for his memories of Bonnington Square in the eighties (those were the days...). Big thanks to my mum for being encouraging from the beginning to the end. Biggest thanks to Andy and my daughters.

The book's title was originally inspired by the beautiful folk song 'Hoy's Dark and Lofty Isle'. John Bremner's memoir, *Hoy, the Dark Enchanted Isle* (Bellavista Publications, 1997), was a lovely read and a useful guide to life in Hoy. I have devoured everything I could find that George Mackay Brown has written about Hoy, including the collections of his weekly columns for the *Orcadian*. Many thanks to the staff at the wonderful Orkney Library – I found details about the Earl's Bu excavations in the Orkney Archive. Background information on the history of MI5 and Special Branch comes from *The Spying Game* by Michael Smith (Politico's Publishing, 2003).